THE MILL RIVER RECLUSE

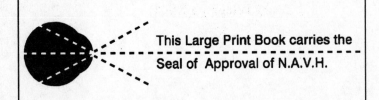

This Large Print Book carries the
Seal of Approval of N.A.V.H.

THE MILL RIVER RECLUSE

DARCIE CHAN

THORNDIKE PRESS
A part of Gale, Cengage Learning

GALE
CENGAGE Learning·

Farmington Hills, Mich • San Francisco • New York • Waterville, Maine
Meriden, Conn • Mason, Ohio • Chicago

Copyright © 2011 by Darcie Chan.
Reading group guide copyright © 2014 by Random House, Inc.
Thorndike Press, a part of Gale, Cengage Learning.

Thorndike Press® Large Print Core.
The text of this Large Print edition is unabridged.
Other aspects of the book may vary from the original edition.
Set in 16 pt. Plantin.

LIBRARY OF CONGRESS CATALOGING-IN-PUBLICATION DATA

Chan, Darcie.
   The Mill River recluse / by Darcie Chan. — Large print edition.
     pages ; cm. — (Thorndike Press large print core)
   ISBN-13: 978-1-4104-7209-0 (hardcover)
   ISBN-10: 1-4104-7209-4 (hardcover)
   1. Widows—Fiction. 2. Secrets—Fiction. 3. Family life—Fiction. 4. Cities and towns—Fiction. 5. Large type books. 6. Psychological fiction. I. Title.
PS3603.H35558M55 2014b
813'.6—dc23   2014021319

Published in 2014 by arrangement with The Ballantine Publishing Group, a division of Random House, LLC, a Penguin Random House Company

Printed in the United States of America
1 2 3 4 5 6 7 18 17 16 15 14

To my husband, Tim, my son, Gavin,
my family, and the extraordinary
Ruth Uyesugi, my teacher,
"other mother," and dear friend

■ ■ ■ ■

PART 1

■ ■ ■ ■

We can easily forgive a child who is afraid
of the dark. The real tragedy of life is when
men are afraid of the light.

— PLATO

CHAPTER 1

As she gazed out the bay window in her bedroom, Mary McAllister knew this night would be her last.

Outside, the February darkness was suffused with light from the town. Thick snowflakes floated past the window. Only the Mill River itself, for which the small Vermont village was named, escaped the snow covering. Its center flowed, black and snakelike, along the edge of the sleeping town.

With her left hand, Mary stroked a large Siamese cat curled next to her on the adjustable bed. With her right, she tucked a few strands of fine white hair behind her ear. Mary's eyes, one clear and blue, the other gray and cloudy, were fixed on the storm outside.

She wondered what they would think of her when they discovered what she had done.

9

The bedroom was dark, but the few lights from the town shone upward, enough to support a faint reflection of her face on the window glass. Mary looked at the reflection through her good eye. Pale and thin, she was the face of death superimposed on the darkness.

She drifted in and out of sleep, awakened every few minutes by the excruciating pain in her abdomen. Finally, her hand shaking, she reached for the bottle of pills and the cup of water at her bedside.

Mary poured the pills into her hand and then swallowed them all, a few at a time, with the water. She would leave this world in peaceful solitude. She would do so before her pain was so great — before her mental faculties were so diminished — that she couldn't leave on her own terms.

She thought of Michael. The priest had left, as he had promised, but she wondered if he was still awake in the parish house. He would find her tomorrow. She knew it would be difficult for him, but he was prepared for the inevitable. They both were.

Still, she feared what death might bring.

Would she see her husband again? In her dim bedroom, Mary's gaze focused on the outline of a figurine that stood on her bureau. It was a horse, carved elegantly from black marble. She thought of Patrick, of the first time she had seen him when he had come to her father's farm, of the horror that followed.

Mary shuddered and forced her mind to focus on memories of her father instead. She remembered him standing in the round ring, his hat pushed back off his forehead, teaching young horses to be gentle. His belly laugh still rang in her ears.

Even now, having been a widow for more than seventy years, she still feared Patrick, but she longed to see her father again, and Grandpop, too. Perhaps soon she would.

Mary touched Sham's furry head beside her, and the cat mewed and curled his paws in his sleep. Michael had promised to find a good home for him. She had no doubt that he would, and that fact comforted her. Tears ran down her cheeks as she whispered a loving goodbye to her faithful feline companion. Silently, she wished him the happiest of lives, however many he had left, and waited for the final, heavy sleepiness to surround her.

In Mill River, a handful of others were also awake. Officers Kyle Hansen and Leroy Underwood had been on patrol for more than an hour. The police department's old

Jeep Cherokee churned through the new snow as they made their way along the country roads surrounding the town. They had been looking for stranded motorists, but the roads were deserted. Most folks had been sensible enough to stay at home during the storm. Even with the snowfall, the evening, like most evenings in Mill River, had been uneventful.

Leroy was bored. He fidgeted in the passenger seat, squinting out the window. His hair was sandy brown and straight — and a little too long for a man in uniform, in Kyle's opinion. His default expression was one of openmouthed confusion, and his shoulders were rounded forward. *Hell, anyone unfortunate enough to see Leroy peering out the Jeep's window might easily mistake him for an orangutan,* Kyle thought.

Leroy turned from the window and held up an almost empty box of chocolate doughnuts.

"You care if I eat the last one?"

"Nah," Kyle replied. "They're stale, you know."

This fact was lost on Leroy. "You think we should drive through town again?" he asked, with his mouth full.

Kyle glanced at Leroy and shrugged.

Leroy crammed the last of the doughnut

into his mouth and struggled to open the thermos. As they started down the hill back into town, Leroy tried to pour the remaining coffee into the thermos cup, but most of it sloshed into his lap.

"Aw, shit. Take it easy with the potholes, would you?" he complained.

Kyle rolled his eyes. What Leroy lacked in intelligence and compassion, he made up for in appetite.

Their route took them over the covered bridge spanning the river and onto Main Street. Through the snow, Kyle could just make out the faint white glow of the McAllister mansion high on a hill past the other end of town.

"You ever seen her?" Leroy asked, following Kyle's gaze.

"Who?"

"The Widow McAllister," Leroy half whispered, as if he were speaking of a ghost.

"No," Kyle said.

"I have," Leroy said. "Once. Back when I was in high school, outside the bakery. She was all wrinkled and hunched over, with a patch over one eye, like a pirate."

Kyle stared straight ahead, trying to focus on driving through the storm.

"I heard that some folks in town's convinced she's a witch or something," Leroy said. "Creeps me out, thinking of her up there watching everybody." Leroy flashed a taunting grin at Kyle. "Maybe someone should make her walk the plank."

Kyle clenched his jaw. Leroy was trying to irritate him, he knew, and he wasn't going to give him any satisfaction.

It was easier for Kyle to tolerate Leroy's crudeness when he thought of how difficult it must have been for the junior officer growing up. According to the police chief, who knew almost everyone in town, Leroy was the son of an absentee father and an alcoholic mother. He had an older sister who lived in Rutland. That sister, apparently, was unique in the Underwood family, having finished college and taken a job as an accountant with the city government.

Then there was Leroy. Nearly a high school dropout, he had somehow received his diploma and bungled his way through training at the police academy. He had an ego the size of Texas, and Kyle had yet to see him show real kindness toward anyone. Why Leroy had been hired, Kyle didn't know. Maybe the town had been desperate for another officer, but by Kyle's standards, Leroy was hardly good officer material.

The old Jeep churned through the snow as they drove back into Mill River. Small, older houses and assorted trailer homes lined this end of Main Street. Most of the residences were dark. One mobile home, though, was brightly lit. In contrast to most of the other trailers, this one was shiny and new. The front yard was filled with ceramic ornaments protruding from the snow — a pair of deer, several rabbits, some gnomes, and a large birdbath.

"I guess Crazy Daisy's still awake," Leroy said. "Probably up fixing a new potion."

At that moment, the front door of the trailer opened and a dumpling of a woman skipped out into the yard. Kyle slowed the Jeep. Daisy was spinning around, face upturned and tongue stuck out.

Leroy hooted with laughter. "Lookit that fat cow!" he shouted, oblivious to Kyle's frown. "She keeps that up, and she'll trip over one of them rabbits an' bite off her tongue!"

"Shut up, Leroy," Kyle said. He rolled down the driver's side window.

"Ms. Delaine, you know it's late, almost one in the morning, and you shouldn't be outside in this storm," he called to her.

Flushed and breathless, Daisy stopped her twirling and looked at them. A dark port-wine birthmark curled up from her jaw to her cheek, and her gray curls fell over her eyes. She teetered dizzily and brushed her hair from her face. "You should try the snow, Officer! I've been working on a spell for it all evening, and it's delicious!" she shouted. "It'll be perfect in my potions too, but I'm in an awful hurry. I'm cooking up a new one tonight!" Smiling, she scooped up a handful of snow, flung it into the air, waved at Officers Hansen and Underwood, and went inside.

Kyle sat shaking his head, but Leroy roared even louder.

"Aw, c'mon, Kyle. You know she's nuts. What's the harm in enjoying the entertainment?"

"She can't help it, Leroy, and you don't have the good sense to keep your mouth shut when you should," Kyle snapped. He was watching the door of the trailer, making sure Daisy stayed inside.

"Ooh, touch-y," Leroy replied. "Hell," he said, chuckling again, "that show alone makes me sorta happy that she survived that fire. When I heard her trailer'd burned, I thought we'd finally be rid of the old bat."

Kyle said nothing, despite his disgust, because it would have been useless. He had eight years on Leroy, but given Leroy's level of maturity, it seemed more like eighty. During his time on the force in Boston, he'd seen more than a few young officers like Leroy. They were all arrogant and stupid and attracted to the position because they liked the power the uniform and the gun gave them. Most of those guys ended up dead or behind bars themselves, victims of their own bad intentions.

In Mill River, there were four police officers — himself, Leroy, Ron Wykowski, and Joe Fitzgerald, the chief. The problem was that in a town where nothing ever happened, three decent cops were more than enough. Leroy, lacking opportunities to jeopardize his career in a town that had trouble finding officers willing to work for what it could offer in salary, had great job security.

They continued down Main Street, through the quaint business district, past the white town hall building, and followed the bend in the road past St. John's Catholic Church. One window was lit in the parish house.

"Preachie's up," Leroy chirped. This was nothing unusual, though, as Father O'Brien's light was often on late into the night.

At the next house, there was another bright window.

"Teachie's up, too," Leroy said in a different tone. "Maybe we should stop by and read her a bedtime story." He raised his eyebrows and slowly ran his tongue across his upper lip.

"Teachie" was Claudia Simon, the pretty new fourth-grade teacher at Mill River Elementary.

"You can read? That's news to me," Kyle said.

Leroy scowled but kept quiet until Kyle pulled up to the police station. As they got out, Leroy stared back down Main Street.

"Damn," he said. "Snow like this makes even those shitty trailers look good."

Again, Kyle didn't respond. All he wanted was a hot shower and a warm bed. It had been a long night.

Claudia Simon was reading bedtime stories of a sort. Each of her students had written a short composition titled, "What I Want to Be When I Grow Up." Of the twenty-three fourth-graders, ten wanted to be President of the United States. Six wanted to be movie stars or singers. Four wanted to be doctors or nurses. One a policeman. One a fireman. And one a counselor.

Rowen Hansen was the little girl who wanted to be a counselor. Her father, Kyle Hansen, was a police officer in town. Claudia had learned from the principal that he was a widower. His little girl had written that she wanted to be a counselor, as her mother had been, because she liked to "listen to people and help fix their problems." That simple. From a fourth-grader. *But,* Claudia thought, *Rowen is an exceptional kid.*

Claudia stood up and stretched. It was after one. But this was Saturday night — no, now Sunday morning — and if she lost herself grading papers, she could sleep late. Dressed in a jogging suit and socks, she padded down the hall to the bathroom to brush her teeth. She examined her reflection in the full-length mirror on the back of the bathroom door. Only a few months ago, her reflection wouldn't have fit in the mirror.

Single, obese, and lonely, Claudia had resolved, on her thirtieth birthday, to get herself into shape. She had made that resolution many times before. She had been overweight all her life, or as much of it as she could remember. She had never had a boyfriend, a prom date, or even so much as a man with a romantic interest in her. After that long, most people would have resigned themselves to a lifetime of solitary cheese-cake. Instead, Claudia threw out the cheese-cake, chips, ice cream, and pizza. She purchased a treadmill and Reeboks. Then, over the next year and a half, Claudia literally ran her ass off.

Now, ninety-two pounds lighter, Claudia examined her reflection with approval and headed to bed. She had a new wardrobe in a size ten. She had a teaching job in a school in a new town where people didn't know her former fat self. She was alive. A single ready to mingle. She would get over her social awkwardness. She wouldn't get flustered when she saw an attractive man. She wouldn't avert her eyes. She was no longer ashamed of herself.

That night, Claudia fell asleep smiling.

It was well after midnight, but Jean Wykowski couldn't sleep. Her husband, Ron, lay snoring beside her. His shift at the police station would begin at seven, and he was oblivious to her tossing and turning. But Ron's snoring rarely bothered her, and it was not the reason that she experienced insomnia. Finally, she slipped from under the covers and tiptoed out of the bedroom.

On her way to the kitchen, she paused at her sons' room. Jimmy and Johnny, ages nine and eleven, took after their father where sleep was concerned. Both were out cold, their breathing slow and rhythmic. Jimmy looked just as she had left him at bedtime. He lay on his back with the covers pulled up to his chin. Johnny, though, was turned around with his feet on his pillow and his head very close to falling off one side. How he had managed that Jean didn't know, but she was able to coax him back under the covers in the proper direction without fully waking him.

Jean continued to the darkened kitchen, wincing every time the floor creaked. She poured a cup of milk and put it in the microwave. While the microwave hummed, she smiled to herself as she remembered how the boys had done the dishes that night, Johnny washing and Jimmy rinsing, each using the pull-out spray nozzle as a microphone to impersonate his favorite singer.

The microwave, too, was special, having been Ron's Christmas present to her. It wasn't the most romantic gift, of course, but it was functional and something the whole family could enjoy. She stopped the microwave, before its final loud beep, and removed her cup of milk.

She was lucky to have such great kids. They were stout little buggers and full of life, not like most of the unfortunate people she saw each day. Her husband of thirteen years was loving and loyal. He and the boys were the reasons she continued her emotionally draining work as a home health nurse for Rutland County.

Her patients were paraplegics, people recovering from surgery or major accidents, and the terminally ill. She watched them struggle and suffer, day after day. With her help, and that of doctors and therapists, some got better or at least learned to live with their impairments. But many didn't, and it was the face of Mary McAllister, the patient to whom she was currently assigned, that kept sleep from her tonight.

She spent most of each shift with the old woman. Mrs. McAllister had only days left, maybe a week. Yesterday, Jean had hardly been able to look at her. The cancer had left Mrs. McAllister withered and jaundiced, and pain medication ensured that she slept most of the time. Jean had given her a sponge bath, changed her garments, and tried her best to make her comfortable. It wasn't much, but it was all she could do. Today, Sunday, there would be no visit because she had the day off, but she knew the relief nurse who would cover her shift was gentle and caring. Attempting to console herself with those thoughts, Jean set her empty cup in the sink and walked back down the dark hallway to her bedroom.

In the parish house next to his church, Father Michael O'Brien was in his office, packing. Not books or files, only spoons. Father O'Brien was obsessed with spoons. He had accumulated close to seven hundred spoons during his lifetime. No two were alike. Tenderly, he lifted each one from a tattered cardboard box, examining it before placing it in a sturdy shipping box on his desk.

He collected the spoons in violation of his vow of poverty, and for this he felt guilty. When he thought about how he had obtained the spoons, he felt even worse. Still, there was something about a spoon — silver or stainless, elegant, frilly, or plain — that comforted him. He needed them. He had never been able to part with them.

Until now.

From his top desk drawer, he retrieved one final spoon. He placed it, a shiny silver teaspoon, in the shipping box. For a moment, he looked at it resting on top of its box-mates, and then retrieved it. He would not part with this one. On the back of the spoon an inscription read, "To my dear friend, love, MEHM."

The one person who knew of his collection, who had been his closest friend for more than seventy years, had given this spoon to him. It would not be a sin to keep just this one.

He eased himself into the chair at his desk. It was late, and his arthritis was acting up. He set the spoon on the desk and put on his reading glasses. There was a small package wrapped in brown paper on his desk, accompanied by a sealed envelope. He didn't know what was in the package. As for the envelope, he knew that there was a letter inside, written on fine linen stationery. He longed to read the letter, but it was not for him to read . . . yet. With a sigh, he picked up the envelope and pressed it to his chest.

He looked out the window toward Mary's mansion on the hill. The darkness and the whirling snow prevented him from seeing the big marble home, but he knew it was there, overlooking Mill River as it had for decades. He closed his eyes. He knew the history of that house, the joy and the suffering, especially the suffering, that had taken place — and still took place — within it. He knew Mary was there, and wondered if she was sleeping, as he had left her, or awake looking down upon him. Maybe her soul had already departed.

"Dear girl, may you finally be at peace," he whispered, and looked once more into the storm covering the mansion on the hill.

CHAPTER 2

1940

They were flying.

On a bright Saturday morning in June, the refined whine of a Lincoln Zephyr coupé pierced the serene quiet of Vermont's Green Mountains. The engine of the car powered it effortlessly along the winding country road. The wind whipped through the open windows of the car, through the blond hair of father and son, Stephen and Patrick McAllister.

The calmness of rural Vermont was in stark contrast to the events occurring in other parts of the world. Across the Atlantic, the Axis powers were bound by a common goal of world domination. The Nazis had overrun Europe, forcing France into submission. Britain was conscripting civilian men at a frenzied pace. But these events were an ocean away and, for the moment, even farther from the thoughts of the men in the Lincoln coupé.

Stephen and Patrick McAllister were the second and third generations of a family that had become established in Vermont more than seventy years earlier. The vast mineral deposits of the state, especially the exceptional white marble, had lured a steady stream of immigrants to quarries in the Green Mountains. Hungry for jobs and new opportunities, Italians, Swedes, Finns, Scotsmen, Irishmen, and others followed newly constructed railroads north to West Rutland. They eagerly took on the exhausting and dangerous work of cutting marble.

One of those immigrants had been Patrick's great-grandfather, a young Irishman named Kieran McAllister. He had crossed the Atlantic in cramped quarters in the belly of a Cunard steamship in 1862, and for the next two years endured working as a quarry laborer without serious injury. With decency, common sense, and a little luck, he had earned the respect of the quarry owner and a promotion to the position of foreman. The increased salary had enabled him to join a group of men in opening a new quarry. Eventually, he had established a marble-works in Rutland, where quarries could have blocks of marble cut or carved before their shipment to buyers.

The marbleworks had been good to the McAllister family. Having been the first of its kind in the area during the most prosperous days of Vermont's marble industry, the business had made Kieran a wealthy man. For nearly fifty years, throughout World War I and the Great Depression, the demand for marble had remained steady and had even increased at times. Now Kieran's surviving descendants still enjoyed the fruits of the prosperity that he had sown, evidenced by his grandson's penchant for new and expensive automobiles.

Stephen looked over at Patrick and grinned. "She handles beautifully," he said, patting the steering wheel. "V12 under the hood, hydraulic brakes. She's a keeper."

The new Lincoln was only the latest in a long line of luxurious automobiles that Stephen had purchased. He had five at the moment. When he tired of a particular model, he traded it for whichever new car caught his eye. On Saturdays when Patrick was home from school, Stephen and his son had taken a car from his collection and driven through the countryside southeast of Rutland County. Now that Patrick was finished with college, he looked forward to their outings as routine weekly escapes.

"Maybe I'll see for myself how she handles

on the way back," Patrick hinted.

"What, you mean you don't want to ride your graduation present home?" Stephen asked.

Stephen glanced at Patrick and was overwhelmed with pride. His son, a Harvard graduate, capable, refined, a true gentleman. Someday, after Stephen retired, Patrick would assume the helm of McAllister Marbleworks. Until then, they would work side by side to ensure the continued success of the family business.

On this morning, their drive was more than a leisurely jaunt. Stephen and Patrick were headed to a farm on the far side of Mill River to select a horse as part of Patrick's graduation present. Mill River was located about eight miles southeast of Rutland, where Kieran had established the family business. While Rutland had become a bustling center of commerce, thanks to the marble industry and the railroad, Mill River remained a sleepy, quaint throwback to the early days of New England.

The winding road finally cleared the green hills and straightened out. Stephen guided the Lincoln over an old covered bridge and onto Main Street. They glided past a number of small houses, a hardware store, a post office, and a beauty salon. A stone church stood on the right side of the street. The road curved sharply, past the town hall building on the left and past a few other businesses and houses, before they were once again driving through the countryside.

Stephen couldn't understand why his son found horses so alluring. He knew that Patrick had taken up riding when he arrived in Cambridge, Massachusetts, his freshman year and that many of his son's classmates, some from the most respected families in New England, were avid equestrians. To Stephen, horses were dirty, unpredictable, and more trouble than they were worth. Certainly, a horse could never compete with any car in his personal collection.

Still, he had never denied his son anything and was not about to deny him the thing that he seemed to love most. When Patrick arrived home after finishing college, Stephen had surprised him on a drive just outside Rutland. Stephen had purchased several acres of pasture, the contractors had just put the finishing touches on a stable on the property. All that they needed were some horses. Patrick would select them, of course. He had told his father that first he wanted a Morgan and a Thoroughbred. They would select the Morgan this morning.

"Look, there it is," Stephen said, pointing. Ahead was a small sign by the side of the road that read SAMUEL E. HAYES. MORGANS. An arrow on the sign indicated that they should turn right, and he swung the black car onto a narrow driveway. After a quarter of a mile or so, the driveway opened into a clearing surrounded by sugar maples. An old pickup truck was parked beside an enormous weathered red barn. Acres of pasture enclosed by a split-rail fence stretched beyond the barn, and a footpath faded up a hill toward a small farmhouse.

Stephen and Patrick stepped out of the car, frowning. "What a dump," Patrick muttered as they looked around at the run-down farm. A small herd of horses grazed at the far end of the pasture, and a short whinny echoed from the barn, but no human inhabitants of the farm were in sight.

"Well, we're here, anyway," Stephen said. "When I called yesterday, Hayes said it'd be fine if we came by this morning. Wait here. I'll go up to the house." He put on his hat and snapped his suit jacket to straighten it, then started up the footpath. He looked rather out of place, a man dressed in a fine three-piece suit and wing tips walking up a dirt path toward what was little more than a shack.

Patrick went to the fence and crossed his arms over the top rail. A gate in the fence was padlocked. The barn door was open and inside he could see long rows of stalls. He looked up at his father, picking his way along the path to the house, and grew impatient. He was eager to see if there were actually any decent horses in such a shoddy structure, and it was a simple matter to climb over the fence.

Patrick stepped tentatively into the barn. The familiar smell of horse manure and hay hung in the air. It was dark, especially coming in from the bright morning sun. Still, Patrick could see the rafters and the loft stocked with bales of hay. The occasional creak came from above his head, and Patrick grew nervous at the thought of the old roof collapsing. A pitchfork and wheelbarrow leaned against another stack of straw bales at the end of the barn. The wooden walls and beams were rough and unfinished. The ancient barn was hardly the neatly painted stable at Harvard, but at least the smell was the same, and it reassured him.

There was a tack room immediately to his left. The three saddles inside were well oiled, but worn. An assortment of bridles and halters hung from pegs on the walls, and several brushes and currycombs rested on a shelf.

Across from the tack room was a large area filled with bags of feed and bales of hay. A Mason jar containing sugar cubes was nestled on top of an open bag of oats. Patrick unscrewed the lid and shook a few cubes into his hand.

The loose boxes at the front of the barn were empty, but he could see several horses toward the rear of the barn. As he walked down the aisle, he heard a low nicker. A horse in a loose box immediately to his left pushed its head over the door of a stall, perked up its ears, and snorted. *The horse is young, maybe about three,* Patrick thought, *but its build already reflects superior bloodlines.* He walked closer. The horse tossed its forelock out of its eyes and eagerly accepted the sugar cubes. It was a blood bay with fine, straight legs and deep shoulders. Its rich, red coat blended gradually into black legs and contrasted sharply with a thick black mane and tail. The horse nuzzled Patrick's hand for more sugar, and, finding none, snorted again and struck its front hoof against the door. "You're a feisty one," Patrick said, and rubbed its forehead. He smiled grudgingly to himself. The old barn certainly belied the value of this inhabitant.

A sudden *thump* came from behind the straw stack at the end of the aisle, and the pitchfork fell to the floor.

"Hello?" Patrick asked, startled. "Is someone there?"

Silence.

He didn't notice that someone was watching him from a small crack between the straw bales.

"Patrick!" a voice called from outside the barn. He turned and saw his father and another man standing in the doorway.

"Son, this is Samuel Hayes," his father said as Patrick came over to them.

The stout horse breeder wore dirty overalls and a wide-brimmed hat pushed back off his forehead. His hair was just beginning to show strands of gray, but the deep crevices in his face made Patrick think that he was older than his barn.

"Mr. Hayes. It's a pleasure to meet you," Patrick said, extending his hand. "I've heard that your Morgans are the finest around."

"Pleasure's mine, and please call me Sam," he replied, clasping his hand. He was obviously pleased by Patrick's compliment. "I don't raise as many as I used to, just a few a year now. Quality over quantity, you might say. Plus, there hasn't been much of a market for 'em for a few years now.

People've been pretty hard up." He paused a moment, looking at Patrick's fine attire with hopeful eyes. "Your pop here tells me that you're the horseman of the family. Well, you can't go wrong with a Morgan. 'Course I'm sure you know that. They're the sturdiest horses you could ever have. Smart, too. An' their temperament's usually steady an' sensible. All my Morgans' pedigrees go back to Justin Morgan's stallion. I break 'em in myself, teach 'em manners, an' I don't sell 'em 'til they're four. Don't believe a horse is full grown 'til it's four, so I keep 'em 'til then to be sure they all get a proper start."

"You said you had several horses for sale?" Stephen asked.

"Yep, there are four, two colts an' two fillies."

"I'd prefer a colt," Patrick said.

"I've got 'em all in the barn there," Sam said. "I'll take each one out separately, so you can see how they're built an' ride 'em, if you want. There's a small paddock on the other side of the barn." He went into the tack room and emerged carrying one of the old saddles and a saddle pad. "If you could take this around the side," he continued, handing the tack to Patrick, "I'll bring the first one out for you."

Stephen and Patrick turned and walked

around the barn to a circular training paddock adjacent to the pasture. Content to let his son handle the selection, Stephen leaned awkwardly against the fence. Sam came out of a rear door of the barn leading a chestnut horse behind him. Patrick set the saddle over the top of the fence and looked closely at the horse. It was a beautiful animal, with a build much like that of the blood bay he had seen in the barn. This horse had a bright white blaze down its forehead and nose.

The horse wore a bridle with a long rein, and Sam stepped to the center of the paddock with the rein in his hand. He shook it gently. The horse began to trot in a circle around him. Its movement was fluid and powerful. A chirrup prompted the horse to canter, toss its head, and swish its tail. After a few minutes, Patrick held up a hand and entered the paddock.

Sam stopped the colt and held its head up so that Patrick could examine its overall conformation. Patrick ran his hands down its neck, sides, and legs, and picked up each of the horse's feet. The colt was obviously accustomed to being handled. It waited patiently until Sam released its head, and then turned its attention to the grass growing in the paddock.

"You want to saddle him?" Sam asked Patrick.

"Could I see the other one first?" Patrick responded. He was thinking of the blood bay he had seen in the barn.

"Sure thing." Sam led the colt outside the paddock, looped the end of the reins around the fence, and walked back into the barn. He returned with the second four-year-old — not the blood bay, but a dark brown horse. Patrick again watched as Sam worked the horse in a circle within the paddock. This colt, too, had impeccable conformation and appeared to be trained as well as the first. Having refused a ride on the chestnut, he felt obliged to saddle this one. He rode the horse several times around the paddock. The ride was smooth and effortless, and the colt obeyed all of his commands without hesitation. Still, with this horse and the chestnut, there was something missing.

He dismounted and handed the reins to Sam.

"They're both fine animals," Patrick told him. He paused. "I couldn't help but notice another one in the barn earlier, a bay? Is that horse for sale?"

"He's a three-year-old, nah, three an' a half, really," Sam replied. "He's a spirited little devil. I kept him in his stall this morning so I could work with him this afternoon. I just started him under the saddle, an' I can already tell he's going to be a handful. Not mean, mind you, but definitely spirited. I wouldn't sell him until he's four, like the others. But I can bring him out for a look, if you'd like."

"I would like to see him," Patrick said. He looked over at his father for a second opinion, but Stephen, oblivious to their discussion, was gingerly stroking the nose of the chestnut tied outside the paddock.

"Mary, could you bring out the bay?" Sam called toward the barn. He began to unbuckle the saddle on the brown colt. "Mary's my daughter," he explained. "She's pretty shy, doesn't really get involved with the sellin' much, but otherwise, she helps out quite a bit with the horses. She's even better with some of 'em than I am, an' the bay in there really behaves for her."

Patrick had neither seen nor heard anyone except Sam since they had arrived at the farm. Then he remembered the noise in the barn. Apparently, he had not been alone.

A loud whinny captured their attention, and the blood bay appeared at the barn door. The colt was tall for a Morgan and almost completely obscured Mary as she walked on the other side of the horse. She kept a firm hand on the lead of the halter as she brought the colt to the paddock.

The bay colt was even more spectacular in the morning sun than he had looked in the dim light inside the barn. The colt seemed to know it, too. He tossed his head repeatedly, shied sideways, as if to flaunt his mahogany beauty. They came closer, through the gate of the paddock. If Patrick had looked closely, he would have noticed a certain spark in the deep brown eyes of the colt, that something that had been missing from the previous two. But despite his fine eye for horses, he didn't notice the spark at all.

He couldn't tear his gaze from Mary.

She led the colt into the paddock and stood almost motionless beside it, still holding fast to the lead. Patrick heard Sam telling him about the bay, but the voice was little more than a monotonous hum occasionally punctuated by a few intelligible words.

". . . an' he's got one of the finest heads I've ever seen on a Morgan, deep-set eyes, an' a fine arch in his neck . . ."

Patrick nodded, shifting his attention to the colt, but his gaze kept being drawn back to Mary. She had dark brown, almost black hair. Most of it was pulled into a loose ponytail at the nape of her neck, but a few tendrils fluttered around her temples. Her cheekbones were high and delicate, under fair skin tinged with the palest pink. She looked up at him with blue eyes rimmed by the longest black lashes he had ever seen. He got an especially good look at the lashes, because Mary averted her eyes downward only a second after he looked into them. She turned her face toward the bay colt. Her unobtrusive manner made her easy to overlook, but once noticed, she was exquisite.

". . . straight legs, an' you'll notice that his build is just as good as that of the four-year-olds, an' he might end up a bigger horse, over fifteen hands when he's full grown . . ."

Mary wore a gray cotton blouse and old work pants cinched with a brown leather belt. Her pants were tucked into scuffed riding boots that came up to her knees. Patrick hardly noticed her attire. He was much more interested in what was beneath her clothing. He caught a glimpse of her throat exposed at the top of her shirt, the outline of her breasts, the slim waist hidden beneath the belt. She looked to be a few inches over five feet tall, but her petite frame made her appear much smaller. *Such fine breeding,* he thought.

Aside from Mary's beauty, though, there was something else about her that appealed to Patrick: vulnerability. Her meekness would be apparent to anyone, but to a man of society who could sum up everything about a person from a thirty-second introduction, and to whom the exercise of power over another was recreation, it was an invitation for pleasure. Patrick was a hawk that had spotted a sparrow.

"He's just green broke now, an' he needs several months of training before he'd be fit for a gentleman such as yourself," Sam finished. "An' as I said, I don' sell 'em 'til they're four, anyhow. But he's a good'un, for sure."

Patrick forced himself to concentrate on the farmer. "I'll be honest with you, Sam. The colts are all exceptional, but this bay tops them all. I don't need to see you work him to know that this is the one I want, assuming he checks out with our veterinarian. Surely we could work out an arrangement. He'd be almost four at the end of the summer. Could I give you a deposit for him and take him then?"

Sam pushed his hat more firmly onto his head and smoothed his grizzled beard. "I've never done that before," he said. "Mary, why don' you put the others in the field?" Mary slipped over to the four-year-olds and led them away toward the gate in the pasture fence. Patrick watched her go. He pictured her on his arm, wearing a fine gown as they made their entrance at a social engagement, saw his parents smiling their approval, saw the looks on the faces of the other guests, especially the other men, as he escorted her. He had always had the best of everything. She would be his perfect match — a shining but submissive partner in his world of wealth and prestige. He clenched his jaw, overcome with a sudden sense of desperation at the thought of not seeing more of her, until an idea hit him.

"I'll pay you double what you normally ask for one of your colts," he blurted, "and I'd gladly come out here on weekends to help with the training. That way, you could be sure that he'd get a proper start, as you describe it. I've been riding for years, but I've never helped train a horse before. Judging from the manners of those four-year-olds, you must be pretty good at it." Patrick smiled, trying to look pleasantly hopeful and fighting the urge to stare at Mary's backside as she walked farther away.

"Well," Sam finally said, "that's a little

sooner than I usually let 'em go, but I don' know that I could refuse an offer like that. I s'pose if you work with him some, he could get used to you, an' I could make sure everything goes well with him . . ."

"Then we have a deal?" Patrick asked.

"I'll expect you here on Saturday mornings, about ten," Sam said, as they shook hands.

Patrick's father strolled up to them. He looked first at Patrick, then at the bay colt grazing beside him. "This the one?" he asked. "Nice color. When shall we send a truck for him?"

"Oh, around the first of September or so," Sam said, smiling.

"Come again?"

"He's the best of them, Pop, but he's not fully broken yet," Patrick explained. "So Sam is going to keep him for the summer, work with him, and we'll get him in a few months. And, I'm going to help with the training on the weekends."

"Oh." Stephen's mouth drooped slightly, and his brow furrowed. "I suppose we won't have our Saturday drives, then." His voice was whiny. "But Patrick, you were so excited to get a horse. Are you sure you want to wait all summer? The other two looked like fine specimens to me," he said.

43

"Of course they are," Patrick said. "But a few more months for the right horse isn't really long to wait. Besides, there's something about this one. I have to have this one." *And,* he thought to himself, *I'll have more from this farm than the bay colt.*

"Whatever you want, son," Stephen said, forcing a smile. He pulled out his checkbook and a pen.

Stephen gave Sam a deposit for the bay colt, and he and Patrick walked back to the Lincoln. Father and son were quiet as they headed down the driveway of the farm, back toward the main road.

"I must say, I still prefer good horsepower to a good horse," Stephen finally said. "If you think that red horse was a real find, I trust you. It must be if you'd wait 'til the end of the summer for it, being as horse-crazy as you are. But," he added, stepping on the accelerator with a satisfied grin, "to each his own."

"A real find," Patrick said, but he wasn't speaking of the bay colt.

CHAPTER 3

As darkness continued to embrace the town of Mill River, Father O'Brien struggled to come up with a sermon for the morning's service. The various themes running through his mind lingered for only a few minutes before his thoughts drifted back to Mary.

In an effort to redirect his thoughts, he looked at the large box of spoons sitting on his desk. It was a box of joy and guilt and sin. He had taped it shut and printed his return address in the upper left corner of the top surface. The address for the box's destination was another matter. It didn't have a destination yet, and he was too tired to worry about it now.

Of far greater concern to him was Mary. He intended to go back up to her mansion at first light. Mass would not begin until ten-thirty, so he would have plenty of time.

He had a dreadful feeling that he would

need it.

Officer Kyle Hansen was quiet as he opened the door of his apartment. He hung his coat on a hook by the door and went to check on Rowen.

His nine-year-old was sound asleep in her bed, surrounded by a zoo of stuffed animals. *I'll surprise her with Mickey Mouse pancakes in the morning,* he thought. He liked to spoil her with special breakfasts on mornings after he worked a late shift and wasn't home at her bedtime. Rowen turned and sighed in her sleep. He bent down and kissed her lightly on the cheek before heading to the bathroom to take a shower.

Kyle relaxed as the torrents of hot water streamed over him. He smiled, remembering the peaceful expression on Rowen's face as she slept. He remembered, too, the first time he'd made Mickey Mouse pancakes for her and her mother years ago, after a vacation to Disney World. It was amazing how much Rowen was beginning to look like her mother. That thought saddened him, though, so he reminded himself of how far they had come since his wife, Allison, had lost her battle with cancer.

Kyle had met her when he was working as a detective with the Boston Police Department, and Allison was a counselor with the city's Department of Children and Families. Allison had been an absolute natural in her job. Her kind, caring nature put almost anyone at ease and made her a favorite when children were involved. When Kyle and his partner had arrested a husband and wife in South Boston on child abuse charges, Allison was called in to interview the two little boys. It was a tragic case, like many others in which Kyle had been involved in his years on the force. But unlike the others, two good things came out of it. Custody of the boys had been awarded to their loving grandparents, and he and Allison had begun a relationship that eventually led to their marriage.

After Allison died, Kyle found himself a single father with a seven-year-old and a job that regularly required forays into the most dangerous parts of Boston. The excitement of being a big-city detective disappeared. He couldn't bear the thought of something happening to him and Rowen losing both her parents. He began looking for a job in a safe place, preferably a quiet community where people felt no need to lock their doors at night. When a buddy told him that he'd heard there was an opening for a police officer in a small town in Vermont, Kyle applied immediately.

Mill River was nothing like Boston. A fender bender or an occasional act of vandalism made for an exciting day in the small town. Pulling someone over for a traffic violation was a major incident. In Boston, people scurried; in Mill River, they strolled. For Kyle, the move was well worth a steep pay cut. The chances of his being injured or killed on the job were extremely low. Even with the rare emergencies that required his help when he was off duty, life was now leisurely and refreshing. Of course, he had to tolerate Leroy, who was nothing compared with the experienced and hardworking colleagues he'd had in Boston, but Kyle considered that a minor price to pay.

Kyle and Rowen lived in a small apartment in a building owned by Joe Fitzgerald, the police chief, and his wife, Ruth. There were two units on the second floor of the building, and the Fitzgeralds lived in the other apartment. Fitz, as everyone in Mill River called him, offered the apartment to Kyle when he accepted the position with the town's police department. It was clean and cozy, and the rent was cheap. Plus, there were other advantages.

Kyle's schedule often required him to work irregular hours, and Ruth, whose own twin daughters and several grandchildren lived several states away, insisted on looking after Rowen when Kyle wasn't home. When Kyle was on duty after Rowen went to sleep, a baby monitor in her room (or, as Rowen referred to it, a "daughter monitor") allowed Ruth to keep tabs on her from the apartment across the hall.

Then, there were the smells. Ruth ran a bakery out of the first floor, and everything she made was delicious. Fresh bread. Cakes. Chocolate chip cookies. And pies, especially the pies. Pecan, Boston cream, strawberry-rhubarb, pumpkin, coconut-custard, apple. By the time Rowen left for school each morning, Ruth had the ovens downstairs full of the day's baking. The fabulous aromas rose through the floorboards of their apartment and made getting up on chilly Vermont mornings almost pleasant.

Kyle was surprised and relieved at how well Rowen had adjusted to their new life. True, there were plenty of tears and hard questions to answer about Allison's death, but his daughter showed a steely resilience in being able to understand and accept it. She loved her school and her new teacher. He worried about Rowen being lonely, but since they lived in town, she could go play with other children who lived only a few blocks away. She had recently asked for a pet. Kyle figured that a dog or cat would also be good company for her, and that he'd eventually give in to her request.

Kyle finished rinsing and stepped out of the shower. After he dried himself, he tied the towel around his waist and wiped his hand in a circle on the steamy mirror. His reflection stared back at him through the porthole. He had baggy eyes and a few days' worth of stubble. On a whim, he struck his best bodybuilder's pose. With the veil of steam coating the rest of the mirror, his biceps didn't look too bad. Satisfied, he left the bathroom seeking boxer shorts and bed.

Jean Wykowski managed to fall asleep beside her snoring husband, but her rest was wrought with vivid, piercing dreams. She was in the white mansion, walking up the stairs to check on Mrs. McAllister. The stairs went on and on, curving and twisting, and as she struggled to reach the top, she heard the old widow calling for help, calling out for her. She could see the bedroom at the top of the stairs, the light from inside leaking beneath the door. She climbed faster.

"I'm coming, Mrs. McAllister," Jean called in her sleep. "I'm almost there." With superhuman strength, she vaulted the final four stairs and burst into the bedroom.

The old woman was out of bed, standing at the window.

"Mrs. McAllister, how did you get —" Jean began, but she stopped speaking as the woman turned slowly to face her. The eye patch the widow usually wore was gone, revealing her cloudy, unseeing left eye.

"I know you have it, Jean," Mrs. McAllister said, shaking her head. "You're too late."

"Oh, but Mrs. McAllister, I don't, let me help you," Jean stammered, rushing toward the frail widow, but before Jean could grab the old woman, she felt a strong hand gripping her own arm.

"Jeanie, hey Jeanie, you're dreaming. Wake up, hon."

She felt the hand shaking her now, and opened her eyes. Ron was sitting up in bed beside her.

"Are you all right? You were thrashing around and yelling, having some sort of nightmare. Thought I'd rescue you."

"Sorry. Did I wake the kids?" Jean asked. Her heart was still beating heavily.

"Nah. You yelling has never done much to get them up."

"Thanks a lot," Jean said, playfully elbowing her husband. He grunted and lay back down on his pillow.

"So, what were you dreaming about?" Ron mumbled.

Jean thought of Mary McAllister's sad face, her deliberate stare. Somehow, the old woman knew.

"I don't remember," Jean said, but Ron was already snoring again.

Leroy Underwood sat in his rusty 1986 Chevy Camaro in front of Claudia Simon's house. The air inside the car reeked of smoke. Without taking his eyes off the teacher's home, Leroy lit another cigarette and inhaled deeply. He had really become comfortable with this house-watching habit. Sit, smoke, relax. Hope to see Claudia. He pictured her wearing only her panties, waving to him from her brightly lit bedroom window, inviting him inside.

Frustrated, he took another drag on the cigarette. She was probably asleep, but even if she wasn't, the damned snow would prevent him from seeing her. His camera resting on the passenger's seat would be useless tonight.

Leroy pulled a cell phone from his pocket, dialed *-6-7 to prevent his number from appearing on caller ID, and selected Claudia's number from his list of contacts. Since he couldn't see her, he decided to permit himself the occasional indulgence of hearing her voice. He felt his pulse quicken as he waited for the connection. Claudia answered after the third ring.

"Hello?" Her voice was soft and low, with just a touch of confusion. "Hello? Who's there?"

He held his breath until she hung up and then exhaled a long, steady stream of smoke.

A part of him felt guilty for waking Claudia, but hearing her throaty voice only intensified his need for her. That voice, and the images of her that ran through his mind during these late-night spying sessions, sustained him. They also supplemented the real pictures of her that he had at home.

Leroy sighed, started the engine, and twisted what was left of his cigarette into the ashtray.

The alarm clock on his nightstand read 3:15, but Father O'Brien was still awake. He turned over onto his stomach and buried his face in the pillow. In this position, he wouldn't have to see the red glow of the clock as the minutes passed. He lay this way for almost half an hour, but it was no use. At 3:41, he climbed out of bed, put on his robe, and went into the dark living room.

The furnishings were sparse. There was an old sofa and matching recliner, a coffee table in need of refinishing, and a television, but those few things were enough. He rarely took anyone into the parish house. When he was home, he preferred to sit in the kitchen or at his desk in the office. What little time he spent in his living room was usually during the middle of the night when he had trouble sleeping.

He squinted down at the television. It was old, too, an RCA from the early seventies. He had received it as a gift when it was brand-new. Sparing use had ensured that it remained operational more than forty years later, although he'd recently had to replace the antenna and purchase some sort of digital converter box for it. He reached out and turned the channel dial carefully, flipping through the stations. Since he had neither cable nor a satellite dish, he could get only two or three clear channels. His choices tonight appeared to be an infomercial, a *Three's Company* rerun, and several channels of static.

Opting for none of those, Father O'Brien returned the dial to off and sat down in the recliner. The footrest of the cranky old chair came up beneath his legs even though he had not pulled the lever to extend it, but he didn't care. *In fact,* he thought as he rubbed his eyes and hoped for sleep, *it's quite comfortable.*

There was just enough light coming from his bedroom down the hall to create a reflection in the dark television screen. It was more like a silhouette, really, because he couldn't make out his features. The outline of his balding head, with the the few remaining hairs on top that refused to lie flat, were all that he could see in the glass.

He remembered well the day before Christmas in 1973, the day he had received the RCA. He remembered it because on that day every household in Mill River had received a new television just like it.

His mouth turned up in a slight smile as he closed his eyes. It had been such a pleasure, hearing his parishioners wonder aloud who had given so generously that Christmas. For children in town, and for perhaps a few of the adults, the delivery of the TVs had reinforced or restored beliefs in Santa Claus. Many of them had come to him with their questions, convinced that he and the church were behind the surprise. He had answered honestly that neither he nor the church was the gift-giver.

By that day in 1973, it was widely known that strange things happened in Mill River. Gifts for people seemed to appear out of nowhere — usually clothing or household goods, or an occasional money order to help cover bills for someone having a hard time. But the delivery of the television sets was the beginning of a series of larger gift-giving events that occurred every few years or so.

In 1975, there was the check for ten thousand dollars that arrived at Rutland County Hospital just in time to pay for Edna Wilson's open-heart surgery. In 1983, a new home had been delivered to Josie DiSanti after she and her two young girls had arrived in town after the loss of her husband. Twice during the eighties, a brand-new school bus had been delivered to the Mill River Elementary School, even though the school board had lacked the funds for such a purchase. In 1993, a few days after a group of delinquents had driven through town in the cover of night, slashing tires as they went, a truck from the Sears auto store arrived with replacements for everyone. And not a week after faulty wiring had caused the McGregor family's house to burn during the frigid winter of 1997, Stan and Claire McGregor and their five children had been presented with an estimate from a contractor to rebuild their home, along with an escrow account containing the full amount needed for the reconstruction.

The townspeople didn't know how or why the kindnesses were bestowed on them. No recipient was ever told the identity of the benefactor — they were simply left to wonder.

Over time, the occurrences became town legends, stories told by the old-timers as they sat on porches drinking lemonade or in the bakery lingering over lukewarm cups of coffee. The television bonanza especially was rehashed dozens of times. Each time it was told, to a newcomer or after another person in town had received an anonymous gift, the number of televisions given on that Christmas Eve increased slightly. The last time Father O'Brien had heard the story, well over four hundred TVs had been given, even though the actual number had been three hundred thirty-six.

It was after four in the morning when, in the comfort of his recliner, Father O'Brien felt sleep come to him. His rest would be brief, he knew, for dawn was only a few hours away. He would have to go back to the marble mansion then and face whatever truths were hiding there, but for now, he clung to those happy memories of the past and what benefactions were yet to come.

CHAPTER 4

1940

In her nineteen years, she had never met anyone like him.

Mary lay in bed, staring at the ceiling. The image of Patrick, tall and blond, standing beside her father and the young Morgans earlier that day, was seared in her mind. Mary blushed at the memory of how he had stared at her, and, cringing, she pressed her face into her pillow. She had been paralyzed by her shyness. She remembered what she had been wearing and felt her face burn even hotter. Not that she even owned a fancy dress, but if she had known that someone like Patrick was arriving at the farm, she would have at least worn a skirt instead of her work pants and the tall boots she wore to muck out the stables.

And now, he would be at the farm every Saturday.

She didn't know how she would be able

to avoid him, but she would try.

That Saturday, and for the next several that followed, Mary managed to slip away with her black mare, Ebony, before Patrick arrived. One Saturday morning in July, though, as she was leading Ebony through the gate, Patrick pulled up beside the barn in a dark green sedan. He got out of the car and smiled at her.

He was early.

"Good morning, Mary! It's nice to see you again! Looks like we're in for a great day, don't you think?"

She stood, frozen on the spot with Ebony's reins in her hand. She swallowed. Her mouth was dry.

"Yes," she said, her voice barely audible. "Good morning."

"So, you're headed out for your Saturday ride? Your father told me you do that often," Patrick said. "Hey, maybe we could take a quick ride together before we start working him? My colt, I mean. I haven't settled on a name yet. I've been riding him in the training ring, but there's not much room in there. Here comes your father now, I'll ask him."

Mary saw her father coming down the footpath from the house. Before she could say anything, Patrick intercepted him and then turned to face her as she stood with the black mare.

"Let me just get the saddle on him. We can take a walk around the pasture," Patrick called, and went inside the barn.

Mary's heart was racing. She climbed into the saddle. She could escape on Ebony before Patrick could even get the bay colt out of his stall. She wheeled Ebony around and then stopped her. There was that strange feeling, the feeling of wanting to be around Patrick. *Stop it,* she told herself. *Get out of here while you have the chance.* Still, she hesitated.

"Mary?" a voice beside her asked. Startled, she flinched in the saddle. Her father stood beside her horse, looking up at her.

"Are you all right?" he asked.

"Yes," she said, "I just, well, you know."

"Patrick's all excited 'bout wanting to ride around the pasture. I told him that'd be fine. The colt's not ready to ride outside the fence, but inside he'd be safe. You feel like you could do that? Jus' once around, to have another horse with some sense next to the colt?" her father asked. "You're all ready to go with Ebby. It'd save me the trouble of saddlin' up another one or walking with him myself."

Mary's hands were shaking. "He makes me nervous," she said, looking toward the barn.

Sam rested a hand against the mare's neck. "Aw, Patrick's a nice fella, an' it'd jus' be once around. Then you can take off like you usually do."

Her father knew well what happened to Mary when she was around a stranger. She had never grown out of her childhood shyness; instead, it had become worse, especially after what Mary had gone through during high school. Still, he did what he could to encourage her to interact with people. He did his best to understand the fear and anxiety that gripped Mary in the presence of strangers and hoped that somehow, with his encouragement, she might become more outgoing.

Mary sat astride Ebony and didn't say anything. Sam took her silence as acquiescence and went to see if Patrick needed help saddling the bay.

When they emerged from the barn, Patrick was in the saddle. Her father kept a firm grip on the colt's bridle near the bit. With a nod to Patrick, he released his hold on the rein and opened the pasture gate so that Mary and Patrick could ride through it.

"Remember, Patrick, jus' once around.

Try to work on his gaits and keep him with Mary's horse — she's a sensible mare," he called after them. Then Patrick and Mary were alone, headed out into the vast green pasture.

The blood bay colt was eager for exercise. He tossed his head, champing at the bit. Then he tried to break into a trot and bolted to the side. Patrick moved in the saddle with him. He had his hands full for a few moments. The bay colt arched his neck and pranced under the tight rein, but Patrick finally managed to restrain him. Mary and Ebony walked just ahead of them, seemingly oblivious to the battle being waged. The black mare stepped lightly with her ears pricked forward.

"He's full of himself this morning," Patrick said, as he and the colt drew alongside Ebony. "He should settle down in a bit, though. Your mare sure has manners. What's her name?"

Mary glanced quickly at Patrick to her left, and felt the panic start to well up inside her. "Ebony," she replied. She knew Patrick was looking at her and focused on watching the fence posts pass on her right. It took so long to go from one to the next.

"Suits her," Patrick said. The bay colt suddenly half reared, but Patrick managed to stay in the saddle. He turned the colt in a tight circle and came up beside her again. "You think we could trot a little?" he asked. "It might help get some of this friskiness out of his system."

"Sure," Mary said, and lightly touched her heels to Ebony's sides. The mare immediately broke into a smooth trot, leaving Patrick and the bay colt behind her. She didn't notice that Patrick held the colt back a moment longer to watch her firm backside posting up and down in the saddle in perfect rhythm with Ebony's movements.

It is as if she were part of the mare, Patrick thought to himself. Mary didn't talk much, but she was great on a horse. Still, he had to find some way to get her to open up. Even with looks like hers, it would not do to have a woman who said only one word at a time. Patrick loosened the reins just a little, and the bay colt surged forward until they were once again even with Mary and the black mare.

"You sure can ride," Patrick said to her. "Your father taught you?"

"Mostly," Mary answered. She stole another look at him. "But I've practiced for years."

Patrick was encouraged. That was the most she'd said to him yet.

"How old's your mare?" he asked.

"Twelve," Mary answered. "She was born here, when I was seven, and I raised her." Mary patted Ebony's neck. For a moment, she forgot about watching the fence posts.

Patrick did the math in his head. *So she's nineteen,* he thought. *Perfect.*

"I've been riding almost four years," he told her. "Started just after I went to college. They have some pretty nice equestrian facilities in Cambridge, and riding is quite popular. I'm not good enough to compete, not like you, or some of the others up there who've been riding all their lives. But now that I'm home, I miss being able to take a horse out and forget about real life for a while. Pop's setting up a stable for me just outside Rutland."

"I go riding for that same reason," Mary said. *Maybe Papa was right about Patrick,* she thought. She felt her abdominal muscles begin to relax. They were coming around the far corner of the pasture. "You said that you were home now?" she asked, surprised to hear the words spill out of her mouth.

"Yes. I'm going to help at the marbleworks, with my father and grandfather. McAllister Marbleworks, in Rutland. You've heard of it?"

"Oh, yes," Mary said. She hadn't the

slightest idea what he was talking about.

"Grandpop is technically in charge, but my father pretty much runs the whole thing. Pop's done a lot to expand it. Now we have representatives who travel all over the world marketing our products. He also put up two new buildings to help meet the demand. One's for cutting marble into tile for floors and things, and the other's for carving statues and figurines."

"Oh," Mary said, because she could think of nothing else to say. She hadn't known that floors could be made of marble.

"Someday," Patrick continued, "I'll be in charge. My father expects me to take over the business once he retires. And, if I can find someone to settle down with, I might have a son of my own who could run it with me."

Mary only nodded. His green eyes were piercing, demanding. She felt a familiar heat beginning to creep onto her face.

Mary's bland response to his mentioning his prestigious future position bothered Patrick. He would try another subject.

"Has it always been just you and your father?" he asked. "I don't mean to pry. I was only wondering."

"Oh. Yes. I never knew my mother. She died giving birth to me," Mary said. "So it's

66

just been Papa and me. And the horses."

"Well, Mill River's a nice place to grow up," Patrick said. "Nice and quiet, pretty countryside. Not too far from Proctor or Rutland. You're really lucky to have had horses your whole life. Hey, let's speed up a little. I don't want to keep your father waiting much longer." Besides, he was eager to show Mary that he, too, was an able horseman.

Patrick finally relaxed his hold on the reins, letting the bay colt loose. The horse tore off toward the gate and then veered back into the pasture. Patrick managed to stop him, but the bay colt reared up and pitched him onto the grass. As the colt flung its hind legs into the air and galloped away, Patrick cursed and wished he had been carrying a riding crop. He was in a mind to go give the colt a good lashing.

Mary urged Ebony into a canter and rode quickly over to Patrick. "Are you hurt?" she asked. She saw her father running through the grass toward them.

"No, no, he just caught me a little unprepared," Patrick said. "Your father was right. He is a handful."

Mary noticed that his face was the color of a ripe tomato.

"If you want to start back to the barn, I'll

get the colt for you," she offered.

"Sure, thanks," Patrick said, rubbing his hip.

Mary rode over to where the bay colt was grazing contentedly, pulled the reins over his head, and led him back to the barn. Patrick and her father were already there, laughing. Mary saw her father slap him on the back good-naturedly. When she reached them, she handed the reins of the colt to her father. Patrick looked disheveled and sore.

"I was jus' tellin' Patrick here that that was the finest show of horsemanship I've seen in a while," her father said, smiling. "Don' you think, Mary?" Still chuckling, he led the bay colt toward the training paddock.

"Yes," she said. Patrick's final moments aboard the bay colt had been quite comical. Strangely, the panicky feeling inside her was gone. She looked at Patrick, really looked at him for the first time, and smiled. He returned the smile.

Mine, Patrick thought.

"Well, seeing as how you're so impressed by my riding prowess, perhaps you would go riding with me again next Saturday, to allow me to give you a few pointers? Assuming, that is, that my trusty steed is, well, a little more trusty?" he asked.

"All right," she said, and turned Ebony onto a riding trail that led into the sugar maples.

Patrick stood for a moment, watching the black mare disappear into the woods. Maybe falling off the damned horse hadn't been such a bad thing after all. He smiled to himself in cold satisfaction and walked back toward the training paddock.

Patrick and Mary went riding the next time he came out to the farm, and the next, and the next. At first, they stayed inside the pasture. As Mary's father worked his magic on the bay colt, however, they began riding around the farm, in the forest, and along the country roads outside Mill River.

Patrick learned that, despite being exceptionally shy, Mary was articulate and had a keen mind. Because of her anxiety and the shortened school years during the Depression, Mary's attendance at school had been sporadic. Still, she loved to read. She had read every book in the school library and could converse knowledgeably about many topics. Books were her primary link to the world that she found so difficult to enter.

To Patrick, Mary was the supreme challenge. He knew that the trust he earned from her each week was fragile. He built it gradually, showering her with attention and repressing any impatience or irritation he felt in prying her out of her shell. Several times, he came close to abandoning his attempts to win her over. As a young man of high standing, he was expected to complete his education and marry. He didn't know how much more of his parents' incessant urging to "find a nice young lady" he could take, and Mary would require some time. True, he could choose a wife from among a good two dozen twittering socialites who regularly fawned over him. His parents would approve of any of them since, unlike Mary, they all came from moneyed families. But those women, and the many who had already succumbed to him, were easy. And none were as beautiful or difficult as the horse breeder's daughter.

Mary had never been happier in her life. She so looked forward to Patrick's visits. To her surprise, she felt more and more comfortable with him. He listened with interest to what little she said and always knew exactly what to say in return. She finally had a friend, and human interaction with someone other than her father. Mary didn't understand why a gentleman like Patrick would want to spend time with a shy farm girl like her, but she did not dwell on the issue.

She swore to herself that she would never reveal to him her darkest secret — the horrific event she still struggled to overcome.

The summer passed quickly. On the first Saturday in September, the bay colt was ready to go. Patrick, his father, and two hired men drove up to the farm in a horse van. A veterinarian from Rutland pulled up behind them in another car. Mary wanted to go down to the barn to say goodbye to Patrick and the colt, but the sight of the other men sent her into a state of panic. It had been months since her fear of strangers had surfaced, and the intensity of it took her breath away. She stayed inside the farmhouse, watching her father and the other men inspect the bay colt and load him into the van.

Patrick's father wrote a check to Sam for the remainder of the purchase price for the horse and got in the van to leave. Patrick looked around for Mary, but she was nowhere in sight.

"Sam, you wouldn't know where Mary is, would you? I'd hate to leave without saying goodbye to her," Patrick said.

"Last I saw, she was up at the house," he replied. "You know how shy she is, an' since your father an' the vet came with you this time —"

"I was hoping she'd be over it enough to meet my father properly," Patrick interrupted, frowning. "I've told him what a pleasure it's been getting to know her these past few months, and I know he wanted to meet her. Would you mind if I went up to the house, to see if I could get her to come down?"

" 'Course not," Sam said. "But good luck."

Carrying a small bag, Patrick bolted up the footpath to the farmhouse. He was about to knock at the door when Mary opened it, wide-eyed and pale. "Mary, I'm so glad I didn't miss you," he said to her as he stepped inside. "I couldn't leave without saying goodbye, and I've told my family so much about you. Won't you come down and meet my father?"

"I can't," Mary said in a hoarse whisper. She was trembling. "I wanted to come down, but I couldn't."

This isn't going as planned, Patrick thought. He tried to ignore a dart of frustration as it shot through him and held up the small bag in his hand.

"Actually, I brought you something, a present. I wanted to get something for you to thank you for your company over the summer." He reached into the bag, as if to remove the gift, and then hesitated. "It's fine if you don't feel comfortable coming down right now," he continued. "But you must promise me that you'll come to Rutland to visit me and meet my folks. They know all about you and have been asking to meet you."

He pulled his hand out of the bag. In it was something wrapped in a soft cloth. He handed the lump to Mary.

"Go ahead, unwrap it."

Mary took the parcel. It was solid and heavy. She peeled back the cloth and gasped. It was a horse, carved from black marble and polished to a high shine. Mary stared at the small version of Ebony in her hands.

"Do you like it?" Patrick asked, watching her face. "I had it carved for you at the marbleworks."

"It's beautiful," she said. Grasping for the words to tell him how much she loved the figurine, she finally looked up at Patrick. He took her face in his hands and kissed her.

Mary would have dropped the miniature Ebony had it not been pressed tightly between them. After a moment, Patrick pulled away and looked down at her.

"Mary, you must know that I've looked forward to seeing more at this farm than the bay colt," he said in a low voice. He ran a finger down her cheek. "Just because he's coming with me now doesn't mean we can't continue to see each other. Promise me that you'll come to Rutland next Saturday and have dinner with my family. I'll drive out in the afternoon to get you. Please, Mary."

Mary was dizzy. The room was spinning. Everything except Patrick standing in front of her was a blur. She so wanted to please him, but to go to a strange place with strange people! His green eyes looked at her, and her mouth tingled where his had touched it only a few seconds before. Mary finally nodded, and Patrick smiled.

"I'll be here at five. Don't worry, it will only be my family, and you'll be with me," he said, turning to leave. Halfway down the footpath, he looked back and waved at her. Then, he shook hands with her father, climbed into the van, and was gone.

"Well, son, you finally have your Morgan. Never did get to meet that girl you were telling us about, though," Stephen McAllister said as the van strained to pick up speed.

"She was up at the house, Pop. She wasn't feeling well. But she's agreed to have dinner with us next weekend."

"Ah, splendid!" Stephen said. "It's strange — you say she was there the day we first came for the colt, but I can't remember seeing her. Oh, well. You remember, of course, that your mother has invited the family to the house next Saturday. It would be an excellent time for you to introduce us to this little hayseed we've all been hearing about."

Patrick ignored his father's belittling reference to Mary. Despite her country upbringing, she was well-spoken and lovely — something his family would surely realize once they met her. He had, however, forgotten about his mother's plans. Such a large gathering might prove problematic with Mary, if he could even get her out of the house. Still, Mary had promised to visit, and visit she would.

A loud stomping and a whinny came from the van's cargo compartment behind them. "Son, have you named this colt yet?" Patrick's father asked.

A regal power coursed through Patrick as he remembered the feel of Mary's face locked in his hands and the sweet taste of her mouth. He, a gentleman and heir to a great fortune, would have all to which he was entitled, including the queen of his choice. "Funny you should ask, Pop," Patrick said. "I just decided on it. His name's Monarch."

CHAPTER 5

In the gray February dawn, Father O'Brien drove slowly up the hill toward the white marble home. Even with all-wheel drive, his truck strained as it rolled through almost nine inches of new snow. He pulled around to the side of the house and removed his key to the back door from his coat pocket. His hand trembled as he inserted it into the lock.

The house was still and silent except for the faint ticking of the grandfather clock in the parlor. Father O'Brien wiped his shoes on the doormat and proceeded quietly through the house, up a sweeping staircase to Mary's bedroom. He could have walked this route blindfolded. But today was different. He took each step carefully, keeping a hand on the banister. He paused for a moment at the door before stepping inside.

Her adjustable hospital bed faced the bay window opposite him. The bed was in a slightly upright position to enable her to see out the window, and Father O'Brien had to step in front of the bed to see her. His breath caught in his throat as he came around and whispered her name.

"Mary?"

There was no movement or sound in response, not even the quiet sonance of breathing.

She was gone.

Mary lay in the bed, her eyes closed and her hands resting gently in her lap. He took one of her hands in his. It was still warm and pliable. Her skin had a grayish pallor tinged with the yellow of jaundice, but her illness had cast this tone over her skin for so long that now, in death, Mary looked to him as if she were only sleeping. The absence of her breathing revealed the truth.

For a long moment, Father O'Brien looked at her. He let go of her hand to smooth a strand of hair out of her face. His lip quivered as he noticed the empty prescription bottle on her nightstand. As he prayed over her, his voice cracked and fell to a whisper. His tears fell freely onto her. He prayed for her soul, suspecting how she died and hoping that her soul would be allowed into heaven. When he finished, he made the sign of the cross and knelt by her bedside. In the stillness of the mansion, the sound of weeping joined the ticking of the grandfather clock.

Kyle was a pancake master.

Since his wife's death, his abilities in the kitchen had vastly improved. Through trial and error and frequent advice from Ruth Fitzgerald, he had developed a limited repertoire of meals that he could prepare successfully. Pot roast and mashed potatoes, for example. Slap the roast in the Crock-Pot for eight hours — simple. Boil peeled potatoes until soft, add milk, salt, and butter, and beat the heck out of them — easy. Hot dogs, hamburgers, and other things that he could boil or fry were no problem. Most vegetables could be boiled or eaten raw, and he forced himself to eat them so that he sounded more credible when he insisted that Rowen eat hers, too. But pancakes were different. Easy and comforting, they were his longtime specialty and Rowen's favorite.

This Sunday morning, after mixing up a bowl of batter, Kyle stood in front of the stove. He was armed with two spatulas and a turkey baster. When the oil in the frying pan reached the proper temperature, he used the turkey baster to squirt batter into a large circle in the center of the pan. Then he added two smaller circles in the ten and two o'clock positions at the top of the large circle. The small batter circles ran together with the large one to form — *voilà!* — Mickey Mouse. He used the two spatulas to flip the edible Disney character as Rowen stumbled into the kitchen.

"Morning, sleepyhead."

"Morning, Dad." She wore a long flannel nightgown and slipper booties. Her light brown hair was rumpled. Rowen rubbed one of her eyes and crawled into a chair at the table. Kyle had already set two places.

"I poured you some OJ," Kyle said. Out of the corner of his eye, he saw her reach for her glass. "I hope you're hungry. I'm making us something new for breakfast. Mouse pancakes."

Rowen swallowed a mouthful of juice and looked at her father.

"Nuh-uh," she said, smiling, but her eyes revealed just a hint of uncertainty.

"Oh yeah. I was talking to Ruth the other day. She said that when she gets a mouse in one of her traps, she skins it and puts it in the freezer. When she has a few of them stored up, she minces them and puts them in pancakes. Says it's convenient because you get some meat for breakfast without having to fix sausage or bacon on the side.

Pass me your plate, will you?"

"That's really gross, Dad." Rowen handed Kyle her plate. She had apparently decided that he was kidding. "Besides," she said, matter-of-factly, "I'm old enough to know Ruth wouldn't cook something like that."

Kyle put the Mickey Mouse pancake on her plate and handed it to her.

"Yeah, I guess you are," he said. "But we really are having mouse pancakes."

Rowen looked at her plate. "Oh, it's Mickey Mouse! I love it when you cook these!" She reached for the maple syrup.

"Seriously, Ruth did give me a few pancake pointers, even though I can make these pretty well, and I listened to be polite. But hey, next time you see her, will you stick up for me a little? Like, tell her how good your dad's pancakes always are?"

"Okay," Rowen said, smiling with her mouth full. "They *are* really good, Dad. I'll bet even Ruth can't make pancakes as good as yours."

"I'm sure she could give me a run for my money," he said with a satisfied grin. "By the way, the paper should be here. Why don't you bring it in? We can read the funnies."

Still chewing, Rowen slipped off her chair and skipped over to the front door. She opened it to retrieve the *Rutland Herald* lying outside in the hall.

"Hi, Fitz!" Kyle heard her say. He'd just flipped another Mickey likeness with the spatulas, but he took the frying pan off the hot burner and walked over to Rowen. Fitz was standing in the hall.

"Hey, kiddo! Morning, Kyle," he said, pulling on his gloves. "So you guys didn't sleep in?"

"Nah, we're up," Kyle replied. Rowen grabbed the Sunday paper and scampered back into the kitchen. "You want some pancakes?"

"No thanks. I'm kind of in a hurry. I just got a call from Father O'Brien. Apparently, Mary McAllister passed on last night, and he's up at her house now. Wykowski's on duty this morning, but he's several miles out on patrol, so the dispatcher called me. Looks like a suicide, and the father wants me to come by to make sure and get what we need for a report before the medical examiner comes to collect the body. It shouldn't take long. All I really need to do is take a look around, enough to gather information for the report."

Kyle glanced at the clock on the wall; it was almost nine o' clock. He wasn't keen on the idea of giving up a cozy Sunday morning with his daughter to deal with a suspected suicide, but Fitz was his boss. He felt obligated to offer assistance.

"Are you sure you don't need a hand? If Ruth would be here in case Rowen needed anything, I could go with you."

"Well," Fitz said, "I suppose you could come along. It'd give you a chance to see how we handle something like this, and I'm sure we'd be done pretty quick. If not, Ruth could take Rowen to the church with her when she goes." He backed out of the doorway. "I'll start the car. Come down when you're ready."

"I'll be just a second." Kyle closed the door. Rowen was finishing her pancake. He set the frying pan back on the burner and finished cooking the second Mickey.

"Rowen, hon, something's come up, and I have to go with Fitz to check up on a lady who's been very sick. Ruth will be across the hall. If I'm not back before she has to leave for church, she'll take you with her and I'll pick you up there a little later." He plopped the second pancake onto her plate and went into his bedroom to get dressed, talking all the while. "Go ahead and finish your breakfast but get dressed in case I'm late, okay?"

"Yeah." She was rifling through the center

of the paper in search of the comics. "Aren't you going to have any breakfast?"

"I had some juice, but I've got to hurry," Kyle said as he came back into the kitchen hastily buttoning his shirt. "Don't worry, I'll have an extra-big lunch." The truth was, he had lost his appetite knowing what he would be dealing with when he and Fitz got to the old woman's house. Even though he'd seen all manner of deaths in his line of work, the sight of a dead person, even one who had apparently passed in a nonviolent way, was something he'd never really gotten used to. It was a mystery to him how so many officers on the force in Boston had been utterly indifferent around the deceased. Although he had learned to hide it well, seeing someone's body always deeply affected him.

Kyle stepped into his boots and threw on his coat. "Now don't putter — you need to be ready if I'm not back or Ruth will squawk at you."

"I know, Dad," Rowen said. Kyle kissed her on the top of her head and hurried out the front door.

Daisy Delaine had hardly slept.

After Kyle had admonished her to go inside during the snowstorm, she had returned to her front yard and gathered two pots of the fluffy new snow. By the time the morning light revealed her mobile home to be half-buried in snowdrifts, the kitchen counter was littered with ingredients — rose hips, cinnamon, molasses, crushed cranberries, and a number of unlabeled bottles of herbs and powders — and two pots of potion simmered on the stove. Daisy tended her cooking pots carefully, humming to herself and occasionally bursting into full song. She directed her lyrics toward a charcoal-colored mop of fur that watched her from a kitchen chair. In response to Daisy's serenade, the mop sat up and wagged its tail.

By late morning, the red substance in the larger pot had thickened to the consistency of raspberry syrup. Crimson bubbles puckered to the surface, releasing puffs of a sweet cinnamon scent. Daisy stirred the mixture vigorously and lifted a spoonful to her nose. "Smells done to me! Nice and thick, too. We'll just let our Valentine's Day potion sit for a while to cool, won't we, Smudgie?"

Smudgie whined and lay back down on the chair. Daisy turned off the burner beneath the pot of red liquid and focused her attention on the smaller pan.

Its contents didn't smell nearly as pleasant as the red Valentine's Day potion.

Daisy whisked the watery, brownish-green mixture that simmered in the smaller pot. "Needs more sassafras," she muttered. She glanced around her kitchen, finally reaching for an unmarked jar of brown powder. She unscrewed its lid and shook a small heap of the powder into the murky mixture.

"Not long now, Smudgie, not long at all," Daisy cooed to the dog as she resumed her stirring. "We'll get this to Mary, and she'll be better in no time."

Once the powdered root had dissolved, Daisy sniffed the steam rising from the pot and removed a clean jar from her cupboard. *This has to help,* she thought as she poured ladlefuls of the liquid into the jar. *It's my strongest batch yet!* After she had carefully sealed it, Daisy gazed at the jar for a moment. She leaned over and planted a light kiss squarely on its lid.

As she switched off the second burner, her face brightened and she turned again to the little gray dog. "Maybe after I take the healing potion to Father O'Brien, I should take some samples of the Valentine's Day potion to the neighbors. We could even get some advance orders this year, couldn't we?" Smudgie yipped and wagged his tail.

Daisy ladled some of the fragrant red

liquid into a few other empty jelly jars and screwed the lids on tightly. She then put on a parka.

"Now Smudgie, you'll be a good boy, won't you?" Daisy said with mock sternness. "Mommy will be back in a little while." She grabbed the jars on her counter and lowered them into the deep side pockets of her parka before disappearing out the front door.

Standing on his hind legs at the front window of the mobile home, Smudgie watched Daisy trudge up the street through the thick snow.

Claudia awoke slowly, keeping her eyes closed to the winter sunlight that shone through the blinds. She stretched under the covers and felt the stiffness of sleep in her legs and back. She would have loved to doze awhile longer, but her mind had begun to race. It was no use now. Besides, it was time for the treadmill.

She swung her legs over the side of the bed and began the daily argument with herself. It would be so tempting not to exercise. She could draw a hot bubble bath and soak for a while. Maybe treat herself to a nice chocolate milkshake in the tub. Wasn't Sunday supposed to be a day of rest?

Of course. But no exercise and a chocolate breakdown would be a boon to the cellulite that threatened her thighs. She had come too far to slack off now.

Claudia reluctantly pulled a sports bra, spandex shorts, and socks out of her dresser drawers. Only the fear of regaining the weight she had lost kept the million excuses from winning the argument. She put on the workout clothes and pulled her hair into a neat ponytail. Her running shoes waited for her on the treadmill in the spare room.

She stood next to the black machine for a moment, stretching her legs and back. Then she sighed and stepped onto the belt on which she would run for the next thirty minutes. The motor hummed, straining to get the belt moving. She began to walk. Even after the stretches, her legs were stiff. *No excuses,* she told herself. The belt turned faster, and she began to jog. Sometimes she listened to music while she ran, but many days, like today, she started exercising and lost herself in the treadmill's whine and the rhythm of her breathing.

The first ten minutes were the worst. It took that long for her body to come to grips with the fact that it would have to work. Once she really got going, though, she knew her brain would release a surge of endorphins that would give her an "exercise high." Running was much better after that. She felt the first beads of sweat pop out on her forehead. She hated the initial sweat. It made her feel damp and filthy. Left, right, left, right. Keep going. No excuses.

Claudia glanced down at the timer on the treadmill. She had been running for ten minutes and forty-two seconds. Left, right, left, right. Not a moment too soon, she suddenly felt fully awake. Her legs were limber and strong, not the heavy deadweights she had swung over the edge of her bed. The sweat was beginning to pool in the little indentation at the base of her throat, but now it felt good, almost purifying. A sense of well-being came over her. She punched up her speed two levels and easily adjusted as the treadmill belt rolled faster. Perhaps she *would* have chocolate today, skim milk with Hershey's low-cal chocolate syrup. A healthy compromise. Claudia smiled, breathing heavily through her teeth. Left, right, left, right. And, she would definitely have that bubble bath.

Why was her alarm clock ringing on a Sunday?

Jean squinted at her nightstand, slapped the clock, slapped it again, then realized it was the phone ringing, not the clock.

"Mom!" Jimmy burst into her bedroom, holding a piece of toast in one hand and the cordless phone from the kitchen in the other. "Mom, wake up. It's Margaret from work and she says it's important." He barely waited until she had grasped the phone before running out of the room.

"Your kid said you were still in bed," barked a woman's voice through the receiver. "Whatsa matter? You sick?"

"I had trouble sleeping last night. What time is it?" Jean croaked, sitting up in bed.

"After ten. Anyway, I'm on my way out for morning rounds, but I had to call and tell you." The voice paused, and Jean could just picture Margaret gripping the phone, giddy with anticipation before spilling a juicy tidbit of information. "Mary McAllister died last night. Or early this morning, I'm not sure exactly when. Sue knows someone in the medical examiner's office, and they said she overdosed on her meds. So that's one you won't have to worry about on your next shift." Margaret paused, waiting for her response. "Jeanie? You there?"

"Yeah. I thought she was close when I saw her yesterday. At least she isn't suffering anymore."

"I wonder who'll get all her stuff," Margaret said. "She's probably got millions in her bank account, don't you think?"

"Probably."

"And she doesn't have any kids, and her husband's dead, right?"

"I think so."

"Well, there's got to be somebody. Hell, Jeanie, you took care of the old broad for months. Maybe she left it all to you."

Jean snorted into the phone. "That's impossible, Marge, and you know it. She hardly ever said a word to me, even before she went downhill. When she wasn't asleep, she kept to herself, like she was afraid to look at me. Besides, I'm sure she could afford to have someone do her will. Even if she doesn't have any family, I'm sure her estate's already spoken for."

"Well, whoever gets it is damned lucky. What I wouldn't give for a fortune to drop into my lap. I'm coming, just a sec," Margaret said to somebody, and then back into the phone, "Jeanie, I gotta go. I'll see ya tomorrow."

"Okay," Jean said, and hung up the phone. After finding her glasses, she spied her purse sitting on the chest of drawers and felt a pang of shame. At the bottom of a little zippered pocket inside that purse was a stunning diamond ring. Mrs. McAllister's diamond ring.

She had carried the ring with her for eight days, feeling secretly glamorous at having possession of it, telling herself each day that she would return it the next. She had never intended to keep it. But now, the old widow was dead. If she didn't return it, she really would be stealing, and the thought of taking anything from a dead woman disturbed her. Jean resolved to return the ring to the mansion as soon as she could.

From the kitchen, the sound of breaking glass seized her attention.

"Mom! Jimmy busted a glass!"

"Liar! It was Johnny, Mom! He knocked it off the counter and now he's blaming me!"

Jean sighed and again reminded herself how wonderful her boys were, how lucky she was to have them.

CHAPTER 6

1940

Mary stood in front of her dresser mirror, staring at herself. The long blue dress she wore matched the color of her eyes. She had curled her hair as best she could manage. Her beige stockings were tight and itchy and only encouraged the unease she felt every time she looked in the mirror. It was almost five o'clock, and Patrick would soon arrive to take her to dinner with his family.

She couldn't believe she had agreed to the date. Her father had been ecstatic when she told him of Patrick's invitation and her acceptance. In fact, he had driven to Rutland to buy the blue dress and shoes as a surprise for her. She knew that her father wanted so much for her to be able to interact with people. *If only I could spend the evening with Patrick alone,* she thought.

Mary looked out the window toward the driveway. A black Lincoln had just pulled up beside the barn. Patrick would be at the door in a few moments. She swallowed hard as a great tightness rose up into her throat. Feeling faint, she sat down on the bed.

She felt the familiar knot in her stomach, the fear that spread upward, raking her insides. It surged down her arms to her fingertips until her hands were ice-cold and trembling. Fighting a strong current of nausea, Mary lay down and closed her eyes. Since her first bout with severe anxiety three years ago, it had been the same every time. In its grip, she was powerless.

Taking deep breaths, Mary tried to calm herself. She remembered well that day in her junior year of high school when this torment had taken hold of her. There had been a new English teacher, an older man who had immediately focused his attention on her. He'd called on her often. He developed a seating chart and assigned her a desk at the front of the classroom. Mary had often felt him staring at her, even though she dared not look up at him. She had begun to dread English class.

Mr. Snee had preyed on her increasing discomfort. One Thursday afternoon, he asked to speak to her at the end of the school day. He'd smiled as she entered his classroom, closed the door behind them, locked it. Told her in an unsteady voice that she was so bright and beautiful, that he so enjoyed having her in his class. That he loved her. Caught her by the wrist when she tried to move past him to the door, pushed her against the blackboard, stifled her scream with his wet mouth. Pinned her against the cold linoleum as he took her innocence. Threatened to kill her if she told anyone of their secret.

In shock, she'd picked herself up from the floor, wiped her eyes, denied to herself that anything serious had happened. She vaguely remembered walking home, staying in bed the next day, telling her father that she didn't feel well. During the weekend, she busied herself with the horses, helping to break a new filly and taking Ebony on long rides in the evenings.

On Monday, though, everything changed.

As she stepped again into Mr. Snee's classroom, she began to tremble. She felt his stare as she took her seat and fumbled with her notebook. She refused to look at him when he announced that he had completed grading the compositions turned in the previous week. She shuddered when he announced that he had selected a few of the better ones to be read aloud.

"Miss Hayes," Mr. Snee said, leaning

forward and placing her graded composition on her desk, "you earned the highest grade on this exercise, so you'll go first."

Finally, she glanced up at him. He was so close that she could see the pupils of his dark, beady eyes and the shimmer of sweat on his upper lip, could smell his sickeningly familiar musk tinged with aftershave. Mr. Snee took a step backward, beckoning her to stand. With hesitation, she had risen and turned to face the other students.

"Now, don't be shy, Miss Hayes. Step up a bit more, to the center here, so that everyone can see and hear you." Mr. Snee settled himself behind his desk as Mary edged away from hers. He smiled again and waited for her to begin.

Feeling her cheeks redden under the stares of her teacher and classmates, Mary had looked down at her composition and tried to focus on her own handwritten words.

" 'Frankenstein's Monster: A Lesson in Humanity,' " she read. "A primary theme of the novel *Frankenstein; or, The Modern Prometheus,* by Mary Wollstonecraft Shelley, is the failure of man to recognize the humanity in a being of his own creation."

Mary remembered how, at that point, she had begun to feel dizzy. She had stopped a moment, knowing that everyone was waiting for her to continue. She had tried.

"Victor Frankenstein, a young scientist obsessed with the miracle of life, assembles a creature using myriad discarded body parts. He is successful in animating the monster but finds its physical appearance so disturbing that he abandons it. In doing so . . ." She paused, trying to steady her voice. "In doing so, he sets in motion a chain of events whereby a kind, innocent creature is mistreated . . . mistreated and misunderstood by almost everyone who encounters it."

Mary stopped reading to look over at Mr. Snee. The teacher had been watching her intently. She felt again his hot breath on her neck, the suffocating pain of him pressing on her and in her. Her hands began to shake. She gazed from student to student, from one face to another, each frowning at her, or smirking, or smiling nervously. She dropped her gaze and focused on the floor. With a start, she realized that she had lain precisely where she now stood, struggling and screaming into Mr. Snee's large hand clamped over her mouth. She gasped as the room started spinning.

For the first time, she'd felt the icy fist of anxiety closing around her stomach. From somewhere in the room, she heard Mr.

Snee's voice asking, "Miss Hayes? Is there a problem, Miss Hayes?" But at that point, she had cared only about getting out of the classroom, away from the raw memory of violation reflected in the taunting eyes of her teacher.

"I have to leave," she said, and burst out of the classroom. She remembered turning left and sprinting down the hallway, past the lockers and closed doors of other classrooms. She needed to be alone, in a dark place, where no one could hurt her again.

At the end of the hallway, she'd frantically turned the doorknob on the janitor's closet. There, among the mops and brooms and buckets, she felt safe. The pungent odors of the cleaning solutions masked the smell of her own fear, while the darkness protected her from seeing anything else that might upset her. She cried then, muffling her sobs with her hands and feeling the warmth of her tears on her fingers.

It had taken them nearly an hour to find her. The school called her father, who rushed over to pick her up. She would never be able to forget the tortured expression on her father's face once they were back home and she finally revealed what had happened. She could still hear the sharp click as her father, overcome with rage, had loaded his shotgun and snapped the barrels back into place. It was nothing short of a miracle that she'd been able to persuade him not to go after Mr. Snee and take matters into his own hands.

She'd had no way of knowing, though, that although her father swore always to protect her, the panic that had driven her from Mr. Snee's classroom had taken root and would force her to suffer through fits of fearful agony for the rest of her life.

Patrick walked up the footpath, reviewing a plan in his head. Tonight he would begin in earnest the process of acquiring Mary. She was the final piece in the puzzle — the last thing he needed before he could ascend to his rightful place in society. He knocked on the door of the old house, and Sam opened it.

"Good evening, Sam," Patrick said. "Is Mary ready?"

"Hello, Patrick, come in. I think she's almost ready, 'least she was a few minutes ago. I'll go up an' check, though. Why don' you have a seat for a minute?" He motioned toward a brown, moth-eaten davenport.

"Of course," Patrick said. The thought of his suit touching that upholstery displeased him, but he did as he was asked. Sam smiled, then turned and practically ran up the stairs. He found Mary on the bed, curled into a fetal position.

"Mary! Mary, he's here. What's wrong?" he said, bending over her.

"Papa, I can't go with him. I feel sick. Please tell him for me."

"Mary, I thought you were goin' to be all right with this. You were so excited when you told me about it earlier, an' he really cares about you, you know." He paused. "Mary, you're nineteen years old, an' you can't go on like this. You need to be with other people, especially people your own age. I know you like Patrick. You went ridin' with him all summer. You should spend more time with him. I'm not goin' to be here forever, an' you can't be by yourself for the rest of your life."

Mary remained motionless on the bed.

Sam sighed. "Patrick'll be disappointed, you know. I'll tell him you're not able to go, but I wish you would try, Mary. You know I only want the best for you," he said, and went back downstairs.

Patrick jumped to his feet as Sam reached the bottom of the stairway. He suspected that getting Mary out of the house would be difficult, and one look at the farmer's face confirmed his suspicion.

"She's too nervous, isn't she?" Patrick asked before Sam could say anything.

"Well, you know how she is," he replied. "When she freezes up like she does, I jus' don' know what to do. I tried to talk her into comin' down, but I don' believe she will."

"Perhaps I could go up?" Patrick offered. "Maybe if I talk with her a little, reassure her, she might relax."

"That's good of you, Patrick, but I don' think it would do any good. She's pretty upset. I asked her to go tonight, but . . ." Sam shrugged and shook his head. For a moment, he and Patrick stood silently in the dim living room.

Patrick struggled to mask his frustration. "Well, please, tell Mary that I'm sorry she couldn't make it this evening," he said as he turned to leave. "I'll try to come out to visit after work one night this week, and —"

The wooden stairs were creaking behind him. Mary stepped hesitantly into the light of the living room. She stopped on the bottom step and faced him, trembling and clutching a dainty black pocketbook. There was no color in her face.

"Mary," he said. He would have an opportunity to work on the first obstacle after all. He rushed over to her, took both of her hands in his. "Your father said you weren't feeling well. Are you better now? Do you think you're up to this evening?"

"I suppose so," Mary replied, looking up at him. Only then did she realize he was holding her hands, and she blushed. She glanced over at her father, but he was smiling with approval.

"We won't be out late. Don't worry," Patrick told Mary and Sam. "But we should be going. Mother's expecting us by six-thirty."

Mary felt herself cringe when Patrick mentioned meeting his mother, but she allowed him to take her arm and lead her to the door. Her father patted her on the shoulder as she left.

"You two have a good time," Sam called to them as they headed down to the car.

Patrick opened the passenger side door of the Lincoln for Mary, then ran around to the other side and got in himself. Mary occasionally rode into Mill River with her father in their old truck, but riding in the Lincoln was a completely new experience. The smooth hum of the engine was nothing like the rough idle of the pickup. The tan leather seat was buttery soft, and it cradled her. Mary folded her hands over her pocketbook in her lap, afraid to touch anything lest she leave a smudge on the polished interior of the car.

Patrick smiled down at her. She was sitting calmly, but her face betrayed the anxiety she felt. She continually looked out the window. Mary reminded him of a little bluebird, perched and ready to fly away. *Not this evening, not ever,* he thought.

They were a few miles outside Rutland when Mary started shaking uncontrollably. She leaned forward in her seat and whispered to him.

"Patrick, I can't do this. Please go back. I thought I could, but I can't."

Patrick reached over and placed his right hand over both of hers. At the same time, he stepped more firmly on the accelerator.

"Mary, please try to relax. It's only my family, and I'm sure they'll like you."

"Can't go, please stop, I'm going to be sick —" She pulled one of her hands free of his and clutched at the passenger's side window.

"Mary, we're almost there. Take a few deep breaths. You have nothing to fear from this evening. It's only dinner, and I'll have you home before you know it. Do you trust me?"

She was curled against the door, whimpering. Patrick focused on keeping his voice calm.

"You'll be with me. If you start to feel anxious, squeeze my arm, and we'll try to get away for a few minutes until you feel better."

Mary's cries quieted a little as she listened.

"That's better. I won't leave your side, I promise," he said, gently rubbing her hand.

Mary remained silent as they drove into Rutland. Patrick pointed out several of the more prominent buildings, including a complex composed of the tall structures of McAllister Marbleworks. "Here's the downtown district," Patrick said as Mary stole a glance out the window, "and here's Main Street Park. The house is just up ahead." The Victorian-style homes were growing larger and larger. The house at the end of the street was the grandest of them all, a great yellow mansion set against a backdrop of autumn maples. Patrick pulled into the circular driveway.

Mary looked around. There were at least six other cars parked around the house. Several young men stood on the porch, talking over drinks and cigars. The wide front door of the house was open, leaving only a screen door that did nothing to conceal the voices of other guests already inside. The windows and door spilled light into the evening. Mary fought to keep from retching. The house was a great gaping monster from which she might not emerge.

"I thought you said this was only a family dinner."

"It is. Everyone here is family."

Mary's face lost all trace of color, and her hands suddenly became so clammy that her fingertips ached. Her violent trembling returned, and she seized Patrick's arm before he could open the driver's side door.

"Please, Patrick, I can't go in there," she said, her voice rising to a fevered pitch. "I'm not ready for this, I —"

Patrick glanced at her, and, for just a second, his eyes flashed a strange hostility. His voice, though, was as soothing as ever.

"Mary! Mary, you are ready, and everyone is expecting us. Don't worry. It won't be as bad as you think."

He extricated his arm from her grasp and quickly got out of the car. When he came around to her side to help her out, she again grabbed his arm and squeezed it as hard as she could. Patrick gasped in surprise and shook his head as if she were a naughty little girl. "Now now, I told you not to worry," he said, patting her hand and pulling her toward the house.

Waves of nausea washed over Mary.

"Hey, Patrick!" said one of the men on the porch through a cloud of cigar smoke. "We were beginning to think you weren't comin'. Yeah, we thought you mighta got lost out there in the country, if you know what I mean." The men sniggered, and the speaker winked and elbowed the man standing next to him.

"Right," Patrick said. He patted Mary's hand again. "Fellas, I'd like you to meet Mary Hayes. Mary, these are two of my cousins, Phil and Donovan Leary." The cousins nodded to her. "The loudmouth is my brother, Jacob."

Mary took a deep breath and looked up at them. She managed to smile. Immediately, the faces of the three men lit up with dopey grins.

"Call me Jake," the younger McAllister said. "And if I'm a loudmouth, it's only because I've had an older brother to set a great example for me. Isn't that right, Patrick?"

Patrick scoffed and guided her into the monster's mouth. "It's a pleasure to meet you, Mary," Jake called after them.

A butler held open the screen door for them, and Patrick and Mary walked through the grand foyer of the McAllister home.

They made their way into a large sitting room in which people were gathering. Patrick proceeded to make the rounds, introducing Mary to more cousins, aunts, and uncles. Patrick noticed his father across the room, pouring himself a brandy. He smiled at Stephen and glanced proudly down at Mary. It gave him a thrill when his father gaped at her so long that he overfilled his glass.

Through all this, Mary looked up only occasionally, and she gripped Patrick's arm with such ferocity that her knuckles turned white. She was thankful that Patrick moved between introductions quickly enough to prevent anyone from saying much to her. When the arm supporting Mary finally began to ache, Patrick bent down and whispered in her ear.

"Would you like to take a break?"

"Please, yes."

They turned to exit the great room, but were blocked by two stunning redheaded women. They wore different gowns and hairstyles, but their faces were mirror images.

"Patrick, we've been looking all over for you," one of them said.

"We've been dying to meet your little friend," the other chimed in.

"This is Mary Hayes," Patrick began. "Mary, meet my sisters —"

"— Sara," one of the twins said.

"— and Emma," the other finished.

They smiled together.

"Hello," Mary said.

"That's a lovely dress," Sara observed, looking wistfully at Mary. "The color's good on you."

"Much better than it would have been on us," Emma agreed. "We saw that very dress in the window at Carolyn's downtown several months ago. Both of us wanted it, but the store had only one left."

"No matter," Sara said. "It was headed for the sales rack — styles change so quickly these days. Besides, that shade of blue looked absolutely ghastly with our complexion. But it looks very nice on you." Both sisters smiled sweetly and walked away arm in arm.

Mary was mortified. She gasped, unable to speak.

"I'm sorry about them," Patrick said. "You're so beautiful, and they're just jealous of you. Let's go get some fresh air."

Again they tried to escape, but an elegant blond woman appeared in the doorway of the great room and announced that dinner was ready. She saw Patrick and Mary coming toward her and intercepted them.

"Patrick, darling, there you are!" The older woman clasped her hands together. "And you must be Mary! Patrick has told us so much about you. I'm Elise McAllister, Patrick's mother."

Mary had rehearsed a hundred times what she would say to Mrs. McAllister upon meeting her. Still, speaking to her reflection in her bedroom mirror paled in comparison to addressing the genuine article. Mary's tongue was a thick ball of wax in her mouth. She hoped the effort she exerted to speak didn't contort her face.

"It's a pleasure to meet you, Mrs. McAllister," Mary said carefully.

Patrick's mother smiled, unaware of Mary's concentrated effort. "The pleasure is mine, Mary. You must come by and have tea with me one of these afternoons." She looked at Patrick. "Why don't you two take your seats with the others? I've got to make sure there are enough places set, so if you'll excuse me . . ."

"Of course, Mother," Patrick said as she hurried away. "She's a real perfectionist," he whispered to Mary.

All the guests filed into the dining room. An enormous table, set for dinner and illuminated by a sparkling chandelier, stretched the length of the room. Patrick selected two seats near one end of the table and pulled Mary's chair out for her. She sank into it.

The dinner passed in a haze. Uniformed house staff continually refilled glasses and cleared away dishes. Mary tried to eat, but her stomach was increasingly unsettled. She pushed her food around on her plate, hoping to make it look as if she had eaten something. She politely nodded and smiled throughout the meal but spoke very little. The words and laughter from the others seated at the table swirled incomprehensibly in her mind.

"Is anyone ready for dessert?" Patrick's mother finally shouted. In the midst of the family's enthusiastic response, Mary asked Patrick where the washroom was and excused herself from the table.

Mary walked to the bathroom as quickly as her wobbly legs would carry her. Once inside, she locked the door and slid to the floor with her back against it. She couldn't take much more.

She stayed several long minutes inside the temporary sanctuary, listening to the muffled conversation coming from the dining room. She couldn't go back there, at least not yet. Mary opened the washroom door and slipped out into the hallway. She walked away from the dining room, looking into open rooms as she passed them. Library, parlor, guest bedroom. A door at the end of the hallway was closed but not latched. She listened for a moment, and, hearing no one inside, slowly pushed the door open.

It was an office. An executive desk covered in books and papers faced the doorway. Bookshelves surrounded the desk. Framed photographs sat on top of the bookshelves and filled almost every inch of open wall space. Mary recognized the people in many of the pictures as Patrick and his parents and siblings. There were several shots of McAllister Marbleworks. One of those pictures in particular caught Mary's attention. The photo hung behind the desk apart from the others, and was smaller and more yellowed than those nearest it.

Mary recognized neither of the two smiling men in the picture, although they looked enough alike to be father and son. She leaned closer to the picture. The older man had his arm around the shoulders of the younger, and a bronze engraved plate attached to the bottom of the picture's frame read McAllister Marbleworks, 1894.

"Ah, to be a young man again," a voice

said behind her. Mary whirled around. A tall, white-haired bear of a man stood in the doorway of the office. His neatly trimmed beard matched the color of his hair, and he watched her with curious green eyes of the same shade as Patrick's. Mary froze.

"I didn't mean to startle you, my dear," the man said gently. "I'm Conor McAllister, Patrick's grandfather. You must be Mary Hayes."

"Y-yes."

"I saw you arrive with Patrick and intended to come over and introduce myself, but I couldn't quite get through the crowd before dinner. I don't move as quickly these days as I used to."

Mary said nothing. She shrank backward as he approached, but he stopped after only a few steps and squinted at the picture.

"That picture was taken a very long time ago, on the first day our marbleworks opened for business. The older man in the picture is my father, Kieran. I was in my late twenties at the time."

"Oh."

"That picture is one of the few that I have of my father when he was younger. He was the most honest, hardworking man there ever was. Came all the way from Ireland with barely two cents to rub together and still managed to do well for himself." Conor watched the quivering girl in front of him. He had been observing the poor shy creature all evening, clinging to Patrick's arm, trying valiantly to maintain some semblance of poise during dinner. He tried to think of something he could say that would put her more at ease.

"I came in here to get away from all the commotion. Families as large as mine can get pretty rowdy sometimes. Oh, don't get me wrong. I love all of them out there, but sometimes I just have to take a time-out in a quiet place to have a few minutes to myself. I imagine tonight would be pretty overwhelming for someone who's not used to a crowd."

Mary swallowed hard and looked up at Conor. "Yes, actually. I didn't mean to intrude. I was — I guess I was only looking for a quiet place, like you."

"That's quite all right, my dear. If I hadn't found you here, I might never have escaped my jumble of a family to make your acquaintance." Conor smiled down at her. When Mary saw the crinkles around his kind eyes and felt the gentleness that he exuded, her anxiety drained away.

"Mary, there you are! I've been looking all over for you. Oh, hello, Grandpop. I didn't know you were in here."

Conor and Mary turned to see Patrick standing in the doorway of the office.

"I was just showing your lovely friend some of my pictures," Conor said. He winked at her.

Patrick looked curiously at Mary. He had expected to find her hiding in a closet somewhere, but here she was, relaxed and smiling. "The pie's almost gone, and Mother's been wondering where you went," Patrick said to his grandfather.

"Yes, well, tell her I'll be along in a few minutes. And Mary, I hope you'll come visit us often." The crinkles made another appearance.

"I will," Mary said as Patrick led her away by the hand.

"We've got to say goodnight to Mother and Pop, and then I'll take you home if you're ready," Patrick said when they were halfway back to the dining room. "So what do you think of Grandpop?"

"I wish I had a grandfather like him."

CHAPTER 7

The medical examiner's van was already parked outside the McAllister house when Fitz and Kyle arrived. Father O'Brien met them at the door. His eyes were puffy and bloodshot.

"Good morning, Father," Fitz said. "Or maybe not so good," he added grimly.

"Yes, well, she's upstairs," Father O'Brien said, as he led them through the house toward the staircase. "The people from the medical examiner's office are here already — Peterson and Gray I think their names are — but I asked them not to touch anything until you got here and looked around."

Kyle remembered what Leroy had said about the old woman who lived, isolated, in the white mansion overlooking the town. He was inclined to dismiss Leroy's comments about her as he would any other of his nasty remarks. *She was certainly no witch,* Kyle thought as he took in the grandeur of the marble home.

The stale air in the house smelled of musty fabric and furniture polish. Although long, heavy drapes artificially darkened the rooms through which they passed, a few cracks of sunlight allowed Kyle to see that the furnishings of the house were mainly antiques. The floors were covered with ornate Persian rugs. Everything appeared to be spotless and unused.

Fitz, too, looked at everything as they passed. "My Ruthie's done shopping for Mrs. McAllister for years," the police chief whispered to him, "but neither of us has ever been in here. It's always been that way — Ruthie just sets the groceries on the back stoop, rings the doorbell, and leaves. Mrs. McAllister never took visitors, see. It upset her too much. So Ruthie's seen her only once, but she didn't get to meet her, even though she would've liked to."

They walked up the stairs to Mary's bedroom. The curtains surrounding the bay windows were wide open. One man stood at the window, looking out over the town below. There was a raised hospital bed behind him, and another man wearing latex gloves bent over it. They both turned toward the doorway as the priest entered the room.

"Here we are," Father O'Brien said. "Mr.

Peterson, Mr. Gray, these are Officers Fitzgerald and Hansen. They just need to look around a little."

"Of course," Peterson replied. He backed up and leaned against the bay window.

"Everything is as we found it," Gray said. "Go ahead and do what you need to do."

Kyle and Fitz came around to the front of the bed and looked at the body resting upon it. Kyle's heart skipped a beat when he saw Mary. Images that he struggled to suppress flooded his mind. *So pale and thin, like Allison was before she died,* he thought. He turned to Father O'Brien.

"Was it cancer?"

"Yes." The priest looked surprised at Kyle's question. "Pancreatic. She was diagnosed about a year ago. The doctors told her she had maybe six months at the time, and she made it twice that long." Father O'Brien paused a moment. "How did you know?"

"My wife died of ovarian cancer."

The priest nodded silently. He knew too well the appearance of cancer patients in their final days of suffering.

"Say, either of you boys ever heard of MS Contin?" Fitz asked. He held up an empty prescription bottle from Mary's bedside table.

"Oh, sure," Peterson said. "It's a synthetic form of morphine. A slow-release pain-killer."

"Looks like you might be right about suicide, Father," Fitz said, squinting at the fine print on the label. "This prescription was filled two days ago for a two-week sup-ply. It's empty now."

"Overdose," Gray said softly. "We see that type of suicide in terminal patients all the time. A tox screen could confirm it."

Kyle said nothing. He was closely watch-ing Father O'Brien. The priest's face re-mained expressionless. Yet, every few min-utes, he blinked several times and pursed his lips. Rowen did the same thing when she tried to keep from crying.

"Did you know she was going to do this, Father?" Kyle asked.

Father O'Brien looked up at the three men facing him.

"I wasn't sure. I suspected she might, but I picked up that prescription for her, any-way. She was in so much pain," he whis-pered.

"Well, she's not hurting anymore," Fitz said. "I've seen enough. Mr. Peterson, if your office will do the toxicology tests you mentioned and send a copy of the results down to the station, we'll include it in our report."

The men from the medical examiner's office took this comment as a signal and readied a stretcher beside Mary's bed.

"I'll be making arrangements for her," Father O'Brien said as Peterson and Gray transferred Mary's body to the stretcher. "Should I ask the funeral home to contact you directly?"

"That'd be fine," Peterson said, pulling a sheet up over Mary's face.

"I guess we're done here, then. Father, you let me know if you need anything else," Fitz said. He looked over at Kyle. "You ready?"

"Sure." Kyle looked at his watch; it wasn't even nine-thirty. He turned to leave, eager to get back to Rowen. Out of the corner of his eye, he saw a flash of chocolate and cream dart through the open bedroom door and under Mary's bed.

"What was that?" Kyle asked.

"What was what?" Fitz responded, looking around.

"Something ran under the bed."

"I didn't see anything."

"Oh," Father O'Brien said. "I almost forgot. Sham." He stooped down and looked beneath the metal bars and wheels supporting the hospital bed. The Siamese cat yowled as it stared back at him with crossed blue eyes. "Mary's cat," the priest said, straightening up. "I promised her I would make sure he found a good home. I would keep him myself, but I have allergies."

Kyle's face brightened. "You know, I could take him. My daughter's been asking for a pet. It'd be a great surprise for her."

"Well, I guess that'd be all right. He's usually pretty friendly, but all the strange people here must be upsetting him. Just like Mary," Father O'Brien mused under his breath.

"Then I'll take the cat with me?" Kyle asked.

"Fine with me. Just make sure you give him lots of attention. He may take a little while to adjust to new surroundings. I don't think he's been out of this house in years. There's cat food in the pantry downstairs — you can take it with you," the priest said.

The grandfather clock chimed to mark the half hour. Father O'Brien watched as Peterson and Gray transferred Mary's body to the stretcher and covered it with a white sheet. Then he squatted down beside the bed and hauled the Siamese out from under it. The cat protested loudly, but, once hoisted off the ground, sat peacefully in the priest's arms.

"I'll carry him for you," Father O'Brien said. Fitz and Kyle followed him out of the bedroom.

Kyle stood fumbling with the keys at the door of his apartment. At his feet were two large bags filled with cat food and supplies he had collected from Mary's house. Holding Sham with one arm, he had just managed to isolate the correct key on the ring when Rowen opened the door. She took one look at the cat and squealed in delight. Although Sham had offered little resistance to being removed from the mansion and driven to Kyle's apartment, Rowen's shriek prompted the cat to claw at Kyle and frantically launch itself from his grip. Once freed, Sham dashed through the open door of the apartment and took refuge behind the sofa.

"Ooh, a kitty! Is he mine? Can we keep him?" Rowen rushed over to the sofa and began calling to the cat. Kyle picked up the bags and set them inside.

"Yep, he's yours, kiddo. He's gonna be pretty shy at first, though. He doesn't know us. We're strangers to him, and he's scared." Kyle shut the front door and went to sit on the floor next to his daughter.

"Where did you get him?" Rowen asked,

still looking behind the couch.

"You remember I said I had to go check on a sick lady?"

"Yeah."

"Well, the sick lady didn't get better, and she died. Her name was Mary. Do you know that big white house on the hill? The one that looks out over the town?" Rowen nodded. "That's where she lived. This was her cat. Since he didn't have anyone to take care of him anymore, I thought we could give him a new home. His name's Sham."

"He must be sad about his owner," Rowen said. As if on cue, a mournful meow came from the thin space between the back of the couch and the wall. Rowen stretched her arm into it, but the cat retreated until he was out of reach.

Kyle crawled over to one of the bags and removed a small pouch of tuna-flavored kitty treats.

"Here, try to lure him out with these," he said, handing them to Rowen. Kyle backed away to watch, not wanting to spook the cat if he decided to come out.

"Tuna flavor," Rowen read from the front of the pouch. She opened the bag and grimaced. "These smell really bad."

Rowen placed a line of treats on the floor, beginning as far behind the couch as she could reach. Then she sat back on her knees, her legs folded beneath her, and waited. After a few minutes, a dark brown nose poked out around the edge of the sofa. A single treat was left on the floor in front of Rowen.

The cat slowly crept forward, watching her all the while. When he came close enough, Rowen gently reached to touch him. Sham backed up slightly as her fingers grazed his head, but instead of hiding again the cat tentatively sniffed at her hand. Apparently reassured, the cat shoved his forehead against Rowen's hand and purred.

"Look, Dad!" Rowen said in an excited whisper. Sham sat in front of her as she scratched behind his delicate brown ears. She grinned at Kyle and began talking to the cat in her most soothing counselor's voice.

"You poor kitty. Are you worried about being in a strange place without your mama? You probably miss her a lot. Don't worry, Sham, I'll take care of you. I know just how you feel."

Father O'Brien had watched the medical examiner's van disappear down the driveway of the mansion before he climbed into his own truck. There were so many arrangements to finalize. He would have to call the funeral home and the visiting nurse's service.

Somehow, he would have to tell Daisy.

But first, he would have to put all of that and the whole miserable morning out of his mind for a few hours. There was only an hour until Mass, just enough time to drive back to the church and collect himself.

When he reached the parish house, he quickly washed his face and changed into vestments for the service. He fumbled through the items on his desk, looking for the notes he had scrawled the previous evening. As he crumpled papers and shoved aside books, he realized that he was angry.

He was angry with Mary.

At once, he felt a crushing shame. It was selfish of him to feel this way, especially after everything Mary had endured. But he was angry, and hurt, because he hadn't had a chance to say goodbye. Worse, by apparently taking her own life, Mary had made a decision that should have been left to God.

Father O'Brien stopped his searching and leaned against the desk. He lowered himself to his knees and prayed that Mary's soul be saved despite her suicide. He pleaded with the Lord to make an exception for a woman who had known so little happiness and yet had given so much of it herself. He asked for the strength to continue, to keep his promise to her, to leave his anger behind.

Only one other time had he ever been angry with Mary. The anger had come about a decade into his tenure at St. John's. After that long with one parish, most priests would have been given new assignments. They might even be permitted to pursue advanced degrees to better serve their parishioners. He had entertained thoughts of someday teaching in a seminary.

But that was not to be. Father O'Brien knew that, as a favor to Conor McAllister, Bishop Ross had made his assignment to Mill River permanent. He knew that future bishops of the Diocese of Burlington would honor that edict. Even though he loved Mill River and his close-knit congregation, he felt trapped.

It seemed that all of the unknown opportunity had been removed from his future.

On his knees beside his desk, Father O'Brien recalled how that feeling had fueled a smoldering resentment within him. Before he knew it, the resentment had become anger. It had become so intense that he could hardly bear to read the newsletters from St. John's Seminary in Massachusetts, his alma mater. The mailings always included a column on new accomplishments and reassignments of alumni. He had even burned one issue that announced a vacancy on the teaching staff. The school had wanted a lecturer on the Old Testament, with particular emphasis on Psalms.

Father O'Brien had a special fondness for Psalms.

It was true what one of his old professors had said, that psalms were songs of the people of God. They mirrored lives. In the psalms, it was easy to find inspiration or guidance for almost any situation. Father O'Brien knew most of them by heart.

But his life's work had been decided. Because of Mary, he would never be in a position to teach psalms at Saint John's or anywhere else.

Then, as now, he had prayed for help in dealing with his emotions. Then, as now, he had felt guilty for his anger and had known deep down that he had no right to be angry with Mary. And finally, one day, as he drove up to the mansion, his prayer had been answered.

It had occurred to him that perhaps God wanted him to remain in Mill River. Perhaps it was no coincidence that he had been assigned to a new church with the same name as his seminary. He might have been brought to Mill River just in time for Mary and Patrick's wedding so that he would be there to protect her through everything that followed. Maybe, in some way he didn't understand, his watching over this one woman was somehow more important than teaching or being transferred to a new parish. If that was true, then perhaps his future held some opportunity after all.

Thanks to his epiphany, the anger had faded away. In its place, a sense of relief, then gratitude, had developed, as his friendship with Mary became an important part of his life. Now, he wished only that Mary's soul would somehow find its way to heaven and that he might never be upset with her again.

Father O'Brien rose from his knees and made his way from the parish house into the sanctuary. No one had arrived yet. The chamber was cool and dim, illuminated only by light filtering through the stained-glass windows. He stood at the altar, looking down the silent aisle traversed by rainbow-colored beams.

He had spoken from this altar thousands of times before, but the memory of one particular day seized him. He remembered a striking couple as they waited before him, a tall blond man and a stunning, blue-eyed brunette. He remembered the church filled to capacity, with all but the first row on the left side of the aisle taken up by the McAllister family. He remembered how Mary had looked into her bridegroom's face with such trusting innocence and how Patrick had looked down at her as if he were about to be awarded a trophy. He remembered how he had known at that moment that theirs would be a marriage filled with darkness.

CHAPTER 8

1941

On a warm Saturday afternoon in late April, Patrick McAllister paced between the front door of the yellow Victorian home and the parlor, where his parents and Mary sat waiting patiently. Every so often he pulled the curtains at the front window aside and looked out.

"Now, son, Father O'Brien is new to the area. Give the man a little leeway, won't you? He might have had some trouble with the directions," Stephen said as Patrick again passed through the room.

"It's a simple drive from Mill River to Rutland," Patrick snapped. "I still can't believe Bishop Ross will be in Rome on my wedding day. He should have postponed the trip."

"I'm sure he would have liked to, but to be invited to a conference at the Vatican, well, I doubt he could postpone that. And

129

we can't reset the date, not with the invitations having gone out. Besides," Elise McAllister said, smiling at Mary, "it's Mary's wedding day, too, and Mill River is her hometown. I don't think it's such a bad thing to have the wedding there, and to have the priest from Mill River marry you."

Patrick crossed his arms and frowned. "No, I suppose not."

Through all this, Mary sat on the couch and said nothing. She had met Bishop Ross, the head of the Diocese of Burlington and a longtime friend of the McAllister family. Now, though, she and the others were waiting to meet Father O'Brien, the new priest in Mill River. She felt a slight fluttering in her stomach.

Over the past several months, she had grown accustomed to Patrick's immediate family. She was still reserved, but she no longer experienced extreme anxiety when she spent time with them. Meeting strangers was another matter. Patrick had seen to it that Mary had been introduced to more people than she could count, certainly more than she ever met during the several years before Patrick arrived at the farm. With each new introduction, she struggled to maintain her composure. To her credit, she had become better at presenting a serene appearance. Patrick expected as much of her, but even her desire to please him didn't completely diminish the anxiety she felt. She never knew for sure what might trigger her inner turmoil, or when it might surface and overwhelm her.

Patrick walked in slow circles around the room, stopping only when he heard the low rumble of a car pulling into the driveway. "Finally," he muttered, when the doorbell rang. The butler showed a tall man with a white collar into the parlor.

"Father O'Brien," Stephen said, rising and extending his hand. "It's a pleasure. Please, come in. I'd like to introduce my wife, Elise, and my son Patrick and his fiancée, Mary Hayes."

The young priest had a boyish face and a build so slight that the thin arms protruding from the sleeves of his black suit jacket looked almost unnatural. A prominent Adam's apple hovered above his white collar. Still, his fine auburn hair had already begun to recede, and a calm maturity radiated from his eyes. He shook Stephen's hand and smiled warmly at the group.

"I'm very happy to meet all of you." Father O'Brien shifted his gaze to Patrick and Mary. "I've been in Mill River only a few months, as I'm sure Bishop Ross has told you, but it would be an honor to perform your wedding Mass." He waited for some sort of acknowledgment, but Patrick only clinched his jaw and glared. Mary trembled silently from her place on the couch. Finally, Patrick's mother swooped into the awkward silence.

"Why don't we all sit down for a cup of tea?" she said, motioning to one of the house staff and casting a stern look at Patrick.

Patrick took his mother's cue. "Yes, Father, do sit down."

"You're very gracious, thank you," Father O'Brien said. Mary couldn't help noticing that the chair in which he sat was so wide that his thinness seemed a mere stripe down the center of its cushions.

"So, Father O'Brien, did the bishop tell you that he married Elise and me when he was a priest here in Rutland?" Stephen asked.

"He did, Mr. McAllister," Father O'Brien replied. "I understand Bishop Ross and your father have been friends for more than forty years."

"Yes, that's true," Stephen said.

"I know Bishop Ross felt badly that he wouldn't be here to marry you," Father O'Brien said to Patrick and Mary, "but under the circumstances, well, he didn't believe he had a choice."

"Of course we understand," Patrick said, with a conciliatory glance at his mother. "He'll be with us in spirit, and I'm sure you'll conduct a wonderful ceremony."

"Speaking of which," Elise said, "we should discuss some of the details. I've found a number of beautiful hymns that may be suitable."

"And we'll want to be sure to schedule a rehearsal," Stephen said.

Everyone was soon engaged in discussing the particulars of the wedding — everyone except Mary.

She sat on the sofa, sipping her tea and trying to concentrate on something other than the new priest sitting in the chair across from her. Unlike the many young women who had every detail of their weddings planned before they met their husbands, Mary didn't worry about her wedding at all. Just in being the object of Patrick's affection, she had already seen her wildest fantasy come true. It was no matter that during each discussion of her upcoming marriage, she seemed to be relegated to the position of an observer. She was perfectly content to let Patrick's mother fuss over the details of the ceremony, and especially relieved that she wouldn't have to deal with people over the many arrangements to be made.

Mary turned her attention to the feeling of the diamond engagement ring encircling her finger. She couldn't quite believe that she was to be married to Patrick, that she would be part of a real family. There was also the issue of money. Each time she visited Patrick, she experienced again a sense of amazement at the grandeur of their home. After a childhood of near-poverty and an even greater struggle during the years of the Depression, she would never have to do without again.

"Is that all right with you, Mary?" Stephen's voice jarred her from her thoughts.

"It must be. She's not stopped smiling since we sat down. I suppose having the ceremony in the bride's hometown is the traditional thing to do, anyway," Patrick said, with another glance at his mother. "You say the church can hold two hundred?"

"Oh yes. Not that I've ever had that many people in it at once. It might be a little cozy, but I'm sure all of your guests can be accommodated," Father O'Brien said, bending down to retrieve his napkin from the floor. Mary stole a glance at him. "In fact, yours might be the biggest wedding the town has ever seen."

He reached for his teacup, and another sparkle caught Mary's eye. The end of a teaspoon protruded from the sleeve of Father O'Brien's jacket. Mary blinked. Surely she was mistaken. When the priest set the teacup back on its saucer, the silver shimmer was gone.

Mary looked at Father O'Brien's face, but the priest's expression was as calm and relaxed as when he first entered the parlor. She was perplexed. A priest wouldn't steal. Besides, why would anyone, especially a priest, steal a spoon? Her eyes must have played a trick on her. He was wearing a silver watch, or perhaps a bracelet of some sort. Surely, that must have been it.

"So, where will you live once you're married?" Father O'Brien asked. Patrick and Mary looked at each other.

"Well," Patrick said slowly, "Mary's father will still be in Mill River, of course, but the marbleworks and my family are here, in Rutland . . ."

Mary nodded, but the problem disturbed her. Naturally, Patrick wanted to live in Rutland, but she could not bear the thought of her father living alone in the old farmhouse in Mill River. She was all the family that her father had left, while Patrick's parents had three other children and an enormous extended family nearby.

When she explained this to Patrick, he had refused to speak to her for the rest of the day. It was a side of him she'd never seen, a stubborn, sulking immaturity.

They had yet to resolve the issue.

"I've already made arrangements for their new home." Everyone turned to see Conor McAllister standing in the doorway of the parlor. He smiled at Mary in a most reassuring way, as if he sensed her worry. "I'm Conor McAllister," he said as the young priest rose to greet him. They exchanged the typical formalities before Conor headed toward the door.

"As I was saying, I've taken care of their first home. Call it a wedding gift. It's a lovely afternoon for a drive, don't you think, Stephen? I'll pull one of your cars around, and we'll all go have a look. A pleasure meeting you, Father O'Brien." Conor left the room before anyone had an opportunity to question him.

"What's he talking about?" Patrick demanded.

"I have no idea," Stephen said. "I assumed we'd help you and Mary find a nice place when you decide where you want to live, but this is the first I've heard of Pop getting involved."

Mary didn't know what Patrick's grandfather had in mind, either, but she felt a knot begin to twist and tighten in her stomach.

"Stephen, we'd better go see what he's up to," Elise McAllister said. "He's unpredictable, to say the least," she continued, turning to the young priest, "and he loves surprises. Patrick will be the first of his grandchildren to be married, so there's no telling what he's planned."

"Something wonderful, I'm sure," Father O'Brien said as he stood up. "But I do have another appointment, so I'll leave you to investigate." He paused at the door. "I look forward to seeing you at the Pre-Cana sessions," he said to Patrick and Mary. "And thank you, Mrs. McAllister, for the tea."

Mary watched the back of the skinny young priest as he walked away. She liked him. He was quiet and disarming, someone around whom she might eventually feel comfortable.

The visitor had no sooner driven away than Conor pulled up to the front door in the black Lincoln. He left the car running as he herded Mary, Patrick, and Patrick's parents out of the house.

Stephen headed for the passenger side when Conor stopped him. "No, son, you drive. I'll tell you how to get there." Conor climbed into the front seat as Stephen got behind the wheel. "Hurry up now, that's it."

Patrick took Mary's elbow, guided her into the backseat beside his mother, and got in himself. "Grandpop, I wish you'd tell us what you've done," he said. His respect for his grandfather barely kept his annoyance at bay.

"Patience, Patrick! I intend to show you," Conor said, grinning. "And we can take Mary home afterward. It will save you the drive."

"But Mary lives in Mill River," Stephen said.

"Indeed," Conor replied. "That's exactly where we're going."

"A charming view, isn't it?" Conor said. Mary and the four McAllisters stood atop a hill overlooking Mill River. A good portion of the land had been cleared of trees and leveled, and a dirt access road connected the site with the main road through the town.

"Yes, Pop," Stephen said, "but why are we up here?"

Mary said nothing, but she noticed that Conor looked as if he were about to burst.

"Patrick, Mary," Conor said as he turned to face them, "I wanted to give you something special for your wedding. But what? What could I give to you, especially you, Mary, to welcome you into our family?" Conor's eyes twinkled, and Mary felt her cheeks begin to burn. "Then, it came to me. I've arranged for a house to be built for you, here, overlooking Mill River. A house in Mary's hometown, so that she may stay close to her father, plated by the finest white marble cut by our marbleworks. The location of her family and the legacy of ours. Construction is scheduled to start this week. With good weather, it should be ready for you to move into in August, right after your wedding."

Conor's announcement stupefied the others. It was Patrick who first recovered his voice.

"You mean, we'll live here? In Mill River?" This time, there was no masking his frustration. "But that means I'll have to drive into Rutland for work every day. And what about my new stable?"

"Pish, it's only a few miles, hardly fifteen minutes away. You'll get used to it. Besides, there were no locations closer to Rutland that compared to this one. Think of it, Patrick — your own country estate! I even purchased several acres back that way," Conor continued, motioning toward the stretch of land down the hill from the construction site. "There's plenty of room for horses. I'll have another stable built for you and Mary."

"Oh, Mr. McAllister, this is a dream!" Mary said, as she fought back tears. "It's perfect! I never expected — we never expected — oh, Patrick, isn't it wonderful?" Her elation had been building from the moment Conor had announced his surprise, but her joy at his mention of a new stable was too much to contain.

Elise shook her head in disbelief. "You certainly outdid yourself this time, Conor."

"I'll say," Stephen said. "It is a bit of a drive into Rutland, Son, but I suppose I could supply you with transportation as a wedding gift from your mother and me." He winked. "Besides, this is a gorgeous place for a house."

Patrick crossed his arms and frowned. He wasn't used to being overruled, but there was no avoiding it this time.

"I don't know what to say, Grandpop. Thank you."

"Yes, Mr. McAllister, thank you so much!"

Mary said. She felt a surge of relief when she realized that she wouldn't have to fight with Patrick to decide where they would live — his grandfather had decided for them.

"It's 'Grandpop' to you too, Mary," Conor said. "And you're both very welcome. Now, my dear, we'd best be getting you home before your father starts to worry." As he turned to walk back to the Lincoln, Mary linked her arm through his and squeezed it, smiling. Conor patted her hand and chuckled. Stephen and Elise followed them, but Patrick seemed to hesitate. He stood glowering for several moments at an invisible target in the sky above Mill River before trudging back to the car after his family.

The warm spring and summer months flew past, and Mary's August wedding day arrived more quickly than she ever imagined it would.

Just before the ceremony, her father stepped back to get a better look at her in her wedding gown. "I don' know what to say, Mary. You look beautiful. I wish your mother were here to see you."

"I'm sure she would be happy for us," Mary replied. "You look good, too." She smiled, prompting the stocky horse breeder to fidget with his bow tie.

"I don' reckon I've worn a suit like this since I married your mother," he said. "Feels sorta strange. An' these shoes are a little tight." He looked over at Mary, but she was staring into the mirror, smoothing the veil that drifted down over her shoulders. Her gown was silk crêpe, with a sweetheart neckline, lace sleeves, and a matching lace train that extended at least three yards behind her. Her dark hair was pulled back into a low elegant twist and held in place by an arched tiara. The veil attached to the jeweled headpiece and flowed down her back.

"I think this might be a bit much, but Patrick insisted on it," Mary said as she lightly touched one of the larger crystals on the tiara. "It's his mother's, and he says it's been worn by every bride on her side of the family for four generations."

"Well, I like it," Sam said. "Besides, this is your wedding day. I don' see any reason why you shouldn' look like a queen."

"I suppose." She continued to stare at herself in the mirror, but her eyes were glazed, locked in place as her mind traveled. Organ music played in the sanctuary outside the door of the dressing room in which they stood, and every once in a while, the voices of people being escorted to their seats also filtered through. Sam glanced nervously at the door, then back at his daughter.

"Fifteen minutes to go," he said. "Mary, are you . . . do you think you will be all right during the ceremony?"

"I think so, Papa. It's been a long time since I've felt really panicky. I thought I'd be anxious right now, but I'm not." That wasn't quite true. Deep down, she could still feel a simmering core of unease, but she was determined that nothing would ruin her wedding day.

Sam shook his head and took his daughter's hands. "I never would've imagined that you'd be able to walk into a roomful of people, much less that you'd be gettin' married." He stopped speaking for a moment and sniffed. "I was so worried that you'd never be right again after . . . well, I won't bring up the past. What matters is the here and now. That Patrick has sure worked a miracle with you."

"I know," Mary said, her eyes clear and bright again. "Sometimes, I can't quite believe it myself. I love him so much. He is . . . he's everything to me."

"Mary, I want you to know that, well, I know you know that I don' have a lot of money. An' you don' know how much I wanted you to have a nice wedding."

"But Papa, look at all of this," Mary said, gesturing toward the door that led to the sanctuary. "In my wildest dreams, I couldn't have imagined anything more than this."

"I know, I know. But it's just that, well, I wish I could've been the one to give you all of this, today."

"Oh, Papa, you've always given me so much," Mary said, embracing her father.

The organ music outside the door grew louder, marking the beginning of the processional. Mary stepped back and wiped her eyes. Sam straightened his tie, tucked Mary's arm around his own, and smiled. It was time.

As the trumpeter played a magnificent fanfare, the congregation rose in a great wave and turned expectantly toward the entrance to the sanctuary. The church was filled to capacity. Patrick stood with his brother and Father O'Brien at the altar, waiting.

The deep chords of the organ joined the clear notes of the trumpet as Mary and her father began making their way down the aisle. Most of the people in the church had never met Mary, but her exquisite beauty caused even those who had already seen her to gasp as she glided past.

Although Mary was anxious, she gave no indication of her feelings. She was smiling, her beautiful face relaxed and serene. Tears slowly trickled from her eyes. Patrick watched her, her hand tucked around her father's arm as they came to a halt before him. When the music stopped, Father O'Brien's voice rang through the church.

"I greet you, family and friends who have gathered here today to witness the marriage of Mary Elizabeth Hayes and Patrick Miles McAllister. Please, join me in prayer." He bowed his head. "Father, we ask your blessing for Mary and Patrick, who today will be united in marriage before your altar . . ."

Mary kept her head bowed, but opened her eyes slightly. She looked down at her father's feet. The stiff dress shoes were moving ever so slightly. His toes were wriggling inside them, she knew, and she had to smile.

Patrick stepped forward and took Mary's hand as her father released it. Sam smiled at his daughter and sat down in the front pew on the left side of the church. The only other occupants of the pew were an older man and woman who wore their Sunday best but who still appeared uncomfortably underdressed. They were Mr. and Mrs. Pearson, neighbors of two decades and the only guests invited by Mary and her father. In fact, they were the only people they could think to invite.

Mary looked up at Patrick, her face more radiant than the crown she wore. Patrick smiled down at her and squeezed her hand as they faced the young priest. Behind him, he felt two hundred pairs of eyes taking in the beauty of this stunning woman who would soon be his wife. He had waited and worked for this moment — their coronation. During the week ahead, they would visit Niagara Falls and New York City. He savored the thought of escorting his glorious bride on their honeymoon. As he felt the softness of her hand in his, his heartbeat quickened and a sudden urgency made itself known. Patrick looked down at Mary again. His eyes were hungry, almost ravenous. Their marble mansion in Mill River was finished. They would spend their first night in it tonight. After waiting for so long, he would finally get from Mary what he wanted most.

CHAPTER 9

Having conquered the treadmill, shoveled her driveway, and treated herself to a hot bath, Claudia Simon drove her old station wagon through Mill River to the grocery store. She smiled with satisfaction at having eaten a healthy brunch to make sure that she would not be tempted by the Doritos in the snack aisle. She was in control of her appetite and proud of it.

She remained firmly in control in the produce section, although that was easy. She didn't feel guilty about eating anything here — fruits and vegetables were her friends, and she piled them into her shopping cart. The dairy aisle was fine, too. Skim milk, low-fat cottage cheese, and yogurt — all acceptable. She picked up a package of boneless, skinless chicken in the meat section and a half pound of salmon at the seafood counter.

Still in control, Claudia ignored the package of Italian sausage that whispered to her and completely bypassed the snack aisle and its crinkly, shiny bags of deep-fried bliss. *A good marinara would be nice,* she thought as she swung through the aisle of dried goods for some spaghetti and pasta sauce. Now the only things that she still needed were low-fat salad dressing and bread. The salad dressing was in the next aisle over. The bread, though, was in the far corner of the store . . . in the bakery section.

Claudia took a deep breath and steeled herself as she pushed her cart toward the bakery. She looked at her watch. It was about noon, which meant that the smells of the morning baking wouldn't be so noticeable anymore. For this, Claudia was thankful.

She would buy a nice loaf of whole wheat bread, the kind that was rich in fiber. She imagined the scent of that whole wheat bread as she passed the bakery area, where behind a glass counter there were birthday cakes, cookies, and rows of doughnuts. Glazed, Bavarian cream, Boston cream, twist. Doughnuts were her greatest weakness, and her control was fading.

She walked faster, swung her cart around the end of the aisle to where the shelves of bread began. Before her stood an enormous

Entenmann's display. Boxes of coffee cakes, pastries, and doughnuts were stacked neatly beneath a sign that read 2 FOR $5.00. She stared at a box of powdered sugar doughnuts and began to salivate. *Stop it,* Claudia told herself. *You're not hungry. You made sure of that before you left the house.* But a little voice in her head asked how long had it been since she had allowed herself a powdered sugar doughnut. A month? Two months? Surely, the voice begged, couldn't you make an exception today?

Well, Claudia thought as she reached for the box, *I exercised this morning and continue to be very careful about my diet.* The little voice encouraged this line of thinking. *You deserve it,* it said. *And besides, a doughnut or two won't cause you to regain ninety pounds.* That was true, Claudia told herself as she set the box in her cart. But it could be a dangerous beginning. She sighed and resolved to try to talk herself out of the purchase, all the while knowing that it wouldn't work.

As she rounded the end of the aisle intent on quickly finding her bread and leaving the store, Claudia heard a male voice that was vaguely familiar and a child's voice that she recognized immediately.

"Here you go, kiddo, be careful not to smash it."

"I won't, Dad. I'll put it on top, by the eggs."

Kyle Hansen was standing in the bread aisle beside a cart and his daughter, Rowen.

Claudia had met Kyle a few weeks before. A police officer, Kyle and his partner, Leroy Underwood, had visited her class as part of the "Explore a Career" project she had started. *No wonder his voice was familiar,* she thought. Her knees had gone weak the moment he had entered her classroom, and, since then, she had replayed his voice speaking to her fourth-graders hundreds of times in her mind.

"We should swing by the deli and get some stuff for sandwiches. And we still have to get a bag of cat food."

"We can put it on the bottom, see, Dad?" Rowen said, pointing down to the wire rack above the wheels of the cart. "That's what it's for, you know. Hey, can I get a doughnut?" Claudia felt herself cringe.

"No, I think Ruth gives you enough treats from the bakery —"

"Miss Simon! Hi, Miss Simon!" Rowen called, spotting Claudia at the end of the aisle. Kyle turned and smiled. Claudia froze. Now, after having succumbed to her sweet tooth, was not the time she wanted to be seen by anyone, much less by this good-looking man who had denied his own daughter a doughnut and would surely think her a pig if he saw the whole box of them in her cart. But it was too late — they were coming toward her. She grabbed a loaf of bread from the nearest shelf, placed it on top of the doughnut box, and forced herself to smile.

"Hi, Rowen," she said, but before she could say anything to Kyle, Rowen interrupted her.

"Miss Simon, guess what? I got a cat! Dad got it from a lady who died and now he's mine!"

"You did?" Claudia said, looking at Kyle, who grinned back at her. "What's her name?"

"*His* name," Rowen said, "is Sham. He's a Siamese and has blue eyes. We have to get him cat food." Rowen was looking curiously into Claudia's cart. Spying the half-hidden Entenmann's box, she pursed her mouth and squinted up at her father. "Hey, Dad, Miss Simon is getting doughnuts, so why can't I get one?"

Claudia thought she would shrivel into a prune. If Kyle noticed her reddening face, though, he didn't show it. In fact, he seemed

151

a little embarrassed by Rowen's antics.

"Oh, all right," he said awkwardly. He looked at Claudia sheepishly as Rowen took off toward the bakery counter. "But only one," he called in the direction of the doughnut case.

"She's got a major sweet tooth," Kyle said as he put another loaf of bread into the cart. "You'd think that getting treats from the bakery all week and pancakes for breakfast this morning would be enough for her."

"Well, I guess when it comes to doughnuts, I can relate," Claudia said with a wry smile. "And you're only a kid once."

"That's true," Kyle said. "So, Miss Simon, how have those fourth-graders been treating you?" He looked at her with genuine interest, and Claudia hoped that whatever she managed to say wouldn't sound idiotic.

"Oh, please call me Claudia. And things are pretty good. I'm getting to know the kids, which is hard when you come in halfway through the school year and they're used to someone else. The kids were disappointed when Mrs. Shultz decided not to come back after her maternity leave. They had a substitute teacher for a month before I was hired, and since I started right after the Christmas break, they came back to class and yet another new teacher. But anyway, I really appreciated you and Officer Underwood coming in to talk to them. The kids enjoyed meeting you."

"That's good. Visiting your class was way more fun than patrolling or checking drivers' licenses. And you should call me Kyle, by the way. None of this, 'officer' stuff."

"Fair enough," Claudia said, smiling, as Rowen returned with what appeared to be a Bavarian cream doughnut in a little wax-paper bag.

"Look, Dad, I got one with custard inside. Can I eat it now?" she asked. "Pleeaase?"

Kyle rolled his eyes at Claudia, and she couldn't help but chuckle. "Well, I've got a stack of papers to grade at home, and it looks like you've got more decisions to make," she told him. "And I'll see you in class tomorrow," Claudia said to Rowen as she turned her cart away.

"Take care," Kyle said. Rowen waved goodbye with her mouth already full.

Claudia headed toward the checkout lines with her heart singing. She hadn't made a fool of herself in front of Kyle, even after the doughnut fiasco. In fact, she thought, as she removed the box of doughnuts from her cart and shoved it onto a shelf at the end of an aisle, she was truly happy, and she didn't need doughnuts to stay that way. At least, not today.

With the end of their shopping trip finally in sight, Kyle and Rowen made their way to the pet food aisle. As they turned around the end of an aisle, Kyle caught a glimpse of Claudia standing at the checkout, rummaging in her purse and chatting with the cashier. It was strange that he hadn't noticed how pretty she was the first time he'd seen her. Then again, he'd been in her classroom, in front of his daughter and twenty-two other fourth-graders.

"Here's the cat food aisle. Dad, come on," Rowen said, tugging at the cart. Her doughnut long gone, she wanted to rush home and play with Sham.

Reluctantly, Kyle tore his gaze away from Claudia and followed his daughter. He was surprised that he actually felt an attraction to someone. He hadn't since Allison had died. He also realized that finding a way to see Claudia again would be no problem at all.

Leroy Underwood was doing some rummaging of his own.

Parked two blocks from Claudia's house, he'd watched her shovel the snow from around her car and drive away. She had cleared the walk around back too, which was just as well, since he had no desire to leave footprints in the snow leading up to the door. Once she drove out of sight, he crept to the rear of the house and let himself in through the back door. Like most other back doors in Mill River, Claudia's was rarely locked. He had watched her for almost a month now. He knew her routine. She worked out every Sunday morning and always went shopping for groceries afterward. She would be gone for at least an hour.

Until today, he had never been so bold as to enter her house. Oh, he had looked into her windows plenty of times, watched as she sat and graded papers at night, ran on her treadmill, lounged on the sofa in front of the television. He had taken some pretty good pictures of her. But he craved her, needed to know more of her. He had worn his police uniform, so that if he were seen, he could simply explain that he was checking out a report of a Peeping Tom. He figured such a situation would be unlikely, though, and fortunately for him, it appeared that he was right. Even in broad daylight, no one was around.

Now he stood in front of her bedroom dresser, running his coarse fingers through her underthings, breathing in the lavender scent of her lingerie sachet. He pulled out silky panties and camisoles and nightgowns, which slid like liquid over his hands. He looked down at her bed, imagined himself beneath her covers. Someday, he would lie here with her.

Carefully, he selected a lacy thong panty from her drawer and put it in his pocket. It was silky black with thin embroidered sides. He would use the thong at night when he looked at his pictures of her.

He grew nervous. She might be on her way home by now, and he needed to leave.

He passed the bathroom where the warm, moist air still smelled of shampoo. In Claudia's orderly kitchen, he opened her refrigerator. Nothing in it appealed to him.

He closed the door and examined the many notes and photos under her assorted refrigerator magnets. There was a picture of her, wearing tight jeans and a low-cut sweater and smiling demurely over her shoulder. Next to it was a picture of the back of an enormous woman, taken so that her face didn't show. He didn't know who this woman was and didn't care — he was much more interested in the picture of Claudia. His eyes were drawn again to the tight jeans. Her ass was firm and round — a perfect cushion for the pushin'. Leroy thought of the black panties in his pocket, and the front of his pants, already uncomfortably tight, felt like it would burst.

Leroy flinched as a someone knocked loudly on the front door. He froze for a moment, listening.

"Yoo-hoo, Miss Claudia, are you home?" a voice called. Whoever it was knocked again.

Leroy stole a glance out the kitchen window and cursed to himself. It was Crazy Daisy, dressed like a damned Eskimo and looking expectantly up at the door.

She'll go away after a few minutes, he thought as he stood in the kitchen, but then he heard a car pull into the driveway and his heart began pounding even faster. He knew well the sound of that car. Claudia was home.

His mind was racing. He heard a car door slam, heard Daisy's singsong voice chattering about some love potion and Claudia politely trying to refuse Daisy's solicitation. He would have to go now and hope that they were too distracted by each other to notice him leaving.

Leroy was out the back door just as Claudia stepped in through the front. He hid behind a thicket in her backyard in case she looked outside. He watched Daisy walk past the house on her way toward St. John's. The woman paused for a moment as she passed the thicket in which he was hiding and then kept going. She probably hadn't seen him. Once Daisy was at the front door of the church, he walked casually around the back, down to where his car was parked. The adrenaline still coursed through him, but he was beginning to feel intense satisfaction at his accomplishment. He stuck his hand in the pocket where the panties were. Though he had never imagined he would, he felt a sort of grudging gratitude toward Crazy Daisy. As batty as she was, her showing up had enabled him to escape with his treasure.

CHAPTER 10

1941

Two months after their wedding, Mary was standing at her bedroom window in her nightgown, watching Patrick leave for work. His new midnight-blue Packard Clipper coupé, the wedding present promised by his father, rolled smoothly down the driveway and disappeared. After a few moments, she caught sight of the car again, moving up the main street of Mill River toward the highway to Rutland.

Although Vermont's autumn glory was at its peak, Mary barely noticed the bright orange and flaming red of the sugar maples. Her gaze bypassed the golden birches interspersed among dark green pines. The rolling hills surrounding Mill River had become a rich natural palette, but one that held no interest for Mary.

She turned her tearstained face from the window and gingerly flexed her wrist. *Per-*

haps some ice would stop it from hurting, she thought. She headed downstairs to the kitchen. There, she pulled a tray of ice cubes from the freezer and slammed it on the counter. A handful of cubes popped loose. She wrapped the ice in a towel and applied the cold, lumpy mass to her wrist.

Mary stood over the sink in the kitchen for several minutes. The ice in the towel melted, spreading coldness through the plush cotton fibers. Water droplets fell into the sink. *Drip. Drip.* In the quiet interior of the mansion, the droplets sounded like sharp blows of a hammer. Mary leaned against the counter and began to cry again.

How could she have been so happy and so wrong at the same time? The two months that she had spent as Patrick's wife felt like two years. The man that Patrick was today was not the man she had married. Or perhaps he was, and she had been too naïve to realize it.

The towel holding the ice cubes was almost completely soaked when Mary finally dropped it into the sink. She held up her wrist. It was slightly swollen. Reddish-purple bruises had appeared on each side, left by the viselike grip of Patrick's hand. She flexed it again and was surprised that it felt much better. Mary took another towel, dried her hands, and pressed it lightly against her damp cheeks.

The tree branches outside the kitchen window twisted gently in the wind. She thought of how that cool breeze would feel on her face and headed back upstairs to get dressed. She really needed to get out of the house.

Mary pulled a long-sleeved shirt and a pair of her comfortable work pants out of her bureau. The first time she had seen Patrick, she had been wearing clothes like this. He hadn't given any indication that it bothered him then, but the last time she dressed this way in front of him, he screamed at her to go change immediately, because no wife of his would dress like a pauper. *A different person,* she thought again, as she peeled off her nightgown. Her injured wrist made it difficult to dress, but she managed. Mary went downstairs, slipped on her riding boots, and headed to the stable through the back door of the house.

True to his word, Conor had had a stable built for Patrick and Mary on the land behind their new home. The barn held three horses — Penny; Patrick's chestnut Thoroughbred, Monarch; and Ebony. The horses turned expectantly as she opened the door.

161

Ebony swung her dark head over the stall door and nickered.

"Good morning, pretty girl," Mary said to the black horse. She rubbed the mare's nose and forehead before she went to the feed room.

While the residents of the barn busied themselves with their morning oats, Mary sat on a bale of straw, her brow furrowed in thought. She had tried so many times to talk to Patrick. Lately, he had been in such a foul mood. He wouldn't open up to her and had taken to staying at work later and later. Perhaps it was just the pressures of his job. He had complained several weeks ago that as the war in Europe escalated, demand for marble was steadily dropping. And, for what orders they did have, they were short on workers since men at the marbleworks were being drafted into the military or transferred to war-related industries.

There was also something else that might have been weighing on Patrick's mind. As much as she tried not to think about it, he could be drafted as easily as any of the other employees at the marbleworks. When his conscription questionnaire arrived, he had filled it out and returned it as required. He had been assigned a number, like all of the young men in Rutland County, and every month, the *Rutland Herald* printed columns of names of the men whose numbers had been drawn by the local draft board.

Her great fear was that it was something about her that bothered him. In the few weeks after they had returned from their honeymoon, he had wanted her to go to dinner or attend some other social function with him almost every night. She had acquiesced. During these outings, Patrick seemed to delight in presenting her to his friends and acquaintances, which made her quite uncomfortable. She had become much better at quelling any anxiety that she felt in those situations, but she now understood that she would never come close to matching Patrick's social prowess.

This morning, over breakfast, when he had mentioned an upcoming dinner engagement, she had asked if they might decline the invitation and enjoy a quiet evening together alone.

"Mary, you know it would be rude to do that."

"Well, surely, Patrick, people don't accept every invitation they receive. Don't you think we could decline this one?"

Patrick's green eyes blazed. He took a last swig from his coffee mug and picked up his briefcase.

"I think that a good wife does what her husband asks of her."

Mary was silent a moment. She couldn't think of what to say, but she felt that she had to say *something* before he left.

"Patrick, wait —" As he opened the side door to leave, she laid a hand on his arm. He turned to face her, and his expression was cold and cruel. He grabbed her wrist, bending it backward as he spoke.

"You will come with me tomorrow night. End of discussion."

"Patrick, you're hurting me. Please," she said. Glaring at her, he released her wrist and walked out the door, slamming it behind him.

She had run upstairs to the bedroom clutching her wrist, her mind reeling. Finally, the tears came. This was her husband, the man she had married. The wonderful man who had been so patient and caring when she had wanted nothing to do with him. He had turned into someone she didn't recognize, and she didn't know what to do.

A shrill whinny came from Monarch's loose box, and Mary looked up, startled. Ebony was still licking the last oats from her feedbox, but Monarch and Penny were finished. One at a time, she led the bay horse and the copper-colored mare outside and turned them into their paddocks. Monarch raced around the field and then lowered himself onto the ground. As Penny grazed, the bay horse rolled, grunting, with all four hooves flailing in the air. Mary watched and smiled. *He still acts like a yearling,* she thought to herself.

She went into the tack room and, taking care not to strain her wrist further, took down a bridle and saddle. She would go riding for the morning, maybe out to her father's. That way, Ebony could still enjoy the afternoon in the pasture.

Mary managed to get the saddle and bridle on the black mare. It took her longer than usual to tighten the girth, but Ebony stood patiently, turning more than once to nuzzle her shoulder. Finally, she climbed into the saddle. She had ridden to her father's several times over the past few weeks. The black mare knew the way. Mary held the reins loosely with one hand, shielding her eyes from the bright sunlight.

Perhaps she would talk to her father about Patrick's strange shift in personality. He could, after all, offer her a man's perspective. She had previously decided against mentioning their troubles to her father — he liked Patrick and was so delighted that she had married. Still, nothing she had tried seemed to make the situation any better. *In fact,* she thought grimly as she looked at her wrist, *it seems to be getting worse.*

Mary swayed in the saddle as the black mare picked her way through the forest. The trail was a shortcut. It would end on the main road almost directly across from the driveway to her father's farm. Mary relaxed and looked up at the multi-colored canopy ruffling in the breeze. The light that found its way through the leaves left moving spots of sunshine on her face, on Ebony, on the ground as they passed by. The milky white trunks of the birch trees stood out against the darker bark of oaks and maples. With each gust of wind, round, gold birch leaves rained down around them.

Mary reached out and caught one of them. When she was younger, during the worst years of the Depression, she had collected these leaves. She had grown up doing without, all the while knowing that her father struggled as best he could to make ends meet. The birch trees had provided for her an escape into an imaginary world of riches. She used to pretend that the golden leaves were coins, and would remove the stems and fill her pockets with them. Several times, she had placed them under her pillow in the hope that the tooth fairy would transform them into real gold while she slept.

She was grateful that she no longer needed to wish for gold to magically appear — Patrick did provide very well for her. Mary sighed. If only her father would let her help him . . . Patrick had already agreed to pay for a new home to be built at the farm, but her father had insisted on keeping the old farmhouse and scraping by on repairs he made himself. Mary thought of him, sitting alone in the creaking house each evening, and was glad that she had decided to visit.

The trail through the forest curved gently and stopped at the main road. Mary urged Ebony across, but the black mare needed no encouraging. She pricked up her ears and broke into an eager trot.

"You know where you are, don't you, old girl?" Mary asked her horse, smiling. "I miss the place too."

The remaining distance to the farm passed quickly. As the huge red barn came into view, Mary noticed that its doors were open. Her father was probably in the training ring. She dismounted and looped the ends of Ebony's bridle around a rail of the fence before walking toward the barn.

"Papa?"

A large cluster of horses grazed in the pasture even though the gate was unlocked. She walked through it and into the barn. It was empty.

"Hello? Papa, are you out here?"

The door at the back of the barn was open, and a snort and short whinny came from the training ring.

"Papa?" Mary walked through the back door, and her breath caught in her throat.

A young colt wearing saddle and bridle stood in the training ring looking at her. Her father lay motionless on the ground only a few feet away.

"Papa!" she screamed, and ran to him.

The horse breeder lay faceup in a smattering of red maple leaves, and a great gash on his scalp had stained the ground around his head to match. His eyes were half closed.

"Papa!" Mary grabbed her father's hand, held his face, shook him by the shoulders. "Papa, wake up! Please!" She put an ear to his unmoving chest and heard nothing but the wind winding through the trees surrounding the training ring. Something in her mind told her to go to the house to call for help, but a frantic sense of inevitability overcame her. She was sobbing, shaking her father, and wiping at her eyes, screaming for someone, anyone, to help her. The training ring spun around her as she collapsed.

Mr. Pearson from the next farm over found her that way, slumped over her father, sobbing and muttering unintelligibly to herself. He had heard her screams and come running, but all he could do was call the sheriff and watch over Mary until her husband and the authorities arrived. The coroner determined that Sam had died as a result of trauma to the head. Most likely, he had been thrown against the fence when he tried to ride the young colt, but no one would ever know quite how it happened.

They held the funeral Mass at the stone church in Mill River. Mary wore a black dress, and the only McAllisters in attendance were Patrick's immediate family. Again, the Pearsons sat together in the front row of the church. And again, Father O'Brien stood at the altar, but he spoke softly, out of respect for the man who lay at rest in the closed casket behind him.

1942

For the McAllister family, May brought none of the joys of spring.

On one of those early spring nights, long after the employees had gone home, a single window at McAllister Marbleworks remained lit. The remnants of winter-chilled

169

air swirled outside the glass, seeping through the crevices, challenging the old steam radiator in the office that sputtered and hissed in response. Conor, Stephen, and Patrick McAllister sat at a table inside the illuminated room. Accounting ledgers lay strewn before them, along with diagrams of machinery and lists of inventory.

"We don't have a choice, for Patrick's sake," Stephen said. "We can keep him from being drafted. He'd be working in a war-related industry. That means he'd be eligible for a deferment."

"I think you're right," Conor said. "And it would make good business sense. I don't see how the demand for marble will do anything but decrease while we're at war. It won't be easy, but we've got to convert to war production, or we won't be able to generate enough income to break even, much less turn a profit."

"Then it's settled. I'll file for a deferment first thing tomorrow," Patrick said.

"Good," Stephen said. "That'll be one less thing to worry about. I've still got to deal with the blasted tires, though." As of January 1, the government had placed a moratorium on the sale of new cars. Not only were Stephen's automobile-buying sprees now prohibited, but the tires on most of the cars he did own had been confiscated by the government for the war effort. Only the Lincoln still had tires, and Stephen worried constantly that one of them would go flat.

Patrick had no interest in listening to his father complain about his inability to maintain his automobile collection. He was far more worried about his own precarious situation. He felt sick every time he thought about the telegram that he had received two mornings ago. It had been an official greeting from Uncle Sam, informing him that he was to report for induction into the army on June 12, exactly a month from today.

The military induction center in Rutland had been busy ever since the attack at Pearl Harbor in December. He drove by it each morning on his way to the marbleworks and shook his head at the long lines of men waiting to enlist. Many of those men had worked at the marbleworks. Some had been drafted, but more had gone willingly, eager for the chance to blast the Japs for their sneak attack.

What others did mattered little to Patrick. He would be lying if he didn't say that, on some deep level, it bothered him that a tiny island nation had the audacity to take on the United States, and that German U-boats were rumored to be prowling just a few miles off the Atlantic coast. There was no doubt in his mind, though, that there were enough foolhardy volunteers and blue-collar draftees available to satisfy the local draft board.

He was unlike those men. He had worked hard to reach the ideal position in life, and his place at the helm of the marble-works was assured. He was educated, intelligent, and privileged. He could not bear the thought of standing in the line outside the induction center, standing beside those men as an equal, and eventually taking orders from some chump officer with only space between his ears. He had no intention of wasting his Harvard degree and placing his life and family's future success in jeopardy to fight a war. His participation would have little, if any, effect on the outcome.

Avoiding the draft, though, would be difficult. He was healthy, in the prime of his life, and could not escape with a deferment for some physical problem. He was not a farmer, and so could not qualify for an agricultural exemption. He supposed his grandfather could twist a few arms, maybe convince the draft board to "forget" that his number had come up. That option was risky, though. If word of such a scheme ever leaked out, his family's social standing would be forever compromised. Working in a war-related industry would be ideal. It would be seen as a legitimate, even honorable, alternative to going to war.

The next morning, Patrick mailed a letter to the chairman of the local draft board. In it, he requested a deferment based on the fact that McAllister Marbleworks would soon be converted to a machine shop. His family's business would produce rifle-barrel drillers, machines to make tin cans, engine parts for Liberty ships, bombsights, and an assortment of other supplies for the war effort. He mentioned that, as the eldest son, he would bear substantial responsibility in overseeing production.

Sending the letter gave him a certain measure of relief. Surely, with his father and grandfather's influence in the community, he would be spared the indignity of being conscripted. Jubilantly, he decided to leave work a few hours early so that he and Mary might go riding before dark.

When Patrick pulled up at the marble mansion, the house was quiet, as usual. The death of Mary's father some seven months earlier had sent her into a deep depression. She rarely left the house, even to go down to the barn. Much of her time she spent in bed, even though she suffered from insomnia. She slept briefly and sporadically. Patrick often awoke in the middle of the night to find her standing at the window, staring silently out into the darkness. She had never been enthusiastic about being intimate with him, but now, she responded to his advances with all the emotion of a slab of cold marble.

Mary had refused to see a psychiatrist, or, despite his urging, almost anyone else. The death of a parent would leave almost anyone grief-stricken, of course. Patrick assumed, correctly, that the death of Mary's father had had a much greater impact on her since Sam had been the one constant throughout her life. For the first few months, this understanding tempered his impatience with her. He went about his business, attended social functions alone, and basked in the sympathetic understanding of society's elite when he explained Mary's continued absences.

And yet, as time passed and Mary continued her downward spiral, Patrick realized that the life of grandeur that he had envisioned for himself and Mary was slipping away. A smoldering resentment of her mental condition, and then of Mary herself, emerged. Twice he had forced her out of the house to visit his parents, but she had been distracted or unresponsive. He had been grateful that only his immediate family had seen her in that condition, and he had resolved not to risk another awkward situation by forcing her out of the house a third time.

Today, however, might be different. Maybe, if he were gentle and persuasive, she would come down to the stable with him. He opened the side door of the house and stepped into the dark entryway.

"Mary! I'm home!" The downstairs of the house was immaculate. Although she had requested that he not hire a maid or any other house staff when they moved into their new home, insisting that she could keep the house herself, Mary had done no cooking or any other housework for weeks. Now a local girl came to the house to cook and clean each morning, and two boys from a nearby farm tended to the horses twice a day. They worked hard for the wages Patrick paid them. It was a good thing, because he would not tolerate incompetent help.

Patrick bounded up the stairs, taking them two at a time. "Mary, are you awake?"

"Yes," came her flat reply. She was in the bedroom standing at the window. Despite the fact that it was past four o'clock, she still wore a rumpled nightgown. "I watched your car coming through town."

"I sent the letter to the draft board today. Pop feels pretty sure I'll get to stay here to help implement our new production plans."

"That's a relief." Mary stood with her back to him. Her voice was devoid of emotion.

"Mary, darling, I stopped on the way home and brought you a little surprise." He reached into his pocket as he approached her. She turned to see him holding out a small, velvet-covered box. "I know I've not been home so much recently with work being so busy, and I thought this might cheer you up enough to feel like going riding with me."

Mary half smiled and reached for the box. She raised the top to reveal an ivory cameo on a delicate gold chain.

"It's lovely. But you didn't have to do this, Patrick."

"I know, but I wanted my wife to have something as beautiful as she is." He waited for some response from Mary, but she seemed as distant and distracted as ever. Still, he smiled at her, gently took her by the shoulders. "C'mon, let's go riding. I came home early, after all." Despite his best efforts, an expectant edge had crept into his voice.

"Patrick, I love the necklace. Really, I do. But . . ." Mary turned to look out the window again. "I just don't feel up to going out." The room was silent for an instant, a vacuum, before it was filled with Patrick's white-hot rage.

"It has been seven months! When will you feel up to it? You cannot spend the rest of your life in this house! Look at me!" Patrick grabbed Mary and spun her around to face him. He lowered his voice to a deep hiss. His red face was but two inches from hers, and he spoke slowly, overemphasizing each word. "I've tried to be patient. I've given you everything I can think of to make you happy and still you're in this sorry state. As my wife, you have certain obligations. If you can't, or won't, fulfill them, you are useless to me." He shoved her away from him. She crumpled to the floor like a rag doll.

Patrick paid no attention to Mary as he changed into his riding clothes and left the bedroom. Still seething, he made his way down to the barn. After leading Monarch out of the pasture and into the barn, he replaced the horse's halter with a bridle. Patrick went to the tack room and retrieved a saddle, which he threw over Monarch's back with a single robotic movement. He cinched the girth with a savage tug. The blood bay squealed and laid his ears back, but Patrick pulled the girth tighter still. He had turned to grab his riding crop when the horse lunged at him. Patrick, still engulfed by his fury, didn't see him coming. He yelled in pain as Monarch sank his teeth into his left upper arm.

With all his strength, Patrick brought his right hand down across the horse's nose. The blow was enough to gain release from the bite. Instinctively, he looked at his left arm. Blood was soaking through the sleeve of his white shirt.

Patrick looked up at the blood bay, barely feeling the ache in his arm. Monarch had backed into an area in the barn where horses were cross-tied and groomed. The horse was worked up and showing the whites of his eyes. Patrick walked backward toward the tack room, watching the horse all the while. Once inside, he grabbed a long leather whip from a hook on the wall. He had found the whip in Sam's barn after the horse breeder had died and had taken it almost as an afterthought. Now he was happy to have it in his possession.

With the whip in one hand, he reached his other hand into a bag on the tack room shelf and scooped out several sugar cubes. Then, slowly, silently, Patrick approached the blood bay. He laid the whip on the floor just outside the tack room door and walked toward Monarch with a few of the sugar cubes in an outstretched hand. The horse shied back even further and half whinnied, but Patrick kept moving, talking in a low, soothing voice.

Monarch flared his nostrils and looked at the sugar. Cautiously, the horse stretched out his head and took the cubes from Patrick's hand. Patrick reached up and took hold of the bridle, still talking, and gently pulled forward. The horse hesitated for a moment before following him. Patrick stopped after only a few steps. Monarch stood between two posts in the grooming area. Secured to each post was a short rope that ended in a metal clasp. Patrick refilled his hand with sugar cubes, and, as soon as the horse accepted them, snapped each clasp to the rings on either side of the bridle. The cross-ties allowed for little movement. Monarch was trapped.

After loosening the saddle and slipping it off the horse's back, Patrick gathered the whip up off the floor. He snapped the supple leather against the barn floor, against a stall, and against the floor again, this time right in front of the Monarch. The crack of the lash startled the horse, but when he tried to rear, he was held down by the straps attached to his bridle. There, finally, was the horse's first display of fear, and Patrick reveled in it. With a sociopath's calm and a vicious grin, Patrick swung the coiled leather snake and advanced on the blood bay.

In her bedroom in the quiet mansion, Mary still lay on the floor, weeping, and heard nothing.

Patrick began an unusually stifling Friday in June as he had most of his days over the past few weeks — recovering from a night of drinking with his cousins in Rutland. The heat only aggravated his headache while the sun nearly blinded him, and he sat in his office with the shades drawn. Despite the wedding band he wore, he thought of himself as a bachelor of sorts. Mary gave him nothing he needed, so he sought to fulfill his needs elsewhere. His wife didn't seem to care. On the rare occasions when he slept in his own home, instead of at his parents' or cousins' houses or in some other place with a pretty young thing he had seduced, she remained isolated in a world all her own. He ignored her, and she scarcely noticed his presence.

Patrick had downed his third mug of black coffee when one of the secretaries knocked on the door. Immediately, he jumped up and threw the door open.

"Damn it, Louise, I told you I didn't want to see anyone —" he scolded. He stopped when he saw the letter that the secretary held out to him. It was an official-looking manila envelope bearing the seal of the Rutland County draft board.

Louise was a mousy little woman with brown eyes and a long nose that spoiled her otherwise pretty face. She quivered and looked up at Patrick. "I know, Mr. McAllister, but this seemed important."

Patrick seized the letter and slammed the door in her face. Once he was alone, he ripped open the envelope and began to read.

June 4, 1942

Dear Mr. McAllister:
We have reviewed the request in your letter of May 12. While McAllister Marbleworks' contribution to the war effort is indeed significant, we have come to the conclusion that Messrs. Conor and Stephen McAllister bear the most substantial proportion of management duties. In the Board's opinion, your abilities would be better put to use serving in our nation's armed forces. Your

education and experience would most surely enable you to enter Officer Candidate School, and we intend to provide notice of your exceptional qualifications to the appropriate induction personnel.

Therefore, please consider this a notice to report for induction into the United States Army not later than June 12, 1942.

Sincerely,
H. Wallace Boyd, Chairman,
Local Board No. 2
Rutland County, Vermont

Patrick's fingers tightened around the edge of the paper as he read the letter a second time, then a third. His eyes focused and refocused on the words on the page, and finally, they registered in his brain. He folded the paper and stormed out of his office.

Conor McAllister looked irritated when his grandson burst into his office in the middle of an important call, but the panic on Patrick's face softened Conor's expression.

"Look, Jack, something's come up that requires my attention. Can I ring you later this afternoon to finish this? You're a good man, Jack. Sure, about three o'clock."

He hung up the phone and looked at his grandson, but Patrick began talking before Conor could say anything.

"Grandpop, they're going to take me." He waved the letter from the draft board wildly as he spoke. "You've got to help me. June 12, that's only a week from now. You know these people. They'll listen to you." He finally shoved the letter in front of his grandfather and began pacing.

Conor put on his reading glasses and read the letter. Finally, he removed his glasses, sighed, and looked up at his grandson.

"I've already tried, Patrick. I spoke with Wally Boyd yesterday afternoon."

"What? And you said nothing to me about it?" Patrick said.

"What's going on here?" Stephen asked as he entered Conor's office. He shut the door quickly behind him. "Son, people can hear you all the way down the hall."

"This is what's going on," Patrick snapped, snatching the letter from his grandfather's desk and handing it to his father. "And Grandpop knew about it!"

Stephen skimmed the letter, gave it back to Patrick, and looked at Conor.

"Pop, you knew this was coming?"

"Look, let me explain it to you," Conor said. "Wally Boyd called me yesterday afternoon right before the board was to meet to make a decision about Patrick. He didn't know for certain what the decision would be, but he had a good idea that the board was leaning toward drafting him." Conor looked at Stephen. "He wanted to know if there was anything that Patrick would be doing at the marbleworks that you or I couldn't handle ourselves. I told him there wasn't."

"Pop, how could you do that? You sealed their decision!" Stephen shouted. "You did."

"I could be killed," Patrick said. His rasping whisper did nothing to hide his accusatory tone.

Conor rose up behind his desk with his fists clenched.

"I've known Wally for most of my life, and we've been friends since our college days. I was not about to lie to the man," he said. "But neither did I intend to let my grandson be placed in jeopardy. I did express my grave concern that if Patrick was taken from us, he might not return. Wally assured me that Patrick is prime officer material, that whether he voluntarily enlists or is drafted, he'll be sent to officer school for specialized training. If the war isn't over by the time he's ready to be deployed, he'll be far behind the front lines, if he's anywhere near action at all."

Patrick looked from his father to his grandfather. "I don't believe it. Haven't you seen the papers? Every day, there are lists of the names of men who've been killed! Lots of them are officers! Lots of them! And God knows what'll happen when the Allies invade Europe! It will happen — it's the only way the war will ever end!"

"We've still got a few days," Stephen said. "We'll appeal the decision. I read something about a District Appeal Board. I'll make some calls —" He stopped as Conor shook his head.

"Son, even if we can appeal the decision of the draft board, how would it look? It would be a disgrace to contest it when the sons of so many of our friends and neighbors are reporting for duty."

"Then you've got to call Wally, Grandpop, get him to set up another meeting of the board and reverse the decision," Patrick said. "He'll do it if you ask. I know he will."

"He won't, Patrick. Wally may be chairman, but he is only one man on the board. And contrary to what both of you may believe, I don't have any special influence over the board members. They are simply men trying to do a difficult job as best they can. I can't force them to make any particular decision. We've all got to make the best of this situation, and it could be much worse for you, Patrick. You could be one of those poor chaps without any education, destined for the front lines as part of an infantry unit. But you won't be, Patrick. You're smart and confident. You'll be an officer, and a good one at that."

Stephen opened his mouth to reply to Conor's lecture, but Patrick beat him to it.

"I most certainly will not," Patrick said, tearing the letter into four pieces. "All my life, I've tried to be what you expect me to be. The best education, the best acquaintances, the best marriage. Now you want me to throw it all away? Well, I'll be damned if I ever do that. I've worked too hard. But I'll tell you one thing. I'm through with trying to please you, both of you." He threw the bits of paper at his grandfather's desk and turned to leave.

"Let him go," Conor said as Stephen started after him. The two older McAllisters watched the youngest disappear out the door.

As Patrick arrived at a tavern to drink himself into a stupor, Mary stood in front of a bathroom mirror in her home. She didn't recognize herself. Her hair was matted and stringy and her puffy eyes had deep circles beneath them. Under the light from the small fixture on the ceiling, the skin stretched across her high cheekbones was ashen, almost cadaverous.

Mary opened the medicine cabinet and removed one of Patrick's razors. With trembling fingers, she pulled out the thin blade. The straight edge cast a scant shimmer against the mirror. Slowly, holding the razor blade lightly against her skin, she traced the length of the vein running down her wrist. She feared the pain, but reminded herself that it would last only a little while. *Do it,* said a voice inside her head, *do it now.* She pressed a corner of the blade into her wrist, barely enough to break the skin, and stopped.

A small bead of red appeared at the tiny incision, grew larger, and stretched into a thin ribbon that ran down her arm. Mary dropped the razor blade into the sink and sank to her knees. Her arm slid along the porcelain basin as she lowered herself against the pedestal, leaving behind a thin stripe of crimson.

There was no escape. She lived in pain and yet could not inflict on herself the hurt that would bring her freedom. Her tears, like the droplets of blood from the wound on her wrist, flowed quickly at first before slowing and stopping altogether.

Mary had no idea how long she had been sitting on the bathroom floor when she finally stood. The razor blade was still in the sink where she dropped it. Now she picked it up and put it back into the medicine cabinet. Shaking, she returned to her bedroom. Her gaze traveled from the unmade bed, to the window overlooking Mill River, to her bureau, finally resting on the small black marble statue of a horse.

When had she last been to the barn? Or out of the house, for that matter? Months, at least two or three months. Maybe more. Her horse might not even recognize her.

The realization coursing through Mary's mind was haphazard, but her fixation on the marble statue triggered an urgent desire to see Ebony. She dressed as if she were in a trance, looking blankly ahead as her fingers fumbled buttons on the shirt. She didn't bother with stockings, but slipped on a pair of boots and went downstairs to the back door.

The crisp scent of fresh air registered vaguely in Mary's mind as she made her way down the path to the pasture. Her eyes were unaccustomed to bright light, and so she walked almost blindly, aided only by occasional glimpses through pupils struggling to adjust to the sun. Her body felt disconnected, as if the commands coming from her brain to her legs were traveling great distances before reaching their destinations. The clothes she wore rubbed uncomfortably against skin that had forgotten the feeling of everything except bedsheets and soft nightgowns.

Ebony and Penny were grazing in the pasture. She walked through the grass toward the fence, fixated on their beauty. It had been so long since she had seen the horses, and the rhythmic swishing of their tails and the way that their glossy coats glistened in the sunlight seemed almost surreal.

"Hey, old girl," Mary said to the black mare. Her voice was little more than a croak, but Ebony raised her head and pricked her ears. "Ebby, come here, girl," Mary said, and the horse nickered and walked to the fence, waiting.

Mary held her hand out. She touched the velvet skin on the horse's nose, ran her hands over the soft black face. Ebony nuzzled her arm and breathed a great sigh through flared nostrils, as if to say, *At last.* Mary threw her arms around the mare's neck and sobbed into the thick mane.

Where was Monarch?

Her question was immediately answered when a loud snort sounded from the barn. She left Ebony and walked through the double doors, toward Monarch's stall, but stopped in shock as the horse came into view.

The first thought that ran through Mary's mind was that this horse looking back at her was not Monarch at all, but some other animal whose rib cage was visible through a dull, dark coat. The next was that the horse had changed color. When she stepped closer, Monarch shifted uneasily. His hooves made an odd suction noise. Mary noticed that the floor of the stall was covered in a layer of soiled straw and manure so deep that it came up well past the horse's pasterns. His eyes were half closed and caked with mucus. Worst of all, the drab hair on his chest and back was streaked with long, half-healed cuts — cuts made by a whip.

For a moment, she simply stood staring at Monarch. She struggled to understand what had happened. *Patrick knows about this,* she thought. Then a bolt of lightning ran down her spine and her mind formulated its first rational thought in months: *Patrick must have done this.* She pushed the thought and accompanying rage out of her mind, though, to focus only on the poor creature in front of her.

Mary slowly opened the door to Monarch's stall. The horse moved backward until his rump pressed against the wall. Talking in a low voice, she spoke to him and stepped forward. He shied away from her hand and she stopped, talking patiently. Finally, she drew close enough to grasp the horse's halter. As she led him out of the stall, Monarch walked with the unsteady gait of an old man.

Once the horse had been secured in a clean stall, Mary pulled an armful of fresh hay from an open bale and filled the hay net hanging there. Judging by the way the horse tore into it, it was probably the first food he'd had in days. She placed a bucket of fresh water in the stall beside him. Then, as the humid air thickened, she began working.

Hours later, after Mary had cleaned Monarch's stall, groomed the horse as best she could, and refilled his hay net, oat bin, and water bucket, she brought Ebony and Penny in from the pasture and headed back up to the house. She concentrated only on Monarch's well-being. It was crucial that she call the veterinarian right away, because in addition to his obvious malnourishment and the cuts from the whip that needed attention, the horse was favoring his right hind hoof. She suspected that an infection, maybe an abscess, had developed after he had stood in filth for weeks.

As she walked back toward the house, Mary noticed neither the wind that had begun to sweep through her hair nor the purplish-green tint of the sky. An approaching rumble of thunder did nothing to distract her, but the rumble of Patrick's Packard coupé coming up the driveway seized her attention. She came around the house and saw the car parked at an odd angle. Patrick was just stumbling out. She felt no fear of him, only the incredible rage that she had suppressed in the barn. Her hair blew wildly around her head as she began to scream.

"Why did you do it? Why? My God, Patrick, he was nearly dead, half starved when I found him, and you knew! You did it!"

Even in his drunken state, Patrick was shocked to see Mary outside at all, much less raving and carrying on as she was. It was so unbecoming of her.

"You sure know how to greet your husband after a hard day's work, Mary." Patrick paused and smiled. "The bastard's still alive, is he? Well, give him a few more days, he won't be." Patrick brushed her aside and staggered into the house.

"You're a monster! How could you mistreat such a beautiful horse? You wanted him especially! You paid double for him, even worked a summer to get him from my father! And you leave him shut up in the barn to starve?" They were climbing the staircase, Patrick pulling himself up and Mary screaming behind him.

"That horse is the monster," Patrick slurred, throwing his hat and jacket onto the bed. "Never learned to do what was expected. Always trying to bite and kick, trying to throw me when I rode him. Never was fully and properly broken." Mary's eyes narrowed at the indirect insult to her father. "He thought he could do whatever he wanted with me. Well, I showed him. He knows now, he does."

Patrick was yelling down at her, and the odor of alcohol on his breath was overpowering. She backed away to escape the smell.

"I helped raise that horse." Tears rolled down her face. "He's a good horse. The only reason he, or any other, would act that way is if he was mistreated. I saw the scars, Patrick. How many lashes did you give him?"

"Enough to show him who was boss," Patrick said, undoing his tie. "And obviously you could do with learning the same lesson. You never learned how to be a proper wife. Never wanted to do what I wanted. You're just like him. You looked really good at first, really good." The words lolled around in his mouth. "Had to have both of you. But you weren't good at all, and neither was he. Not good at all." A crack of thunder sounded over the house as the sky darkened. Patrick fumbled with a lamp, and when his clumsy fingers couldn't find the switch, he picked it up and threw it across the room.

Mary screamed. Her instinct told her to run, but Patrick stood between her and the bedroom door. He lurched forward. His arm caught her and flung her in the same direction as he had thrown the lamp.

As Mary struggled to her feet, Patrick walked purposefully toward her bureau. He reached out for the black marble statue of Ebony and held it up. He ran a finger over the smooth lines of the carving as lightning flashed outside the window.

"You stay away from me!" Mary said as Patrick advanced toward her, but he only smiled and kept coming. "Don't you think it's funny," he said, "how, after months of neglecting me, when I'm about to be sucked into a war and my family won't do a bloody thing to help me, that all my wife cares about is a *goddamn horse!*"

With the miniature Ebony in his hand, Patrick lunged at Mary. She turned her head and tried to push him away, but the black marble figurine he held smashed into her face just above her left eye. She collapsed, struck unconscious, with Patrick swaying above her.

He stood that way for a moment before dropping the black marble statue. It hit the bedroom floor with a deep *clunk,* but he didn't hear it. He didn't know whether Mary was alive or dead, but his inebriated brain told him that he had to get out of there. He would leave, drive away to some place where the draft board and the authorities would never find him. He would rebuild his life, free of his demanding family and sick wife.

Patrick threw open the door to the bedroom closet, pulled a suitcase from the top shelf, and began stuffing clothes into it. Then he grabbed his hat and stumbled downstairs to the car.

Sheets of rain fell as Patrick threw the suitcase into the trunk and got behind the wheel. He cursed when the wipers were barely able to keep up with the volume of water hitting the windshield, but he put the car into drive and gunned the engine anyway. Combined with his blurred vision, the drenched window almost completely obscured his view of the road ahead.

He drove through Mill River and decided to head for Canada. There, out of reach of the government and his family, he could assume a new identity, get a job, and start over. Patrick was thinking about how to access the funds in his bank account as he encountered the first of the road's familiar twists and turns. He confidently steered the Packard around the first sharp curve, but the car fishtailed as he careened around the second. Alarmed, he slammed on the brakes but could not control the car. It skidded off the road toward a cluster of maples.

I'll need a new car, too, Patrick thought in the instant before impact. Then all went black as he was thrown through the windshield onto the midnight-blue hood.

CHAPTER 11

Since the end of Sunday Mass an hour earlier, Father O'Brien had been sitting in his office in the parish house, thinking. Tired and emotionally drained, he was quite sure that the service he had just conducted had been the most difficult of his long career. Worse yet, every time he glanced out the window, Mary's mansion gleamed in the bright sunlight. A white monument surrounded by the new snow, it was a beautiful and sorrowful reminder of her.

A knock at the parish house door startled him. When he opened it, Daisy Delaine stood in front of him, holding up a jelly jar of brownish-green liquid.

"Hello, Father," she began breathlessly. "You know the potion I mentioned last night? The potion for Mary? Well, here it is. It's my healing potion, the strongest I've ever made. I just know it will help her. I thought maybe, on account of the snow, you

197

could give me a ride up to her house."

Father O'Brien fought back tears as he ushered her inside. After the priest closed the door behind her, Daisy stood in the foyer of the parish house looking up at him with wide, worried eyes.

"Daisy, I —" he began, but his voice broke as the pent-up tears began dripping down his cheeks. "Daisy, I was about to come see you. She passed on last night, my dear. Mary died last night."

Daisy flinched as the shock of his words registered on her face. "Oh," she said, looking down at the jar in her hands. "Oh. I'm too late. After I got the snow to start falling, I hurried, but I just needed a little more time to give her . . ." She began to shake, and Father O'Brien took the jar from her so that her unsteady hands wouldn't drop it.

"Come sit with me a moment, my dear," he said, placing an arm around Daisy's shoulders and nudging her toward the sofa in his living room. He sat down beside her. "Daisy, look at me," he said, and she raised her teary eyes to meet his own. "You have to understand something. As much as we wanted Mary to get better, there is nothing that you or I could have done to make her well. God decided that it was her time to go, and not even your strongest potion could counteract that decision. It's not your fault that she's gone."

"Father, I don't know what I'll do without her. Other than you, I don't have anybody. She was . . . she was my . . ."

"Shh, I know," Father O'Brien said as he reached out to the sobbing woman. "It won't be easy for either of us. But Mary wouldn't want us to be sad. She'd tell us to be strong and happy, and to remember all the wonderful times we had with her, yes?"

Nodding and sniffling, Daisy sat back and wiped her eyes and face with her sleeve. Moistened by tears, the red birthmark on her cheek seemed especially noticeable.

"Will we have a funeral for her?"

"In the spring, my dear. Mary wished for her final resting place to be at her father's farm. Will you help me plan a burial service for her?"

Daisy nodded again.

"Would you like to stay for a little while? I was just about to fix some lunch," Father O'Brien said, even though he didn't feel like eating.

Daisy sniffed loudly and shook her head. "No, thank you. I was planning on taking some advance orders for my famous love potion. For Valentine's Day. Maybe it'll help keep me from thinking about . . . about her."

"She wouldn't want us to be sad," Father O'Brien said again. He handed Daisy the jar of brownish-green liquid, which she returned to her pocket.

"I know." Daisy stood and walked slowly to the foyer. As she reached the front door, she stopped with her face a few inches from it. Very slowly, instead of opening the door to leave, she took the doorknob in her hand and leaned her forehead against the heavy wood. Father O'Brien saw the little woman's shoulders tremble as she tried unsuccessfully to compose herself. He waited, understanding the profound nature of the loss she felt and giving her the space and silence to make it through the wave of grief. Finally, she straightened up and looked back at him.

"Father, I forgot to ask — could I put you down for your usual order?"

Father O'Brien had to smile. He usually humored Daisy with purchases of her strange concoctions, but she had never tried to sell him her love potion.

"Well, Daisy," he began gently, "I don't remember ever buying any love potion from you in the past. And you know that, since I'm a priest, I, um, really couldn't use it myself. But," he added, seeing the dejection beginning to appear on Daisy's face, "why don't you put me down for one jar, a small one, and I'll pass it along to someone in need."

"Okay," Daisy said, with the faintest, fleeting glimmer in her eyes. "I'll come by with it in a few days. And," she said in a whisper as the glimmer disappeared, "I'll try not to be sad. Mary wouldn't have wanted that." Her eyes overflowed again as she trudged outside toward the next house on the street.

Father O'Brien closed the door with tears leaking down his own cheeks. He knew Daisy's pain was as great as his own.

As much as he tried not to think about how he had found Mary earlier, the scene replayed itself in his mind. She had been so . . . still. And then, as he sat down again in his office chair, he was overcome by a terrible sense of déjà vu. His mind reached back in time, to another day more than seventy years earlier, when he had discovered Mary in the mansion. He tried to deflect the powerful memory, but it invaded him, its similarities with this morning's awful experience rising and fading, and he was helpless to stop it.

On that stormy evening in June 1942, he had been summoned by the Mill River police. Patrick McAllister had been thrown through his car's windshield and killed. "Father," the police chief had asked him, "could you go with one of our officers to tell his wife?"

The side door to the marble mansion had been left open, which was strange, because the storm outside had been ferocious. When no one came to the door, he and a police officer a few years his junior ventured inside. The house was dark and quiet, and they assumed that Mrs. McAllister was upstairs in bed. They were half right.

She was upstairs, slumped against her bedroom wall. At first, they didn't see her. Then the young officer spotted her, rushed forward, and immediately recoiled, saying, "Sweet Jesus, my God, oh my God, I'm sorry, Father, but I've never seen anything like this."

What Father O'Brien had seen of Mary's face hadn't looked human. Her left eye was lost in a great purplish-black swelling that extended to her hairline. He caught only a glimpse of her before the officer, quickly overcoming his shock at seeing her, snatched her up in his arms to carry her downstairs, screaming, "Go, Father, she's hurt bad and we've got to hurry!" His stomach churning, he ran back down the stairs with the officer carrying Mary right behind him.

They took her to the Rutland County Hospital, where Patrick's body had been sent. There, doctors determined that the upper rim of the orbital bone surrounding her left eye had been shattered. An injury such as that could only be caused by a blunt-force blow with a hard, heavy object. The doctors were puzzled, too, by the fact that their patient was a member of one of the wealthiest and most prominent families in Rutland but wore clothes smeared with dirt. Her matted hair looked as if it hadn't been washed or brushed in weeks.

Father O'Brien had no answers for them, nor for Patrick's parents and grandfather, who had arrived at the hospital to identify Patrick's body. The family had been allowed to see Mary for a moment. It was for the better that she remained unconscious, unable to see the fresh shock on her in-laws' faces.

"They may have had an argument," he suggested to the McAllisters as they all stood numbly in the hospital waiting room.

"We know Patrick was drinking," Conor had said. "And we know he went back home before the accident because he had a suitcase with him. Maybe he lost his temper and —"

"My son wouldn't do something like that," Elise cried into Stephen's shoulder.

"Well, look at the state she's in," Conor

had continued angrily. "She's obviously been far worse than he let on for quite some time."

"So she neglected him! Drove him out of his own home," Elise retorted between sobs.

"Maybe it's better not to discuss the hows and whys right now," Stephen said, still holding Elise. "We can talk to Mary when she comes to . . ."

"If she comes to," Conor said.

"And she will, Pop, we have to believe that, but in the meantime, we should go home. There are arrangements to make."

"You two go. I'll wait here in case she wakes up. If she does, I'll call you right away," Conor said. Patrick's parents left, leaving Conor and Father O'Brien alone in the waiting room.

Even more than seven decades later, Father O'Brien's ensuing conversation with Conor McAllister remained clear in his memory. The conversation had changed his life entirely.

"Father," Conor began, "I want to tell you that I love . . . loved my grandson very much. There's not anything in the world that I wouldn't have done for him." He still remembered the tremor in the patriarch's voice and the way that several glistening tears had worked their way down the creases of his face into the thick white beard.

"However, I know, have always known, what Patrick was capable of. He was brilliant, handsome, confident. His father made sure he had everything he ever wanted, whenever he wanted it. He wouldn't listen to me when I tried to keep him from spoiling the boy. I was so busy with the marbleworks and thought it best not to interfere, but I was wrong. I should have done more to prevent Patrick from turning out as he did. Patrick grew into a determined young man, determined to succeed and determined to have the world accede to his every demand. He wanted control over every aspect of his life, from the woman he married to his responsibilities at the marbleworks. And he couldn't have it. At least, not all the time."

Conor looked up at him, his eyes watery and bloodshot. "This morning, Father, Patrick received notice that he was going to be drafted into the army. He and his father believed that I could have prevented it. And I could've. I could've pressured the draft board to defer him, but I shouldn't have, and I didn't. It wouldn't have been the right thing to do. And yet . . . ." Conor's voice faded as he struggled to maintain his composure. "Patrick left the marbleworks right before noon. I thought he needed some time alone, to cool off, so we didn't go after him. Now, I wish we had. We didn't know . . ."

The tone of Conor's voice changed as he dropped his gaze to the floor. "I have always worried about Mary, however. From the moment I met her, from that first time Patrick brought her to the house, I knew that she was innocent and vulnerable, a poor shy thing. I worried that Patrick might seize on that weakness and feed off it, or lose patience with Mary, or try to make her into something she was not. I should have suspected that they were having serious problems when he stopped bringing her to the house. He told us she was having a hard time with her father's death, that she was spending time with friends, but we had no idea." Conor paused for a moment before continuing. "You saw Mary this evening, Father. As much as I don't want to, I believe Patrick did that to her. If she survives, she will be forever scarred on the inside and the outside. And," Conor said, his voice breaking, "I blame myself. I should have protected her." The tears were coming faster now. Conor covered his mouth and chin with a shaking hand.

"Mr. McAllister, you mustn't blame yourself for this. Despite what you may believe, you are not responsible for Patrick's behavior. There is no way you could have predicted that this would happen."

For a long while, they had sat together in silence. Finally, Conor looked at him square in the eyes again.

"Father, I need your help. If Mary lives, I want to be sure that she is cared for and protected for the rest of her life. Part of that I can do. All of my grandchildren have trust funds. Patrick's currently contains several hundred thousand dollars. As Mary will be his sole heir, she will be entitled to that money. In addition, I intend to bequeath to her another substantial sum. If invested properly, those amounts, taken together, should sustain her for the rest of her life."

"That is very generous of you, Mr. McAllister," he said, but Conor continued.

"But, I will not be on this earth long enough to ensure her security. Mary will be utterly alone if she survives. You know how close she and her father were, but he's gone now, and I can't imagine Elise will ever reach out to her if she believes that Mary had any role in Patrick's leaving the house tonight. That is why I need you, Father. You're about the same age as Mary. You will be alive long after I'm gone. You can look after her for me," Conor said.

Father O'Brien remembered the over-whelming feeling of responsibility when the enormity of Conor's request sunk in. "Mr. McAllister," he said, "of course I will do everything I can to ensure Mrs. McAllister's well-being. But, you have to understand, she may choose to leave Mill River. The church may assign me to a different parish. So many things over which I have no control could change."

"I can talk with Bishop Ross about your situation and ask him to request a dispensation for you. With permission from the Vatican, he could make sure you wouldn't be transferred from Mill River. As for anything else that might come up, well, no one can predict the future, but I trust you, Father. I've trusted you ever since I met you, and I trust you will find a way to do this thing for me. You will, won't you, Father?"

He hadn't had a chance to reply, for at that very moment, Bishop Ross burst into the waiting room.

"Conor, I came as soon as I heard. I can't believe it, and his wife is here, too, injured?" the portly bishop asked, slightly out of breath. "Father O'Brien, it's good of you to have come."

"Yes, she's here," Conor said, "but she is

still unconscious. We don't know much about what exactly happened with Mary yet. Stephen and Elise went back to the house a few minutes ago. Could you go to them, perhaps? I'll follow after I speak with the doctor, and I think Father O'Brien should stay with Mary tonight, in case there is any change in her condition."

"Of course, of course. I'll go immediately, and I'll come back here in the morning," Bishop Ross said, and hurried out the door.

Conor turned to face the father again, waiting for his answer. Father O'Brien didn't know how he would do what Conor wanted, but he couldn't refuse.

"I will protect her as best I can, Mr. McAllister, for as long as I am able. That is the most I can promise."

And he had kept his promise to Conor, kept it for some seventy years, until today. He looked at the envelope and package on his desk for the hundredth time. Now that Mary was gone, he would do what was necessary to keep the last, secret promise that he had made to her.

■ ■ ■ ■

PART 2

■ ■ ■ ■

Give light, and the darkness will disappear of itself.

— DESIDERIUS ERASMUS

CHAPTER 12

1942

The window of the dim hospital room was open a crack, and the ribbon of fresh air that slid inside cut through heavy odors of sickness and sterility. Mary lay in the bed, her petite form outlined under tight white sheets. A bandage around her head hid the swollen purple mass that was her left eye. She was still unconscious.

Father O'Brien also slept. He had spent most of the night slouched in a wooden chair at her bedside. Now the rush of fresh air brushed his cheek and swept through his hair, and he opened his eyes.

"Good morning, Father," a nurse said as she entered the room.

"Good morning, Miss . . ." Father O'Brien said, straining to make out the nurse's name on her name tag.

"Clarke," said the nurse, as she took Mary's pulse. She glanced up from her wristwatch as Father O'Brien shifted stiffly in the chair, rubbing the back of his neck. Her brown eyes were sympathetic. "Did you manage to sleep there all night?"

"I was here all night. As for sleep, well . . ." Father O'Brien sighed and looked at Mary. "Let's just say that I didn't get nearly as much as she did."

"She still hasn't come around, then," said Nurse Clarke, reading Mary's chart. "The doctor will be here soon to check on her." She shook her head as she hung the chart back on the end of the bed. "If her husband really was the one who did this to her —"

"Papa?" Mary groaned, and turned her head on the pillow. Her right eye fluttered open.

"Mrs. McAllister, it's Father O'Brien," said the priest, jumping up from the chair. "Can you hear me?"

"I'll get the doctor," the nurse said, and hurried from the room.

Mary turned her head slowly toward the priest. "Can't see," she said, and raised her left hand toward her injured eye. Father O'Brien grabbed the hand before it touched the bandage.

"No, you mustn't touch it. You're in the hospital. You've been hurt," Father O'Brien said carefully. Her hand was limp and fragile. "Do you remember what happened to you?"

For a moment, Mary's expression was one of confusion. Her mouth opened slightly as her sleep-numbed mind struggled to respond. Then she flinched, as if someone had startled her. Her body became rigid. The hand that Father O'Brien held suddenly clenched tight around his fingers.

"He's starving him," she whispered desperately.

"Who's starving who?"

"Patrick," Mary said, her frenzy growing. "Monarch. In the barn for weeks. Beaten and starving." She pulled on the priest's hand, attempting to sit up. "He'll kill him, you've got to stop him."

"It's all right, Mrs. McAllister, Patrick isn't going to hurt anyone."

Tears flowed out of her uninjured eye. "He'll kill him. Please, Father."

A man in a white coat came into the room, followed by Nurse Clarke, carrying a small silver tray. He approached the bed slowly as the nurse went around to the other side.

"Mrs. McAllister, I'm Dr. Mason. Do you know where you are?"

Mary turned toward him, grimacing slightly. "In the hospital."

"Do you remember how you were injured?"

Mary blinked, shuddered again, and looked up at the doctor. "Ebony, the miniature marble Ebony," she said, in a faraway tone. She sucked in her breath sharply, her exposed eye racing from side to side, reviewing some unknown event. The doctor looked at Father O'Brien and raised his eyebrows. The priest shrugged.

"Who's Ebony?"

"My horse. And Monarch. You have to keep him away from them." Mary's voice rose again.

"Keep who away?" Dr. Mason asked.

"Patrick, I already told him," Mary said, turning again toward the priest, "Monarch needs help. You've got to call the veterinarian. His foot is infected, and he's starving, please . . ." Mary was thrashing and babbling now, the right side of her face tear-streaked.

Dr. Mason nodded at Nurse Clarke, who nodded in return and picked up a syringe from the tray. She quickly injected the tranquilizer into Mary's upper arm.

"You need to relax, Mrs. McAllister," Nurse Clarke said softly, smoothing Mary's hair away from her face. After a few minutes, Mary quieted down.

"Mrs. McAllister," said Father O'Brien, still holding her hand, "don't worry about the horses. I'll call Conor, and we'll see to them." His words seemed to soothe her, for she nodded and closed her eye.

Father O'Brien stepped away from Mary's bed, motioning for the doctor to follow him. "Do you think she remembers what happened?" he whispered once they had moved out of earshot.

"If she doesn't already, she may remember in the next few days. But apparently, it's too stressful for her to handle right now, or she is more concerned about something else — the horses, I suppose," the doctor replied.

"It's good that she woke up, though?"

"Oh yes, of course. Her speech and ability to move appear normal, which indicate that there may be no serious physical damage to her brain. But it will take longer for her to recover from the mental shock of the incident. And as for the eye, well, we know from the X-ray that her eye socket is fractured, but we won't know the extent of the damage to her eyesight until the swelling goes down."

Father O'Brien looked at his watch. It was just after eight. As Conor had left last night, he had promised to come by first thing in the morning. Maybe Conor would be willing to go with him back to the marble mansion. Maybe they would learn what had happened, and what Mary had been unable to tell them herself.

"Just be careful, now. I'll have to ask you not to touch anything. We don't want to disturb something that could be evidence before we finish our investigation." The young police officer who, with Father O'Brien, had discovered Mary the previous evening escorted Conor and the priest into the master bedroom. "We really can't stay too long, either. My boss said I'm just supposed to let you have a quick look around."

"We won't be long," Conor said, "and we do appreciate your letting us see the place. Do you have any idea as to how long your investigation will take?"

"Not more than a few days, probably," the officer replied. "I know two other officers are due out here this afternoon to gather up everything."

Only in the bedroom were there signs of struggle. The remains of a lamp lay shattered on the floor. The closet door was open and several items of Patrick's clothing were strewn across the bed. Conor and Father O'Brien stepped carefully around the room. It was Conor who finally noticed the small marble figure on the floor.

"I wonder," he said as he pointed to the miniature Ebony. "At the house last night, Elise was adamant that Patrick would never have hurt Mary. She's convinced Mary's injury was an accident, that Mary somehow hurt herself. She has never seen, had never seen the side of Patrick that I saw." He paused, staring down at the black marble figurine and the droplets of blood on the carpet surrounding it. "I wonder if that was what he used . . ."

"Maybe," Father O'Brien said. "It's small enough to be grasped in one hand."

Conor did not reply, but continued to stare downward. After a moment, the police officer cleared his throat.

"I don't know what more we could see here," Father O'Brien said, nodding at the officer. "Shall we have a look in the barn? Mary seemed very concerned about the horses."

"Yes, yes, of course," Conor said. "But do me a favor, would you?" he asked the officer on their way out. "Make sure that marble figurine on the floor gets fingerprinted, and have it returned to me once you're done with it." The officer nodded.

If there had been any doubt in Father O'Brien's mind as to Patrick's true nature, it was erased once they saw the blood bay horse in the barn. The whip marks and malnourishment were shocking. As Father O'Brien approached Monarch's stall, the horse showed the whites of his eyes and bolted backward, stumbling as he tried to avoid shifting weight to his infected hind hoof.

"Dear Lord," Father O'Brien muttered, "who could do this to an animal?"

Conor was at Mary's bedside when she awoke again later that afternoon. Thanks to the injected tranquilizer, she was groggy but much calmer than she had been when she had first regained consciousness.

"Grandpop?" Mary said, looking up at him.

"Mary, dear, how are you feeling?" Conor replied, taking her hand.

"Sleepy. My face hurts. My eye."

"I know it does, Mary. Your eye socket is broken, but you're safe now."

"Safe," Mary said, and then suddenly, "the horses —"

"Are just fine," Conor said. "Father O'Brien and I went out to the house this morning. The horses are fine. We called the veterinarian for the red one, and he'll be taken care of, don't you worry."

"Oh, Grandpop, it was Patrick. He beat Monarch, starved him, and I had no idea. Promise me you'll keep Patrick away from all of them, please, Grandpop."

Conor hesitated before saying anything else. Mary's one visible eye pleaded with him. He wondered how much he should tell her, how much she was capable of handling in her fragile state of mind. To someone who did not know her, she would appear to be perfectly rational, if a little sluggish. But he could see right through her calm demeanor, and Father O'Brien had told him what had happened when she had first awakened that morning. Mary was fighting to hold on to her sanity as a child might struggle to keep hold of a kite on a blustery day. It would not take much more to rip it away from her.

"I promise, Mary," Conor said. "And you mustn't blame yourself about the red horse. You didn't know. None of us knew."

Mary was quiet for a moment. When she spoke again, her voice was reduced to a whisper. "Grandpop, I'm afraid of him."

"Of Patrick?"

"Yes."

"Mary, I don't want to upset you, but we need to know how you were hurt."

She paused. "It was the miniature Ebony. He hit me with the miniature Ebony."

"Mary, do you mean the small horse statue in your bedroom?"

"Yes."

"Patrick hit you in the face with the figurine?"

"Yes." Slow tears slid from Mary's right eye down over the curve of her cheek. "He was drunk, screaming at me, said I wasn't a good wife." Conor's green eyes flashed. "I love him so much. I've tried to be a good wife, but he always wants more. He's never happy with me. Please, Grandpop, you won't let him hurt me again, will you?"

Conor looked into Mary's bandaged, tear-streaked face. Her expression was one of great love and fear, inextricably mixed. He decided after several moments of wavering that he would tell her of Patrick's death.

"Mary," he began softly, taking her other hand, "there is something I need to tell you. Last night, after Patrick hurt you, he tried to leave town. There was an accident. He was already gone when the police found him." Conor paused, watching as Mary's expression shifted from fear to shock to disbelief. "They think it happened quickly. Mary, do you understand me?" Conor squeezed Mary's hands between his own. "Patrick died last night, my dear. I'm so sorry. Mary?"

Mary looked at him, her visible eye glazed and bloodshot, and said nothing.

"For the life of me, Pop, I don't know why you had to tell her about Patrick so soon," Stephen said as he and Conor left Rutland County Hospital. "She was already in a feeble mental state. And now, twelve days without so much as a word to anybody. How much longer can she stay in that . . . that trance or whatever she's in? A week? Two weeks? A month?" Conor did not reply as they got into the black Lincoln.

Stephen slammed the door and inserted the key into the ignition, but did not turn it. For a moment, the two sat silently in the plush leather seats. Stephen gripped the steering wheel and seemed to be wrestling with his words.

"Pop, I think we should really consider sending her to Brattleboro —"

"Absolutely not. We've already had this discussion, and you know I have no intention of shipping her away to some asylum."

"But, Pop —"

"She's your daughter-in-law," Conor snapped. "Your family. And mine. The doctors say the best thing for her right now is to be near her family and people she knows. If it were Sara or Emma in that hospital room, you'd never think of Brattleboro."

"If I thought it would help —"

"Horseshit. You'd do nothing of the kind. And in Mary's case, she's so shy and fearful that moving her to a strange place would prevent her from ever recovering."

"I wish you'd thought of her recovery twelve days ago, before you decided to tell her all of what happened."

Conor sighed as Stephen finally started the engine. "Perhaps I made a mistake in telling her so soon, but at the time . . . she was terrified. I was only trying to calm her, to make her feel safe by letting her know Patrick couldn't hurt her anymore."

"We don't even know for sure that things really happened as Mary said they did. Given her current state, she could have been confused. She might even be inventing the whole thing." Stephen glanced sideways at his father and saw immediately that he had gone too far.

"What, then?" Conor roared. "Do you think she decided to crack her own skull? Decided she didn't need sight in one of her eyes?"

"No, Pop, but —"

"She's blind in that eye! Her eye socket will heal but the doctors can't do anything to restore her sight." A brilliant fuchsia crept over Conor's face as he brandished his forefinger at his son. "No, I'll tell you exactly where your line of thinking is coming from. I know Elise is having a hard time with this. We all are. But she won't accept that Patrick did anything wrong. She's blaming Mary for some horrific thing that Patrick did, that was his fault alone. And now, it sounds like she's actually starting to convince you of that as well."

Stephen cringed behind the steering wheel.

"I knew it!" Conor said. "And I'll bet she's also behind this renewed push to send Mary to Brattleboro! A simple way to get rid of the one reminder of what really happened. Of what Patrick did."

"She . . . *we've* lost a child, Pop. Patrick was our son. Try to imagine what we're going through, and how Elise might feel right now. Mary is the least of her concerns."

"Well, I'll tell you, we're the only family Mary has left. Her recovery and well-being are our responsibility. As much as we all loved Patrick, it's shameful that we had no idea of the cruelty he'd been inflicting on his wife. We sure as hell aren't going to abandon her now."

Stephen turned the Lincoln into the driveway of the yellow Victorian mansion, and the father and son entered the house without another word. Stephen went immediately into the sitting room where Elise was waiting for him. Conor heard them speaking in hushed tones as he made his way down the hallway to his office. Once there, he switched on the light and closed the door.

As always, the pictures on the wall greeted him with a flood of memories. He remembered the evening when he had first discovered Mary here, staring at the old photo of him and his father. He had worried about her even then, when she could have been any one of the many girls Patrick used to see. Now, he appeared to be the only one in his family who cared what happened to her. He would not fail her again.

Conor picked up the phone and dialed the number of Jack Gasaway, the attorney who handled the McAllister family's legal affairs. He needed to make some changes, and soon.

If Mary knew Father O'Brien was in the room, she didn't show it.

Three weeks after her injury, Mary remained at Rutland County Hospital, staring blankly, speaking to no one, and displaying no emotion except for an occasional sigh.

She recoiled when anyone approached her, but offered no significant resistance to the nurses who tended to her. An intravenous line kept her nourished and hydrated, although the nurses regularly brought her food in the hope of coaxing her out of her stupor. Her glazed expression hadn't changed at all as Dr. Mason removed the bandages from her eye and examined it.

Dr. Mason felt with some certainty that her left eye would never be the same. The swelling had gone down, revealing a slightly misshapen supraorbital ridge that had started to heal. But the blunt force of Patrick's blow had been so great that the retina of her left eye was almost completely detached. That damage was permanent.

Father O'Brien visited Mary every few days. He felt that he was obligated to do this as part of the promise he had made to Conor. He also visited because it provided him some measure of relief. With Rutland County boys being drafted into the war, he often found himself visiting the soldiers' families, feeling helpless, as if his words of comfort were incapable of penetrating their worry. Seeing Mary was a silent reprieve from those more unpleasant visits.

As usual, he sat at her bedside, making polite conversation with no one but himself, attempting to elicit a response from her. He was persistent and patient. It didn't seem to matter.

He had just finished describing to her the beautiful roses that were blooming on the hospital grounds. He mentioned that he had been out to her home in Mill River, that Conor had made sure it was being kept up, and that her horses were doing well. At the mention of the horses, Father O'Brien thought that he might have detected a faint upturn of the corners of her mouth, but he could have been mistaken.

It was almost noon when Nurse Clarke came into the room with a tray of food for Mary. Father O'Brien looked at it with some interest, but not because of the watery soup and glass of juice.

"Hi, Mrs. McAllister. Are you hungry? I brought you some lunch," she said with a bright smile, setting the tray on a wheeled stand by the bed. Mary did not respond.

"And how are you today, Father?" the nurse said, turning to him. She seemed happy to speak to someone who would answer her.

"I'm very well, thanks. I was just telling Mary here about those lovely roses outside. The most beautiful I've seen in quite some time."

"They are gorgeous," Nurse Clarke said. "Mrs. McAllister, the doctor will be in to see you soon. If you would eat some of your lunch, I think he would be very pleased." She bent forward, hoping for a reply. Mary stared at the wall.

"Well. I'll be in to check on you in a bit. See you later, Father." Nurse Clarke smiled and shut the door lightly behind her.

Father O'Brien rose and walked around the hospital room. For a few minutes, he stood at the window, staring out. Mary was still quiet and unresponsive. Circling back toward the bed, he looked out the small glass window in the door. No one was visible in the hallway outside. Casually, he glanced at the tray on which Mary's lunch had grown cold. Next to the plain white bowl of soup was an equally plain soup-spoon.

With a trembling hand, he reached for it. The spoon was old, slightly bent, and dulled by repeated washings in the hospital kitchen. A *lovely* thing. He held it in front of him, rocked back on his heels to look out the door, to check once more that no one was headed toward the room. The guilt that he always felt about his spoon habit bubbled up inside him, but he pushed it away and pushed the soupspoon up into the sleeve of his jacket. It would make a fine addition to his collection.

"Thou shalt not steal," whispered a voice. Mary was looking right at him. She had seen everything.

In the moment of silence that followed, while Father O'Brien's lower jaw battled gravity and lost, Dr. Mason burst through the door. Mary's trancelike demeanor immediately returned.

"Hello, Mrs. McAllister, how are you doing today?" Dr. Mason asked, nodding to Father O'Brien. As usual, Mary cringed slightly but otherwise did not respond. The priest watched as Dr. Mason took Mary's pulse, very carefully examined her eyes, and listened to her heart.

Father O'Brien wanted so much to tell him that Mary had spoken, but the hard, thin form of the spoon in his sleeve stopped him. What would he say if the doctor asked whether Mary had spoken?

"No change, I guess," Dr. Mason muttered under his breath. "It's good of you to keep coming by, Father. She's just going to take some time, and your visits can't do anything but help. Have you any idea whether Mr. McAllister will be here this evening?"

"Mr. McAllister . . . Conor, you mean?"

Father O'Brien asked, forcing his jaw back into action. Dr. Mason nodded. "I don't know why he wouldn't be. He's made a habit of coming by after work each evening."

"I should still be here, and I'd like to speak to him about Mary's condition. If you see him this afternoon, would you make sure he knows to ask for me when he arrives?"

"Certainly," said Father O'Brien. Dr. Mason smiled, glanced back at Mary, and left to continue his rounds.

"Mrs. McAllister," Father O'Brien began, drawing his chair closer to her bedside, "Mrs. McAllister, can you —"

"I want to go home, Father," Mary said, turning to face him and focusing her good eye on his right sleeve. "Please tell Grandpop and the others that I want to go home."

Her perfect, lucid speech shocked him. "I'm sure that they'll take you home, Mrs. McAllister, as soon as you are well." She seemed to have forgotten about the spoon incident, and he was relieved. "But, how long have you — we didn't know that you were aware of anything around you," Father O'Brien stammered.

"I remember Grandpop telling me about Patrick," Mary said, her voice cracking just a little as she mentioned Patrick's name, "and I felt the anxiety, like I used to have but much worse than it had ever been. It came up over me and everything went blurry. I remember bits of conversations, people coming in and out of the room. I remember the doctor taking the bandage off my eye, and still not being able to see out of it. My thoughts came and went, and I didn't care. Until a few days ago, I wanted to die.

"And then Grandpop came by again. I don't know what day it was exactly, but I remember him saying something about Brattleboro, a retreat there for the mentally ill. He said to me, 'Mary, please come back to us, I don't know what to do. I won't let them send you away, but I just don't know what to do.' " Tears squeezed out of the corners of her eyes — both of them, Father O'Brien noticed — and she was quiet a moment as she wiped them away. "When he had gone, I realized that Patrick wanted to hurt me, maybe kill me, and that if I didn't get better, he would have gotten exactly what he wanted. If something were to happen to Grandpop, Patrick's parents would be more than happy to send me away. No one would be left for the horses." The tears were flowing faster now. "And, most of all, Papa would have wanted me to get better, I know it. I'm trying, really trying, to live again, but it is so hard here, surrounded by strange people who think I'm crazy. I just want so much to be home, Father."

His mind whirling, Father O'Brien leaned back in his chair. He still could not believe that she was so lucid when only a few days before, she had been despondent. "I think I should call Conor," he said. "If we're going to get you out of here, he'll have to be the one to do it. And you'll need to speak to many more people than just me."

"I know," Mary replied. "But Father, please don't tell anyone about my anxiety. Everyone thought it was gone, but it never really went away. I can't control it, I couldn't ever control it, and now it's worse than it ever was. I don't want the doctors or Patrick's family to send me away."

"Of course not," Father O'Brien said, standing up to leave.

"Father . . . why do you steal spoons?" She looked up at him with watery eyes and, for the first time in weeks, smiled. Despite her words, the tone of her question was not accusatory. She spoke lightly, as if amused by a magician performing a trick. Father O'Brien opened his mouth to reply, but she continued. "I wondered, when you took a spoon from Patrick's mother the day you came to the house to help plan our wedding, whether you regularly pilfered fine silver. I thought that maybe it was because your church stipend was so modest . . . but today, well, the hospital spoons are surely worthless."

Father O'Brien stood at her bedside, feeling more than ever the way his right sleeve hung more heavily than his left. She had seen him that day at the McAllisters'. He thought about what excuse he could give her, but even with only one good eye, she would most surely see through any lie. He sighed, sat down again. She waited.

"The truth is, Mrs. McAllister," he began.

"Please, just Mary."

"Mary, then." He paused. "Considering what I'm about to tell you, perhaps you should call me Michael." And he told her of his sins, a hundred and twelve of them, collected in a box in his office, with the one hundred and thirteenth up his sleeve. How his attraction to spoons began shortly after he entered the seminary. How it intensified after he took his vows and drove him to steal the spoons, one by one. His voice cracked as he spoke of his guilt, how he always confessed his most recent transgressions and was still powerless to stop. Expecting her to react with disappointment and disgust, he begged her not to tell anyone.

Her response surprised him. "No one is perfect, Michael, not even priests. Some are less perfect than others. Overall, you are a good person. You are caring and kind. In our world, even small gestures of kindness are remembered, and you've done so much more. Your coming here over the past days and weeks has helped me, probably more than I realize right now." Father O'Brien felt his lower lip begin to quiver and he bowed his head, blinking rapidly. Mary reached out a hand to comfort him. "Michael, yours is a minor flaw. I won't tell anyone, I promise."

CHAPTER 13

Claudia watched the minute hand of the clock on her classroom wall creep toward the six. Seventeen minutes until snack time. It was the last period before the school day ended at three-thirty, and her fourth-graders were working on multiplication problems in small groups. The last period was always the hardest because the kids were eager to go home and were easily distracted.

"Miss Simon! Miss Simon!" wailed a girl's voice. Claudia looked up and saw Mia Wallace writhing in her seat. Several boys sitting behind her were sniggering to themselves. "Travis wiped a booger on my back!"

Mia Wallace was the class outcast. She was twice the size of a normal fourth-grader, and Claudia knew that most of the other kids called her "Mia Walrus." She had even caught Travis Shay imitating Mia at recess, slithering along the ground shouting "Me a walrus!" to anyone who would listen. Claudia empathized with Mia. She remembered well her own school days as a fat child, and it was even more painful watching the nine-year-olds' cruelty being inflicted on someone else. She would not tolerate it.

"Travis!" Claudia said, standing up.

"I didn't do it, Miss Simon! I was only pretending! See? There's nothing on her!"

Claudia inspected Mia's back. There was no sign of any booger.

"Just the same, Travis, that's a horrible way to treat people. I think Ms. Finney would be interested in hearing about this. Go down to her office," Claudia said, walking over to her classroom intercom. "And don't dawdle in the hallway. I'm going to tell her you're on your way."

Mia smiled at Claudia. Travis rolled his eyes and left for the principal's office. For him, it was nothing new.

After a few moments, the students resumed their discussions. Claudia tried to focus on grading the stack of papers in front of her, but she found herself instead thinking about the carrot sticks and peanut butter she had in her desk drawer. Her stomach rumbled almost loud enough to be heard over the chattering of her students. Lunch had been three hours ago.

"Miss Simon, we can't get this one," said Rowen Hansen, carrying her math book and paper up to the teacher's desk. The two other girls with whom Rowen was working followed.

"Let's see," Claudia said, looking at Rowen's paper and the multiplication problem. She recognized their error immediately. Very slowly, Claudia worked out the problem, showing the girls how to indent the proper number of spaces, until the girls smiled with comprehension. She handed the book back to Rowen, but as she let go of it, the bound pages slid out of the spine and fell to the floor.

"Uh-oh, I think your book came unglued," Claudia said, reaching for the pages.

"I know. It's been that way since last semester," Rowen said. She held out the cover for Claudia to see. "I told Mrs. Shultz about it. She tried to get me a new book but the school didn't have any more. Then she glued the pages back in, but they fell out again last week."

"Oh. Well, you'll need it tonight for your homework," Claudia said, "but first thing tomorrow morning, I'll try to glue it for you again. And I'll double-check about getting you another book. Maybe there's an extra one now that wasn't available when Mrs.

Shultz asked about it. Would that be okay?"

"Okay." Rowen smiled and carefully carried her things back to her seat.

Claudia looked at the clock again. Two minutes until the bell rang. One minute. Then her students were jumping up, stuffing their books and papers into their backpacks, running for the hall where their coats and snow boots waited. "See you tomorrow," she called as the last children filed out the door.

Claudia lunged for her lower right-hand desk drawer, pulled it open, and fumbled inside for her insulated lunch bag. She removed a plastic sandwich bag full of carrot sticks and a little Tupperware container of peanut butter. Best snack in the world, she thought to herself as she dipped one of the carrots into the peanut butter and popped it into her mouth. That particular carrot was a little large to be eaten in a single mouthful, but she didn't care.

"Claudia, hi," said a voice to her left. Claudia turned to see Kyle Hansen coming through her classroom door. He was wearing his police uniform and smiling at her. The carrot and peanut butter stuck to the roof of her mouth, and she realized with some degree of alarm that she could not finish chewing in time to reply properly.

"Oh, hi," she said, standing up and putting her hand over her mouth. She chewed ferociously and swallowed, hoping that part of the half-chewed carrot wouldn't lodge in her throat. "I didn't expect to see you back here so soon. You just missed Rowen. I think she's putting her coat on in the hall."

"Yep, I already saw her. I'm on the evening shift tonight, and I told her I'd pick her up at school before I left for the station. But actually, I wanted to say hello to you while I was here." He stuffed his hands in his pockets and shuffled his feet. "And, actually, I, uh, I was wondering if you might like to have dinner with me sometime this week. Something simple, maybe, like pizza."

"Oh." Claudia swallowed one more time, to make sure that there were no little bits of carrot that might fly out of her mouth.

"Or, we could make it just coffee, if you'd like," Kyle said. "I know you're probably swamped with papers to grade in the evenings, so we wouldn't have to go for dinner if you'd rather not."

He took a step backward, and Claudia realized that he assumed her hesitation to be a prelude to rejection.

"Pizza sounds great," she said, with more honesty than Kyle realized.

"Really?" His face brightened. "How

about tomorrow? I'm on tomorrow at eleven, so there'd be plenty of time for dinner before my shift starts. I could pick you up at about six."

"Perfect! Do you know where I live?"

"You're renting the house next to St. John's, aren't you?"

Claudia smiled and nodded. "Yeah. Mill River's so small. I keep forgetting that everybody knows where everybody else lives."

"Dad! Come on! I want to go home and check on Sham!" Rowen said, sticking her head into the classroom.

"I'll be right there, kiddo," he said, and Rowen disappeared back out the door. He followed his daughter, pausing to grin at Claudia again. "See you tomorrow, then."

Claudia sank back into the chair at her desk. In slow motion, she reached for another carrot and twirled it in the peanut butter. She actually had a real date. With Kyle. And pizza. Each of those facts was exciting and terrifying, but sitting in her empty classroom crunching carrots, Claudia resolved to get over the terrifying parts and thoroughly enjoy herself.

By Monday afternoon, Daisy's kitchen counters were covered in canning jars of all sizes, each filled with her red love potion. Trying to keep her mind from lingering on the news of Mary's death, she had worked all day to ensure the purity and consistency of the thick liquid, sterilizing her jars and carefully simmering the potion until it was ready. Now that the jars were sealed, all that was left to do was perform the final magic spell.

As Smudgie watched from a kitchen chair, Daisy cleared a space on the counter between two rows of jars. She moved three candlesticks from her kitchen windowsill, each holding a red tapered candle, into that space. The middle candle was the tallest. Very carefully, Daisy struck a match and lit it first. Then, she touched the wick of each side candle to the center flame so that all three were lit. She stepped back and began chanting.

"St. Valentine, great saint of affection, and Venus, goddess of love, Cupid, winged dearie, who foils rejection, come down from the heavens above. I ask you three to come to these flames and bless my crimson potion, with the magic of love — by whatever name, the most important emotion." Waving her arms in time with her words, Daisy went through the verse once more. Smudgie stood on the kitchen chair, wagging and yelping.

"Shhh now, Smudgie," Daisy whispered, scooping up the little dog and sitting down, "we must be very, very quiet. Valentine's Day is the fourteenth, so we have to wait fourteen minutes for the spell to take hold before we put out the flames." As the candles flickered, she sat silently in the kitchen, watching the second hand of the clock on the wall gliding past the numbers. Drops of red wax slipped down each candle. Daisy's gaze never left the red tapers for more than a few seconds.

She had always been cautious with candles. Her vocation required that she use them from time to time, but since the fire just after Thanksgiving, she had become especially prudent. It still bothered her how everyone in town was convinced that her trailer had caught on fire because she had left a candle burning unattended. She knew better.

It disturbed her even more that no one had taken her seriously when, after the flames had engulfed her mobile home, she had told them of the man she had seen running from her backyard. She had tried to answer the officers' questions as best she could. No, she hadn't imagined the man.

She couldn't describe his face — he'd been wearing a black ski mask. She didn't think she could estimate his height, except to say that he'd been taller than she. No, she'd never seen a man in a black ski mask lurking around before. No, she didn't have fire insurance.

In the end, the fire had been ruled an accident for which she'd been blamed. The police found no evidence of the man she'd seen, and it was determined that her candle *had* started the fire. She hadn't been the one to light it, though, and she had managed to escape with Smudgie and a few notebooks containing her handwritten spells, but nothing else. She knew what she had seen, and she loved her little home. The last thing she ever would have done was destroy it.

Father O'Brien had offered her a spare room at the parish house until she could make arrangements. For three days, she had wondered what to do. She had no one, except Smudgie, of course. She had no savings to speak of, no home, no hope. All she had was her magic. For three days, she had tried spell after spell to no avail. But what had happened after those three days had been nothing less than magical.

"Let's go for a walk, shall we, Daisy?"

Father O'Brien had asked her on the fourth day after the fire. "I'm sure Smudgie would like the exercise, and I have a little surprise for you." They had walked down the street to Daisy's yard, where the ruins of her burned mobile home were. Or should have been. But on that fourth day, the blackened heap was gone, and a brand-new mobile home was waiting in its place.

"Surprise, Daisy," Father O'Brien had said, producing a pair of keys from a pocket in his robe. "It's yours. Let's have a look inside."

She remembered the shock of it, walking through her new front door for the first time, seeing the beautiful little kitchen in which she now sat. It had been fully furnished, down to a sparkling new set of canning jars in her kitchen cupboards.

"Father," she had said, "I never knew my magic was this powerful. I mean, I've tried for the last three days to conjure up some kind of solution to my situation, but this! This is by far a personal best!"

"Ah, well, Daisy," Father O'Brien had replied, "I guess none of us ever knows what will appear in our lives from one day to the next."

Father O'Brien was absolutely right, Daisy thought, and she smiled, feeling a delicious anticipation of what this Valentine's Day might bring. She looked up at the clock on her kitchen wall just as the second hand brushed past, completing the fourteenth minute.

"Oops! Up we go, Smudgie, that's a good boy," she said, jumping to her feet and setting the dog back on the chair. She wet her fingers under the faucet and pinched out the flame of each candle, leaving the middle candle for last. "There! All ready for delivery! I think I'll take care of a few orders right now, before it gets dark outside. Looks like a humdinger of a batch, doesn't it, Smudgie?"

From the chair, Smudgie wagged his approval.

Daisy placed several jars of the red potion in a plastic grocery sack and put on her parka and boots. Her nearest customer, Mrs. Murray, had ordered two jars and lived only a few blocks away.

The Murrays' home was modest, a beige rancher with a carport and a bay window in the front. Daisy stepped onto the worn welcome mat and rang the doorbell. After a moment, the front door opened. A little girl with huge brown eyes and long pigtails peered up at her.

"Well, hello there, Lindsey. Is your mother

home?" Daisy asked, bending down to speak to the child.

The little girl nodded as the door opened wider.

"Watch out, sweetie," Mrs. Murray said, nudging her daughter behind her leg. "Hello, Daisy. What brings you by?"

"Oh! I've got the love potion you ordered, Mrs. Murray. Two jars, right here. Just finished it, I did, and I thought I'd get it to you while it's still warm." She pulled two jars of the red liquid from her grocery sack.

Lindsey stared at the jars in Daisy's hand. "Mom, is it Kool-Aid?" she asked, looking up at Mrs. Murray.

"No, sweetie, this is something for grown-ups. You know, you left your dolly in the kitchen. Why don't you go play with her?" Mrs. Murray said, taking the jars. "Uh, how much do I owe you, Daisy?"

"Eight dollars," Daisy said, smiling as the little girl retreated back into the house. "You get a discount since you ordered more than one. Your daughter's awfully cute, by the way. She's lots bigger than the last time I saw her."

"Um-hmm, they don't stay small for long. Excuse me just a minute while I get my purse." Mrs. Murray backed into the house and closed the front door, leaving Daisy standing on the porch.

A light tapping noise caught her attention. Daisy turned to see Lindsey, clutching a baby doll, smiling and waving to her from the bay window. The little girl darted behind the curtain before peeking out once more.

"Peekaboo!" Daisy called as the front door opened again.

"Here you are." Mrs. Murray leaned out and pressed several bills into Daisy's hand. "Thanks for coming by!" She followed Daisy's gaze to the window, half smiled, and quickly shut the door.

"Thank you for your business," Daisy called, shoving the bills into her pocket. She looked at the bay window one last time as she turned to leave. Lindsey was still there, peeking out from behind the drapes, when an adult hand abruptly moved her aside and pulled the curtains across the window.

Observing the quiet, closed-up house, Daisy wiped her eyes and lingered a moment longer before continuing her deliveries.

Leroy was in no mood to go to work, but he had no choice. His head was pounding. The brightness of the new snow hurt his eyes and made his head feel even worse. He was hungover and nicotine-starved. He had run out of cigarettes that morning but hadn't been able to leave the house to get a new carton for fear of puking in the damned convenience store. Only in the last few hours had he felt better, and he stopped for Lucky Strikes on his way to work. Holding another fresh smoke in one hand, he swung his Camaro onto Main Street and stepped on the gas. The car quivered and fishtailed before its snow tires got a good grip on the road. A few blocks past the mobile home park on the north side of town, he spotted a squat hooded figure hauling a sack up the sidewalk. Crazy Daisy, no doubt.

The windshield was fogging up, either because of the smoke or because his heater was broken, he didn't know which. Wiping at the condensation barely helped. He slowed the Camaro and lowered the windows to let in some fresh air. As he passed Daisy, he craned his neck to see what was in her sack.

"Hello, Officer! Got my famous St. Valentine's Day love potion here! Only five dollars a jar, or two for eight." Daisy flashed an artificial smile, pulled out a jar, and waved it at him.

Leroy reminded himself that as an officer of the law, he had to be civil.

"Naw, thanks," he said, curling his lip at

the ugly reddish smear along the side of her face. He stepped on the gas as Daisy stared after him with a look of dejection. He didn't give a shit. Like he would ever waste money on that potion crap.

He didn't need love potion — Claudia's panties folded neatly in his pants pocket did more than enough for him. He carried that silky black token nearly everywhere. They were even better than the pictures he had secretly taken of her. They were his constant reminder of her, and he thought of her often — how he would approach her, seduce her, make her scream out for him. He would give her the card and then ask her to dinner on Valentine's Day, where he would call the irresistible Underwood charm into action.

It took all of another thirty seconds to drive through the center of town, up to the police station on the left side of Main Street. His headache was still fierce but felt as if it might be waning. *Eight hours, only eight hours,* Leroy thought to himself as he drove into the parking lot. He pulled a pack of Lucky Strikes from his new carton and stuffed it into his jacket pocket. At least now he had plenty of cigarettes. And, when his shift ended at eleven, he could swing by Claudia's house for a little late-night surveillance.

■ ■ ■ ■

Having dropped off Rowen at their apartment after school, Kyle was already at the station when Leroy arrived. He heard the rumbling of the old Camaro in the parking lot, then a loud *thump* and a fit of cursing. After a moment, Leroy limped through the station door.

"Hey, you don't look so good," Kyle said.

Leroy scowled and headed for the coffeepot. "You care if I make some?" he asked, ignoring Kyle's comment.

"Go right ahead. What's with the limp?"

"Tripped and fell on the curb on the way in. Damned thing's coated in ice. Twisted my ankle."

"I'll salt it. Wykowski probably forgot," said Kyle, heading toward a storage closet. He scooped out a cupful of salt from a bag in the closet and went to scatter it around the entrance to the station. When he returned, the coffeepot was beginning to perk and Leroy was sitting in a desk chair next to it with his eyes closed and legs splayed out in front of him.

"So you had a few too many last night, did you?" Kyle asked. Leroy grunted, half opened his eyes to glare at Kyle, and shut

251

them again.

Kyle chuckled. He enjoyed those rare occasions when he could annoy Leroy, instead of the other way around. "Did you have company or were you drinking alone?"

Leroy ignored the question.

"Alone again." Kyle sighed in mock pity. "You know, I heard Daisy Delaine has been taking orders for love potion. Maybe it's not too late to get yourself some. Valentine's Day's three days away, you know."

"I passed her truckin' a bag of that red goo up the hill on my way in. Crazy ol' bat already tried to sell me some. But," Leroy said, straightening up in the chair, "I don't need any of that shit. And I've already got plans for Valentine's Day, thank you very much."

"Really?" Kyle said. "I'll believe that when I see it."

"I ain't lying. I'm going to have me a hot date for Valentine's Day, you just watch."

"Who?"

Leroy smiled and worked his mouth as if he were savoring something delicious. "Claudia Simon."

Kyle spun around. "She actually agreed to go out with you?"

"I haven't asked her yet, but she will. I've got it all planned out, see. I'm gonna send her a card and some flowers tomorrow and then take her to the King's Lodge in Rutland for a fancy Valentine's Day dinner on Thursday night."

Kyle didn't ask what Leroy planned to do about dessert. The look on Leroy's face told him all he cared to know. "Leroy, man, I gotta tell you, she's way out of your league. And she's older than you. I wouldn't waste any time on her."

Leroy scowled as he stood up and grabbed the keys to the department's Jeep Cherokee. "I don't care how old she is, her hot little ass looks just fine to me. And it won't be no waste of time," he said. "I'm going out on patrol for a few hours. Don't worry none. I'll be back before your shift ends."

Kyle couldn't resist one last dig. "You're setting yourself up for rejection," he called as Leroy disappeared out the door. "And you forgot your coffee."

As the coffeepot sputtered the last of the water into the filter, he sat down at the other desk chair and opened a folder containing incident reports — both of them — from the previous shift. It would take only a few minutes to review and file them. The phone was quiet. His shift would probably end uneventfully.

Kyle poured himself a cup of coffee. It

looked like sludge flowing into his cup. "Must've used half the can," he muttered to himself, and this thought was confirmed when he removed the filter and discovered it was filled with coffee granules up to the very top. He smiled to himself as he pitched the filter into the trash can. Leroy was a jackass and a moron, and Claudia would surely dismiss any overture he might make toward her. Still, the fact that Leroy couldn't even brew a decent pot of coffee reassured Kyle in some strange way.

The massive white house was still and dark.

Just before four o'clock Monday afternoon, Jean Wykowski pushed open the back door to the old mansion. "Hello?" she called, but only the ticking of the grandfather clock in the parlor answered her. She stepped into the kitchen and closed the door. It would take only a moment to return the diamond ring to Mrs. McAllister's jewelry box.

Jean climbed the stairs slowly, recalling her attempts to get to the old woman in her nightmare. *It was only a dream,* she thought, and instead tried to concentrate on the task at hand. When she reached the bedroom door, though, she hesitated before going in. She felt suddenly uncomfortable, as if her entering the old widow's bedroom now, especially carrying a ring that she had taken from it, were sacrilegious. It was almost enough to make her turn away. Almost, but not quite.

The adjustable bed was in its usual position — facing the window — with the top half in a semi-upright position. The curtains on the window were drawn back so that the occupant of the bed could have seen outside. The heavy bureau was still against the wall, with Mrs. McAllister's jewelry box resting upon it.

One day, when the old woman had been asleep and Jean had worked up enough courage to open the small, dark jewelry box, she'd been surprised to discover that it was virtually empty. It contained only a glossy strand of pearls and a matching bracelet, a cameo necklace, a gold wedding band, and the diamond engagement ring. Judging by the luxurious appearance of everything else in the beautiful house, Jean had expected the jewelry box to be overflowing.

She opened her purse and removed the diamond ring from a zippered compartment. It was as stunning as ever. When she had first seen it nestled in the red velvet of the box's interior, she hadn't believed it to be real. Each of the three diamonds in the setting dwarfed that of her own quarter-carat engagement ring.

She remembered how, while Mrs. McAllister slept, she had first slipped the ring onto her finger. No matter that her nails had been uneven, that the skin on her hands had been painfully dry from repeated washings and the use of latex medical gloves. The enormous diamonds had transformed her hand. Even more, it had transformed her, if only for a moment, from a middle-aged, middle-class, average-looking woman into royalty. She had forgotten the disconcerting feeling of certain parts of her body sagging more than they should. Forgotten the hassle of using a weekly rinse on her hair to hide the gray. Forgotten the feeling of wishing for something beautiful and special for Christmas and receiving a microwave oven instead.

She had begun to try on the ring each time she visited, wearing it for a few minutes more each day. And then, last week, instead of replacing the ring in the safety of the red velvet, she had slipped it into her purse. She hadn't asked Mrs. McAllister's permission to take it, but she had never intended to keep it, either. She had wanted only to borrow it for a few days, to be able to put it on and enjoy a few more private minutes of feeling like a queen.

The thought of not returning it, especially since Mrs. McAllister had passed, disturbed her so much that it made her feel slightly nauseous.

Still, when she opened the jewelry box and placed the ring inside, she felt a pang of sadness. She caught one last glimpse of the diamonds before closing the lid. Her secret moments of luxury would be no more.

The stairs outside the bedroom door creaked with footsteps. Jean whirled around to see Father O'Brien standing in the door of the bedroom.

"Oh! Father! You startled me!" she said, thinking wildly for a way to explain why she was standing in a dead woman's bedroom. "I heard about Mrs. McAllister. I didn't know anyone else was here. I still have a key to the back door, and I just, well, I just needed to, to visit one last time, I mean —"

Father O'Brien's expression went from one of curiosity to one of empathy. He came toward her and stood looking out over Mill River through the bedroom window. "I know, Jean. I'm having trouble myself, believing that she's gone. I imagine you're feeling much the same way, having taken care of her for so long. It's quite all right, your being here, I mean. I came to get some information, to start making arrangements for her funeral and for the execution of her estate. But stay as long as you like."

"Actually, I was just ready to leave." She handed him the key to the mansion and put her purse over her shoulder. "Father," she said, stopping just before the doorway, "is it true that Mrs. McAllister had no family at all?"

Father O'Brien was silent a moment. "Well," he said slowly, "members of the McAllister family forgot about her long ago. I don't believe she'd had contact with any of them in decades."

"Then, what will become of all this?" Jean asked, gesturing with the hand that wasn't clutching her purse. "The house, and everything else?"

"I believe it will go to a variety of people," Father O'Brien said carefully, "but exactly who those people are . . ." He hesitated, as if searching for the right words. "Who those people are remains to be seen."

"Oh. Well, I'd better be getting home. Take care," she said, and started down the staircase.

Stupid, stupid, Jean thought to herself as she hurried into her car and started the engine. *You should have gotten in and out. A few more minutes, and he would have seen you with the ring.* She shuddered to think how much worse it would have been if she had been caught stealing, or returning something she had stolen, by a priest. Her heart, which had been racing since the moment she had seen Father O'Brien, slowed down. At least now the ring had been returned and her conscience was clear.

Father O'Brien watched as Jean Wykowski's car disappeared from view down Mary's driveway. He opened the lid to the jewelry box and saw that the diamond ring was back in its usual place. He still couldn't believe that she had actually returned it and that Mary had been right. *Ah, Jean, she knew you would keep it for just a little while,* he thought. He admired the character that Jean must have had to return the ring she obviously loved so much. Throughout his many years of petty theft, he had mustered neither the strength nor the courage to return a single spoon.

Father O'Brien left the bedroom and went across the hall into the room Mary had used as a library. The door creaked when he pushed it open. The layer of dust that coated the shelves and the stale air that hung between the bookshelves revealed how long it had been since Mary, or anyone, had been inside it. A small desk was nestled in the far corner. He went to it and completely removed the top drawer. It was filled with assorted papers and several bundles of old correspondence bound with rubber bands. Near the back of the drawer, he found what he was looking for: a wrinkled manila envelope containing some folded papers, two business cards, and a small leather booklet.

One of the business cards, from Gasaway and Gasaway, Attorneys-at-Law, was yellowed and slightly bent. The other was crisp and new by comparison. It read JAMES R. GASAWAY, ATTORNEY. The booklet was old, and nondescript save for the inscription of "Rutland County Savings and Loan" in the lower right corner.

Father O'Brien placed the envelope in his coat pocket and exited the library, closing the creaky door behind him. He went back to the bedroom and withdrew from another pocket a small notepad and pen. He began making notes to himself, lists of things. The jewelry box and its contents were on the list. The house, the furniture, the old horse farm that had belonged to Mary's father. The millions of dollars in liquid assets. Sham, the Siamese.

Then, he began to list the names. The Mill

River Public Library. Mill River school system. Rowen Hansen. Ruth Fitzgerald. Daisy Delaine. Jean Wykowski would have been shocked to know that her name was on the list, too.

The sun was starting to set, and Father O'Brien looked out over Mill River as shadows began to envelop the little town. Today was February 11. Counting from tomorrow, he had only twenty-two days until March 5.

Tuesday, March 5, would be a very important day. Vermont state law designated the first Tuesday in March as the annual Town Meeting Day. On that day across the state, residents of each town would meet to debate and approve a town budget, elect town officers, and visit with neighbors. Town Meeting Day was always a major social event for Mill River. By the beginning of March, most people in the little town were eager for a change in their winter routines. The meeting was usually held at four o'clock, with a merry potluck supper immediately following.

Father O'Brien thought of the little brown package and the sealed envelope that Mary had given him. They were still on his desk back at the parish house. At Mill River's town meeting, after the debating and voting, he would honor Mary's final wishes by reading that letter and presenting to the town whatever was inside the package.

He looked down over Mill River, watching as the sunlight faded and the streetlights switched on. In the next twenty-two days, he had a lot of work to do.

CHAPTER 14

1942

"Well, here we are," said Conor, holding open the back door of the mansion for Mary. It had been four weeks since she had last been inside her home, and she walked through the door looking at everything as if for the first time. She was not completely blind in her left eye, but she might as well have been. It registered only shadows of movement and was extremely sensitive to bright light. Its color had changed, too, from a clear, bright blue to a murky shade of blue-gray. She had taken to wearing a patch over it.

"How are you feeling?" Conor asked, coming up beside her.

"Fine. A little strange at being back here, but relieved to be out of the hospital."

Conor nodded. For a while, he stood in the sitting room, watching as Mary walked slowly around the davenport and chairs, tracing her finger along the banister. She looked up toward the master bedroom, put one foot on the bottom step, but didn't venture any further. She wasn't ready to go there just yet.

"Grandpop," she said, backing away from the staircase, "I want to go down to the barn."

Conor smiled. "I thought you'd never ask. There's something there I want to show you."

All three of the horses were grazing in the pasture. Ebony and Penny hadn't changed at all, except for having grown fatter. But it was the sight of Monarch that made her gasp with delight. Having been well cared for over the past month, the blood bay horse had regained much of the weight he had lost. His ribs no longer showed, and his coat, though scarred with white whip marks, was beginning to take on a healthy sheen.

"He looks wonderful! They all do," Mary said. The horses were coming closer, ears pricked forward, nickering. Monarch wasn't at all lame. In fact, there was no sign that there had ever been anything wrong with his hind hoof.

"The veterinarian was out almost every day at first," Conor said. "Said he'd never seen a horse in such bad shape. He had him standing with his hoof in a soaking bucket twice a day for the first week. I don't know what else he did, but he managed to get the infection cleared up. He said it was close. Another few days and he wouldn't have been able to do anything for him."

Ebony went immediately to Mary. Monarch, on the other hand, went to Conor and began nuzzling his shirt pocket.

"Yes, yes, I know," he told the horse, laughing.

"He likes you!" Mary said.

Conor retrieved several sugar cubes from the pocket and offered them to Monarch. "I know sugar's rationed — I really shouldn't be giving it to a horse. But I'm afraid I've spoiled him," he explained. "I've been out to see him a number of times over the past few weeks, and we've gotten to know each other. He was pretty skittish at first, but this fella has a sweet tooth. Once I figured that out, he came around pretty quickly."

"Grandpop, I had no idea you liked horses."

Conor chuckled and rubbed Monarch's forehead. "It's been a while since I've been around any. But don't forget, when I was your age, if you didn't want to walk somewhere and you weren't taking the train, a horse was your only other option. I enjoyed them very much when I was a young man. I guess I still do."

"Would you like to go riding with me sometime?" Mary asked.

"I haven't ridden in years. And, mind you, I wasn't all that good at it when I was growing up. But, maybe, when the doctor says you are well enough to ride, I could be persuaded to try it again."

Mary stroked the velvety skin on Ebony's nose and smiled.

After a few more minutes, Conor looked at his watch. "Mary, it's after two-thirty, and I promised Stephen I'd be back at three."

"Oh! Well, you shouldn't be late on my account." Her attention was still focused on the black mare.

"Yes. Well." Conor shifted uncomfortably. "Mary, are you sure that you won't stay at the house in town with the family for a few weeks? Just until you've adjusted to being . . . well, being by yourself?"

Mary sighed and looked into Conor's worried eyes. "Grandpop, I'll be fine, really. I feel fine. Dr. Mason said there isn't any reason why I can't do things around the house, so long as I don't do anything too strenuous for the first few days. And I know how Stephen and Elise feel about me. It

266

would only make things worse, for everybody. I'm much better off here."

"But you'll be all alone. I intend to do
everything I can to see you regularly, but
you have to know, with the war on, gasoline
is hard to come by and driving for pleasure
isn't allowed. I had to get special permission from the county to take you home, and
I don't know how often I'll be able to get
out here."

"Grandpop," Mary said, "please don't
take this the wrong way — you know how
much I enjoy your company — but I'm used
to being alone. I don't mind it. I've always
been that way. You know strange people and
places have always made me anxious. I'd
much rather be safe in the comfort of my
own home or off riding with Ebony. I'll be
fine here, really. As soon as I'm able, I'm
going to start a garden, and go riding, and
redecorate the library. And I know you'll
visit me as often as you can."

"And so will Father O'Brien. He's right
here in town, so he's offered to stop by a
few days each week to check up on you as a
favor to a certain someone," Conor said,
winking. "He also said that you should call
him if you need anything, however small."

"I will," Mary said. She smiled to herself
as she remembered Father O'Brien stand-

ing awkwardly in her hospital room, his face contorted with shame, when she had asked him about the spoons. "He is very kind, having spent so much time with me in the hospital. I do feel comfortable around him."

"Good, good. So, my dear, do you feel well enough to walk an old man back to his car?"

"Of course, but you're not old, Grand-pop."

Conor smiled and offered his arm to Mary. "Oh, I almost forgot. I've hired a local girl to help around the house for a few weeks. She's already been to the market for groceries for you," he said, as they started back toward the house. "Also, I've had two boys from a farm a few miles out coming each day to look after the horses. I'll tell them to continue, at least for the time being, yes?"

Mary nodded. "They've done a wonderful job," she said, but then her brow furrowed. "As long as it doesn't cost too much. I can't imagine how much it was to have the vet out for Monarch all those times." In fact, she hadn't thought about that at all, or about her own hospital bills, or any of the other bills for the house or the car . . . She touched the patch over her left eye.

"Good gracious, Mary, you needn't worry

about any of that, or any of your other expenses, for that matter. I've made arrangements to ensure that you are provided for financially. I just need a few more days to work out the details, and then I'll sit down with you and go over everything." He patted the hand she had linked through his arm. "Promise me that you'll worry about nothing except recovering, and getting your life back."

Mary looked up at Conor and nodded. "All right. If you're sure."

"I am," he said. They had reached the door to the marble mansion, and he extended an arm to open it.

"Grandpop?" Conor looked down at Mary and saw her eye becoming teary. "I just want to tell you . . . I feel as if nothing I can say can thank you for everything you've done, for taking care of me . . ." She wiped the tears that spilled down her cheek.

"Mary, my dear," he said, but his words caught in his throat. He put his arm around her, kissed her on the forehead, and tried his voice again. "Mary, that's what your family is for."

The next day was Sunday, and, true to Conor's word, Father O'Brien stopped by in the early afternoon. Mary invited him

269

into the sitting room and went to put on water for tea.

"It should be ready in a few minutes. I'll hear the kettle when it whistles," she said, joining him.

"I'm in no hurry," he said, settling back into the chair. "I had two visits scheduled after the service this morning but nothing else for the rest of the day. Have you given any thought to attending Mass? Maybe once you've settled back in here?" Father O'Brien asked.

"I have," Mary replied, "but I don't think . . . I don't think I will." Father O'Brien's face registered polite surprise. "Michael, I don't want you to think my decision has anything to do with you. It doesn't. I don't think I could bear being around all those people. And even if I could, my memories of being in the church are painful, the beginning of a year I wish I could forget."

"I understand," Father O'Brien said. "I only thought that it might help you work through everything that's happened. Many people find coming together with each other, and with God, to be comforting."

Mary averted her gaze, glanced down to where her arm rested on the davenport. She looked meek, almost ashamed, as she smoothed the fine fabric beneath her hand. "I've never been comfortable coming together with other people. Well, I suppose that's not completely true. With Patrick, I had started to feel more comfortable, but now, it's so much worse." Mary appeared to be searching for words, but they did not come to her. She shook her head quickly to herself and continued. "As for God . . . I have a lot of questions right now. Patrick insisted that we attend Mass, and at first, I thought doing so might be a good thing. But now, I find myself wondering if there is a God at all. In the last year, I've lost nearly everything — my father, my marriage, my husband. I'm lucky that I didn't lose my life." Mary was trembling, clenching the arm of the davenport, staring at him with her one blue eye. "I feel almost as if I've been punished for something, but what? I've never hurt anyone. I've never wanted to hurt anyone."

Father O'Brien flattened himself against the back of the chair. Questions such as Mary's were to be expected. He had counseled many who had begun to question their faith after suffering personal tragedies. But the intense pain in Mary's voice and the grief that distorted her young face rendered him speechless. He gasped and tried to

271

come up with something to say.

The teakettle beat him to it. Its whistle had an immediate calming effect, much like a bell signaling the end of a round in a boxing match. Mary took a deep breath, straightened the black patch over her left eye, and wiped the tears from her cheeks. "Excuse me a minute," she said, and left for the kitchen.

A few minutes later, she returned with a silver tea tray. She set it down on the coffee table, revealing, in addition to the teapot and two cups with saucers, a plate of cookies, a bowl of sugar cubes, and a pitcher of cream. He noticed that a small teaspoon rested on each saucer.

"Here you are," said Mary, filling the first cup. "I didn't know how you take your tea, so I brought out everything. Please help yourself to whatever you like." She handed him the cup and saucer and proceeded to pour some tea for herself.

"Thank you, Mary," he said, carefully accepting the tea. He was most interested in seeing the spoon tucked on the saucer behind his cup. It would surely be a beauty, made of fine silver and patterned with delicate swirls. Holding his breath in anticipation, Father O'Brien held the saucer in his left hand and grasped the silver spoon handle with his right. He brought the spoon up over the edge of his cup, but it wasn't a spoon.

It was a fork.

He would have thought this an oversight with anyone else, but he knew Mary's choice of flatware was no accident. He swallowed and felt his cheeks begin to burn.

Mary was watching. She herself had a spoon, which she was using to deposit sugar cubes in her own cup. She added cream and stirred. "It's just a little precaution, Michael," she said with an apologetic smile. "I hope you understand."

"Ah, yes," he said, and used the fork to take a sugar cube. This was turning out to be a most unpleasant visit.

Mary set her cup back on its saucer and sighed. "I'm sorry I got upset a few minutes ago. It's just since that, while I was in the hospital, I had time to think about . . . what happened to me. I feel so conflicted. It makes me angry to know that I loved — that I still love — someone I didn't really know at all, someone who would do something like this to me." She paused, waiting for some response from Father O'Brien, but he only nodded. "Part of me . . . the part that still loves Patrick . . . would never want to see him hurting. But, I've thought about how Patrick died, and it doesn't seem fair. The other part of me says that he didn't suffer enough. Not like I did, and Monarch did. Grandpop told me more than a hundred people came to Patrick's funeral. Business associates and prominent couples from Rutland, extended family members. I was still in the hospital, and only his parents and immediate family knew where I was and what Patrick had done to me. He never had to face all those people who came to mourn him. He didn't live to face what he left me with — a life of half vision — or feel any shame or remorse for what he did. Although now, I doubt he would have felt either of those things."

"Mary," Father O'Brien said, "even though Patrick is no longer living, I have to believe that he is being made to atone for what he did. I also believe that everything happens for a reason, although it may not be clear to us what that reason may be."

"You believe that God allowed Patrick to do this to me for a reason?" The edge crept back into her voice.

"Man has free will, and Patrick chose to do what he did. But, yes, I do believe it happened for a certain purpose that neither of us is aware of, at least right now."

Mary stood up and walked to the sitting

room window. "So it's fate, then?" she said, focusing on an indeterminate target outside. "I don't think so. I believe our choices alone lead to certain results. Look at me. My choice to marry Patrick, and not having the ability to see beyond my feelings for him, to realize I was in danger . . ." She lightly fingered the patch over her left eye.

"But Mary, what brought him out to your father's farm in the first place?"

Mary did not reply for a moment. When she spoke again, it was almost to herself, and Father O'Brien had to strain to make out her words. "Spending time with him was still my choice. Who I see, what I do, what I believe. Now all I have is me. I can't afford to make wrong choices anymore."

"Mary, you have me, and Conor, and God. You should especially try to have faith in God. It is all right to ask for His help in making decisions in your life."

"What I believe . . ." she repeated, turning around to face Father O'Brien. "Michael, you have been wonderful to me over the past weeks, and I've come to think of you as a friend. Other than Conor, you're my only friend." She paused a moment as she came back to sit on the davenport. "But going out for any reason would be so painful for me. Right now, that's the last thing I need. Too much has happened. I still have a lot to think about. I have to protect myself and get better. Maybe someday things will be different." Mary's voice and her one visible eye were pleading. "Now that you know how I feel about this, about not going to Mass, I hope you can continue to be my friend."

Father O'Brien swallowed and looked at Mary. "Well, I, uh, of course," he said. "You've been through so much, and I'll do everything I can to help you. But let's look on the bright side, shall we? You're so young. The rest of your life is ahead of you. I know that time is a great healer. And it may be that, with time, your anxiety will subside. Do you remember when you first experienced it? Perhaps, if I knew how the anxiety started, I could help speed up that process, help you overcome it." At least, he intended to try — his promise to Conor required it of him. Besides, she knew about the spoons. Despite her assurance that she would not divulge his habit, her knowing of it had begun to trigger bouts of paranoia in his mind. He dared not give her any reason to go back on her word.

Mary stiffened at his suggestion as a frown settled over her face. "No. I can't," she said. Her terse reply was almost reflexive, and she shuddered and turned her head so that she no longer faced him. "I can't talk about that. I'm sorry, I just can't."

"Oh, Mary," he said, surprised that his innocent question had provoked such a response. He chose his words carefully. "I'm so sorry. I didn't mean to pry. Please know that I absolutely respect your privacy. You've been through so much, Mary, and as your friend, I'm here only to help however you want me to."

She nodded and turned back to him as her expression softened. "Thank you, Michael. I do need a friend right now."

Father O'Brien visited Mary again on Wednesday, and Conor showed up at the house again the following Friday morning. Mary was surprised at how quickly the week had passed. She had spent much of that time reading and resting or with the horses. She had also opened the windows of the white mansion so that the sweet summer air could flush the staleness from her home. The scents of honeysuckle and pine drifting through the rooms rejuvenated her. Her strength was returning.

Mary had just finished dressing when Conor knocked at the door. Wearing her riding clothes, she rushed downstairs to greet him.

"Grandpop!" she said, embracing him. "I didn't expect to see you until the weekend! I was just going down to the stables. I'm taking Ebony for a ride. Would you like to come along?"

"Whoa, wait a minute now! Are you sure you feel up to it? Did the doctor say you could go riding so soon after coming home?"

"He didn't say one way or the other, but I can't wait anymore. And besides, Ebony's so gentle, I'll be perfectly fine. Oh, won't you come with me, Grandpop?"

Conor smiled but shook his head. "I'm afraid I can't today. I have to get back to the marbleworks. I decided to make a special trip out here today to bring you something — this." He removed a fat white envelope from his jacket pocket. "Could we sit down for a few minutes?"

"Yes, of course," she said, looking with a slight frown at the envelope. She took his arm and walked with him into the sitting room. "There's nothing wrong, is there?"

"Oh, no, Mary, not at all," he said, settling himself into a chair. "Here," he said, handing her the envelope. "Go ahead, have a look."

She opened it and removed several folded

sheets of paper. A small blue booklet was wrapped in the center. Slowly, she unfolded the paper and began reading to herself: *Last will and testament of Conor M. McAllister. I, Conor Murphy McAllister, a resident of Rutland County, Vermont, being of legal age, sound mind, and disposing memory do hereby make, publish, and declare this to be my Last Will and Testament . . .* Mary stopped reading and shook her head. "Grandpop, I don't understand."

Conor smiled. "Do you remember last weekend, when I told you not to worry about your bills?"

"Yes."

"Well, I've taken care of everything. I've updated my will, you see. You don't have to read the whole thing. I just wanted to show you a particular passage. Let me see it for a moment." Mary handed him the stack of paper. Conor put on his spectacles and began thumbing through the pages. "Here it is," he said, and passed the papers back to Mary, pointing at the bottom of a page.

"I give and bequeath the sum of one million dollars to Mary Hayes McAllister," she read. Her eyes grew round as she looked at him, speechless.

He laughed, delighted at her reaction. "I wanted you to have a copy of the will. But let's hope you won't get that money for a while, shall we? In the meantime, what's written in that little blue book should take care of anything you may need."

Mary reached for the blue booklet in her lap and dropped Conor's will on the floor. For some reason, her hands were not working very well, and she had a difficult time retrieving the scattered papers. Finally, she set the stack on the coffee table and opened the little blue booklet.

"That is the bank record for Patrick's trust fund," Conor said as he watched her. The first few pages were filled with numbers handwritten in ink. Most of the entries were annual notations of a bank account balance, although several large deposits were also recorded. Mary flipped to the last page, on which the current balance was written, and gasped.

"I've had the trust fund transferred to your name. I've also arranged for you to receive a monthly stipend, which should be more than enough to cover what bills or other expenses you may have. It'll be adjusted from time to time, to reflect increases in the cost of living. But as long as you don't spend much more than the stipends, the balance in the trust fund should accrue more than enough interest to meet your needs."

Mary tried to speak and couldn't. Each of the dollar amounts she had just read was larger than any she had ever imagined having. She felt light-headed and short of breath. She also felt tears threatening to pour down her cheeks, but willed herself to retain them lest Conor come to think that no visit to her would be complete without her having a good cry. When she finally managed to make a sound, it was a mere squeak, and the tears gushed through her self-control.

"Now, Mary, these had better be happy tears," said Conor, coming to sit beside her on the davenport. He removed his handkerchief and offered it to her.

"Yes," she mouthed, accepting the handkerchief. She dabbed around and under the patch over her left eye. It became uncomfortably cold and moist when she cried.

"I knew this would be a bit of a surprise for you. I have an important luncheon meeting in Rutland, so I'll leave you to get used to the idea," Conor said, standing up. "I told you I would take care of everything, and I meant it. You won't have to worry, Mary, because you are a member of my family and will always be taken care of. No, no, don't get up, I can see myself out." His words only caused her to cry harder. She held out his handkerchief, thinking he would take it back, but he closed her hand around it.

"Keep it," he told her. "I'll get it the next time I come out, when we go riding." He winked at her and let himself out through the back door.

CHAPTER 15

"Dad, was the lady who owned Sham a witch?"

It was Tuesday evening, and Kyle sat on the sofa in his living room, folding a clean load of laundry before his date with Claudia. Stacks of clothes were piled on the cushions around him. Now, only the socks were left in the clothes basket at his feet, and he began matching them. Rowen sat on the floor playing with Sham. She pulled a string across the carpet in front of the Siamese, whose eyes grew dark and round as he prepared to pounce.

"Of course not. You know there's no such thing as witches. Why do you ask?"

"I told Jen and Stacy at school about Sham. They said that the lady who lived in the big white house was a mean old witch who never came outside. They said no one had seen her in years, and that she had an evil eye, and all she ever did was stay up in her house and watch everybody out the window. And they said that Sham was a witch's cat."

"Did Jen and Stacy ever see Mrs. McAllister? That was her name, you know — Mary McAllister."

"No. I don't think so."

"Well, I saw her, and she was a perfectly ordinary old woman. Whatever they say about an 'evil eye' is just a bunch of baloney. It's true that she was blind in one of her eyes, though. Fitz told me that she was injured in an accident a long time ago. And," he said, as Sham sprang across the carpet, trapping the end of the string beneath his front paws, "I think Sham looks and acts like a regular cat, don't you?"

"Yeah. But why didn't Mrs. McAllister ever come out of her house?"

Kyle thought about this a moment. "Well," he began, pulling another handful of socks from the clothes basket, "I don't know for sure. She'd been sick a very long time, too sick to leave her house. Before that, it could've been a lot of reasons. Sometimes, people are afraid to go out. It's almost like a kind of disease in their minds. They're afraid that something bad will happen if they go outside, even if there's no reason at all to think that, and they stay in their houses all the time. I suppose Mrs. McAllister was one of those people."

"Oh."

"Now, kiddo, what are you going to tell Jen and Stacy if they start talking about this witch business again?"

"That Mrs. McAllister was just a sick old woman, and there's no such thing as witches." Rowen looked up at him and grinned.

"Attagirl." Kyle leaned over and rumpled her hair. "Let's put these away so we have clean clothes tomorrow. I'll take care of the shirts and pants. Can you take your stuff and put it away in your room?"

Rowen stood and waited for him to gather up her clothes. Before he handed them to her, Kyle held up a pair of his own socks and shook his head.

"Man, Rowen, your feet sure are growing fast. I never saw such big feet on a nine-year-old. If they keep growing, I don't know if we'll have to order special ones to fit you. Maybe they don't make them any bigger than this."

"Gimme a break, Dad. Those are yours," she said, giggling. She pulled his socks out of his hand and threw them back at him.

Kyle laughed as Rowen disappeared into her bedroom. He quickly gathered up his own laundry. It was fifteen minutes before six o'clock, and he didn't want to be late. "I've got to leave in a few minutes," he called, stuffing his underwear into his chest of drawers. "Ruth should be here in a few minutes, but I'll be home to tuck you in before I have to go back to work. Make sure you do your homework. I'll check it when I get home, okay?"

"Okay," Rowen called back from the living room. She had resumed her string-pulling. She looked up at him as he tied the laces on his boots. "I think it's funny that you're having a date with Miss Simon. Are you going to talk about me?"

"We might," Kyle said, winking at her. "But I'm sure anything we say about you will be wonderful."

"You promise?"

"Promise."

There was a loud knock at the front door, and Kyle opened it with one hand as he leaned against the wall tying his bootlaces. Ruth Fitzgerald bustled in, carrying a covered tray.

"Hello, hello!" she said. "I brought you some treats — cinnamon rolls! Have you had dinner yet, Rowen?"

"Yeah, Dad made pizza! There's a lot left in the kitchen, if you want a piece."

Ruth looked at Kyle and smiled. "Well, aren't you a lucky girl! I just had supper myself, thank you. But I guess you're too full for dessert, then?"

"No I'm not." Rowen stood up and looked eagerly at the tray in Ruth's hands.

"I've got to run, Ruth," Kyle said. "I should be back before nine. I'll have my phone with me, and I'll take my radio, too, and leave it in the truck, just in case."

"Okey-dokey," Ruth said. "Have a good time. C'mon, Rowen, let's take these into the kitchen and heat them up so the frosting gets nice and gooey."

Kyle watched Ruth hurry into the kitchen, followed by Rowen and Sham, as he pulled on his coat and left to pick up Claudia.

At five minutes before six, Claudia peered into the mirror for the umpteenth time.

Was she seeing things, or was her lipstick on crooked? Did one eye have more eye shadow than the other? Maybe it was the light. Surely, that was it. Her shiny strawberry-blond hair reflected that light, and, thanks to a little hair spray, seemed to be holding its shape. Claudia locked eyes with herself, pursed her lips, smoothed her hair away from her face and over one ear.

She was wearing her favorite jeans and a

black cashmere sweater. The jeans were her favorite because they were the first she had purchased in a size ten, the first jeans that had ever made her feel slim and attractive. They would remind her of that feeling tonight, when she would be seated in front of a pizza for the first time in months.

Claudia took one last look at herself and stepped away from the mirror. She went out into the kitchen, glanced out the front window for any sign of a car in the driveway. She had removed her "fat" picture from the refrigerator, but she examined the front of the appliance again to reassure herself that the photo was not in sight. She was still having trouble convincing herself that she had a date with Kyle. She could not imagine having to reveal to him the identity of the woman in the photo.

Two bright headlights suddenly shone through the kitchen window. Claudia watched Kyle hop out of the driver's seat of a blue pickup truck and walk toward her front door. He caught sight of her peering through the window and waved. She smiled back and opened the door before he rang the doorbell.

"Hi," she said, as he stepped into the foyer. "Let me grab my coat." She shut the door behind him and went down the hallway to the coat closet.

"Sure. You'd better bundle up. It's pretty much a deep freeze out there. I left the truck running, but it hasn't warmed up much. I heard on the radio on the way over here that the temperature was five degrees, and that's without the windchill."

Claudia reappeared, wearing a long wool coat. "I grew up in upstate New York," she said, fitting her oversized earmuffs around her ears. "I like the cold. You just have to know how to dress for it, that's all."

"I completely agree," he said, grinning at her. "I grew up in Massachusetts." He paused a moment, looking at her. "I've got to tell you, those are the biggest earmuffs I've ever seen."

"Oh!" Claudia laughed. "They were a Christmas gift from my mom a few years back. That's what she said when she gave them to me, and they're really warm." She patted her covered ears and smiled. Talking with Kyle was so easy that just for a moment, she had forgotten how nervous she was.

"Well, shall we brave the elements, then?" he asked, reaching for her front door. Once they were outside, he opened the door of the pickup for her.

"So, where did you go to college?" Kyle

asked as he backed out of her driveway.

"Syracuse."

"Ah! You're an Orangeman! Er, I mean, Orangewoman."

"I guess I am," Claudia said. "Where did you go to school?"

"Boston University."

"Hmm. So that makes you . . ."

"A Terrier." Claudia thought she detected a hint of color in Kyle's earlobes, but the darkness made it difficult to be sure. "BU's a great school, but it's got a pretty lame mascot."

"What was your major?"

"Criminal justice and history, double major," he said. "For a while, I didn't know whether I wanted to be a police detective or a history teacher, so I took courses for both. It wasn't too hard because a lot of the classes overlapped. Obviously, the police option won out in the end."

"When you came to visit my class, you said you'd worked in Boston."

"Yep. I got promoted to detective just a few years before I decided to move up here. It's funny. Sometimes, what you think you want can change so quickly. After my wife died, I didn't want the big detective job anymore. For Rowen's sake, I didn't even want to be in Boston. Cops in the city are hurt or killed all the time, and I couldn't keep taking that risk."

Claudia had heard that Kyle was a widower. Whether he was really ready for any type of new relationship, she didn't know, but she gave him a warm smile as they pulled into the Pizza Hut parking lot. "Well, I think you made a good choice in coming to Mill River. Not that I've lived here all that long, either, but it seems like a great place to raise kids."

Claudia opened her door and was engulfed by the frigid air. She drew a breath and gasped.

Kyle heard her and chuckled. "Makes you realize how cold it is out here, coming from inside a warm house or car. The first breath is always pretty bad — you can feel it all the way down your lungs."

"Yes," said Claudia, but she had not gasped because of the cold. Rather, it was the heavenly scent emanating from the restaurant that had taken her breath away. The warm, rich smell of fresh yeast dough, garlic, tomato sauce, pepperoni. Claudia couldn't remember the last time she had even gone near a Pizza Hut. Her stomach growled.

"There's nothing like hot pizza on a cold night," Kyle said, holding the restaurant

291

door for her.

"That's true," she said, stepping inside.

They were seated quickly. The place was almost empty, which was to be expected on a Tuesday night. The waitress took their drink orders and left them alone.

Claudia opened her menu. The appetizer insert jumped out at her. She would have liked nothing more than to have a few buffalo wings, followed by some breaded mozzarella sticks and an order of cheese-stuffed jalapeño peppers. But all those things were deep-fried.

"I think I'm going to need some of these hot wings," Kyle said. His comment made Claudia's stomach growl again, but she summoned up her willpower. "I'll just have a side-salad first," she said. "And maybe we could share a pizza? I couldn't eat more than a slice or two." This statement further bolstered her resolve, even though it was not exactly true. What she really wanted was a large pepperoni pizza with a stuffed crust . . . all for herself.

After the waitress reappeared and took their order, Claudia started to feel nervous. She had been dreading this moment, after they had ordered and before the food arrived, when they would be left with nothing to do but try to engage in conversation. For a few seconds, her mind raced, attempting to come up with an appropriate topic, but Kyle saved her.

"So, how long have you been teaching?"

"Nine years, if you count this current school year. But it doesn't seem like nearly that long."

"Always fourth grade?"

"No. I've taught second and fifth, but I was teaching a fourth-grade class before I accepted the position here. I think I like fourth grade best, though. The kids are at an age where they're still innocent, but their personalities are beginning to come out. And other things, too — sense of humor, more of an awareness of the world, better social interaction. You can really see them growing into individuals. I like that."

"Yeah, I know what you mean. I see it in Rowen every day. She's growing up so fast. Sometimes she'll say or do something that's so adultlike, it kind of catches me off guard."

"She's a special kid," Claudia agreed. "I mean, all of them are, but Rowen is so quick to pick up on things, and really intuitive for a nine-year-old."

"She likes you a lot," Kyle said. "In fact, she asked me before I left whether we were going to talk about her. I told her we'd only say nice things."

Claudia laughed. "Well, I don't think there is anything to say about Rowen that isn't nice."

Kyle beamed at her, and Claudia couldn't help but notice how proud he looked. She felt so glad for him, seeing how his decision to move his daughter to Mill River had resulted in Rowen being so well adjusted and happy.

The waitress appeared at their table with the wings and salad. Claudia spread her napkin carefully across her lap, relieved that their initial conversation had gone so well.

"I'm curious," Kyle said, reaching for the plate of wings, "what made you decide to come to Mill River? Especially in the middle of a school year?"

Claudia had anticipated this question and was ready with her usual answer. "Oh. Well, it wasn't an easy decision. I was teaching in Dryden, a little town in upstate New York. My two brothers and my parents live there, and I'd been there for a number of years, but I guess the truth is, I wanted a change. I felt as if my life had come to a standstill, and I just needed to be in a new place." For a split second, she looked at her salad, then down at her size-ten jeans, and wondered how she could ever tell him the real reason that she had uprooted herself — that once she had reached her goal weight, she'd felt an overwhelming urge to make a fresh start for the new year in a place where no one knew she had been fat.

Kyle nodded, his mouth full, and she continued. "I found out about the opening at the elementary school here on a job website and applied for it. I didn't expect to get the job, but when I did, I felt horrible telling the principal of my old school that I'd be leaving at the end of the semester. I didn't have any really good reason that would explain my resignation, just that I felt like my life was stagnating, but he was great about it. He told me to do what I needed to do, that he would always give me good employment references, and wished me well."

"Sounds like a great guy," Kyle said. "You never know what kind of people you'll end up working with, but it sounds like you got lucky."

"Yeah, he was really understanding, but I do like the principal and teachers here, too," Claudia said. "Everyone has welcomed me, offered to show me around, that sort of thing. I think it's a good start."

"I like most of the guys in the police department here," Kyle said. "Fitz, the chief, has been so good to me. He rented me the apartment above the bakery. His wife, Ruth, watches Rowen for me when I have to work late or . . . when I'm out for other reasons." He looked up at her and Claudia grinned. "I offered to pay her, but she won't take a dime. The woman's a saint. Wykowski's all right, too. The only one I don't care much for is Leroy. As luck would have it, most of my shifts overlap with his, but I guess everything can't go your way."

"I don't think I blame you. That day you two came to my classroom, Leroy made me feel a little uncomfortable. I'm not sure why, exactly. It was just something about him, maybe the way he looked at me."

"I'm sorry," Kyle said. "It should have occurred to me that it might not have been a good idea to bring him. He has no tact or manners, and he thinks of himself as a ladies' man. As far as I can tell, he doesn't have much success with them, but he'll still chase anything with a skirt, if you know what I mean."

"Yes. But you shouldn't apologize for him. Leroy's behavior is his problem, after all. I can't imagine what woman would want to be with him, anyway."

Kyle's face suddenly took on new radiance, and his brown eyes shone with a wicked sparkle. "You know," he began, "I probably shouldn't tell you this, but Leroy's gearing up to take you out for Valentine's Day."

"What?" Claudia said. Her mouth was full of salad, and she covered it quickly with her napkin.

"Oh yeah," Kyle said, laughing. "He told me all about it yesterday. He's going to send you flowers and stuff this week, then ask you to the King's Lodge in Rutland for a romantic Valentine's Day dinner. Granted, King's Lodge is a nice place, but —"

"Oh, no!" Claudia said, once she had swallowed. "Please tell me you're joking."

Kyle only shook his head and laughed harder.

"Geez," Claudia groaned, putting her hand on her forehead.

"The worst of it is, Leroy can be pretty persistent sometimes if he sees something he really wants," Kyle said. "But, if he calls you, you could tell him you've already got plans for Valentine's Day."

"That'd be a lie," Claudia said, "but it might discourage him."

"Ah. Well, I think I have a better idea. If you went out with me Thursday night, you wouldn't have to lie, and we could both enjoy a nice evening."

Claudia's mouth nearly fell open. She was

mortified to think that she might have baited him into offering to take her out for Valentine's Day. "Oh my gosh, Kyle, I didn't mean to imply, you know, for you to feel as if you should ask me to dinner that day." She felt her face begin to burn.

"Oh, no," Kyle said, and there was no mistaking it this time — his ears were turning pink. "The truth is, I meant to ask you all along, and this just seemed like the perfect opportunity." He grinned sheepishly.

The waitress arrived at their table with the pizza and served each of them a slice.

"Well, what do you say?" Kyle asked when she had left.

"Oh. I'd love to," Claudia said, still struggling to keep her composure. She glanced up at him and managed a shy smile.

"Good." He picked up his pizza and bit into it. "This is good, too," he said, hurrying to wipe away a long string of melted cheese that stuck to his chin.

Claudia just laughed at him. He was so fun and genuine, and she was actually enjoying herself. The pizza was phenomenal. She allowed herself two pieces, even though she could easily have eaten the entire thing.

They had just finished and were still talking when they heard a singsong voice at the carryout counter.

"Hello, there. I've come for my order, small pizza with a stuffed crust and an order of breadsticks. By the way, you wouldn't be interested in trying some of my famous love potion, would you now?"

Almost at the same time, Kyle and Claudia peered over the edge of their booth. A short, stout figure in a hooded parka stood at the counter. Even though she had just eaten, Claudia thought of the warm, doughy, garlicky breadsticks and felt an overwhelming urge to order some to go. *Don't be a pig,* she scolded herself.

"No, thank you, ma'am. Your total comes to fifteen seventy-five." The kid behind the counter shifted uncomfortably at Daisy's solicitation.

"Here you are," Daisy said, offering the cashier a fistful of bills. She sniffed loudly, then pulled a tissue from a coat pocket and blew her nose. "Boy, you know it's cold outside when your nose runs faster than you can." She gave a final loud snort, oblivious to the attention she had drawn. "It's a pity, my love potion's especially effective on teenagers such as yourself. It would even help you with those pimples, too. But I guess it's just as well — I've almost sold out the entire batch. Demand's been pretty strong this year."

The cashier looked at two pretty waitresses standing nearby and blushed before he placed Daisy's bills in the cash register. "Twenty-five cents is your change," he said, handing her a quarter and her receipt. He pushed two flat pizza boxes across the counter. "Your dipping sauces are in the box with the breadsticks. Have a good night."

"Thank you, I will!" she said. "And a good night to you as well." Daisy picked up her pizza and breadsticks and turned for the door, humming loudly. The cashier and waitresses watched her leave, snickering.

"Who is that woman?" Claudia asked Kyle as they lowered themselves back into their seats.

"Her name is Daisy Delaine," Kyle said, "but almost everybody in town calls her 'Crazy Daisy.' It's mean, I know."

"She came to my house a few days ago wanting to sell me love potion, whatever that is. Said she made it herself. I can see why she got that nickname."

"She's not really crazy, at least, not like the people down in Waterbury, in the state hospital. Fitz told me she's lived in Mill River for years and she's always been a little . . . off. People have tried a few times to get her committed, though, and no court

300

has ever found her to be incompetent. From what I've heard, she mixes up a different homemade concoction for each holiday and peddles it all over town. But she's harmless. Mostly people just feel sorry for her."

"That explains the love potion. So she takes care of herself?" Claudia asked. "Where does she live?"

"In a little trailer down the road. She does all right. I guess she lives on disability payments from the government and whatever she can make selling her potions. Hey, would you like to take some of this home?" Kyle said, motioning to the few pieces of pizza left in front of them. "You could have it for your lunch tomorrow."

"Oh, no thanks," Claudia said, thinking how good it would be to have pizza again the next day. But she wouldn't fall into that trap. "Why don't you take it home for Rowen?"

"Okay," Kyle said. He motioned for the waitress to bring the check and a carry-home container for the pizza. When they were ready to leave, he insisted on paying for everything and helped Claudia put on her coat. They had been out for an hour and a half, but it had seemed like so much less.

They sat shivering in the front seat of the

pickup as Kyle started the engine and adjusted the heater. It felt colder out now than it had been when they arrived.

"Well, at least it's a short drive home," Kyle said.

"Yes," Claudia said, trying to keep her teeth from chattering. Even though she was cold, she wished that the drive would be longer. Neither she nor Kyle said anything for a few minutes.

The light from the streetlamps made the snowpack glisten. As they turned onto the main road, the great white mansion on the hill came into view. Like the snow, it, too, glowed, reflecting the light so that it appeared to hover high up above the town.

"Kyle, who lives in that big white house?"

He smiled at her. "I wondered about that, too, when I first saw it. The house is vacant, now. The woman who lived there died two days ago. Her name was Mary McAllister. I don't know much about her except that she'd lived there for most of her life and rarely came out. Fitz and I went up there Sunday morning to do a report for the medical examiner. Father O'Brien was there too, from St. John's. He said she'd been sick for more than a year."

"It's a beautiful house. I don't think I've ever seen one like it."

"The outside's made of white marble. Her husband's family built it for her years ago. The inside's something else, too. All kinds of expensive furniture and paintings, like a palace."

"Wow. It's hardly something you'd expect to find in a little town like this."

"I know. But I've learned that sometimes what you find in a small town can surprise you." He was looking at her again, still smiling. Claudia felt herself blushing.

They were going past St. John's now, and then Kyle pulled the blue pickup into her driveway. She turned to thank him for the evening, but, before she could say anything, he had gotten out of the truck, leaving the engine running. He held up a finger to tell her to wait as he ran around the front of the truck to open the door for her.

"Kyle, you don't have to keep doing this," she said, laughing, as he helped her out of the front seat.

"I insist," he said. "It's our first date, and I have to make a good impression. Especially since I apparently have competition from a colleague of mine."

He spoke with such seriousness that Claudia was worried. "You don't really think I'd go for Leroy, do you?" she asked.

"Well, no, not after talking to you tonight,"

he said, smiling. They had reached her front door.

"I had a great time tonight," she said. She was beginning to feel awkward. Why did he continue to grin at her? With horror, it occurred to her that maybe she had a piece of salad wedged between her front teeth. She returned his smile, but without showing her teeth. "What is it? Why do you keep smiling at me?"

He took a step closer to her. "I'm not sure," he said, putting his hands gently on either side of her head, "but I think it's the earmuffs. You look like a cute little bear."

Before she could reply, he slid his hands a little lower, so that they were cradling her face, and kissed her.

Instinctively, Claudia closed her eyes and wrapped her arms around his waist, pulling him against her. She smelled his cologne and the scent of his smooth leather coat, felt his warm mouth against hers, and thought her knees would give out.

"Oops," he said after he had pulled away, "maybe I should have asked before I did that." Claudia smiled again and shook her head, reassuring him. "Tomorrow, I'll get us reservations for Thursday night, and then call you to let you know what time."

"Okay," she said, and took a reluctant step

toward her front door. She was beaming now — any food in her teeth be damned. "I'm looking forward to Thursday."

"Me too," he said. He didn't go back to the truck until she was safely inside, waving goodbye to him through the kitchen window.

Claudia waited until the headlights of Kyle's truck had backed out of her driveway and turned onto the road. She stood in her kitchen with her heart hammering in her chest, still wearing her coat and gloves and earmuffs. When she was sure that he was gone, she jumped up and down, squealing with delight. She had just had her first date and her first kiss and he had said she looked like a cute little bear. She hadn't made a pig of herself at Pizza Hut, and best of all, she had a date for Valentine's Day!

He couldn't believe it.

The ashes at the end of Leroy's cigarette had built up to almost an inch and had started to crumble onto his lap before he noticed them. Reflexively, he tapped the cigarette on the edge of the ashtray in the police department's Jeep, never once taking his eyes off Claudia's house.

She had been with Kyle. All evening.

He had gone out on patrol earlier in his

shift, had driven by her house hoping to catch a glimpse of her through a window. Her car had been in the driveway and her porch light had been on, but the inside of the house had been dark. She usually came home soon after the school day ended and stayed there, running on the treadmill or grading papers or doing something until she went to sleep. But tonight, when he had driven by a little after six, she had been gone. He had pulled into the parking lot of St. John's, behind some trees not even a block from her house, and waited for her to return.

The backstabbing bastard had actually kissed her, right in front of her house, right in front of him.

Leroy's left hand was clenched on the steering wheel. He held the cigarette in his right hand, and now he ground it into the ashtray. He had arranged to have two dozen roses sent to Claudia's classroom tomorrow, as a surprise to mark the beginning of their relationship. But now she was home safe and sound, and he would have bet anyone his last Lucky Strike that tomorrow, when his flowers arrived, she'd automatically assume they were from Kyle.

Her panties were in his pocket, as usual, but instead of comforting him, they only fueled the raging jealousy inside him. He started the Jeep and slammed it into reverse, then knocked the gearshift into drive and sped out of the parking lot. He had a few hours left before his shift ended, and he needed to drive.

The main road out of town had been cleared of most of the snow, but patches of ice remained. Feeling confident in his four-wheel drive, Leroy didn't care.

Now his bruised ego took over, goading him on, telling him that he could compete with Kyle any day. He was younger and stronger. He didn't have to rent a place from his boss, and he wasn't stuck with a brat. In fact, when the roses were delivered tomorrow, it would be even more of a surprise when Claudia realized they were from him!

Leroy was just outside Mill River when the Jeep hit a patch of black ice going around a sharp turn. He pulled the steering wheel hard, but the four-wheel drive was useless. The next thing he knew, he was flying up over the snow piled along the edge of the road. A telephone pole loomed up out of the darkness, forced itself into the right-hand side of the engine. He felt a sharp jerk across his chest as his seat belt locked. There was a pop and a whoosh as the airbag inflated, and a nasty stinging sensation as his face smacked into it.

"What the hell?"

The lights in the Wykowski household flickered. Ron Wykowski bolted up out of his recliner, nearly tripping over the extended footrest before it snapped back into the base of the chair. He punched the remote control in his hand to turn off the television. A tremendous crash sounded as if it had occurred right on the other side of the living room wall.

"Quick, get your coat. I think somebody had an accident," Jean said, looking out the front window. She didn't realize that Ron was already on his feet, pulling on his boots. "I can't see far enough around the house from here, but I'm going to call for help. There might be people hurt."

Jimmy and Johnny came tearing into the living room. "Mom, Dad, a police officer crashed outside!" Jimmy said.

"We can see the lights flashing from the window in our room," Johnny explained. "I think it's the Jeep from the department."

"You boys stay inside," Ron told them, causing a little of the excitement to leave their faces. He glanced down at his watch as he headed out the door. "Must be Leroy.

Kyle's not on 'til eleven."

Ron came trudging around the house just as Leroy pushed open the front door of the Jeep. The telephone pole in front of the Wykowski house was forced deep into the hood of the vehicle. No siren was sounding, but red and blue lights swirled and flashed on the dashboard.

Leroy swung his legs out of the Jeep, tried to stand, wobbled, and collapsed into the deep snow just as Ron reached him.

"Leroy, can you hear me? Say something if you're conscious."

Leroy struggled to sit up. His face was reddish and rasped in a few places where it had met the airbag. "I'm dizzy. And my ankle hurts like a bitch."

"Jean called for help as soon as we heard the crash. Should be someone here soon. Let's get you up out of the snow." He helped Leroy back into the front seat of the Jeep. "What happened? Did you hit ice coming around the turn?"

"Uh, yeah, I think," Leroy said. "I tried to swerve the other way but the wheels wouldn't stay on the road."

Jean came breathlessly around the Jeep. "An ambulance is on the way. Are you hurt, Leroy?" she asked.

"Not bad," he said. He appeared less

dazed now and more like his usual self. "Just my left ankle. I twisted the other one yesterday morning coming into the station, and now this one's messed up. I may as well be a damned cripple."

"Let me see," Jean said. She squatted down in front of him and, as gently as she could, removed his boot. "Can you move it at all?" she asked, and Leroy gingerly rotated his ankle in her hand.

"Good," she said. "Now see if you can push against my hand." Leroy did this as well. Jean carefully felt all around his foot and then lowered it. "You've got good movement even though it's a little swollen. I don't think it's broken, but you shouldn't try to walk on it until you get it X-rayed."

Leroy grunted and leaned sideways against the back of the seat. The deployed airbag drooped out of the center of the steering wheel, and he brushed it away.

Jean was watching him. "Without that and your seat belt, you probably would've broken your neck," she said. "A lot of the paralyzed people I take care of weren't nearly as lucky as you."

Annoyed at her lecture, Leroy looked away and grunted again.

An ambulance arrived a few minutes later, carefully pulling over near the place where the Jeep had skidded off the road. Assisted by Ron and one of the paramedics, Leroy made his way over to the ambulance.

"I'll follow you into Rutland, Leroy," Ron said. "I need to fill out a report on this, anyway, and you'll need a ride back from the hospital."

"Naw, that's all right," Leroy said. "I'm not really hurt. They'll probably just give me a checkup and send me home, so there's no sense in you coming too."

"Well, maybe it would be better if I took care of the Jeep," Ron said. "Is there anyone you want me to call?"

"My sister lives right outside Rutland City. You could let her know, I suppose, and I'll just have her give me a lift when they're done with me." Leroy paused as he craned his neck up to get one last look at the damaged police vehicle. "You could call the chief for me, too, and tell him about the Jeep. I know he's gonna go off on me when he finds out. Maybe he'll go easier on me if you tell him first."

Ron glanced over at his wife, rolling his eyes, and turned back toward the ambulance. "Sure, I'll get hold of Fitz. And I'll call Kyle and see if he can come in early to cover the rest of your shift."

"Yeah, okay," Leroy said, just before the

paramedic shut the back doors of the ambulance.

"Fitz'll have his head in the morning," Ron said to Jean, leaning against the damaged Jeep. "This is the only four-wheel drive we've got, and it looks totaled to me."

"Well, I'm just glad no one was seriously hurt," Jean said. "He could've hit someone coming the opposite direction. If the pole hadn't stopped him, he might've come through our house!"

"He must've been doing at least fifty when he hit the ice." Ron shook his head. "Leroy drives like a maniac. I guess he was bound to do something like this before long."

"C'mon, let's go inside and call a tow truck," Jean said. "The kids are probably dying to know what happened, and I'm freezing my buns off."

When Father O'Brien awoke the next morning, it was still dark outside, and he shivered as he dressed in the chilly parish house. Even after he put the heat up, he couldn't seem to get warm. He imagined the hot coffee that would be brewing down at the bakery, and the sweet, cozy smell of cinnamon and pastry, and almost felt better. He often hankered for a slice of tart cherry pie. Now, the thought of the warm filling in

Ruth Fitzgerald's flaky piecrust was all it took for him to go to the closet for his coat.

Ruth came out from behind the counter when she saw him enter the bakery. "Morning, Father. Haven't seen you in here for a while!" she said. Her hair was pulled neatly back into a bun, and the large apron she wore was speckled with flour and bits of dough. The warm air that rushed out past him was rich with the scent of baking. "I'm awfully sorry about Mrs. McAllister. Fitz told me what happened."

"Thank you, Ruth. It's been a busy few days, and it hasn't been easy. But when I woke up this morning, all I could think about was hot coffee and cherry pie."

She laughed and went back behind the counter. "Well, you're in luck. I took one out of the oven about a half hour ago, so it's about cool enough to cut."

"It must have summoned me over here," he said, winking at her. "I'll just take my usual seat, then." He started over toward a small table by the front window.

"There's today's paper over there on the counter," she said, handing him a fresh cup of coffee. "I'll bring your pie over to you in a minute."

He nodded and went to sit down, taking the newspaper from the counter as he passed. A steady stream of people were arriving to pick up muffins and Danish for breakfast, or to fill thermos flasks with coffee. He sighed and opened the paper, although it could barely be called that. The *Mill River Gazette* came out three times a week, on Monday, Wednesday, and Friday, usually containing the police blotter, obituaries, and perhaps an article or two. But the news was so slow in Mill River that most issues seemed to contain more advertising than anything else.

"Hullo, Father, nice to see you," said Fitz, setting a large piece of cherry pie in front of him. "You been holding up all right since Sunday?"

"Fitz! I didn't see you come down," Father O'Brien said, putting away his paper. The bakery was really hopping now, and Ruth was busy taking orders from customers milling around the counter. "Sure, I'm all right." *That's not exactly true,* he thought to himself as he remembered Sunday morning, but he supposed he was doing as well as could be expected. "You're off to the station?"

"Yep, and I'm not looking forward to it, either. I guess you haven't heard about the wreck last night?" Father O'Brien's eyes grew wide, and he shook his head. "Well,"

314

Fitz continued, "I got a call at a little after eight last night. Leroy'd taken the Jeep out on patrol, hit a patch of ice out by Ron Wykowski's house, and smashed into a utility pole."

"Oh, my," Father O'Brien said. "Was he hurt?"

"Just a sprained ankle, and a few scrapes on his face."

"Well, that's good."

"Yes," Fitz said, but his expression came very close to contradicting his response. "Anyhow, the Jeep's totaled. Don't know exactly what we'll do now, because that was our only four-wheel drive, you know. And it was old. The insurance payout won't be nearly enough for a new one. I've heard the state sometimes auctions used cars to other state or county agencies, though, and I think there's an auction in a few weeks. I'll go up to Montpelier and see if they've got anything we can afford. Maybe we'll get lucky."

Father O'Brien nodded, and his mind was racing. He thought of the list in his coat pocket. The situation was perfect, but he needed to act quickly. "Everything will work out in the end, Fitz, I'm sure of it," he said to the police chief, who smiled in return.

"If you say so, Father, I'll try not to worry. I suppose stranger things have happened in

315

this little town." Fitz was pulling on his gloves. "I've got to get going," he said, heading for the door. "Enjoy your pie."

"Will do." Father O'Brien finished the pie quickly, along with his coffee. When no one was looking, he slipped the teaspoon he had used to stir his coffee up his sleeve. It would be one more to add to the box in his office. The usual guilt was there, but today, he didn't have time to dwell on it. He had something more important than spoons to worry about. Waving goodbye to Ruth, he put on his coat and braced himself for the cold outside.

CHAPTER 16

1945

As the Allies struggled against Hitler's forces, Mary fought her own private battles against her anxiety.

She had no guests other than Conor and Father O'Brien. Eventually, gasoline rationing forced Conor to curtail his trips to Mill River. He managed to see her once in a while, but they took to writing letters as their primary means of communication.

After spending so much time alone, even Mary's occasional attempts to greet the postman ended in fits of trembling and panicked disorientation. While she gladly did her own cooking and cleaning, shopping and other errands were out of the question. Mary was grateful for the dependable girl Conor had hired, who took care of those tasks and then quickly deposited any packages or groceries on the doorstep before leaving.

On VJ Day, September 2, 1945, she put on her best dress and eye patch but remained in the marble mansion, cheering silently from her bedroom window as the little town celebrated the war's end with a victory parade. She succumbed to her isolation, clinging to society only through letters from Conor and visits from Father O'Brien, the news and music on her radio, and the sight of Mill River from her bedroom window.

Mary loved that view most of all. She watched Mill River on crisp, bright mornings, during the noonday rush of things, at twilight as its few streetlights winked on. It didn't matter that, standing in her home high above the town, she was far removed from the small cluster of buildings and the main road that parted them. Nor did it matter that she knew none of the people who walked up and down the sidewalks each day. Regardless of her affliction, she was a part of Mill River, and the town was a part of her — a steady, calming presence that never changed.

Keeping his promise to Conor, Father O'Brien stopped by the mansion at least twice a week. The young priest came by every Wednesday evening and after Mass on

Sundays, when he often stayed for lunch and a horseback ride.

"I don't think she's big enough for me," he said as he climbed astride Ebony for the first time. Mary had suggested that they stay in the training ring so she could teach him proper posture and position in the saddle. "And what if she gets spooked and takes off?"

"Ebby doesn't spook easily," Mary said, adjusting the length of the stirrup leathers to accommodate his long legs. "She's a good girl. Strong, too. Morgans are smallish horses, but you'd be surprised at how they can outpull much larger ones. Ebby could carry someone probably twice your weight. Just remember, keep your heels down and your back straight. And when she trots, support yourself with your legs and try to move up and down with her."

Father O'Brien nodded, trying to process all of Mary's directions.

"Are you ready?" Mary asked.

"I suppose," he said, looking down. Even though Ebony was a small horse, the ground still seemed far beneath his feet now that he was in the saddle.

Mary flicked the long rein and the black mare began to walk in a large circle. Once he was accustomed to the gentle swaying of the mare's gait, Mary flicked the rein again. As the horse broke into a trot, he lurched and bounced uncomfortably.

"Try to feel how she's moving," Mary called. "Keep your weight in the stirrups." After a few minutes, he managed to post in rhythm with Ebony. Surprised at his accomplishment, he smiled at Mary.

"Good!" Mary called. "Let's try a canter now, just for a few minutes." Mary flicked the rein a third time, and Ebony tossed her head and began a slow, easy canter.

Father O'Brien liked this fluid gait the best. Leaning slightly forward in the saddle, it was almost as if he were gliding around the ring. He marveled as he felt the black mare's strength gathering and pushing with each stride and his own exhilaration in being carried so effortlessly.

After a few times around, Mary slowed Ebony to a walk. "It seemed like you were having fun," she said, watching the young priest settle back into the saddle. His tall, lanky form looked goofy astride the small Morgan. Even sitting properly with his feet in the stirrups, Father O'Brien was all elbows and knees. Mary couldn't help but laugh when, after he dismounted, his walk was slightly bowlegged and he winced with every step.

"Consider it penance," she said, winking at him, and giggling at his openmouthed surprise. "Don't worry, Michael, we'll toughen you up."

She was right. With some practice and more careful instruction, Father O'Brien grew comfortable riding Ebony. He didn't wish to ride either of the other horses, and Mary didn't blame him. Being a Thoroughbred, Penny was a bit highly strung for a beginner. Monarch was a gelding now, but he had retained some stallionlike mischievousness and was sometimes difficult under saddle.

Both Ebony and Penny had delivered foals during the war, a result of Monarch having discovered a weakness in the fence separating his and the mares' pastures. Penny's foal was a colt, a dark chestnut, while Ebony's was a blood bay filly who was a miniature copy of her sire. Mary was delighted at the foals' arrivals, but she decided that five horses were enough. She asked Father O'Brien to arrange a visit from the veterinarian to see to Monarch, and had waited anxiously in the mansion until the priest had come up from the barn to tell her that all had gone well.

Sometimes, they didn't go riding at all, but just walked around the pasture, talking, offering occasional treats to the horses. Father O'Brien had never seen young horses play, and he couldn't get enough of watching their antics.

"They're just like children," he said one afternoon at the pasture, as the filly nipped and squealed at the little colt. The colt squealed back, kicking up his heels and rushing over to hide behind Penny. "Squabbling and fighting! The way they lay their ears back and frown makes them look like they're pouting!"

"They are pouting," Mary agreed. "But they can be very sweet, too. See?" The filly had come to her and was nuzzling her fingers. "And each of them will have a distinct character, just like a person. It's one of the things I really love about them."

"I never thought of horses that way," Father O'Brien said, "but I guess I'll get to see these little ones grow up." He smiled as the filly stretched her nose out to him. "She sure likes attention."

They had named the filly Ruby, for her bright red coat. A name for the colt eluded them for weeks, though, until one day they saw him prance around and around, trying to get the attention of his mother and the other horses. Despite his squeals and circling, the other horses just grazed contentedly, and the little colt had finally flopped onto the grass in a dizzy, uncoordinated heap.

"What a show!" Father O'Brien said, holding his sides. Mary was laughing, too, although baby horse antics were not such a surprise to her. Still chuckling, Father O'Brien wiped at his eyes. "I can't remember the last time I saw something so funny," he said. "He's like a little jester, trying to entertain the royal court."

And so the little chestnut colt was Jester. Mary thought the name especially fitting since his daddy was Monarch.

As American soldiers returned home from the war, Mary's life returned to normal, or, at least, as normal as it could get. She joined the Book-of-the-Month Club, as her appetite for new reading material was voracious. She added more shelves to the library upstairs and lost herself among the titles.

Conor was finally able to resume his frequent visits. Mary eagerly watched for his car and felt a surge of excitement when she spotted it coming through the center of town toward her home. She threw open the door and embraced him before he could even ring the doorbell. "Easy now," Conor said, laughing. "Wouldn't want to topple your grandpop, now would you?" Of course, this was nonsense; he was as tall and stout as ever.

Mary had almost forgotten how much she looked forward to seeing his kind, cheery face. During his first visit back to her home, they talked for hours, with Conor telling stories of being cooped up with his family during the war.

"Stephen was so beside himself. All he seemed to do was complain that he couldn't drive any of those cars of his. He still waxed and polished them every week. Then there was Elise, always fretting and worrying that Jake would be drafted into the military. She about drove us all crazy. The last straw was when Sara and Emma came to blows over who would wear the last unripped pair of nylon stockings. Jake and Stephen had to separate them, if you can imagine that! They insisted on keeping their nylons, you know, even though most other folks were turning them in so the government could use them to make parachutes. Don't get me wrong, I love my family, but I tell you, they're all spoiled and selfish." Conor shook his head. "I had taken to walking in the evenings, just to get away from everything. I think we were all at our wits' end, because the war went on so long and there was really nothing we could do."

"You must have spent lots of time writing," Mary said. "Your letters meant so much to me. I can't tell you how much I looked forward to reading them. Each time I opened one, it was almost as if you were here. And you were so busy at the marble-works. Surely that helped keep you from feeling cooped up at home."

"Well, yes. We haven't done much with marble in some time, though. We've been making gun sights and rifle-barrel drillers and so many other things. As fast as the parts come in, we assembled them and shipped them out. Made my job easy, really. All I had to do was sign the papers at each end of the process."

Mary nodded. "And what will you do now that the war is over?"

Conor shrugged. "Oh, we'll go back to cutting marble at some point, but we've got to get some orders in first. It's a period of transition, I suppose. The country's recovering, but I expect it will be a while before people start wanting marble again. Except for tombstones, maybe."

"Well, I think you should spend your spare time out here while you wait for business to pick up again," Mary told him. She smiled and bounced off the sofa. "Let's go down to the barn. You won't believe how the babies have grown."

The next week, Mary was expecting Conor's visit, but it was a whey-faced Father O'Brien who came to her door.

"Michael! What's wrong? Are you sick?" Mary asked as she pulled him inside.

"No. Well, yes. I have some horrible news." He watched her face shift from surprise to concern. He saw a spark of realization in her good eye, a kind of knowing, as if, perhaps, on some subconscious level, she had already guessed what he dreaded to tell her. "Bishop Ross just phoned me." He lowered his voice and spoke more slowly in an effort to soften the effect of his words. "Conor died in his sleep last night. Oh, Mary, I'm so sorry."

"What?" she gasped. He caught her as her knees buckled, helped her to a chair in the kitchen as she gripped his arm, shaking her head. "It can't be," she said. "He was coming to visit me today, in a few minutes."

"I'm sure that he had every intention of doing so. I didn't believe it myself at first, Mary." Father O'Brien pulled up another chair and sat down beside her. She looked as though she was just starting to get her mind around the idea. At last, the tears began to fall, and her chin trembled when she tried to speak. "I am so sorry," he kept repeating, but his words were pitifully inadequate.

"I don't understand," she finally said. "He wasn't sick at all. There was no reason for him to die."

"No reason known to us, anyway," Father O'Brien agreed. Mary couldn't speak. He straightened up in his chair and cleared his throat. "The bishop said that things are still chaotic at the McAllister house in Rutland, but that it looks as if the wake and funeral Mass might be held the day after tomorrow. I would be happy to drive you, if you'd like."

"No." Her sharp refusal was tinged with terror. "No, I couldn't go, with all the people that will be there, the rest of the family." Her gaze focused on the kitchen floor. "Besides, I don't want to see him that way. I'd rather remember him as he was when he came here to see me."

Her response was exactly what Father O'Brien had expected. He nodded, took her hand, and squeezed it. "I'm sure Conor would have appreciated that," he said. "Here, let me get you a glass of water." When he went to stand up, she shook her head.

"No, no water. Please, just sit here with

me a little while longer?"

"Of course, Mary. I'll stay as long as you'd like."

Conor's death brought to Father O'Brien a new understanding of the immensity of the promise he had made to the head of the McAllister family. He had become Mary's sole source of human companionship and conversation. He still had every intention of keeping his promise, of course, but would he be able to honor it for a lifetime? He worried that something, some decision over which he had no control, some circumstance that he could not foresee, would force him from Mill River. What would become of Mary without him?

It was true, in the beginning at least, that he kept in touch with her purely out of obligation and, perhaps, pity. Now, though, he had come to value the relationship. He had become attached to her, though not in any way that was improper. He was sure that few people, if any, were aware of his visits to the marble house, and he thought this a good thing lest someone make any sort of unfounded accusation against him. Such an accusation would jeopardize their relationship, a relationship that was unlike any other he had known.

To visit Mary was to escape from his normal obligations. Her home was a place of refuge, her personality unique among the people he saw on a regular basis. She was clever and delightful and totally uninfluenced by what others had or thought or did. She took in what information was available to her and formed her own opinions. Within the confines of her home and the boundaries of her property, she was a happy source of stability and confidence.

Of course, all of this changed if he made the slightest suggestion that she leave the grounds of the mansion, or if a person she didn't know was required to stop by to see to a leak in the roof or a portion of fence that needed mending. She would never see the person, always asking Father O'Brien to supervise whatever the business was while she took refuge in her library or bedroom until the stranger had departed. She never answered the phone.

He did as she wished, all the while wondering what could possibly have caused her to develop the anxiety in the first place. Since he had first inquired about it, he hadn't dared ask her again. But he felt confident that, if she would only venture out with him, he could help her. He could introduce her to people who would be accepting of her affliction and her appearance. Perhaps he could show her that she had nothing to fear from her neighbors.

Eventually, he got what he hoped for, but when she finally agreed to try to face people again, the results were disastrous.

One year, he convinced Mary to participate in Halloween. *A good opportunity,* he thought. *She can meet dozens of people while staying in the familiar surroundings of her home.* He brought her an enormous pumpkin, and together they scooped out the seeds and stringy innards and carved it into a jack-o'-lantern. Mary spent all Halloween day baking batches of cookies and wrapping small packages of them in aluminum foil. Toward evening, she insisted that he attend the Halloween celebration at St. John's as he had planned, since she wanted to attempt to give out the cookies by herself.

He never should have left her.

When he came to check on her later that evening, he'd found the jack-o'-lantern smashed, the walkway littered with broken eggs. He still remembered seeing the cookie basket abandoned in the foyer and Mary crying in the closet.

"I couldn't do it," she'd said. "There were so many little children . . . they rang and knocked over and over, and they waited for so long. I wanted to open the door, and I really, truly tried, but I couldn't. And then, a few of them came back. They were yelling horrible things and banging on the door. I was so scared, Michael. And I wanted so much for tonight to be happy."

Between sobs, she told him what happened. All evening, she'd heard their calls of "trick or treat." She stood in the foyer, trembling, with the basket of cookies in her arms. She had never been able to open the door and face them.

It pained him to hear her describe the strange sounds she heard after several hours of visits by innocent trick-or-treaters. Sounds of pumpkins being smashed, wild laughter, shouts of "Stingy old witch!" Every few minutes, someone thumped violently on her front door. She'd seen ominous shadows moving past the windows and was terrified that someone or something would come crashing through. She even considered calling the police, but she decided against it. The thought of using the telephone was as horrible as doing nothing. It had been all Mary could do to crawl into the hall closet and hide.

"Don't worry, Mary dear," he'd told her. "I should have stayed with you. But you tried, you did your best, and that's what matters."

After that day, it had been years before he suggested again that she attempt to interact with strangers.

Still, he often had to squelch the part of him that wanted to drag her, kicking and screaming, if necessary, into the outside world. Despite her assurances to the contrary, he knew that she was sometimes lonely. He had seen the expressions of longing that crossed her face more and more often as she looked down at Mill River. He knew that she was imagining herself as a real member of the community. Surely, he told himself, persuading her to seek treatment would be better for her in the long run. Surely, with proper counseling and support, she could overcome her anxiety and live her life as a normal person. Surely.

But he couldn't, wouldn't do it. She had suffered so much pain in her life already, and she insisted that she was happy, even as isolated as she was. Living as she did kept her from having to suffer through encounters with her anxiety. He couldn't, wouldn't take that security from her.

"Children grow up so quickly."

At the kitchen table in the mansion, Mary sighed and spread in front of her the most recent *Mill River Gazette.* The headline on the front page read "Class of 1968," and she had just pulled out the pictures of the graduating students included in a special insert. "Michael, do you remember the youngest Wilson boy?"

Father O'Brien looked up from scribbling notes for an upcoming sermon. "Do you mean little Eddie? Of course. Why do you ask?"

"He's not little anymore. He's valedictorian this year and has a full scholarship for college."

"If he isn't sent to Vietnam, you mean. Let's hope he's not."

"I can't stand to think of all the kids who are ending up over there. War is always such a horrible thing." Mary sighed again. "I've watched Edward Wilson spend every Saturday afternoon down in the library, and sometimes more than that during the summers. He's done so well. In fact, all these kids have done well to graduate. I feel like they're my own, in a way. I hate to think of any of them growing up and leaving."

"As do I, Mary dear," Father O'Brien said softly. He watched as Mary, smiling and remembering, pored over the senior class portraits. Her joy at seeing the students reassured him that she wasn't being crushed by the weight of her isolation. He brought her news about others in the town, activities at the schools, marriages, and people who had moved in or moved away. She knew the names and ages of most of the townspeople, what they did for a living, whether they were children or had children, when they were ill or doing well. She asked about them, cared about them, and he told her everything he could without violating any of his vows. She remembered it all.

It was only natural, he supposed, that Mary became attached to the people in town, even from a third-party perspective. Her close attention to the graduation issue of the *Gazette* was an annual ritual. But recently, she had begun to do more than observe and listen to his stories of her neighbors.

With his help, she had begun to provide small, anonymous gifts to the people she secretly knew. The gifts weren't very much at first, at least as compared with Mary's wealth. A hundred dollars to help the family of a man who'd been killed in the new war. Packages of diapers and baby clothes for new parents. Birthday cards containing ten-dollar bills for the children in town. He made sure that the gifts were delivered late at night, when the recipients were asleep.

Father O'Brien wished so much that Mary could see firsthand the joy she brought to the townspeople. She was creating within the town a sense of security, a feeling of wondrous gratitude toward an unknown benefactor. He did his best to convey it to her, although his own knowledge of the recipients' reactions to Mary's gifts was usually limited and never as satisfying as seeing them in person would have been. It made no difference to Mary, though. "In our world, even small gestures of kindness are remembered," she often reminded him. Just knowing that she had helped made her happy.

The appreciation of her neighbors was only a small part of what Father O'Brien wished that Mary could see. During the summer of 1972, he figured out a way to change everything.

To celebrate thirty years of friendship, he bought for Mary a brand-new RCA color television set. True, she had always loved her radio and had never expressed much interest in the newer technology, but the times were changing. Most of the programs were broadcast in color, and the screens of the newer TVs were larger than those of earlier models. A television could bring to

Mary a real-life view of the world that her anxiety kept from her.

At once, Mary's radio faced serious competition. She stared at the news anchors' faces, fascinated by every muscle movement and nuanced expression. She told him repeatedly how wonderful it was to be spoken to by a strange person, to be able to listen to and enjoy seeing the new person on the television screen without being overcome by fear.

She delighted in watching Mutual of Omaha's *Wild Kingdom* and loved the Cookie Monster on *Sesame Street.* "It's those googly eyes," she told him as she watched the blue monster gorge himself on cookies after singing about the letter *C.* "I think I could've opened the door for him that Halloween."

Mary raved about *The Price Is Right,* admitted to him how she dreamed of being able to run up onstage in front of everyone and kiss Bob Barker on the cheek. Together, they laughed until their sides ached at the old black-and-white reruns of *I Love Lucy.* Mary had never been outside New England, but she experienced the Old West through episodes of *Bonanza.* She watched cooking shows on PBS, cheered as Secretariat won the Triple Crown in the spring of 1973. She looked forward to watching *A Charlie Brown Christmas* again that December.

It was that Peanuts Christmas special that helped her decide to provide new color televisions for every family in Mill River. "No one should have to miss something as precious as that program. And just think, Michael," she said as they worked out the number of RCAs to order and made sure they would be delivered on time, "what it will mean, especially for the children. They'll be able to see things and visit places they've only imagined."

"Yes," he replied, looking at Mary and comparing her to that poor Christmas tree chosen by Charlie Brown. Like the fragile evergreen, he knew that Mary would thrive if only she could experience the support and affection of others.

Father O'Brien's spoon collection continued to grow.

The stolen utensils came from the homes of his parishioners, from restaurants, from hospitals and picnics and just about every place he visited. Only a sample of Mary's flatware was missing. He hated the thought of what he might do, would do, if she hadn't hidden her spoons from him. He didn't blame Mary for insisting that he bring one of his own spoons to use when he came for lunch or dinner, just in case she had prepared something that required the use of that utensil.

Gradually, the unmatched specimens of his thievery came to number over six hundred. They spilled out of their shoe box, into bigger and bigger boxes, until he was forced to store them in the box that once held his RCA. But the square behemoth was too big to fit under his bed or in his closet. He finally shoved it under his desk so that he would be spared the agony of seeing it out in the open, reminding him of his weakness.

Mary never divulged his secret.

Their quiet trust in each other permeated even their usual greetings. It was always, "Good day, Mary," or "Good evening, Michael." A simple smile, the door held open to allow safe passage, a comforting presence. They noticed the gray hair and wrinkles as they appeared, but those physical signs of age changed nothing between them.

It was with delight that Father O'Brien first presented Mary with a pie from the new bakery in town. "It just opened," he told her upon arriving at her home for dinner. "Joe Fitzgerald, you know, the new police chief? His wife, Ruth, is in charge of it. She says she's saving up to run a bed-and-breakfast after Fitz retires. I don't know how she does it, but her pie is amazing. This one's a tart cherry. I thought we'd have some for dessert." After dinner, he smiled at her reaction — curiosity, then surprise, and finally bliss — as she tasted the first bite.

Pie from the bakery became a weekly treat at the marble mansion.

In time, Father O'Brien, and through him, Mary, came to know Fitz and Ruth. The police chief's wife, especially, was loved by everyone. She never spoke a judgmental word about anyone, never gossiped, never refused to help a neighbor in need. With Mary's approval, Father O'Brien asked Ruth to become an assistant for Mary, to see to her shopping and other personal errands. He knew that Ruth would take as much care in selecting Mary's groceries as she would her own. She would be discreet with what he told her of Mary and, most importantly, would be understanding of Mary's refusal to meet her in person. He wasn't surprised when Ruth wouldn't accept a penny in return for her weekly assistance.

■ ■ ■ ■

It was the idea of finally meeting Ruth that prompted Mary to try one more time to interact with her neighbors. "I'm older than I was the last time," she told Father O'Brien, "and hopefully wiser. I know now that I need to do this. To get away from here, somehow. Maybe this time, I will. It's especially not fair to Ruth . . . I feel I owe it to her to try. She does so much for me."

"Well, why don't we go to the bakery for coffee? It's usually quiet after the morning rush, and I know Ruth would be thrilled." Father O'Brien struggled to keep his excitement from his voice — he didn't want it to scare Mary into reconsidering.

Indeed, Father O'Brien arrived early on the designated morning, for he knew that Mary was likely to change her mind or at least put up stiff resistance to leaving her home. It ended up taking two hours just to get her to come down from her bedroom. Another hour passed before she would go with him out the back door to his truck, and her sobbing and quaking as they left the driveway alarmed him. He pulled over on the main road.

"Mary, dear, it's all right," he said to her.

She was cringing in the front seat of the pickup, wearing her eye patch and a light jacket. "Take some deep breaths. Yes, that's it. You're just fine, now. Mary, dear, look at me. Remember how you told me that you had to do this? Fight the anxiety, Mary! It can't touch you, not this time! Right?"

"Yes, keep driving," she wailed, and then said more to herself, "I have to do this. It can't touch me." He steadied his hands on the steering wheel and stepped on the gas, tearing into town before she reversed her decision.

They pulled up in front of the bakery. Mary was quieter now, but she still trembled in the front seat. He reached over to her. "Mary, we're here. You're doing wonderfully. There's no one around. We can slip right inside. Ruth is waiting for us. I'll come around for you — all you have to do is hold on to me."

He went to the other side of the truck to help her down. She clutched at his arm, shivering. Her face was as white as her hair.

They made it to the front door of the bakery, with Father O'Brien talking to Mary all the while. As they were about to go inside, a group of teenage boys came out. The youths were pulling apart warm cinnamon rolls and stuffing their mouths full. It was nearly ten o'clock. Father O'Brien knew the boys were skipping school, but he didn't dare say anything to them for fear of upsetting Mary.

One of the boys looked curiously at him, then down at Mary, and sniggered. Father O'Brien recognized him at once. "Hey, you guys," the young Leroy Underwood said, pointing at Mary, "it's a real live pirate! Arrrgh, shiver me timbers!"

The whole group stopped and stared. A few boys laughed nervously, looking from Leroy to Mary to Father O'Brien. Others just watched quietly. Only Leroy seemed totally unaware of the gravity of the situation.

Mary's scream shocked all of them. She pulled away from Father O'Brien. He expected her to run back to the truck, but she stood her ground, glaring at the youth who had addressed her so rudely, and then closing her eyes.

"YOU CAN'T TOUCH ME! YOU CAN'T TOUCH ME!"

"Man, she's crazy," muttered one of the boys as they shrank away. Mary kept talking to herself with her eyes tightly closed as they ran off.

"YOU CAN'T TOUCH ME! NOT THIS TIME!"

"Mary dear, let's go inside," Father O'Brien said as he touched her arm, but she opened her eyes and screamed again.

"Can't touch me! Michael, I can't, I can't!"

Through the glass front door of the bakery, he saw Ruth Fitzgerald approaching. He frowned at her, shaking his head, and she stopped and watched from inside.

Trembling, Mary turned to face the door of the bakery and saw Ruth looking on. The police chief's wife took a step forward. Father O'Brien stared as Mary saw Ruth's expression of kindness and pity.

"Oh, Ruth," Mary said, and placed a hand over her heart. Just for an instant, a certain acknowledgment registered on Mary's face, a shard of recognition and gratitude, a wisp of friendship. Then she bolted away from him back toward the pickup.

Father O'Brien met Ruth's eyes for an instant but had no choice except to run after Mary, fumbling for the key to open the door of the truck.

He'd barely stopped the pickup outside the door of the mansion when Mary jumped out and ran inside. Father O'Brien followed her, but she locked herself up in her bedroom. He sighed and looked at his watch. When she finally emerged hours later, he was sound asleep on the sofa in the sitting room.

Her hand on his shoulder woke him. He sat up slowly, blinking, relieved to see that she was finally calm again.

"Michael, I —"

"Mary, I didn't hear you come down. Are you all right? I didn't mean to fall asleep here, I just wanted to make sure —"

"— that I'm all right, I know, and don't worry, Michael, I'm fine. Disappointed in myself, but otherwise fine. But there's something else. I owe you an explanation."

"An explanation? Of what? What do you mean?"

"I've been thinking," she said, lowering herself onto the sofa beside him. "All these years, you've been so patient with me. When I get anxious and do what I do, you always take care of me. You try your best to help me, and look what happens. When I think of all the trouble I've caused you, I feel I've been a tremendous burden."

"That's nonsense. You told me a long time ago that no one is perfect. Well, that's true. We're friends, regardless of our faults. Nothing will change that, and you will never be a burden to me."

Mary was quiet a moment. "That's all the more reason I need to explain something to you. I should have done it years ago. It isn't easy for me to even think about it, but you deserve to know what happened to make me the way I am."

Whatever trace of sleepiness Father O'Brien felt vanished. He straightened up against the sofa back and waited for Mary to continue.

"When I was a girl, in high school, I was shy, but I was normal. I loved school. My junior year, though, there was a new English teacher. He took a liking to me, always called on me, watched me during class, that sort of thing. He asked me to come to his classroom after school one Thursday." Mary was shaking now, but he didn't move for fear of causing her to bolt upstairs again. She spoke her next words slowly, as if she were fighting to force them from her mouth.

"When I got to his classroom, he locked us inside. And then he raped me."

"Dear Lord, Mary," Father O'Brien said. Carefully, he reached out and took one of Mary's hands, but she wasn't finished.

"I didn't say anything about it for several days. Not even to my father. I suppose I was trying to convince myself it never happened. I even managed to go back to the classroom for English on Monday. But the teacher made me stand up and read a

345

composition out loud. All the while, he was looking at me with his cold, dark eyes, and it was as if the whole thing was happening again, right there on the classroom floor. I felt so ashamed. Everyone in the class was staring, the room was spinning . . . it was all I could do to get out of there. I was only sixteen.

"They fired the teacher, but I don't think he was ever prosecuted. My father was determined to protect me, to keep me out of the whole mess once everything came out in the open, even if it meant I wouldn't testify against him at trial. And I don't blame him, with what happened afterward. Even with that teacher gone, I never went back to school after that. I couldn't."

"What a horrible, horrible . . . I'm so sorry, Mary," Father O'Brien began, not knowing what he could say in response to such a dreadful story.

Silently, her eyes full of tears, Mary looked at him. Her chin and bottom lip quivered, and she looked as if she were trying to continue, but couldn't.

"Shh, come here." Father O'Brien slid across the sofa and wrapped his arms around Mary. She sobbed into his chest, heaving decades of repressed torment into his black jacket.

"You don't need to say anything else, dear girl. And you have no reason to be ashamed of anything," he said, his chin pressed into her white hair. "No reason at all."

He held her for a long while, finally understanding why she feared so much.

After the incident outside the bakery, Mary never again expressed any interest in leaving her home.

Father O'Brien often looked up at the mansion and saw her increasingly frail form at her bedroom window. The vision in her good eye was beginning to slip, too, for she told him that the buildings along Main Street looked blurry to her. On her next birthday, he gave her a little spyglass that she could use to look out over the town. Binoculars would have been twice what she needed, and with the little telescope, she could view the goings-on in the town below just as she always had.

Although it had been years since Mary had kept horses, he often saw her gazing out the library windows toward the barn and pasture. After Jester and Ruby had died, she refused to replace the horses, saying that she couldn't bear to love and lose another friend. Together, they had created a horse cemetery, with Ebony's marker in the center. The small circle of stones was visible from the library window.

Upon Ebony's death, Father O'Brien had finally returned to Mary the mare's marble likeness. "Conor gave this to me for safekeeping," he told her. "He wanted me to give it back to you when the time was right."

Mary accepted the figurine without hesitation. "What was done to me was not Ebony's fault," she said, and set the little statue on her bureau where she had first kept it.

Her calm acceptance of the figurine took him by surprise, like many other things Mary did. For his eightieth birthday, she presented him with a beautiful mahogany display rack she had mail-ordered from a company in New Jersey. "For your spoons," she told him, and the case was indeed stunning. It had space for perhaps three dozen. "I couldn't resist getting it for you, seeing as how after all these years, I feel almost like your partner in crime," she said with her most feisty grin.

He reminded himself then how she had sewn pockets into the sleeves of his clothing to help facilitate his theft.

"It's beautiful," he said, admiring the fine grain of the wood in the display rack, but found later that he couldn't bring himself to choose from among his hundreds of spoons the thirty-six that would fit in it. This he hadn't the heart to tell her.

For Mary's eighty-second birthday, Father O'Brien brought her a Siamese kitten. Despite her refusal to replace her horses, he thought that perhaps she would appreciate another companion, one that could be with her all the time. Seeing Mary gasp in delight, he chided himself for not thinking of it sooner. Mary named the kitten Sham, after its tendency to sleep on the sham-covered pillows on her bed.

On a sparkling February afternoon just after Mary's ninety-first birthday, Father O'Brien arrived at the back door of the mansion. She usually met him at the door, but this time she did not. He let himself in, calling to her. Perhaps she was in the wash-room.

She heard him and raised herself up off the sofa in the sitting room.

"Oh, Michael! I'm sorry, I guess I dozed off," she said. "I've got lunch all ready, just have to warm it."

She stood up and walked toward the kitchen, toward him. He started to say something, stopped, and squinted at her. He swallowed and looked again. She saw the concern on his face as she approached.

"Michael, what is it?"

He didn't know why, but in looking at her, he knew that something was terribly wrong.

CHAPTER 17

As Father O'Brien was leaving the bakery after finishing his pie and coffee, Claudia was passing out her class's weekly math quiz. "Ready, set, begin," she said, and twenty-three papers were flipped over and twenty-three heads bowed over their desks. The only sound in the room was of pencils scribbling, erasing, being twirled and tapped. She would now have several quiet, uninterrupted minutes to think about last night's date with Kyle. She smiled.

A soft knock at her classroom door interrupted the beginning of her daydream. Joyce Rennert, one of the secretaries from the office, opened the door and leaned in to speak to her.

"Miss Simon, there's a delivery out front for you," she whispered. "I would have brought them with me, but there were so many."

"So many?"

"Roses," Joyce said, giggling. "It looks like whoever sent them bought out the store."

"Oh," Claudia said, and she realized that Leroy's attempt to impress her must have arrived. "I'll come to the office when my class goes to music. Could you keep them down there for me until then?"

"Oh, we'll be happy to." Joyce smiled wistfully. "Brenda and I'll get to pretend that we were the lucky ones who got flowers!"

If you knew who had sent those roses, you wouldn't feel so lucky, Claudia thought, and went back to her students.

A few hours later, Claudia went to see what was waiting for her. Despite the advance notice, she was still shocked. An arrangement of what looked like at least two dozen huge red roses, complete with baby's breath and ferns, sat on the counter in the office. The vase was enormous. Claudia took the card nestled in the greenery and opened it. On the front of the card was a picture of a heart in flames, while the printed message inside read, "My heart burns for you." There was also a handwritten note:

Claudia,

Roses are red,
Vilets are blue,

352

Wouldn't you know,
I've been thinking about you.

                    Have a nice day.
            Officer Leroy Underwood.

She had to struggle to read the poem, as it was scrawled in terrible handwriting. She noticed right away that "violets" was misspelled. For a minute, she almost felt sorry for Leroy, until she remembered the way he had stared at her in her classroom. She shuddered. The roses were beautiful, but she wanted nothing more to do with them.

Joyce came up beside her and sighed. "They sure are something else. I wonder if they'll even fit in your car?"

"I suppose I could get them in somehow. I think I'll leave them down here until school's out for the day." The truth was, she really didn't want to take them home. She started thinking of ways she could get rid of the whole lot.

"The office already smells like roses! Just think how they'll be in your house! By the way, who sent them to you? What's the occasion?" Joyce's eyes glittered in anticipation of learning a juicy tidbit of gossip.

"Just someone I met recently," Claudia said. "No occasion. I think he wanted to surprise me." She had no intention of letting word get out that she was the object of Leroy Underwood's hot pursuit.

Joyce's expression dimmed.

Just as Claudia turned to go back to her classroom, a man wearing a hat that read KATHY'S FLOWERS AND GIFTS came up to the office. He set a bud vase holding a single, delicate pink rose on the counter. "Hello again," he said to Joyce. "I tell you, this Miss Simon person is popular today. Second order for her, and it's not even noon."

Hearing her name, Claudia backtracked to the office window. "I'm Claudia Simon," she said.

"Well, lucky lady, this was just called in for you." He pushed the bud vase toward her before turning to leave. "Have a good one."

Joyce's eyes were wide with disbelief. She raised her eyebrows and looked at Claudia but didn't say a word.

The little card hanging from the bud vase read, "Just wanted you to know I had a great time last night. Looking forward to tomorrow night. Kyle."

"Another recent acquaintance?" Joyce asked.

"Yes," Claudia said, picking up the bud vase. She never would have guessed that a single rose from one man would outdo two dozen from another, but Kyle's choice had been perfect. She beamed down at it. "I'll definitely take this one with me."

On her way home from school that afternoon, Claudia pitched Leroy's Valentine's Day card and dropped off his mass of roses at a nursing home just outside Mill River. Mission accomplished, she sang along with the radio in her car all the way home. When her phone rang for the first time that night, she was sitting at the kitchen table with the bud vase, grading papers. Still feeling warm and fuzzy, she reached to answer it.

"Hello?"

"Claudia." The drawl said it all.

"Yes?"

"It's Leroy Underwood. How are you doing tonight?" Claudia rolled her eyes at the ceiling. He sounded like a telemarketer with a bad script.

"Fine, thank you," she said. "I was pretty surprised this morning, shocked, really, about the roses. They're beautiful. And the card, too. Thank you." She had to force herself to say the words, didn't care if it was apparent that they were spoken with all the feeling of a piece of cardboard.

"Not as beautiful as you, and I was hoping you'd be surprised. I just wanted to know, are your legs tired?"

"My legs? No," Claudia said, wondering why he could possibly be asking about her exercise routine. "Why do you ask?"

"Well, 'cause ever since Kyle and me visited your classroom, they've been runnin' through my mind. By the way, you had a real pretty blouse on that day." His words came out thick and numb, as if he had been gnawing on them for some time. He paused, and Claudia could almost see his mouth stretching into a slimy smile on the other end of the phone. Revolted, she said nothing, and Leroy blathered on, although he lowered his voice to a husky whisper. "And what that card said was true, you know. I got it on my way to work the other day. So I was thinking, how'd you like to go out with me this week?"

Absolutely not, Claudia thought, but she struggled to remain polite. "Oh. To be honest, I have a lot of papers to grade in the evenings, for my class. And lesson plans to prepare." She hoped her tone of voice would convey the message to Leroy, but he persisted.

"Well, tomorrow night's Valentine's Day, you know," he said. "Let's you and me go to Rutland for a night on the town. We'll go to the King's Lodge. I'll make it your lucky night." He sounded impatient, almost insistent, as if she owed him a date.

Claudia brought out her solid excuse. "The thing is, Leroy, I've got to be at school bright and early Friday morning, and I already have something planned for Thursday. I'm actually seeing someone right now." For a fleeting second, she wondered whether one past and one prospective date qualified as "seeing someone" and then decided that now was not the time to worry about it. "But thank you for asking. And thank you again for the roses and card. They were lovely."

"Oh. Yeah. Sure. Then have a good night," Leroy said. His voice was dry and frustrated.

"Same to you," Claudia said, and hung up. Waves of relief washed over her. *That should take care of Leroy,* she thought.

The phone rang again.

Surely, he wasn't calling back for another attempt?

She would screen the call. After four rings, her answering machine clicked. A friendly voice came through the speaker.

"Hi, Claudia, it's Kyle. I was just calling to —" Claudia seized the phone before he could say anything else.

"Kyle? Hi, I'm sorry about the machine," she said. "I would've answered, but Leroy just called. I thought the phone ringing was him again."

Kyle laughed. "No problem, I understand. I hear he really did it with the flowers."

"Yes, it was quite a scene. The office girls couldn't believe it, especially when the man from the flower shop came back with your rose. Thank you, by the way. It's beautiful."

"My pleasure. I asked for red, initially, but the flower shop was fresh out of red roses. I wonder how that could've happened?"

Claudia had to laugh at his mock surprise. "I didn't even bring Leroy's flowers home. I didn't want anything to do with them. And just now, on the phone, he reminded me why."

"So he wanted to get together this week?"

"Yeah, he was pretty disgusting. He wanted to go out tomorrow night, and he got a little pushy about it, in the end. Unfortunately for Leroy, I already have plans," Claudia said lightly.

"Plans, the plans! Yes! That's what I was calling about! I got reservations at the King's Lodge at six o'clock tomorrow. We could go to a movie afterward if you'd like. I can come by for you at about five-thirty."

"That would be great," Claudia said. "I'll see you tomorrow, then."

"Yup. See you tomorrow."

Claudia hung up the phone for the second time. All was right with the world.

It was sometime during that night that a brand-new Jeep appeared at the police station.

It was parked there in the morning when Fitz arrived to start his shift. Despite the frigid temperature, he stayed outside for a moment to admire it. It was a polished white Grand Cherokee, so white that it humiliated even the deep, fresh snow in which it was parked. Looked brand-new, or close to it. He rumpled his mouth and wondered whose it was. A new Grand Cherokee like that was about thirty grand, maybe more with options. He stepped closer and peered in the side window — it probably had heated seats to boot. The owner of this baby sure was a lucky devil.

Fitz walked through the snow and around the front of the Jeep, heading for the door to the police station, when he noticed the envelope. It was tucked into the base of the windshield, and his name was on it. Taking care not to slip, he grasped the envelope and hurried into the station.

Ron Wykowski was putting on his coat, getting ready to leave. " 'Lo, Chief," he said, and yawned. "Another slow night. I just put some fresh coffee on."

"Morning, Ron," he said, but his attention was focused on the envelope. He opened it and pulled out a thick stack of papers and booklets. On top was another sealed envelope, again with his name written on the front. The next item in the stack was what looked like a bill of sale. Underneath that was an owner's manual. And the last item in the stack was a certificate of registration that listed the Mill River Police Department as the owner of the Jeep.

"Can't be," Fitz muttered, staring at the registration. "Ron, did you see who parked that white Jeep outside?"

"What Jeep?" He came over to the counter where Fitz had spread out the contents of the envelope. "What's all this?"

"There's a brand-new Jeep Grand Cherokee in the lot. You have any idea who parked it there, or how long it's been there?"

"Nope. I mean, it wasn't there when I came on shift last night. That was at eleven, and I didn't leave the station after that. What's going on?"

"I was hoping you knew," Fitz said, as he plucked the registration out of the papers on the counter. "Take a look at this."

Ron's eyes widened as he read the certificate. "There's really a new Jeep out there?" He handed the registration back to Fitz and went to the window. "Holy shit."

"My gut's telling me this is some cockamamie prank, but this registration looks authentic," Fitz said. He opened the second, smaller envelope that had been inside the first. It contained a short typed letter.

Dear Fitz,
Please accept this new Jeep as a replacement for the one your department recently lost. It has been registered in the department's name and has been fully paid for. The title should be issued by the DMV within a few weeks. Your department will need only to cover insurance payments, which should be manageable.

Best wishes,
A resident of Mill River

P.S. Keys are in the glove compartment.

"Ron! Ron, go outside and check in the glove compartment, will you?" Fitz asked. "The doors are open. This letter says the keys are in there."

Ron was more than happy to oblige, and he returned in a matter of seconds with two sets of keys. "It's brand-new, and loaded," he reported. "It's got the new-car smell, and the odometer reads nineteen miles. It must not've been out there too long, because there's not a bit of snow on it, even though we got almost a foot last night."

"Must've been bought in Rutland," Fitz said. "There's a Jeep dealership up there."

"Yeah, but who bought it?" Ron asked.

"Looks like somebody in Mill River," Fitz said, showing him the letter.

"Somebody who knew about Leroy's accident," Ron said, when he, too, had read it. " 'Course by now, that's probably everyone in town."

"I'm going to make some calls. I still don't believe this whole thing is legit." Fitz sat down at the desk and pulled out the Rutland County yellow pages. Then he remembered his conversation with Father O'Brien the morning before, and the priest's confident reassurance that "everything would work out in the end," and wondered if his first call shouldn't be to Father O'Brien.

"Well, if this is for real," Ron said, looking out the window again, "I hope you don't let Leroy anywhere near it."

By late morning on Thursday, Daisy was a wreck.

For more than two hours, she had been looking out the front window every few minutes, checking to see whether the mailman had come. She was wearing her snow boots and hooded parka, ready to dash outside the moment he arrived. He usually reached her house by ten-thirty, but it was nearly noon and he had yet to show up.

Maybe, just maybe, he would bring a valentine for her this year.

Maybe he had already delivered to the houses along her street. Maybe she had missed him and there had been no mail at all for her.

Daisy had been on that dreadful emotional roller coaster all morning, cycling from the memory of bitter disappointment from years with no valentines to the fervent hope of the thought that perhaps this year would be different. Smudgie sensed that something was bothering her. He sat on the sofa, whining occasionally, and watched her with a worried expression as she paced from one end of her mobile home to the other.

With an impatient sigh, Daisy peered again out her living room window. Even the sun hadn't bothered to come out. The sky was dingy and cold and heavy. Although it had snowed heavily the previous night, it looked like they were in for more.

She let go of the curtain and felt a light puff of air on her face as it fell back across the window. Just as she turned to resume her pacing, a shadow became visible through the curtain. It stopped in front of her house. Daisy zipped up her parka and threw open the front door.

Finally!

Taking care not to slip, she scooted down her walkway to the mailbox. The postman was only two houses down the road by the time she reached it. She took a deep breath, pulled down the squeaky mailbox door, and plunged her hand inside.

She pulled out a glossy sheet of Pizza Hut coupons. There was nothing else inside.

Daisy sniffed, glanced around to see if anyone was watching her. A hard knot was forming in the pit of her stomach. Her chin quivered. She leaned back against the mailbox for support, but her feet slipped out from under her. Daisy fell with a thud into the dirty snow piled along the road.

The indignity of her situation was too much. She groaned and squeezed her eyes shut, sobbing the low, miserable heaves of a devastated soul. It was a long time before she felt the sting of tears freezing on her cheeks and heard her neighbor's hound baying almost in unison with her cries.

When she finally collected herself and trudged back to her trailer, Smudgie met her at the door and followed her into the kitchen. He whined again and she scooped him up into her arms. "Oh, Smudgie," she whispered into his gray fur, "Why doesn't anybody love us?"

Daisy set Smudgie on his favorite kitchen chair, removed her parka, and tore off a paper towel to dry her eyes. She tried to be friendly and sociable with her neighbors and other folks in town. The thought of hurting anyone, shunning anyone, had never occurred to her, and she wondered why no one, except for Father O'Brien, was ever friendly toward her. She was even nice to Officer Underwood, although she didn't care for him one bit. No sirree Bob, she would never like anyone who had been mean to Smudgie.

She smoothed the fur on the little dog's head and wondered how she could have even thought that someone might remember her on Valentine's Day. Except for Smudgie and Father O'Brien, she hadn't any real friends, much less anybody who was more than a friend. She wondered if it would always be that way.

A single bottle of bright red liquid sat on Daisy's countertop. It was the only bottle of her love potion that she hadn't managed to sell. Of course, she wouldn't let it go to waste. She looked at it for a moment before she twisted off the cap. She poured a bit into a saucer for Smudgie and took a drink of it herself. Tiny snowflakes began to drift downward from the sky. She swallowed, closed her eyes, took another sip.

There was always next year.

She summoned every bit of her magical power and hoped the familiar hope that next year would be different.

Jean Wykowski was doing dishes on Valentine's Day.

It was already after noon, but Ron was still in bed, recovering from having worked all night. Unfortunately, he was on the graveyard shift again tonight. The previous night's snowfall had caused school and its Valentine's Day festivities to be canceled, so Jimmy and Johnny were sprawled on the living room carpet amid a sea of undelivered cheap pink and red grade-school valentines, taunting each other about who would have gotten more of them from the girls in their classes. In a few years, that teasing would take on a whole new meaning. The boys would actually want to receive valentines from girls, and Jean didn't want to think about that day.

She heard a creaking from the bedroom down the hall, heard the thump of Ron's feet hitting the floor as he got out of bed. After a few minutes, he padded up behind her and slipped his arms around her waist.

"Morning, hon," he said, and kissed the back of her head. His breath was awful.

"Afternoon, you mean," she said, turning around and placing a soapy hand over his mouth. His eyes widened in surprise, and he took a step back. "Morning breath, dear."

"Oh, sorry." Now he covered his own mouth and disappeared back down the hall. Jean heard running water and the quick, rhythmic scrubbing of his toothbrush. She resumed her washing.

"Minty fresh," he said, appearing for the second time. "Can I have a Valentine's kiss now?" She turned from the sink and looked at him standing in front of her in baggy sweats and a T-shirt with his hair plastered straight up on one side.

"Hmm. You do look pretty cute with your hair all messed up," she said, and puckered up.

"Where are the kids?"

"In the living room, looking at the valentines they were going to take to their school parties. Why?"

"Well, I was thinking," he said, "just a kiss is pretty weak for today, don't you think? And since I'm gonna be stuck at the station again tonight . . . do you wanna fool around?"

Jean rolled her eyes at the ceiling. She had the day off, her first after working three days in a row of twelve-hour shifts, and she wasn't exactly feeling frisky.

"We can't do it with the kids in here," she whispered, but, with eerie timing, Jimmy and Johnny streaked through the kitchen to the back door to grab their coats and boots.

"Mom! It's starting to snow again!" Jimmy yelled.

"We're going out to build a snow fort," Johnny said. "We tried during recess at school yesterday, but we didn't have enough time."

"Yeah, and it caved in, anyway," Jimmy said, pulling on his boots.

"Did you boys pick up the valentines you had on the floor?"

"Aw, Mom, we'll do it later."

"Yeah, as soon as we come in, promise."

"Sure, hon, let them go ahead. It's only a few pieces of paper," Ron said, winking and nudging her with his elbow.

She was outnumbered by hopeful faces. "All right," she said. "If you two promise to clean up the mess in there when you come in, because I'm sure not going to end up doing it."

"We will, Mom, don't worry."

"Yeah. Thanks, Mom."

The back door had been closed not even two seconds before Ron was gently pulling her down the hall.

"What if the boys come back inside while we're right in the middle?"

"It's not like we won't be able to hear them come in," Ron said. "Besides, there's nothing like the feeling that you might get caught." They were in the bedroom now, and he was stripping off his clothes with gusto.

"Hmm." She remembered the time in high school when they had sneaked into his father's garage, into the covered back of his pickup truck, to fool around. Ron's dad had come into the garage to get an extension cord and left again without realizing they were buck naked in his vehicle.

Ron turned around, and she found herself looking down at his behind. It still looked pretty good to her, even after thirteen years of marriage. She glanced out the bedroom window facing the backyard. The kids were happily piling up big snowballs outside. She quickly lowered the shades.

"You remember the time we did it in your dad's pickup?" she asked, climbing onto the bed.

"Y-e-es," he said slowly, with a wicked grin. "Why?"

"Oh, I was just thinking, maybe the next time you're on patrol in that new Jeep, you should pick me up and we could . . . initiate it."

"Hell, yes!" he said, sliding under the covers with her. She squealed and giggled as he pulled her against him. "Jeanie Wykowski," he said, nuzzling her face, "I almost forgot what a naughty girl you can be."

Afterward, they dressed quickly, in case the boys came back inside, and sprawled out on the bed together.

"Too bad you have to work tonight," Jean said.

"Yeah, I know." Ron sat up suddenly. "Hey, I've got a little something for you to keep with you while I'm at work." He was grinning now, going to his chest of drawers, removing a small box from the top drawer.

"What do you mean?" Jean sat up as he came back to the bed.

"I can't believe I almost forgot this. I've had it a while now. Here." He offered her the small box. "Happy Valentine's Day."

She didn't know what to expect as she

flipped open the top, but what was inside was something she never expected Ron to give her. It was a three-stone diamond ring — with diamonds far bigger than they could afford.

"Ron, it's beautiful, but it must have cost a fortune." She was staring at it, unsure whether she should even remove it from the box.

"Well, I saved up for it out of all the overtime I've been getting. Besides, I know the microwave wasn't really a romantic Christmas gift, and I've wanted to give you something nice like this for a long time. Do you like it?"

"Yes," she admitted, smiling into Ron's anxious face. She carefully pulled the ring from the foam in the box and slipped it onto the ring finger of her right hand. It fit perfectly. "Wow," she said, holding out her hand. "It's so sparkly."

"The center stone is a half carat and the side stones are quarter carats. I wanted to get you a ring with three stones for the past, the present, and the future." He looked so proud of himself that she dared not laugh at his repetition of the cheesy marketing pitch.

"Honey, it's really, really beautiful," she said, and kissed him. "I think it's the best Valentine's Day present yet. But I don't have anything for you," she said, frowning. "I didn't think we were doing anything this year . . ."

"Oh, don't worry. You can give me my Valentine's present a little late."

Ron was grinning suggestively. Jean raised her eyebrows. "You look as though you already have a present in mind."

"Indeed I do," he said, pulling her back down on the bed to cuddle. "Actually, it was your idea."

"Oh, really?"

"Yeah. I want to go for a ride in the new Jeep with you."

Claudia was determined that everything be perfect.

Her hair was under control. She was wearing her favorite skirt with sheer tights and a new, low-cut mauve sweater. Underneath them, she wore a new lacy bra and matching thong underwear. This would be her first romantic date, after which there might be a very real possibility of finally, finally being with a man for the first time. She wondered what it would be like, if it happened.

But no matter. She resolved not to worry about it and to enjoy the evening. She glanced over at Kyle sitting behind the wheel as they drove into Rutland. He was squinting as snowflakes peppered the wind-shield like powdery moths, slowing the pickup to turn into the parking lot of the King's Lodge.

It was a cozy restaurant, with French provincial styling on the outside and crack-ling fireplaces inside. The hostess checked their coats and showed them to a small, out-of-the-way table in the dining room.

"This place looks wonderful," Claudia said once they were seated. While Kyle ordered a bottle of wine, she looked up at the dark-stained beams running across the ceiling and the tables spaced nicely to allow for private conversation. A little candle lamp glowed on each table. Other than the fire-places and a few soft overhead fixtures, the candle lamps provided the only illumina-tion.

"It does," Kyle agreed. "I haven't been here before, but I've heard it's got good food and the nicest atmosphere in Rutland." He grinned across the table at her. "Given his usual taste, I'm surprised ol' Leroy even suggested it to you."

"I'm just glad I'm not here with him," Claudia said. "He definitely would've ruined the atmosphere." She laughed as Kyle's brown eyes twinkled at her. It occurred to her that she was flirting, and it felt perfectly natural.

"So, I'm curious. What exactly did he say to you on the phone?" Kyle asked. The waiter returned with a bottle of merlot and poured a glass for each of them.

Claudia repeated the conversation with Leroy as best she could remember. Kyle just shook his head and chuckled. "One bad pickup line after another. Well, now you understand why he can't get women to go for him."

"Yeah. But I think I pretty much discouraged him. And I told the truth — I did already have a date." Claudia batted her eyelashes at Kyle over the top of her menu.

"Hmmm." Kyle smiled at her again, looking proud of himself.

As Kyle focused on his own menu, Claudia discreetly studied him. She wasn't so nervous, and not nearly as flustered as she had felt at the Pizza Hut. He was wearing a thick, oatmeal-colored sweater with a crew neck. She noticed the way his square chin curved into his clean-shaven jaw, how his dark hair was cut closer at the temple. The light from the flickering candle lamp cast shadows that played across his face and hands.

She especially liked his hands. His palms

and fingers were well proportioned. They were neither too big nor too small, and he kept his nails neatly trimmed. The silver band of his wristwatch peeked out from under his left sleeve and sparkled in the candlelight as he casually tapped his fingertips on the table. She watched the outline of the tendons on the back of his hand that extended from his wrist to his knuckles. Kyle's were strong, capable hands, the type that could keep a viselike grip on someone under arrest or gently wipe away a little girl's tears.

She wanted him to touch her with those hands.

The waiter arrived to take their order, and Claudia hoped that the dim light would disguise her blushing.

Claudia discovered that the food wasn't just good — it was unbelievably good. Having decided to make an exception and eat as she pleased, she helped herself to the hot bread the waiter brought, smearing it with the heavenly shallot butter that accompanied it. She ordered salmon with sorrel sauce, rice pilaf, and baby peas. Kyle opted for a New York strip steak and baked potato, with a side of asparagus. The house specialty dessert was something called "pyramid cake," and they decided to split one after they had finished their main courses. The waitress brought them a dish to share, along with two forks. What was placed before them was something out of Claudia's wildest, most fattening cravings — a four-layered, chocolate pyramid of sin with custard between each layer. A rich ganache topped with elegant, curled shavings of chocolate flowed from the peak down over the triangular sides.

"Ladies first," Kyle said, pushing the dish toward her a little. Claudia smiled, lifted her fork, and carefully scooped up a bite. The sweet, moist cake and rich chocolate icing were heavenly. She couldn't help but close her eyes and sigh as she savored the taste.

"That good, huh?" Kyle asked.

Claudia half opened her eyes to see his bemused expression. "You have no idea," she said.

They were still raving about the meal, and especially the dessert, as they put on their coats.

"I can't remember the last time I've eaten like that," Claudia said.

"Yeah," Kyle said, groaning. "I feel like I'm in a food coma."

"A what?" Claudia said, laughing, even though she'd heard him perfectly well. It was such a clever, funny description.

"A food coma. You know, when you're so stuffed that you can't think," Kyle explained. "Like you just want to sack out on the sofa."

"And become a couch potato," Claudia said, still giggling. "Oh, I hope I don't fall asleep during the movie."

Kyle opened the heavy wooden door to the parking lot, and they were confronted by sharp wind and whirling snow. What had been lazy flurries only a few hours ago had become a major snowstorm. Already, the cars in the lot were covered.

"Let's run for it," Kyle said, grabbing her hand. At the pickup truck, he helped Claudia inside and started the engine to clear the windows before shutting the door.

"I didn't hear anything on the weather about another storm," Claudia said once he had joined her. "If it keeps up like this, we won't have school tomorrow, either."

"I heard we were supposed to get only a dusting," he said. "This doesn't look good, though. If we stay for a movie and the snow doesn't let up, we might have trouble getting back. What do you say we leave now and stop to rent a movie instead? Even though it's a school night, I made an exception and let Rowen sleep over at her best friend's house on account of our date. So, it'd just be us and the cat."

"Fine by me," Claudia said, but inside, she was euphoric. Whether it was caused by the warm buzz from the merlot or her raging attraction to him, she didn't know. And she didn't care.

After a quick stop at the local video store, they arrived at Kyle's apartment. It wasn't fancy by any means, but it was clean and neat and nicely decorated. As they came in, she saw a large Siamese cat slink away down the hall.

"Would you like some coffee?" he asked. "I've got decaf."

"Sure. Um, could I use your bathroom?"

"Down the hall on your left. I'll start the coffee and set up the movie."

She didn't really have to use the restroom — she only wanted a moment alone to think. She stood quietly in front of the mirror. Through the door, she could hear the noise of the coffee grinder. It was obvious to her where tonight could lead, if she wanted it to. And she did want it to, desperately. But now, she was starting to think that maybe she shouldn't. A part of her felt that it was too soon. For a few seconds, she looked into her own eyes, noticing the enthusiasm and indecision they held.

And then the lights went off.

She groped around for the doorknob, found it, and walked with little steps into the hallway.

"Kyle?"

"In here." He was still in the kitchen but now digging through a drawer. "I've got a flashlight somewhere. The whole street's black."

She felt along the wall until she came to the armrest of the couch. A faint beam of light shone from the kitchen, and she followed it. When she got there, one working flashlight was lit on the counter, and Kyle was fiddling with a second.

"I think the batteries in this one are dead," he said. "I should've remembered to get new ones." He leaned back against the counter, looking a little disappointed. "I guess someone doesn't want us to watch any movies tonight. However," he said, pausing to hold up the carafe of the coffee-maker, "I am happy to say that I have available for your enjoyment a little less than a cup of freshly brewed decaf."

Claudia giggled as he slid the carafe back under the coffee filter. In that moment, she took a deep breath and pushed her indecision aside. She stepped in front of Kyle, shyly traced her hand up over his fingers, leaned into him just enough so that he put his arms around her waist.

"I don't really want to watch a movie, anyway."

"You don't?" His voice was playful, and with the help of the flashlight, she could see that he was smiling a little, but his eyes were dark and serious.

"No. And the coffee can wait."

He drew her tight against him as he kissed her. She felt his hands at the small of her back, moving up to cup her face. She pulled back a little and opened her eyes, then turned to glance down the hallway toward his bedroom. When she looked back at him again, her eyes told him what she was too timid to say aloud.

In the darkness, there was only his mouth and his hands. The shock of his hands, *those hands,* on her bare skin nearly took her breath away. They unsnapped her bra, slid gently over her breasts, guided the thong down over her hips. He eased her on the bed beside him and found her mouth with his. She felt his fingertips brush her inner thigh.

The wind howled outside, shrieked and rattled against the windowpanes, but Claudia was oblivious to it all.

■ ■ ■ ■

Leroy was in an unusually foul mood.

Since his return to work after the Jeep
mishap, Fitz had relegated him to desk duty.
Except for when the photographer for the
Gazette had come to take a picture of the
officers around the new Jeep, he had been
prohibited from going anywhere near it.
Both his ankles were still sore, one from the
accident and the other from slipping off the
damned curb outside the police station. It
even hurt to drive his Camaro.

But that hurt was nothing like what he
wanted to inflict on Kyle, the asshole. It was
bad enough that Claudia had flat out rejected his Valentine's Day plans.

He could've handled a simple rejection
from her. Could've taken a few days to
regroup and come up with a different approach. Now, though, Kyle was interfering
in his business, and by the way Claudia had
eagerly followed him up to his apartment, it
would take an extra-special effort to distract
her.

Leroy squinted out the windshield, trying
to see through the snow into the window of
the apartment above the bakery. The windows had remained black since the power

went out, but he didn't dare turn on his headlights while he was parked in the idling Camaro.

He had a pretty good idea of what was going on up there.

It was just his luck to be stuck with a partner who'd turn out to be a backstabbing son of a bitch. The fact that he had Claudia's panties in his pocket but that at that very moment Kyle was probably helping himself to what was normally in those panties, well, that was more than he could tolerate. Especially when Kyle knew, *knew,* that he was set on having Claudia, and then went and hit on her before he had the chance. Scooped her out from under him. Burned him. The bastard.

Leroy lit a cigarette, closed his eyes, tipped his head back against the seat. He tried to remember the last time he'd been this angry. It wasn't difficult to recall, that day in November when the witch-bitch Daisy had filed a complaint against him for threatening to get rid of her dog. Like he'd put up with a runty little mop pissing on the wheel of his Camaro! Nothing had come of the complaint, of course. Nobody'd heard his threat except Daisy, and nobody ever believed a word she said.

He tapped his cigarette into the ashtray.

Now he had worked himself up even more. He forced his thoughts back to the matter at hand. He loved remembering the day he'd visited her classroom. When he'd introduced himself, Claudia had looked into his eyes and smiled. He knew immediately that there was a connection there, something he'd never had with any other woman. But now, Claudia was distracted by Kyle. The question was, what did he intend to do about it?

If only Kyle were gone, out of the picture, he would have Claudia to himself. As much as he wished he could just bump off his partner, he didn't expect he could get away with it, not with Fitz watching him so closely. The old man always seemed to have it in for him, criticizing, harping about his driving. Telling him to grow up and lecturing about manners. He would've liked to see how Fitz would've handled the Jeep on that ice. Probably would've flipped the thing, or kept going right over the snowbank into Wykowski's house.

There had to be some way to get Claudia's attention, some fantastic way to convince her that she'd be crazy to choose Kyle over him. A way to show her how much he loved her, that he'd do anything for her. A way to make her realize, as he had, that they were meant to be together. Leroy looked out into the darkness again, but still couldn't see anything except the faint outline of the bakery.

He ached for her.

Leroy took another drag on the cigarette, watching the embers on the end turn bright orange as he inhaled. He marveled at the power in those embers, their potential to explode into flames, to engulf everything around them.

For a moment, he sat, struck by how simple it would be. He would build upon his Valentine's Day seductions. This time, though, he'd do it right. He'd use fire to make his surprise delivery to the school look like nothing. He'd wait for the perfect moment to prove to Claudia just how serious his feelings had become. She'd finally understand that they were meant to be together.

He switched on the headlights and revved the engine.

From now on, Leroy Underwood would be doing the burning.

CHAPTER 18

2012

Mary was yellow.

At first, he thought his eyes were deceiving him, that the unnatural sallowness of her skin was merely the result of the way the light was dispersed within the mansion, or a result of a strange mixture of color and shadow reflecting off the sitting room walls. Then, in one terrifying instant, he realized that the interior of the house had nothing to do with the color of Mary's skin.

"Mary, are you all right?"

Confused, she looked at him. "Why, yes, Michael, I'm fine. I'm a little tired, but other than that . . . Why do you ask?"

He didn't know exactly how to describe her appearance to her. "Mary, have you looked in the mirror today?"

"No, you know I don't like mirrors. What's wrong? Why are you acting this way?"

"I'll show you," he said, taking her hand.

He led her to the washroom and flipped on the light. "Look at yourself, Mary. Do you see it?"

She stepped in front of the mirror, hesitating before looking into it. When she did, she saw immediately the contrast between her skin and the white wall behind her. She raised up a hand in front of her face and examined it.

"Michael, I . . . I don't know what's happening. I don't feel any different than I normally do."

"Your coloring isn't normal," Father O'Brien said. "I think people turn yellow when there's something wrong with the liver. You remember me telling you about old man McGee? He was yellowish for years before he died. They said it was liver disease, on account of his drinking."

"You know I never touch alcohol, Michael."

"Of course I know that."

"Then why would anything be wrong with my liver?"

"I don't know." He lowered his voice, preparing for her reaction at what he was about to suggest. "I know you've never had much use for doctors, but I really think you should see one." She shot him a fearful look, but he pressed on. "You wouldn't have to go anywhere. Doc Richardson's an old friend of mine. I'm sure he'd come by to see you if I called him."

"No, oh, no," Mary said, backing out of the washroom.

"It wouldn't be so bad, Mary," he said, following her. "And I think whatever is happening to you is serious." They were back in the sitting room now, facing each other.

"I can't, Michael."

"You can. And I think you must. A simple exam won't take very long. I'll stay with you the whole time. Please, Mary. I'm so worried about you. Do it for me, if for no other reason."

Eventually, to Father O'Brien's great relief, she agreed to a quick visit from Dr. Richardson. Two days later, he brought the doctor to the back door of the mansion, warning him again of Mary's extreme reaction to strangers.

"Why don't we leave our coats here, Fred," Father O'Brien said as they stood in the kitchen. He took the doctor's coat and draped it with his own over a chair. Dr. Richardson looked around the room with great interest.

"I've always wondered what it was like in this house," the doctor said. His hair was graying but still thick, and the bifocals he wore augmented his expression of wonder. He rolled the sleeves of his white shirt to his elbows. "I don't suppose, given what you've told me, that many people have seen it."

"No," Father O'Brien said.

Mary was waiting for them in the sitting room, clutching the ends of a shawl that she had wrapped around her shoulders. She didn't even turn to greet them as they entered the room, although Father O'Brien felt sure she had heard them come in. She was quivering, and wearing a black patch over her left eye. *She hasn't worn that patch in years,* Father O'Brien thought.

He also noticed that her skin was slightly more yellow.

"Mary, this is Dr. Fred Richardson," he said, coming around in front of her.

"It's good to meet you, Mrs. McAllister," the doctor said, looking carefully at her.

"Hello," Mary whispered. She did not make eye contact. In fact, she kept her head down, and her quaking increased.

"Mrs. McAllister, there's no need to be afraid of me. I'm here to help you," Dr. Richardson said, taking a step toward her. She recoiled at his advance. Unsure how to proceed, the doctor looked over at Father O'Brien.

Father O'Brien had seen Mary in this agitated state many times. He hoped that she wouldn't bolt upstairs and lock herself in her room. She had done just that three years earlier, when contractors had come to the marble house to reshingle the roof. It occurred to Father O'Brien that they should sit, so that they appeared less threatening. He lowered himself into an armchair and motioned for the doctor to do the same.

"Mary, I told the doctor you've not felt bad at all, just that a few days ago we noticed your complexion looked a little different," Father O'Brien said.

Mary glanced at them and nodded.

"I also told him that you never drink anything alcoholic." He looked at the doctor and raised his eyebrows in a silent prompt.

Dr. Richardson took the hint. "Mrs. McAllister, have you ever had any medical procedure that required you to receive a blood transfusion?"

"No," she whispered, and drew the shawl tighter around herself.

"Have you had any unusual pain in your abdomen recently?"

"No."

"Are there any particular foods that give you an upset stomach?"

"No."

"Have you noticed any weight loss over the past few months?"

"A little." She stole a glance at Father O'Brien before he could hide the new surprise and worry that clouded his face.

"Have you noticed any change in your appetite?"

She was quiet a moment before she answered. "I'm eating a little less, I suppose."

Dr. Richardson paused before he spoke. "Mrs. McAllister," he said gently, "I think it would be very helpful if I could examine you. It won't take long, and you could stay on the sofa right where you are."

Father O'Brien watched Mary. Her whole body jerked twice, and he knew she was fighting an instinctive urge to run away. Yet, she surprised him by staying put as the doctor slowly went over to her.

Dr. Richardson sat on the sofa beside her and drew a penlight and stethoscope from his medical bag. His movements were careful and deliberate. He kept his voice low and soothing. "First, I just need to look in your eye with this little light. It won't hurt at all. Do you think you could look at me for just a second?"

Keeping her face turned downward, Mary slowly rolled her gaze up to his chin. She still wouldn't look him in the eyes. The doctor shone the light into her eye, highlighting the yellowing of the sclera. He made no attempt to remove the patch to examine her other eye.

"That's good," he said, clicking off the penlight. "The next thing I'd like to do is listen to your heart and lungs." He put on the stethoscope and slowly, slowly placed the end on her chest. "Try to take deep, steady breaths," he said. Mary cringed, breathing rapidly.

"You're doing great, Mrs. McAllister," Dr. Richardson said, although she didn't look as if she were doing well at all. The doctor moved off the sofa and knelt on the floor. "The last thing I need you to do is stretch out here so I can examine your abdomen. It will only take a minute, and then we'll be done."

Mary slowly acquiesced, drawing her legs up onto the sofa and lying down flat on her back. She turned her face away from him. Her hands were clenched into tight fists on each side of her.

"Good," he said. "Now, all I'm going to do is feel to see if everything is okay." He placed a hand on her abdomen and pressed down ever so slightly. She didn't move. With both hands, the doctor palpated her abdomen, moving down each side. When his hands reached Mary's right side, just below her rib cage, he hesitated, felt more carefully.

"Does this hurt at all?" the doctor asked.

"A little." Her whispered reply was muffled by the fabric of the sofa back.

"Okay, then, we're all finished," he said after another moment. He retreated to the armchair while Mary sat up and pulled the shawl back around her shoulders. She did not speak but kept her head bowed, waiting. Father O'Brien got up and sat next to her on the sofa.

"Mrs. McAllister," Dr. Richardson began, "I can't be sure exactly what is happening to you without some additional tests, but there are several possibilities. What we know is that jaundice — the yellowing of the skin — is caused when the blood supply isn't being cleansed properly. Usually, your liver filters all the blood in your body and removes waste products that build up. Then it dumps the waste products into the intestine through a little tube called the bile duct. People become jaundiced when either the liver isn't working as well as it should, or when the bile duct is blocked, preventing the waste products from leaving the body. Both of those things cause the waste products to enter the bloodstream and make the skin appear yellow." He paused, watching Mary's face.

"Do you understand all that, Mary?" Father O'Brien asked. Mary nodded.

"We can't say for sure what's causing your jaundice," Dr. Richardson continued. "Based on your history, I don't think it's because of hepatitis or some other liver condition. I'd say it's more likely that you have something blocking the bile duct, maybe a gallstone. If it's a gallstone causing the problem, we can take care of it, but like I said before, we can't be sure that's what it is without some other tests."

"What other tests?" Father O'Brien asked.

"Well, I'd suggest a CT scan," Dr. Richardson said. "It's not invasive — it's just having a big camera take a picture of your insides. We'd run a blood test, too. But the best thing, I think, would be to also have a procedure called an ERCP. I'm not going to try to pronounce what that stands for because I'll just get tongue-tied. Basically, it involves putting a little camera down through your mouth and stomach to the bile duct to see exactly whether and why it's blocked. But you'd be asleep for it, so you wouldn't feel anything."

Mary shivered as if she were submerged

in ice water.

"Couldn't the first test, the scan, do that?" Father O'Brien asked. The look of concern on the doctor's face worried him. It was the look of a man who knew or suspected more than he was revealing.

"It might, but it varies from person to person," Dr. Richardson said. "The CT scan is quick, and takes a detailed picture of the inside of the body. But the good thing about the ERCP is that while the camera is down in there, if a gallstone is blocking the bile duct, it can be removed. Or, they can put a stent, a little tube, into the bile duct to keep it open. Everything could be scheduled at the clinic in Rutland. And it's done on an outpatient basis, so you'd be home the same day."

Mary had reached her breaking point. Suddenly, with swiftness uncommon for her advanced age, she flew off the sofa and up the staircase to her bedroom.

"I think she needs some time to think about all this," Father O'Brien said. "And she'll need some time to calm down."

"You sound like you've seen her do this before."

"I have."

"Well." The doctor took a last look around the sitting room and reached for his medical bag. "Let me know what she decides, then, and I'll be happy to give her referrals or help her however I can."

"I'll walk with you to your car," Father O'Brien said as they retrieved their coats from the kitchen.

Once they were outside the mansion, Father O'Brien turned to the doctor. "Okay, Fred, let's have it."

"What do you mean?"

"I mean, what do you really think is going on with her? I've known you for years, and something serious is all over your face."

Dr. Richardson sighed and shoved his hands into his coat pockets as they neared his car. "Look, I can't make a definitive diagnosis on the basis of that limited examination."

"But you've got an idea of what's wrong."

The doctor paused. "She's got an enlarged gallbladder. That in and of itself isn't so uncommon. But the thing is, I think there's something else there. A mass of some kind. I couldn't tell what it was, and didn't want to scare her any more than I already had, but . . ." They reached his car, and he sighed again as he leaned against it. "Some years ago, I had another patient who came in with jaundice like hers. Had about the same history — no drinking or anything that might cause liver disease. It wasn't good. I think the oncologist who treated him is still in Rutland. I'll look up his name and call you with it."

"An oncologist?" Father O'Brien said.

Dr. Richardson nodded.

It was as if the doctor's words hit Father O'Brien's chest with the force of a charging elephant. He took a step backward, struggling to speak. "Do you really think she has cancer?"

"It may not be that at all. I'm just worried because of the mass, and also because gallstone blockages of the bile duct usually occur after a patient has had a history of trouble with gallstones. She doesn't show any symptoms of gallstones. But she's obviously a very sick lady. It's critical that she have those tests done so we can determine why she's in this condition. Do you think you can persuade her to do it?"

"I don't know. Just getting her to agree to see you was nearly impossible."

The doctor shook his head. "I don't think I've ever seen such a severe case of social anxiety disorder. Has she always been that way?"

"As long as I've known her. More than seventy years now." *Social anxiety disorder,* Father O'Brien thought. A three-word description of a lifetime of suffering.

"She's probably progressed to full-blown agoraphobia . . . which means she's so afraid of panicking that she'll avoid leaving familiar surroundings for fear of having an attack. And her eye . . . I wasn't about to ask to see it. But that's just a damned shame." The doctor opened his car door and got behind the wheel. "Look, Michael, do your best to convince her to have the tests. She really needs to get them right away. I can prescribe some sedatives for her so it's easier for her to leave her house."

Father O'Brien nodded. "I'll be in touch," he said. He waited until the doctor had driven down the spiraling driveway before returning to the back door of the mansion.

He was so old now, in the waning portion of his life. He straightened up his skinny, arthritic frame and adjusted his white clerical collar. A slight, cold breeze ruffled the sparse hair on his head. His jaw was clenched tight with determination.

Mary's condition was no toothache, or flu virus, or any other minor health problem that she had endured by herself in the past. This time, she truly needed help, even if she didn't think she did. He smoothed the wisps of hair back down on his head. It was almost amusing to him that at this time in his life, as an old man, he felt like David about to confront Goliath. He knew he would face the battle of his life in trying to convince Mary to leave her home to receive the medical care she needed. It was a battle he resolved to win.

Father O'Brien opened the back door of Mary's home, took a deep breath, and closed it softly behind him.

The scenery outside the window of the truck was finally visible in the thin light of the winter sunrise.

Mary blinked and tried to focus on something. The houses and trees and everything else shifted from blurry to clear to blurry. She was unaccustomed to taking medication, except for an occasional aspirin. The effects of Valium were strange and disturbing.

The anxiety was still there and had been ever since Michael had helped her into the front seat of his old pickup. Now, though, it was blanketed by the sedative, compressed into a little ball that spun around and around inside her, confined and harmless. Even the constant chatter of Daisy Delaine in the backseat didn't disturb her.

"I really like going to the doctor, Mrs. McAllister," she said over the back of her seat. "Father O'Brien's so nice to take me when I need to go. I usually have a checkup and get some new medicine. Are you going for a checkup and medicine?"

"I suppose," Mary said. She felt odd when she spoke, as if her own thoughts were being expressed in someone else's voice.

"I really like my doctor, too. His name's Dr. Mann. It's an easy name to remember, since he's a man, not a woman. I've been seeing him for a long time. Let's see," Daisy said, counting to herself, "I think about twelve years now. Whoo-wee! Time sure flies, doesn't it, Father O'Brien?"

"It does, Daisy," he said, glancing at her in the rearview mirror. Then he looked at Mary next to him. "Are you doing all right?" he asked.

"I'm fine," she said. Waves of sleepiness were flowing over her, even as the sun climbed higher. She leaned her head against the window.

"We're coming into Rutland now," he said. "The clinic is only a mile or so from here."

"Oh, goody!" Daisy said from the backseat. "I can't wait to show Dr. Mann my new spells." Mary heard the sound of notebook pages turning and smiled to herself.

Michael had told her years before of how Daisy had taken up residence in Mill River after the death of her elderly parents. The Delaines were dairy farmers who had adopted Daisy as an infant. Her birth to a young, unwed mother had been long and difficult, and not without lasting effects for Daisy. Nevertheless, they'd taught her to be self-sufficient and outgoing, but they worried about what would happen to their daughter once they were gone. With Michael's help, they had arranged to move Daisy from their farm outside Rutland to Mill River, where she could live safely on her own. He'd helped her find a place to live and tried to ease her transition into the community. Daisy had always been naïve, almost childlike.

Mary had seen Daisy several times from a distance, usually walking up Main Street carrying potions or groceries. Most people in town treated her politely, and enough of them bought her potions to provide a supplement to her government checks. Even so, through Michael, Mary knew that Daisy was still treated differently, and Daisy probably didn't understand why.

Now, though, having met her in person, seeing her unforgettable face and knowing her history, Mary felt a special bond with her. It was no wonder that they were quite alike — she and Daisy wanted so much to fit into the community. Even though Daisy sought out people in her attempts to gain acceptance while she herself avoided them, were they not both completely isolated from others in Mill River?

It was only for a moment that Mary was lost in her thoughts. The white winter haze of rural Vermont had become the houses and businesses of Rutland. She squinted out the window.

It had been more than seventy years since she had last been in Rutland.

Father O'Brien slowed the pickup as they entered the town. With Daisy scribbling in the backseat, Mary focused her gaze on each building, tree, and street sign, searching for something familiar. She recognized nothing. Father O'Brien turned left at a stoplight, heading toward the county hospital.

And then, she saw it. Just a glimpse before the image disappeared from the limited view of the pickup window, the creamy exterior of McAllister Marbleworks.

Mary looked over at Father O'Brien. He was watching her. He took one of her hands in his and squeezed it. "I couldn't think of any route to avoid it completely," he said.

Mary didn't say anything. She didn't have to.

Within a few minutes, they were pulling into the parking lot at the clinic. Daisy squealed with excitement, bouncing on the backseat until Father O'Brien got out and bent the front seat forward to allow her to exit. He went around to the other side for Mary.

The dulled anxiety threatened to bubble up inside her. She was experiencing a strange sense of déjà vu, the feeling of being parked outside a new place, a yellow mansion, of being pulled from a vehicle against her will. The memories were coming quickly now, through more than seven decades, the din of conversation spilling out of the McAllister home, the stares of the brothers and sisters and cousins as she faced them. Mary tried to protest as Father O'Brien opened the door and helped her down from the front seat, but she was so unsteady that she lost her balance when her feet touched the pavement. Everything whirled around her, and she leaned heavily against him. He steadied her with his arms and his voice.

"Daisy has one of the first appointments of the day, so it won't take too long before she sees the doctor, but I can't leave you out here in the truck. It's too cold, and someone is supposed to be with you while the sedatives are working."

Mary nodded. Even with images resurfacing after so long, she felt only a shadow of the old anxiety. The medication kept an umbrella above her, shielding her from it. She pulled her coat together and felt to make sure her eye patch was in place.

With Daisy skipping ahead, they approached a door in a row of office buildings. Mary noticed a discreet sign on the door that read DRS. RICHARD R. MANN AND KRISTIN A. MORRIS, PSYCHIATRISTS. Daisy held the door for them as they went inside.

Despite the nondescript exterior of the office building, the small waiting room was quiet and elegantly furnished. A beautifully upholstered sofa and loveseat were placed against two of the walls. Polished cherry tables held neat stacks of magazines. The carpet was plush, a deep blue that made Mary feel as if she were sinking into velvety water as she stepped onto it.

A receptionist smiled a greeting over a counter on the left side of the room. There were two other people waiting. Mary looked at each of them. The people seemed ordinary enough, and only glanced up from reading their magazines for a moment as the front door of the office opened.

As Daisy approached the receptionist to sign in, Father O'Brien led Mary to a pair of chairs in the far corner of the room. She felt more brief stares as they passed, though the sedative kept them from bothering her. He eased her into the more sheltered inside seat and sat down beside her.

"This isn't too bad, is it?" he whispered.

"No."

Daisy walked over to them then, clutching her notebook and smiling. "They said Dr. Mann will be ready to see me soon. I can't wait!"

Her enthusiasm was loud enough to cause the others in the waiting room to look up at her again.

"Well, Daisy, why don't you sit for a few minutes until they call you?" Father O'Brien asked. "There's an open seat right behind you."

"Okay." Daisy backed herself into the open seat, next to a woman with mussed blond hair and bloodshot eyes. The woman was engrossed in reading a magazine article. She did not look at who had sat down next to her until Daisy leaned in close. "Hello there," Daisy said. She peered at the magazine over the woman's shoulder and read aloud the title of the article. " 'Get to Know

Your Sexual Self.' " The blond woman startled, snapped the magazine shut, and glanced around the room. "Looks like a very interesting article," Daisy continued. "But I actually prefer articles about potions and magic." Daisy smiled and waited for a reply. The blond woman managed a half smile before abruptly moving to another seat on the opposite side of the waiting area.

Daisy's jaw dropped down in surprise, and Mary was certain that it was only a matter of seconds before she said something even more embarrassing. She sat in her corner, feeling guilty for wanting to laugh, not knowing what to do about poor Daisy.

The little woman looked at Father O'Brien, but before she could say anything, he put a finger to his lips and motioned for her to approach.

"Father, is she mad at me?" Daisy asked.

The priest stood up and whispered to her. "You see, Daisy, some people who are waiting to see the doctor don't like to talk to anyone in the waiting room. For them, seeing a doctor is very private. Not everyone is like that, but some people are. Like that lady," he said, looking over at the blond woman. "It doesn't mean she's angry at you. She just wants some privacy."

"Oh. I can understand that, I guess. I like

405

to keep my potion recipes private."

"Exactly," Father O'Brien said, sitting down again. He persuaded Daisy back into the open seat. It was only a few more minutes until the receptionist called Daisy to see Dr. Mann. After she left, Father O'Brien helped Mary to her feet. "We've got a little while until she's finished, so we'd better get you over to the outpatient clinic." Mary shuddered but followed him back to the truck.

The next hours were a surreal nightmare. Father O'Brien stayed with her as she signed the consent forms. Mary knew he could not be with her through the medical procedures. Alone, she and the Valium fought back terror as unfamiliar nurses removed her eye patch, revealing her cloudy gray eye and misshapen brow bone. They helped her into a hospital gown and took a blood sample. She couldn't look directly at any of them. Although the tranquilizer had muted her anxiety, she felt the fear begin to seep through the sedative's shield. Her body inched through the cold metal cylinder of the CT scan.

Terror finally overtook her when she was surrounded by the stainless steel of the operating room. The silver walls reflected light and sound and trapped astringent odors of alcohol and iodine. The surgical technicians transferred her to the operating table and turned on the bright overhead lights. The cruel beams penetrated her sensitive left eye. She screamed. Her arms were bound to the sides of the table, unable to shield her face. She jerked her face away, crying out until one of the nurses covered the eye with a soft piece of gauze.

She vaguely heard a man's voice speaking to her, telling her about the ERCP procedure, that she was going to sleep, that it would be over in no time. The last thing she felt before the anesthesia took effect was her heart thumping through her back against the hard operating table.

When she opened her eyes, two faces looked down at her.

"Mary? Can you hear me? How are you feeling?"

She blinked. The two faces blurred and changed. She struggled to focus on them.

The man above her bed spoke again. "Not too close, Daisy. She's just barely awake."

"Hello, Mrs. McAllister," Daisy said. "I hope you're feeling better."

"Mary, can you hear me?"

She knew it was Michael now. She tried to speak but managed only a croak. Her throat was painfully dry.

"Everything went well, Mary," he told her. "You're in the recovery room."

"I want to go home."

"I know, Mary dear. It won't be long. Right now you just need to rest. The doctor will be by to check on you in a while."

Daisy leaned over the edge of the bed, holding up a Styrofoam cup. "Do you want some ice, Mrs. McAllister? The doctor said you could have some when you woke up, if you wanted."

Daisy spooned a small ice chip into her mouth. Mary held it there as it melted, providing cool, exquisite relief to her sore throat.

As the minutes passed, the anesthesia continued to wear off, and Mary felt herself becoming more alert. She squinted up into Daisy's eager eyes. When Daisy turned her head, seeing the birthmark curled over her cheek brought Mary an unexpected calm and a rush of love.

Daisy looked up at Father O'Brien as he whispered something Mary couldn't hear. It didn't matter, though, because Mary's attention was still focused on Daisy's face.

"Look, Mary," Father O'Brien said. He touched her hand as it rested atop the white sheet covering her. "Your skin isn't nearly as yellow as it was."

Mary looked down at her arm. It was true — the improvement was readily apparent. She smiled a little. "Maybe everything is all right now."

It has to be all right, Mary thought to herself. Perhaps nothing serious had been wrong with her. She fervently hoped that the procedure had cured whatever the problem was and vowed to do everything she could to fight her anxiety and recover her health. As she looked up at Daisy and Michael, she knew now that she needed more time to live.

Her hope was short-lived. The look on the oncologist's face as he entered her room a few minutes later told her all she needed to know.

CHAPTER 19

It smelled of pastries in the darkness.

Claudia opened her eyes. Her initial belief, that it had all been a dream, was quickly disproved as Kyle stirred in his sleep beside her.

She had made a horrible mistake.

What time was it? Claudia raised herself up on one elbow, just enough to squint over Kyle toward the digital alarm clock on the nightstand. Its flashing neon numbers read 2:28, as it waited to be reset after the power outage. She sniffed again, and her stomach growled. If Ruth Fitzgerald had the baking going downstairs, it was probably closer to six. She carefully slipped out from beneath the blankets, feeling goose bumps rise up on her bare skin. She listened for the howl of the storm outside, but the apartment was quiet. With any luck, she could get dressed and walk home before Kyle awoke and started asking questions.

Claudia tiptoed around the bedroom. Her purse was on the floor, and she nearly tripped over it. She fished her arm down inside it until she found her phone. It was a relief to see the text message on the screen notifying her that school was again canceled for the day.

Thank goodness. I need a day off just to process everything, Claudia thought as she gathered up her clothes. She fumbled with her bra in the darkness, but she couldn't find her thong or her tights and decided to put her skirt on without them. She pulled the sweater over her head and felt around on the floor for her boots.

Why, why had she given in and done it? Especially since she had never been with anyone else and hadn't said anything to Kyle about it being her first time. That fact had, of course, become apparent to him, and he had been surprised. What he must think of her now she could only imagine. She had done too much too soon. She had been too eager, had gone from being a formerly fat virgin to an easy broad who slept with men after having dated them for only a few days.

No matter that Kyle had been her first date, the first man to genuinely reciprocate her interest, her first intimate experience,

her first everything. A wonderful first everything.

Plagued by morning-after regrets, she felt
cheap and ashamed. Now that she had given
him everything, he might not want her
anymore. She had no intention of sticking
around to hear this from him once he
awoke.

Having found both boots, she stepped into
them. She felt an urge to cry and inhaled
sharply to stifle it. She felt a more powerful
urge to gorge herself on the doughnuts and
pies and fresh bread whose smells emanated
from beneath the floorboards. She thought
of a warm, gooey cinnamon roll, of unwind-
ing its spiraled layers and biting into the
spongy, spiced center.

She would go home and cry and eat.

Claudia stepped quietly toward the bedroom door and pulled it open. It creaked,
as if to warn the man sleeping in the bed.
Kyle rolled over and opened his eyes.

"Claudia? Where are you going?"

"Home."

"What?" He sat up, blinking, but she was
already down the hall, grabbing her coat
from the hook by the door. He jumped up
to follow her, looked down at his naked-
ness, and yanked a blanket off the bed to
wrap around himself. "Claudia! What's

wrong? Wait, don't leave! It's freezing outside! Claudia?"

She was out of his apartment and had almost reached the exit to the building. He stood at the top of the stairs above her. She turned and looked up at his sleepy, confused face. "I think I made a big mistake. I'm sorry," she said.

"Claudia, wait a minute, whatever's wrong, let's talk about it," he pleaded, but she pushed the door open and hurried outside.

Early Friday morning, just after Claudia fought her way through the fresh snowdrifts and up Main Street to her house, Father O'Brien opened the front door of the parish house to retrieve the copy of the *Mill River Gazette* on his doorstep.

He walked with it into his little kitchen and set the teakettle on the stove. Some mornings, he liked tea more than coffee, and this was one of those mornings. He sat down at the table and removed the thin newspaper from its protective plastic wrapper.

There on the front page, just as he had expected, was a story about the new Jeep. The headline read, "Mystery Donor Rescues Police Department," and next to the story was a picture of the new Grand Cherokee, surrounded by Mill River's four police officers.

The town was in an absolute tizzy. Word of the new Jeep had spread quickly. Even the *Rutland Herald* had sent a reporter down to cover the story. The article in the *Gazette* contained several quotes from Fitz, talking about how he had discovered the Jeep, wondering about the identity of the benefactor. The old-timers in town had done their part, too, rehashing the TV story for anyone who would listen. There was a picture of some of those older gentlemen printed with the article. Father O'Brien skimmed the story, smiling to himself. He was glad to see that Fitz had kept his promise not to reveal any of his own involvement in the matter.

It hadn't been ten minutes after Fitz's shift had ended on Thursday when he'd knocked at the door of the parish house and asked, "Do you have a minute, Father? Something mighty strange happened this morning, and I thought you might know what's going on."

In the end, he hadn't lied, but he hadn't told Fitz exactly who was behind the purchase of the Jeep. It was not yet time to disclose that information. He had, however, explained that he'd arranged to have the

Jeep delivered to the police station on behalf of someone whose identity would be revealed in due course. That yes, the gift to the police station was in fact a sure and proper thing. Being a man of patience and integrity, Fitz had held his curiosity at bay and promised that their conversation would remain confidential. His interview for the *Gazette* was proof that he had kept his word.

The teakettle on the stove whistled, softly at first, then more shrilly. Father O'Brien pushed himself up out of his chair and took the kettle off the burner before it sounded its most incessant, high-pitched shriek — something he just couldn't handle at such an early hour.

He dropped a teabag into a mug and poured the hot water over it. For a few minutes, he stood at the counter, preoccupied, moving the teabag up and down in the darkening liquid.

The town meeting was now only eighteen days away. Sometime during the next week, he expected to see the agenda for the meeting printed in the *Gazette,* including a notice that he intended to make a special announcement. It would be unusual, and would surely pique the interest of the residents of Mill River. But after the stir caused by the appearance of the police department's new Jeep, and considering the fact that many in town suspected his involvement in the years of anonymous gifts, he didn't think the problem would be attracting people to hear what he had to say.

The real problem was that he might not finish the arrangements in time. On the legal side of things, Gasaway, the attorney, assured him that all was on schedule. The package and the letter waited, unopened, in his office. But, there were still many decisions that he himself had yet to make. He had added the Mill River Police Department to his list of names. In fact, he'd taken care of everyone who he knew had some immediate need, but for a little town like Mill River, Mary's wealth could do so much more. It *would* do more.

The money would, of course, be held in trust for the benefit of the town. It could be divided among separate accounts and reserved for different uses. He and Mary had discussed ways to ensure that the money could benefit the greatest number of people, but she had passed on before they had been able to make all of the specific decisions that were required. Now, he had less than three weeks to make those final decisions and have all the legal documents in place. He put his hand lightly around the handle of his mug and closed his eyes. The comforting steam from the hot drink silently rose up over his face.

He remembered lying in bed the previous night, listening to the storm assaulting the thick walls of the parish house, feeling thankful to be warm and healthy and happy. He had few possessions, but he had everything he needed. Not everyone was so lucky, he knew.

Just like that, it came to him.

He opened his eyes.

It was so simple. With Mary's fortune, he would make sure that everyone who lived in Mill River was warm and healthy and happy.

Jean yawned and looked toward the bedroom window.

The faintest morning light shone through the curtains, enough to be caught and reflected by the new ring on her right hand.

She still couldn't get over how the ring Ron had given her was almost exactly a miniature version of Mary's. There was no way he could know how much she had loved the old woman's ring, or even that such a ring existed. He had never seen it.

Maybe, after thirteen years of marriage, he was learning to read her mind.

The most surprising thing was that, even

though Ron's diamonds were tiny compared with the massive diamonds in Mary's setting, his meant so much more to her. She would always remember how he had looked when he had given the ring to her — his rumpled hair, stubbly beard, and pleading brown eyes. Her dear Ron.

She loved him so much. It wasn't his fault if her life was at times mundane.

She was incredibly lucky.

Her husband was the sweetest man in the world.

It took Kyle only a few moments to pull on his clothes and coat and run outside to his truck. When he saw the two feet of snow that had accumulated around it, he almost decided to follow Claudia's example and walk up to her house. Almost. It was just up the street, and the snowplows had already cleared the road. He had no idea why she had decided to leave and was eager to find out. Then it occurred to him that perhaps it wasn't such a good idea to approach her immediately. He had obviously done something wrong and didn't want to drive her further away.

He went back to his apartment for a snow shovel and began to dig out the truck. Once he was able to open the driver's side door, he started the engine to warm up the cab. He resumed his shoveling with dogged determination until the truck was free and a path from it to the road was clear. He broke through the barrier of snow that the plows had pushed against the side of the road. Finally, in the pale light of early morning, he drove carefully up the main road to Claudia's house.

The driveway was occupied by her snow-covered car, so Kyle left his truck at the side of the road. A trail of deep footsteps led through the snow to the front door. Claudia had made good time getting home, but now her house was quiet and dark. If only she would open the door when he knocked.

Claudia had never felt more stupid in her life. She had been so convinced Kyle would think poorly of her after their night together, but the look of his face staring down at her as she left was surprising. He had seemed genuinely concerned that she was leaving. She didn't know what to think. Cold and confused, she had staggered safely into her living room and burst into tears. After twenty minutes of bawling, she still felt miserable.

Now, she was attacking the treadmill. The belt turned and whined beneath her running shoes. The perspiration was coursing down her face and neck. She didn't care. She would finish a strenuous workout, and then she would eat. French toast, with real maple syrup. As many pieces as she could hold.

She had been running for almost thirty minutes when her doorbell rang. She tried to ignore it. It rang again. Then there was loud knocking.

Of course, it was Kyle.

He was calling to her now, still knocking and ringing. Pleading for her to open the door, apologizing for whatever he did to upset her. She didn't want to see him yet, in her disgusting, post-workout state, but he persisted. Finally, she decided to face him, if only to avoid having him jolt her neighbors from sleep.

She flung open the front door. Kyle's hand was raised in midair, poised to knock again. He pulled it back down and looked at her with surprise.

"Hi," she said.

"Claudia," he began, and then hesitated. "I . . . I don't know what I did, but I'm sorry if I upset you. I would've come sooner, but I had to shovel out the truck." He was babbling, as if he was caught off guard at being face-to-face with her so soon. "Can we talk?"

"Okay," she said after a moment. With her hand, she wiped the sweat from her forehead. She hadn't the slightest idea what she would say to him, but she stepped back and motioned him inside.

They left the chilly entryway and went into the kitchen. For a moment, Kyle looked down at her without saying anything. His hair was disheveled, and droplets of sweat were clinging to the edges of his face. Still silent, he removed his coat and sat down at the breakfast table. When he spoke, his words were awkwardly genuine. "Whatever I did, I'm sorry. I didn't mean to upset you or make you uncomfortable. But I don't understand why — I mean, I had such a great time last night, uh, you know, with dinner and everything."

His face was turning red, Claudia noticed, and he was becoming more flustered. "I didn't mean to imply that the only thing I liked was, well, you know," he said. "I just really enjoyed your company. I really like you, and I'm sorry if —"

"You didn't do anything wrong, Kyle," Claudia said. "It was me. Before now, I'd never even had a boyfriend or anything, and things happened so quickly." She crossed her arms and looked down at her running shoes.

"That's still really hard for me to believe," he said. "I'd think you'd have no problem dating whoever you wanted. Hell, it took Leroy all of ten seconds to decide you were the one for him. You're so pretty, and smart, and fun. To tell you the truth, I almost didn't have the guts to ask you out because I didn't think I had a chance."

"I never thought you'd be interested in me that way."

He was incredulous. "You're nuts! Why would you ever think that?"

She couldn't look at him, didn't see his brow furrowed in confusion. Instead, she walked straight to the drawer beside the refrigerator. Although she couldn't quite believe what she was doing, she took out her fat picture, the one she had hidden there a few days earlier, and handed it to him.

"This is why." He stared at the picture, as if trying to understand what she was telling him. "That was me, eighteen months ago. Until now, no one ever wanted to go on a date with me."

"Wow," he said slowly. "You've . . . really changed."

"I know." His words seemed to confirm her worst fear, that, eighteen months ago, he would have been repulsed by her, that his interest in her now was only superficial. She began to cry. It was as if her emotional dam, the one that she had patched and reinforced during all those months of dieting and running and wishing, had burst. "I guess that after last night, I was afraid you'd think I was easy, or desperate, or something. I've never been in that situation before. I mean, I thought you liked me for me, but what if I was wrong? What if I were still fat? Would you have wanted anything to do with me? What if you were one of those guys who sleeps with a woman and never calls her again? You didn't seem like that kind of person, but I had no past experience, so how should I know? I was worried that in the morning, everything would be different." The words gushed out along with her tears. Her nose was beginning to run, too. She finally took a breath and sniffed loudly.

"Claudia." Kyle's voice was soft and reassuring. He stood up and began fumbling around, feeling in the pockets of his jeans and jacket. "I want to show you something." After a few moments, he produced his wallet, which he opened and handed to her.

She was looking at a picture of Kyle, Rowen, and a woman that could only be Allison. The resemblance that Rowen bore to her late mother was startling, but that wasn't what surprised Claudia the most.

Allison was chubby. Really chubby.

"That's a picture of Allison," Kyle said. "It was taken when Rowen was six, but that's about how she looked when I met her. I loved her very much." Claudia heard the effort in his words and looked up at him. "I fell in love with her for the person that she was. Everybody liked her. She was awesome with kids down at the precinct. She was spunky and gentle at the same time. She had this warm presence, you know? I always felt comfortable around her. When I met her, I just knew there was a good possibility that we could have something special." He paused, looking at his hand resting on the kitchen table. "She died about two years ago."

"I know," Claudia said. "The principal gave me what background information he had about Rowen and a few of my other students when I accepted the position here."

He nodded. "When she was really sick, right before she died, she didn't look like that picture at all. She was all skin and bones, maybe about eighty pounds. I used to carry her around the house, from the bedroom to the sofa or bathroom. I think I loved her even more at the end. How she looked never had anything to do with it."

Claudia stood silently, listening.

"I didn't know how long it would take to get over Allison. At first, I couldn't imagine being with someone else. Then the first year passed, and we moved up here, to Mill River, and I started to think that maybe I could love somebody again. If I met somebody, that is. The day that Rowen and I ran into you at the supermarket, well, it was the first time I'd had that same, I don't know, the same kind of feeling about any woman since Allison. I really wanted to get to know you. You have that same kindness. I know we've only gone out a couple of times, but I thought we clicked, and I've been really happy." He paused to run a hand through his disheveled hair. "To be honest about last night, a part of me was wondering whether I was ready for that, too."

"Were you?"

He smiled a slow smile. "I wouldn't have gone through with it if I hadn't thought so. And now I know so. Yeah, it was kind of soon for us, but then again, I don't think there's anything wrong in two adults feeling attracted to each other and acting on those feelings."

He made it sound so simple and right.

He didn't think she was a slut.

He didn't like her only for her appearance.

"Yes," she said, nodding in agreement. "I guess I made a lot of stupid assumptions. I'm . . . I'm really sorry."

He caught her in a tight hug before she could say anything else. After a moment, she pulled his face down to hers and kissed him.

"Kyle?" she said, with her eyes still closed.

"Hmm?"

"When do you think Rowen will be home from her friend's house?" Her arms were around his waist now, and she could feel the dampness of his shirt. Neither of them smelled particularly pleasant.

"About noon, I guess," he said against her mouth. "I suspect they'll sleep in, since school's canceled. Why?"

"I think we need a shower. We're both stinky."

"We?" He was kissing her face, which was wet with tears.

"Yeah. We."

"One shower?"

"Uh-huh."

He smiled again. "As long as you promise not to run out and leave me naked and alone again, I think that's a good idea."

She laughed and wiped at her eyes. "Don't worry, I won't."

■ ■ ■ ■

Kyle and Claudia were inseparable over the next couple of weeks. They spent time together going to dinner, watching movies, playing in the snow with Rowen. Several times, Kyle left for work a bit early, stopping by Claudia's house on his way to the station.

Leroy discreetly monitored their activities, struggling to remain focused on his ultimate goal. It was all he could do to act civil when he and Kyle were in the same room. During their last encounter, he'd muttered something to Kyle about how Claudia was butt-ugly compared to Jessica, a new woman he'd met in a bar in Rutland just after Valentine's Day. Of course, Jessica didn't exist and Claudia was by far the most beautiful woman he'd ever met. He'd worked out his plan to win her heart. The next time she spent the night with Kyle above the bakery, he would be ready.

For two weeks, he waited. In order for his plan to work, he needed Claudia to be at Kyle's apartment on a night when he wouldn't have to work the graveyard shift. Everything fell into place on the first Friday in March. He'd worked the evening shift, and was heading home just after eleven o'clock when he saw her car parked outside the bakery. Wykowski was on duty for the rest of the night. The town was quiet, as usual. Even the weather was cooperating, providing bursts of fine snowflakes that resulted in a kind of moving fog. It was the perfect sort of weather to help him avoid being seen. The temperature was fifteen degrees and dropping, according to the weather report that blared from the radio in the Camaro, but he wasn't worried about that. Soon enough, it would be plenty warm in a certain downtown portion of Mill River.

Leroy drove home to prepare. He changed into black clothing and gloves and put into the trunk of the Camaro a small jug of gasoline, a flashlight, an old rag, a can of black spray paint, and several large bottles of beer. His cell phone was charged. He always carried a cigarette lighter, and Claudia's black thong — his ever-present good luck charm — was in his coat pocket. All he needed now was his ski mask.

Everything was still quiet when he drove back into town around midnight. As he passed the police station, he saw Ron Wykowski tipped back in a chair with his feet crossed on the front desk.

Lazy ass, Leroy thought. *He'll be awake*

soon enough.

After circling the block, Leroy swung the Camaro onto an unlit street well off the main road and parked. He put on the ski mask, gathered the supplies from the trunk of his car, and began walking along the back streets toward the bakery.

He crossed through a thicket of pine trees, approaching his targeted building from the rear. As he expected, the building was dark, its upstairs occupants apparently sound asleep. He set the gasoline container and other items at the base of a large spruce. Carefully, he took out the flashlight and stepped up to the building.

There was a small window at the back of the bakery. He peered in through it, shone the flashlight around the darkened first floor. The place was absolutely still. The stainless steel ovens and countertops gleamed, and farther inside, the neat wooden chairs were turned upside down on the tables, waiting for morning.

Kindling.

Leroy walked back to the gasoline and bag of supplies. He squatted down with his back against the tree, fished in the bag for a beer, and used his teeth to open it. Next, he removed the can of spray paint and shook it several times to mix it. He looked at the back of the bakery, took a long swig of beer, and smiled to himself.

His plan was brilliant, really: Spray-paint some graffiti on the back of the bakery. Lure Kyle out of the building with a bogus 9-1-1 call so that Claudia would be left alone. Set the building on fire. Enter the burning building and rescue Claudia while Kyle was still out on a wild goose chase. Coupled with the graffiti, the fire would appear to be an act of vandalism. His only apparent involvement in the matter would be the heroic rescue of the woman he loved.

Of course, it wouldn't hurt that he might be able to redeem himself in Fitz's eyes by helping someone escape a raging fire. And Kyle, the asshole, would look like a total loser when he finally showed up. Best of all, after he saved her life, Claudia would surely, surely, realize that she was with the wrong man.

Leroy drained the first bottle of beer and opened a second. After another long drink, he pushed the open bottle into the snow, belched, and hauled himself to his feet. Like an artist approaching an empty canvas, he shook the can of paint again and headed toward the vast back wall of the bakery.

■ ■ ■ ■

Daisy's alarm clock screeched at exactly midnight. She threw off her covers and switched on the lights, calling to her little dog as she dressed. "It's the first Saturday in March, Smudgie! Time to start the St. Patrick's Day potion! We've got to get some fresh wintergreen, the fresher the better! Oh, yes, little green leaves, touched by the moonlight, seasoned by snow! Are you awake, Smudgie?"

The little gray mop rolled over on the bed and groaned.

"Fine, you stay inside. I won't be long, and we'll have a nice breakfast when I get back. But if you miss seeing a leprechaun, you'll be sorry!"

Daisy scrambled into her parka and boots, wrapped a thick scarf around her neck and face, and put on her gloves. Waiting by the front door to her trailer was a snow shovel, a nine-volt floodlight, and a large metal colander. She gathered them together and ventured outside into the night.

The best place to find fresh wintergreen was in the thicket behind the buildings in the center of town. The snow there was often more shallow than in other areas, and something about the soil, or perhaps the shade of the large spruces and white pines, seemed to help the shrubby wintergreen plants to flourish. Every year, early in the morning on the first Saturday in March, Daisy awoke to pick wintergreen.

She didn't mind the cold, or the tiny, crystalline flurries that flew at her face. She trudged through the snow, pulling the shovel behind her. It actually stayed on top of the snow, making a slight grooved indentation beside her deep footprints. Leaving this trail in the darkness, with the back of her parka spread out behind her against the snow, Daisy resembled a strange sort of winter snail.

Upon reaching the thicket, she positioned the floodlight on the colander and began digging. She had to clear two feet of snow before she uncovered a short clump of waxy green leaves. "Ooh," she squealed to herself, slightly out of breath. She threw down the shovel and stooped to pick them.

Wintergreen was the primary ingredient in her St. Patrick's Day potion. Before adding other magic ingredients, she would ferment the fresh leaves for a week in her kitchen to produce a fragrant, minty tea.

In no time, her colander was half-full. She was humming to herself, alternatively shoveling and picking, when she heard a deep, guttural noise from within the thicket. It was unlike anything she had ever heard while gathering wintergreen. Perhaps it was an animal — a bobcat, or maybe a bear? She grasped the snow shovel defensively. The backs of the town buildings were quite close. Surely, a bear would be wary of approaching them.

Daisy took up her floodlight and walked slowly in the direction of the sound. Again, the noise rattled through the darkness, a deep, gurgling growl that sent shivers down her spine. Only a short hill separated her from the final cluster of trees behind the buildings. A little voice inside her head told her to turn back, but she summoned all of her courage and pressed on. Using the snow shovel for support, she came up slowly over the hill and shined her floodlight directly ahead.

There, squatting against a large pine tree, was a man dressed in black. As the beam of the floodlight washed over him, he opened his mouth and released another enormous belch. Daisy was at once disgusted and relieved. At least it wasn't a bear.

The man turned to stare at her but was forced to shield his eyes from the glare of the floodlight. In the split second she stood watching him, Daisy noticed several empty beer bottles glimmering in the snow. When she saw his black ski mask, she recognized him immediately.

It was the same man she had seen running away from her burning trailer.

"Oh!" she gasped. Too shocked to scream, Daisy staggered backward, abandoning her shovel. She followed her broken path back through the thicket, snatched up her colander, and continued as fast as she could go until she burst through the front door of her trailer.

Smudgie was waiting for her, now fully awake and wagging his tail happily. Daisy ignored him. She slammed the door and locked it, grabbed the phone off the kitchen wall, and dialed 9-1-1.

"Rutland County 9-1-1, what is your emergency?" asked a woman in a monotonous voice.

"I'm in Mill River. I need to talk to the police," Daisy cried into the handset.

"If you'll tell me what's wrong, ma'am, I'll try to help you."

"Please, just let me talk to the police in Mill River."

"One moment, I'll transfer you." Daisy heard a series of clicks and then a man's voice.

"Mill River police, Officer Wykowski speaking."

"Officer, Officer, this is Daisy Delaine. There's a man in black in the woods behind town," she said, gasping. "It's the same man I saw when my house burned down in November."

"Hold up a minute, Ms. Delaine. Are you sure you saw someone?"

"Oh, yes, Officer, and heard him, too. He was drinking and burping. At first I thought he was a bear, but then I saw him burp and realized it was a man."

"I see." There was a pause at the other end of the line. "Just out of curiosity, Ms. Delaine, could I ask what you were doing out in the woods at this hour?"

"I was gathering fresh wintergreen for my St. Patrick's Day potion. It has to be picked on the first Saturday in March, you know, before the sun comes up. I always go right after midnight to make sure I have time to find enough. After dawn, it loses its magical properties."

"Ah." Ron Wykowski was quiet a moment. "Well, I suppose I'll drive by and have a look," he finally said. "About where did you say the man was?"

"He was sitting in the woods behind the bakery, or was it the hardware store? He

435

was wearing all black, even a black mask. I ran away once I realized who it was."

"You say you'd seen the man before . . . do you have any idea as to his identity?"

"No, Officer. He wasn't very tall, but he wasn't really short, either. And I've never seen his face."

"Okay, Ms. Delaine. I'll swing by and check things out. If you think of anything else, give us a call back."

"Thank you, Officer, I will." Daisy hung up the phone and went back to make sure that the door to her trailer was locked. She also lowered the window blinds and pulled the curtains closed. If the strange man in black had followed her home, she would see to it that he couldn't get inside to hurt her or Smudgie.

Claudia opened her eyes.

As Kyle shifted beside her, she raised her head to look at his alarm clock. They'd been sleeping for only a few hours, but she felt wide awake.

Is this what being in love does to people's sleep schedules? she thought, sliding her arm around Kyle's waist. She snuggled up against his side, breathed in the delicious scent of him, kissed him lightly on the mouth.

In the dim bedroom, he opened his eyes slowly before he turned his face toward her.

"What's wrong?"

"Nothing. I just woke up."

"What time is it?"

"Some wee hour of the morning."

"And you just woke up?" Kyle flipped onto his side and pulled her closer.

"Uh-huh. But it's too early to get out of bed." Claudia heard his quick intake of breath as she slipped her hand down his boxer shorts.

"You're right," Kyle said, nuzzling her cheek. "Much too early."

Having that witch find him sitting in the woods was the last thing he needed. At least, it had looked like Crazy Daisy. With the damned floodlight shining in his eyes, he wasn't positive whom he had seen.

At least no one else had come by.

Warily, Leroy waited in the thicket for a good half hour after Daisy had stumbled upon him. He had expected her to tattle on him, but no one had driven through the town the entire time he'd been waiting. Wykowski was a pretty serious guy, but if Daisy had called the police station, even he would've dismissed her story. Things would be so much easier with that idiot woman out of the picture.

He'd almost done it. Almost. Even now, he still couldn't believe how his plan to burn up her yapping kick-dog and scare the bejesus out of Crazy Daisy had almost become much more. It was so easy — reaching through her open kitchen window, lighting one of her candles, moving it beneath the curtains. The old trailer'd gone up in flames like a rocket in the night.

He hadn't counted on the old bitch being home napping, though, or the damned dog alerting her to the fire.

But no matter. He and Kyle had taken the report from her, once the firefighters had doused what was left of the burned mobile home. Turns out she'd seen him running away — wearing a black ski mask — after the dog started yapping. Of course, no one believed her that time, either.

She'd told them she didn't have any homeowner's insurance, so how she'd gotten that new trailer he didn't know. Some charitable fuck must've helped her, and now she was better off than before. If she had any sense at all, she'd go home to her trailer and stay there for the rest of the night.

Leroy looked at his watch and saw that it was nearly one in the morning. His random doodles and choice phrases had thoroughly defaced the back of the bakery. He was feeling better now that he'd had another beer and was no longer breathing paint fumes. It was time to take care of the next part of his plan.

Leroy took his cell phone from his coat pocket and cleared his throat. He smiled as he pressed *-6-7 and then 9-1-1.

"Rutland County 9-1-1, what is your emergency?"

"Yeah, I'm at 744 Mitchell Road in Mill River," he said in an artificially low, panicked whisper. "We need the police out here quick. Someone's in my house, maybe more than one person. I heard glass breaking and woke up. I think whoever it is is still downstairs."

"You're at 744 Mitchell Road in Mill River?" the operator repeated. Leroy detected some confusion in her voice. "That address isn't coming up . . . are you on a cell phone?"

"Yeah, the landline's not working," Leroy said, thinking quickly. "Maybe whoever's downstairs cut the wires. Can you tell the cops to hurry?"

"Yes, sir, I have officers en route. Would you like me to stay on the line with —"

Leroy hit the "end call" button and slid the phone back into his pocket.

439

Ron was trying to convince himself that it was really worth going out into the frigid night to investigate Daisy's call, when the dispatch radio crackled to life.

"Officer Wykowski, this is Rutland County. We have a report of a burglary in progress at 744 Mitchell Road with the possibility of multiple intruders. Do you copy?"

Ron sat up in his chair. Doc Richardson lived at 744 Mitchell Road.

"That's an affirmative. I'm on the way." Ron stood, grabbed his coat and gloves, and bent back toward the radio's microphone. "Rutland County, could you contact Chief Fitzgerald at his home and apprise him of the situation? He'll need to arrange for another officer to assist on this, and he might want to be there himself."

"No problem, Officer Wykowski. We'll divert other units from Shrewsbury and Proctor if you need additional backup."

"Copy that, and thanks. I'll let you know. Wykowski out." Ron locked the station door and ran to the Jeep.

"Who'd be knocking at this hour?" Claudia said, pulling the covers up around herself.

A loud pounding at Kyle's front door continued.

"Oh, crap," Kyle groaned. He got out of bed and put on a pair of jeans as quickly as he could. "It's Fitz, I'm sure. Which means that something serious is going down."

"Aren't you off duty?" Claudia said, but Kyle had already left the bedroom.

"I'm awful sorry about this," Fitz said when Kyle opened the front door. The police chief had baggy eyes and was fumbling with the zipper on his coat. "We've got a burglary in progress out at Doc Richardson's. Maybe two or three of 'em in the house, Doc said. Ron's on his way now, but he needs backup, and there's nobody from any other department who can get there faster than we can. I radioed him to let him know we'd meet him at Doc's place. We can take my truck, and Ruth offered to come stay with Rowen until we get back."

"No need for that, she's at a slumber party," Kyle said. "Just let me grab my gear. I'll meet you downstairs."

Fitz nodded and started downstairs as Kyle ran back into the apartment.

"What's going on?" Claudia asked. She had switched on a bedside lamp.

"Burglary," Kyle said, removing his service revolver from the nightstand drawer. "I've got to go help, but it shouldn't take too long." He finished dressing, buckled on his duty belt, and slid the revolver into its holder. "Maybe you can keep the bed warm for me?"

Claudia smiled. "Okay, but be careful."

"Don't worry," Kyle said. He leaned over to kiss her. "Everything will be fine."

Fitz's truck was just beginning to warm up inside when Kyle climbed into the front seat. "I hope Doc's okay," Fitz said as they pulled out of the parking lot. "Stuff like this doesn't usually happen out here."

"How long have you known him?"

"Old Doc? Years and years. Ever since Ruthie and I moved to Mill River. He was one of the first people we met and he's been a good friend ever since. His wife and Ruthie are real close."

"Is Leroy meeting us there, too?"

"Nope," Fitz said. "He went off shift a few hours ago, but he isn't home and he didn't answer his cell. Who knows where he is."

"I can think of a few places," Kyle said, and then added cautiously, "You know, maybe it would be better if you just let him go. It seems like he's getting to be more trouble than he's worth."

Fitz snorted. "I've come really close, let

me tell you. But it's hard to find anybody willing to work here. We can't pay what people deserve. We've barely got the staff and resources to scrape by, which is why you and I are doing what we're doing right now."

Kyle nodded but decided not to prolong the conversation. Fitz was driving fast, focusing on the curving road ahead of them. The police chief didn't need any distractions.

Leroy crouched against the large spruce in back of the bakery until Fitz's truck had disappeared.

Department policy required at least two, and preferably three, officers to respond to a burglary in progress. As always, Fitz had followed that policy to the letter. The old man was so predictable.

Mitchell Road was a winding mountain trail, and the address he'd given the emergency dispatcher was a good three miles from the center of town. With the snow reducing visibility and making the roads slick, it would take the officers at least ten minutes to reach the right house. They'd probably take several more minutes to realize there was nothing wrong and another ten minutes to get back to the station. By his best estimate, he had at least twenty-five minutes to execute the rest of his plan.

Plenty of time.

Leroy reached for the two nearest empty beer bottles and stood them upright in the snow. Next, he lurched to his feet and grabbed the container of gasoline. After the beers, a good dose of paint fumes, and almost an hour in the bitter cold, he was wobbly and seeing double. His hands shook as he positioned the mouth of the gas container above the empty bottles. Filling them with fuel was even more difficult. His old gas jug didn't have a nozzle, and he had forgotten to bring a funnel. He struggled to hold the container steady as he poured the gasoline. Once the bottles were almost full, Leroy reached into his sack for the old rag.

He ripped the cloth down the middle, twisted each of the two halves into a cylinder, and stuffed them into the mouths of the beer bottles, making sure to leave some of the material hanging outside each glass neck as a fuse. *Just enough,* he thought as he shook the nearly empty gasoline container. He turned it upside down and watched the last of the gas drip out onto the protruding fabric.

He was ready to show Claudia just how much he loved her.

Giddy with pride and an exuberant sense of anticipation, he felt like doing a dance under the big spruce tree. Grasping the loaded beer bottles, he almost bolted out of the thicket toward the bakery, but he remembered the supplies and other bottles strewn around his resting place. He would need to return them to his car so that no one would suspect him of starting the fire.

Somewhat grudgingly, Leroy set the Molotov cocktails in the snow and gathered up his mess.

Doc Richardson's rustic log home was set back off the highway. The department's Jeep was parked in front with its lights and sirens turned off. Ron got out to meet Fitz and Kyle as they pulled up.

"It's been dark and quiet since I got here," Ron said. "I don't see any suspicious vehicles around, either. But, there's no telling what's going on inside."

"It's been at least fifteen minutes since the call came in," Fitz said. "We'd better hurry. Ron, you go around the left side. We'll go around the other way and meet you in back."

The officers branched off, examining the windows and doors of the house for signs of forced entry. They reconvened in the dark backyard.

"I don't see anything unusual," Ron whispered.

"Me neither," Fitz said, "but dispatch told me the phone lines were cut. I think we'd better announce ourselves and see what's going on. Ron, you stay back here. Kyle and I will cover the front."

Kyle and Fitz went back to the front porch and took up positions on each side of the door. They drew their service revolvers, and Fitz nodded and pounded on the door.

"This is the police! Open the door and come out with your hands in the air."

A minute passed, and they heard footsteps inside the house. The porch light flickered on.

Kyle and Fitz stepped backward, crouching with guns raised as the front door opened. An older man wearing thick glasses and pajamas stood in the entryway with his hands held up near each side of his head.

"Don't shoot, don't shoot! What's going on? Fitz?"

"Doc, you all right? We got a report of a burglary in progress out here," Fitz said. He lowered his weapon, and Kyle did the same. "Did you hear anyone break in?"

"What? No, nobody broke in. Jane's out of town visiting her sister, and there's no

446

one here but me."

"You're sure about that?" Fitz said. "You didn't call 9-1-1 about twenty minutes ago?"

"No, I've been asleep since around ten o'clock. I didn't even hear you drive up." The doctor looked drowsy and perplexed. "You can come in and look around, if you want."

"It must have been a crank call, Chief," Kyle said. He placed his service revolver back in his duty belt as Fitz sighed and shook his head.

"Goddamn punks. Ron, false alarm. Come on back around," Fitz called. "Doc, I'm sorry to bother you. There's gonna be hell to pay for this, I promise."

"No, no problem," Doc said. "I'm sorry you boys drove all the way out here for nothing, though. Would you like to come in for a bit? I could make some coffee."

"That's nice of you, but I think we'll pass. I have to get back to Ruthie, let her know everything's okay, and then get hold of dispatch and see if we can't find out who called us out here." Fitz started back toward the Jeep. "But stop by the bakery if you're in town tomorrow . . . er, today," he said, over his shoulder. "You've got some coffee and pie on the house."

"Will do." Doc Richardson smiled and raised a hand in thanks before closing his door.

Leroy stood beneath the big spruce tree with the loaded beer bottles at his feet. He adjusted his ski mask and looked up at the windows of the apartments above the bakery. His heart was beating hard.

She'll love me for this, he thought

Leroy flicked the cigarette lighter and smiled at the tiny, perfect flame.

Two things he knew for sure: he was meant to be with Claudia, and he wouldn't get another opportunity like this one.

He held the lighter to the tip of the rag extending from the first Molotov cocktail. The rag ignited. Leroy dropped the lighter, picked up the bottle-bomb, and heaved it through the window in the bakery's back door.

The sound of the glass shattering made him flinch. For a moment, he stood without moving, transfixed at the sight of the puddles of fire on the floor of the bakery.

One more, he thought, snapping himself back into action. Then he would run to his car, drive around the block and onto Main Street, and arrive at the bakery just in time to come to Claudia's rescue.

Leroy lit the second Molotov cocktail and lifted it into the air.

Startled awake, Claudia rolled over in Kyle's bed.

She held her breath, listening for whatever it was that woke her. There was another loud *pop,* and then nothing.

Fitz's truck backfiring? Maybe Kyle's back, she thought. She snuggled down beneath the blankets, listening for footsteps coming up the stairs to the apartment, but the building remained quiet.

Claudia had almost dozed off again when she smelled smoke. She sat up, sniffed to make sure, and scrambled out of bed. She jumped as an alarm began to screech, two alarms, smoke detectors in Kyle's apartment and in the bakery downstairs. She grasped around for her clothes, a robe, something to put on, but the air inside the apartment was growing more and more uncomfortable to breathe. She threw open a window. Frozen air spilled inside, cutting through the fumes, and she took several deep breaths.

Kyle's bathrobe was draped over a chair near the bed. She took one more breath and put on the robe before dropping to her hands and knees.

Stay low to the floor, she thought as her lesson plan for fire safety ran through her head. Crawl to the door and check whether it's hot or cool. She was on her hands and knees in the hallway now, heading toward the living room and front door. Once there, she pressed a hand against it.

The door was warm.

It's not hot, Claudia decided, and she touched the back of her hand to the metal knob. When she felt that it, too, was still cool enough to handle, she opened the door a crack. More smoke poured in through the opening, but she didn't see any flames. *Go, go, go,* she told herself, and she crawled out of the apartment. The smoke was still thickening. She began to cough. Her eyes were burning and watering, but she could see the door to the apartment across the landing.

Ruth!

Claudia crawled to the Fitzgeralds' door and knocked. "Ruth, are you there?" Gasping for breath, she twisted the doorknob. It was locked, so she banged on the door again.

"There's a fire and we have to get out of here. Ruth?" Even kneeling in front of the door, she felt dizzy. The smoke was suffocating, pressing itself down her throat and into her eyes.

"Ruth," she called, before she coughed again. She couldn't catch her breath. Her field of vision darkened from gray to black as she collapsed against the door.

Following Ron, who was driving the department's Jeep, Fitz and Kyle rounded the final curve in the highway as they came back into Mill River. Sirens blared in the distance.

"Wonder what's going on," Fitz muttered.

They turned onto Main Street. Even several blocks away, they could see the flames shooting from the bakery.

"Oh, God, Ruthie," Fitz said. The lights and sirens on the department's Jeep came to life as it shot forward ahead of them. Fitz stomped on the accelerator.

"Claudia's in my apartment," Kyle said. He grabbed the radio in Fitz's truck, but Ron's voice came through the speakers before he could say anything more.

"Dispatch, this is Officer Wykowski in Mill River. We've got a building on fire at 130 Main Street. Requesting fire personnel and paramedics, over."

"Officer Wykowski, this is Rutland County dispatch. Roger that, building on fire at 130 Main Street. We've already got fire and medical on the way, over."

451

"We can't wait," Kyle said as Fitz slammed on the brakes outside the bakery. A few people were beginning to gather on the street. Fitz and Kyle jumped from the truck and pushed them aside as they sprinted to the building's entrance. Fitz unlocked the door and opened it, releasing a stream of smoke into the cold.

The stairwell to the apartments was fully walled off from the rest of the first floor, but it was still full of dense smoke. Grasping the handrail for guidance, Fitz and Kyle climbed toward the apartments with their gloved hands over their noses and mouths.

Kyle was about to turn toward the door to his own apartment when they nearly tripped over Claudia slumped against Fitz's door.

"Ruthie!" the police chief yelled. He unlocked the apartment door as Kyle bent to lift Claudia. "Take her! I've got to get Ruthie!" Fitz rushed past him into the apartment.

Struggling to breathe, Kyle carried Claudia down the stairwell to the outside exit. Two fire trucks and an ambulance had just stopped in front of the bakery.

"I need help! Get some oxygen!" Kyle said, his voice raspy and hoarse. He coughed as two of the firefighters took Claudia from his arms. A third guided him closer to one of the trucks and put an oxygen mask up to his face. Several members of the fire and rescue unit began pulling out long lines of white hose while another group, wearing protective gear, raced past him up into the stairwell.

"Take deep breaths. Is there anyone else in the building?" the firefighter holding the mask asked.

Kyle nodded and pulled the mask from his face so that he could speak. "The police chief. And his wife. He went in after her. Second floor apartment, right side." The firefighter radioed the information to the men inside the building. Kyle looked around, trying to see where the men had taken Claudia.

"There," the firefighter said, pointing behind him. Kyle turned to see Claudia lying on a stretcher with a mask strapped to her face. She'd come to and was nodding slightly in response to questions from one of the paramedics.

Thank God, Kyle thought, but then he worried again about Fitz and Ruth. He watched the fire crews working, the jets of water dousing the bakery. Most of the flames appeared to have been extinguished, but the fire department wasn't taking any

453

chances.

There was another flurry of activity as the group of firefighters that had entered the building came back out. Fitz was between two of the men with his arms around their shoulders, while Ruth was supported by two others. Both were coughing and gasping for breath.

"She was standing by the open window," Fitz wheezed to Kyle as a firefighter prepared to fasten an oxygen mask around his face. "She said the door was hot and she was afraid to open it, so she sealed it up with wet towels. Said she knew we'd come for her."

"I never heard Claudia," Ruth said. "Is she all right?"

Kyle lowered his oxygen mask. "I think she will be. I'll be right back." He walked over to Claudia and took one of her hands.

"Kyle," she said, her voice barely audible. "Ruth —"

"They're all right. I just spoke to them. Everybody got out okay." He saw one of the paramedics coming back toward them. "You breathed a lot of smoke. They'll probably want to take you to Rutland to make sure you're okay, but I'll see you there in a little while, all right?"

Claudia closed her eyes and nodded. Kyle

squeezed her hand and walked back toward Fitz.

"Hey, we've got one more!" The last firefighter had exited the building with a bundle of beige fur in his arms. "We need to get him to a vet, though." Sham the Siamese yowled and panted as the firefighter placed him in a portable cage.

Everybody got out, Kyle thought. The relief sank in as he leaned against the shiny red fender of the fire truck.

"Hey, Kyle! Chief! Are you guys okay?" Ron made his way through the center of activity.

"We're good," Kyle said. Fitz removed his oxygen mask and nodded.

"You'll never believe what we found on the other side of the building." He motioned for Kyle and the police chief to follow him.

They approached a second ambulance where another stretcher was being readied for transport. Ron pointed at the man on the stretcher. "Guess who we have here?"

Kyle and Fitz stepped closer to the stretcher. The unconscious man had severe burns to the right side of his face, and part of his right hand was gone.

"I've got a hunch it's someone we all know," Kyle said, frowning. He leaned in to get a good look at the victim, then shook his head in disgust.

"Son of a bitch," Fitz said.

"He was stretched out in the snow wearing a black ski mask when we found him," Ron said. "Obviously up to no good. And you should see the fresh mess spray-painted around back. I guess ol' Daisy's story was for real."

"About the man in black, you mean?" Kyle said. "The one she insisted she saw the night her trailer caught on fire?"

"Yep. She called the station a few hours ago and said she saw the same guy who burned her trailer hanging out behind the bakery," Ron said. "I didn't get to check it out, though, because the fake burglary call came in right after hers."

"What do you want to bet he made that bogus call?"

"Wouldn't surprise me." Ron looked at the bakery and sighed. "I hope you got plenty of fire insurance, Chief. And you, too," he said to Kyle. Kyle nodded as Fitz grimaced and squinted up at his blackened building.

"We all got out okay. That's all I care about," Fitz said in a gruff voice. "But what the hell do you think Leroy was doing here?"

"Maybe some sort of revenge," Ron said. "We found him in back of the building in an area with a lot of shattered brown glass. He might've been messing with bottle-bombs to set the bakery on fire, but the idiot didn't get it right. There's no neck on a beer bottle, not like a wine bottle, anyway. If he filled it with gas and lit it, he might not've had enough time to throw it before it exploded. I'm going to take a better look back there to see if he left anything else." Kyle and Fitz nodded at Ron before turning their attention to Leroy.

"He must've still been after Claudia," Kyle said finally. "But something this dangerous, I never thought, I mean, even Leroy —"

"He holds a grudge longer than anybody I know," Fitz said. "He might've been real sore about you dating Claudia. He was hot on her for a while. Maybe he was trying to get rid of you. We'll get warrants to search his car and his house, see if we can find out what he was trying to do. And then I'm going to make sure he gets what he deserves, even more than he already has."

Kyle nodded, only half hearing Fitz's comments. He was thinking about how grateful he was that his daughter hadn't been in the building and how thankful he was that Claudia, Fitz, Ruth, and even Sham were safe.

The paramedics loaded Leroy into the

ambulance and closed the back doors. As the vehicle sped away, Kyle couldn't help but remember his own words to Claudia: "Sometimes what you find in a small town can surprise you."

CHAPTER 20

2012

The marbleworks hadn't changed.

It was still the same stately building, down to the bronze plaque at the front door engraved with its date of completion. From the front seat of Father O'Brien's truck, Mary was too far away to read it, but she had committed the inscription to memory years ago: "McAllister Marbleworks, est. July 22, 1894."

She had made up her mind upon leaving the outpatient clinic that she would get a good look at the marbleworks. She had asked Michael to drive past it so that she might see it again. It was the one part of Rutland that stood out, a grand structure from a different era. Seeing it brought back memories of her youth — memories of her relationship with Patrick. She remembered the yellowed picture of Conor as a young man, standing with his father on the front steps of the marbleworks. He had been the closest thing she had ever had to a real grandfather, and even now, she missed him.

"One of Conor's great-great-grandsons is in charge now," Mary said, still peering out the window. "Brought it back from financial collapse. I read it in the *Herald* a while ago."

Father O'Brien grasped the steering wheel, waiting. Daisy was sound asleep in the backseat. Finally, Mary sighed and turned to him. "I'm ready," she said. The priest nodded and shifted the truck into drive.

Mary looked again at the marbleworks as they pulled away. She focused on the buildings in Rutland, too, trying to absorb each image of the town. It would be the last time she would see any of them.

A part of her refused to believe what the doctors had told her — that she had metastatic pancreatic cancer and had perhaps six months left to live. She was a little groggy from the anesthetic and tranquilizers, but otherwise felt fine. The yellowish tint to her skin was rapidly disappearing. The doctors had inserted a stent in her bile duct to keep it from being blocked off by the primary tumor. The stent would prevent her from becoming jaundiced again for at least a few months. Apparently, her last few months.

Mary had a vague recollection of her oncologist mentioning a schedule for follow-up visits and some experimental treatments of last resort, but she knew without a doubt that she would refuse all of them. She would only return to Mill River, to her quiet, peaceful home, and live out the remainder of her life.

Mary looked over at the elderly priest. His eyes were fixed blankly on the road ahead, but she was sure that his thoughts were far away from the highway. His shoulders were a little more stooped than they had been on the way into town that morning.

The worst part of learning her approaching fate was realizing that Michael would be left without her. It pained her to imagine him sitting in the parish house, eating supper by himself. She could envision him reading in his office, counting his spoons, having no one he could really talk to. She knew that he would want to tell her of his day, to confide in her, to seek her advice. He would be alone.

A loud snort from the backseat startled her. Daisy shifted position and muttered something that was unintelligible except for the words "magic snow." Mary turned to gaze fondly at her, quite as if she were seeing Daisy for the first time. Daisy in person was exactly how Michael had described her. The endearing misfit was childlike and socially awkward, yes, but Mary knew now that she was also much more.

"We're almost home," Father O'Brien said as they rounded the final bend in the highway before it straightened out into the heart of Mill River.

Mary looked up at her mansion. It felt odd to see the house through the windshield of the pickup instead of looking down through her bedroom window at vehicles on the main road. She was shocked at the degree to which her white marble home stood out among the leafless trees surrounding it. *This is what everyone else sees,* she thought. A huge white house that bears no resemblance to anything else in town. Mary closed her eyes, trying to remember whether she had ever noticed that contrast. She didn't recall having seen it during her disastrous bakery outing more than a decade ago. Perhaps she had seen it when the mansion was first completed or after returning home with Patrick from an evening out. She concentrated on the distant past, but could only remember sitting in Patrick's new car, trying to avoid seeing anyone.

Michael had told her how her own seclusion in her beautiful white mansion was a topic of great curiosity for others in Mill River. That she was an object of mystery had never bothered her, but what if the people in town, the people she watched and had come to love, thought of her as she thought of her marble home now? Cold and distant?

True, they didn't know that she had been responsible for the decades of anonymous surprises in Mill River or that she felt so invested in their lives. She had given them no way to know her. They knew nothing of her likes or dislikes, her sense of humor, her dreams. But she was a real person, a person who knew the difference between being alone and being lonely, who wanted so much to be accepted, to have coffee at the bakery, to come face-to-face with someone she didn't know without feeling fearful.

It occurred to her then what she could do, a way she might be able to tell the people of Mill River who she was and how much she cared for them.

She breathed a sigh of relief as the pickup stopped outside the back door of the mansion. Even with the Valium, she hadn't felt right since they had left early in the morning. She took Michael's hand as she stepped down from the truck. It was a good thing. Her legs were weak and wobbly.

"Steady now, I've got you," Father O'Brien said, helping her stand.

"I can help, too, Father!" Daisy said as she clambered out of the backseat. She hurried around to Mary's other side and slipped an arm around her waist. "Two is better than one, isn't it?"

"Well, yes, in this case, it is," he said, managing a weak smile.

They helped her up the stairs to her bedroom. Father O'Brien sat on the side of the bed as she lay down. "I know you're exhausted," he said. "Just try to rest. I've got to take Daisy home and then I'll be back." Mary didn't like the expression on his face. It was the expression he wore when he told her of his most difficult experiences as a priest. She knew that he was pushing his own emotions away, trying to temporarily free himself from the knowledge of her condition.

"It was wonderful meeting you, Mrs. McAllister," Daisy said. "And don't you worry, you'll be feeling better in no time, I just know it! Oh! That reminds me — how would you like a free bottle of my Sick-Away Potion? Works like a charm, it does, and I know I've got some left at home."

"That would be very kind of you, Daisy, thank you," Father O'Brien said, before

Mary could reply. Daisy hadn't been in the room when the doctors had given their diagnosis, and Mary was grateful for his answer. But now she laid a hand on Father O'Brien's arm and smiled up at Daisy.

"Daisy, you have been so kind to me today," she said, ignoring Father O'Brien's gasp of surprise. "I wonder if you might come by to see me from time to time. I'm sure Father O'Brien could bring you. I would so enjoy your company."

Daisy could hardly contain herself. "Oh, Mrs. McAllister, I'd love to come see you again! And I just know the potion will help you feel better," she said, clapping her hands. She bent down and kissed Mary on the cheek. "Goodbye, Mrs. McAllister! Get well soon!"

Father O'Brien squeezed Mary's hand and followed Daisy out of the bedroom.

With tears in her eyes, Mary listened for the sound of the back door opening and closing. Only when she was finally, mercifully, alone, did she stop fighting the overwhelming truth and begin to cry.

Father O'Brien was gone only about an hour. He dropped Daisy off in front of her mobile home before he stopped for a few groceries. He found himself rushing down the supermarket aisles, grabbing at bread and fruit and cans of soup. Deliberately, he walked slower. Mary was probably sound asleep, he told himself, and there was really no reason to rush. Then again, time was precious now, and he didn't want to waste it.

In the dry goods aisle, between the egg noodles and the neat blue and orange boxes of macaroni and cheese, he almost broke down.

He took several deep breaths and squeezed his eyes shut. He resolved not to think any more about Mary until he arrived back at her house. Methodically, he finished his shopping.

Her house was dark when he again parked outside the back door, but she had turned on the porch light. Perhaps she was awake. He left the groceries on the kitchen counter and went upstairs, calling to her.

Mary was standing in front of the large bay window in her bedroom. She pulled a shawl wrapped around her shoulders a bit tighter as he came up beside her.

"How are you feeling?" he asked.

"Fine. I'm glad to be home." She was still wearing her eye patch. When she turned toward him, he noticed that her face was tear-streaked and felt his own emotional control start to slip again.

"I knew you would be. Mary, I'm . . . I'm so sorry. I want so much for this whole thing to go away, for it never to have happened, but I just don't know what to do." He was struggling now, pursing his mouth and blinking rapidly.

"So much has changed," she said in a distant voice. "But we'll go on, just as we always have. I've still got some time left. Other than that, I'm not sure there is anything else either of us can do." She paused to wipe at a tear that had slipped out from under her eye patch. "When we left here this morning, I just kept telling myself that whatever was wrong with me would be something a doctor could fix."

"We were both hoping that."

"And I was so scared, even with the Valium. When the doctors came in afterward, I knew what they were going to tell me just from their expressions. But hearing it was still an awful shock." She was trembling.

"Hearing something like that would be difficult no matter the circumstances."

"Yes. And Michael, I should have told you this earlier, but I wanted to thank you for taking me to Rutland. I know I made it anything but easy for you. Going in, I didn't think I'd want to see the marbleworks, but coming home, knowing that it would be my last time in Rutland . . . I'm glad I got to see it again."

"And you got to meet Daisy."

Mary smiled faintly. "I can't tell you how grateful I am for that, too. After all these years of hearing about her, buying her little jars of strange concoctions —"

"— and pouring them down your sink." Father O'Brien added with a weak smile.

Mary sighed. "Yes, she's just exactly as you described her to me, and yet so much about her was . . . unexpected. Seeing her in person was the only way I would have realized just how special she is. And meeting Daisy today really taught me something. That, and seeing my own house from town, like everybody else does." Mary's expression became more serious as she looked again out the window.

"How do you mean?"

"I've lived in this house for so many years and, until today, not once did I think of how it appears from down there — a monstrosity, isolated and different from everything around it." She frowned and shook her head. "Thanks to you, I know everything about everyone in Mill River, but I don't know them personally. And it's too late for me to do much to change that. But those people down there, they don't know me. All this time, I've felt like I've been part of their world, but I know now that that's not really true."

Father O'Brien looked at her with raised eyebrows. "You know, you surprised me earlier, asking Daisy to come by. I never thought I'd hear you invite someone to visit you. But it's not too late for other people, Mary. You can still meet some of the other folks in town, if you'd like."

"Oh, no, I couldn't. I didn't mean that," she said, with an anxious expression. "What I mean to say is that, well, look at Daisy. She's never met me before, and here she is offering me her friendship and her potions, the only things she really has to give. I never expected someone to reach out to me like that — so selflessly and with such kindness.

"All my life I've been terrified of people. I still am, except for you, and now maybe Daisy." When she turned to him, her visible eye was bright with excitement. "And still, for so long, I've tried to help them the only way I could. You've said many times that Mill River is full of decent, hardworking people, the kind that don't have a lot but would give everything they have to a neighbor in need."

"Yes, with a few exceptions," Father O'Brien said. "And I haven't yet given up hope on the exceptions."

"Like that awful kid outside the bakery . . . but I know you're right, Michael." Mary's smile faded into serene certainty as she looked again at the lights of Mill River below. "Daisy and the other kind, caring people in this town deserved a much better neighbor in me. They deserve to know that someone has cared about them all these years." Before Father O'Brien could interrupt, Mary continued. "I think I know what I need to do before I die, how I can make up for lost time." She reached out and touched his arm. "Will you help me?"

When he looked down at her, it was as if he were looking into Conor's face again, into that same pleading expression he had worn when the patriarch had asked him to look after Mary. He had no more power to refuse Mary's request now than he had had to refuse Conor's on that sad night so many years ago.

"Of course, however I can, but what do you intend to do?"

"I have so much, Michael, much more than I need. Soon, I won't need anything at all." She raised a thin, wrinkled hand and pressed it flat against the bedroom window.

Her gaze was still fixed on the oasis of light shining up from the darkness. "I want to take care of Daisy and all the others. I want to give them everything I have."

Father O'Brien struggled to come to terms with the fact that Mary was dying.

In the first few months after the diagnosis, her illness did not progress as rapidly as the doctors had predicted. For this, he was grateful. He found himself examining her each time he visited the house, looking for any sign of a faltering step or increased fatigue. Once in a while, Mary mentioned feeling more tired than usual, but Daisy's frequent visits helped keep Mary smiling.

When the deep snow of winter finally gave way to moist earth and tender new leaves, they reveled in the springtime. The property behind the mansion was mostly pasture, surrounded by a forest of pine, oak, birch, and sugar maple trees. On the warmer days, they walked down to the barn and around the greening, empty pastures, sometimes talking, sometimes not.

When Daisy was with them, they couldn't get a word in edgewise.

Daisy delighted in gathering herbs for her potions during these outdoor treks. She insisted on explaining the medicinal use of the plants she collected, the proper way to preserve them, and their uses in certain potions, but Mary and Father O'Brien always listened attentively.

"You know, Michael," Mary whispered as Daisy spotted a cluster of clover and rushed over to it, "we must keep coming here with her as long as we can. Even when I start to feel poorly. She's so happy here. She mustn't know what's happening to me until she has to."

"Of course, Mary dear," Father O'Brien replied. He blinked several times as she went over to Daisy. Mary put an arm around her shoulders and whispered in her ear. Holding up a four-leaf clover, Daisy smiled and hugged Mary around the waist.

They've become so close, he thought. A hint of wonder lit up his eyes as he watched them together.

"Come look, Michael!" Mary called. "Every clover in this clump has four leaves!"

Daisy examined the leaves in her hand and then looked up at him. "It's a miracle!" she said. She smiled at the sun as she waved a fistful of green in the air.

"Don't forget the library, Michael," Mary said one August evening as they discussed her plan, "and the schools. The children will need books. There were never enough books when I was in school."

"Books," Father O'Brien said. He was sitting at her bedside, dutifully taking notes.

"Make sure there's enough for new ones each year."

"There's more than enough, Mary."

"And we need to do something for the police," she said, clutching at her abdomen and wincing as she shifted position on the sitting room sofa. Dr. Richardson had written her a prescription for MS Contin, a narcotic painkiller, and Father O'Brien had become a regular customer at the pharmacy. The medication dulled the pain enough to permit her to focus on the disposition of her estate. "What do they need?"

"I'm not sure. I can talk with Fitz, if you'd like," Father O'Brien said.

"No, no, no one can know until I'm gone. You'll have to think of something, Michael."

"All right."

"Who else is there? Think of who else we can help, Michael." She fell asleep after that, with her head on the arm of the sofa and an expression of concentration still on her face.

Father O'Brien gazed at Mary. She seemed to have aged immeasurably since the start of spring. He noticed the deepened creases in her cheeks and forehead, the white hair that had grown even lighter in color, the frail form that collapsed in exhaustion after walking around the house for only a few minutes. He noticed her paling complexion, for the only sunlight that warmed her face now came in through the bedroom window as she looked down at Mill River.

He stood and gently pulled a crocheted throw over her. She spent so much of her time sleeping. The medication contributed to this, but Father O'Brien knew that her constant exhaustion meant that the cancer was slowly overcoming her.

Seeing her in such a weakened condition, Father O'Brien never would have believed that, each day, she waited for the mailman despite her anxiety, and that she struggled down the stairs to see whether a certain package had arrived.

He never would have guessed that she could carry the large box from Sears upstairs and open it. But she did. Somehow, Mary found the strength and courage to assemble and use what she had ordered. It took all her strength to repackage the equipment and hide it in her closet, but she managed to do this as well.

Father O'Brien would be surprised once

he learned that she had kept this secret from him.

Sometimes secrets were necessary, though, and she didn't feel guilty for keeping this one.

All would be revealed in time.

By September, Mary couldn't properly care for herself, and it became necessary to explain her illness and prognosis to Daisy.

"My cancer isn't something the doctors can fix," she had said in response to Daisy's first question. "I am going to die because of it. There isn't any medicine, or any potion, that can stop it. But the doctor gives me medicine to make me feel better. That way, I can enjoy the time I have left."

With moist eyes, Daisy looked from Mary to Father O'Brien and back to Mary. "When are you . . . how much time do you have left?"

"I don't know for sure, Daisy. Months, maybe. Yes, I think several more months."

"Oh." Daisy bit her lip and twisted her hands in her lap. "I always thought a month was a long time. But now, even several months feels too short." She grabbed Mary's hand and began to sob. "I don't know what to do."

Struggling to keep her composure, Mary

looked up at Father O'Brien.

"Daisy, my dear, we must make the most of the time Mary has left," he said, nodding at Mary. "We'll all spend lots of time together. And Mary will need our help, too. Will you help me to take care of her and keep her spirits up?"

Daisy squeezed Mary's hand and nodded.

She proved to be a selfless caregiver. Daisy spent hours in the marble mansion, keeping Mary company, fixing simple meals, and attending to her more personal needs. Father O'Brien also devoted his every spare moment to Mary and spent only a minimum amount of time on his congregation. As Mary's condition worsened, though, he knew that it still wasn't enough. Mary needed more assistance than he and Daisy could provide.

He ordered an adjustable hospital bed and had it moved into her room. Additional personal help for her, though, would be more of a problem. Mary required someone with a medical background, but he would never force her into a hospital. She wanted to die at home, on her own terms.

The only viable option was Rutland County's home health service. Father O'Brien remembered that Ron Wykowski's wife was a visiting nurse and arranged for her to come out to the mansion most days. Jean was honest and caring. More important, she was sensitive to Mary's anxiety problem.

To his surprise and great relief, Mary accepted Jean's presence without complaint. *If only she had a few more years,* he thought, *she might just get used to meeting people.*

"She likes my jewelry," Mary said to Father O'Brien one evening, smiling.

"Who?"

"Jeanie. She really likes to wear my engagement ring."

Father O'Brien put down his book and looked at her. *A strange topic of conversation, at least for Mary,* he thought. "You showed it to her?"

"No, not really. She found it herself, while I was napping."

Father O'Brien gasped. "Found it? Don't you keep it in your jewelry box? Did you give her permission to wear it?"

"Well, no, but I don't mind." Mary wasn't upset at all. On the contrary, she was settled comfortably against the raised back of the hospital bed. "That ring holds bad memories for me — I don't know why I kept it, really. She wears it around the house, when I'm asleep, or while she thinks I'm asleep, but she puts it back before she leaves."

"Well, if she puts it back," Father O'Brien

said. He was still disturbed to think Jean would actually help herself to Mary's possessions.

"Oh, she won't steal it. Even if she borrows it for a while, which wouldn't surprise me, she'll bring it back. She's a good girl. She only wears the ring to escape, to pretend she's a princess or a movie star. I know how it feels to be a woman watching her youth slip away. It's not easy to do her job, taking care of people like me. If my ring brings her a bit of happiness, so be it."

"Hmmph." There was a certain tone in Mary's voice that made him drop the subject. After all, someone they both knew had pilfered spoons all his life and never returned them.

Father O'Brien dreaded the autumn. The days of summer had looked much the same, enabling him to pretend that time was no longer against them. As the reds and oranges of the trees grew more vibrant, though, Mary's condition continued to deteriorate. Often, he sat with her at her bedroom window. As she slept, he held her hand and watched the gradual emptying of branches. The reappearance of the dark, barren limbs reminded him that Mary had so little time remaining.

■ ■ ■ ■

The fire that destroyed Daisy's mobile home that November provided Mary another opportunity to help someone in need. Father O'Brien made the arrangements for the purchase and delivery of a new mobile home. Mary wrote an anonymous letter for him to give to Daisy explaining the gift, but she was surprised when he brought it back to her the evening after the mobile home was delivered.

"I just couldn't bear to give it to her," Father O'Brien said. "Daisy was so excited, thinking she had conjured it up herself. I decided to let her keep believing that."

"The poor dear," Mary said, clutching her side and alternatively laughing and wincing. "Then it's good she didn't see my letter. Eventually, she'll find out what really happened. I'm just glad she's happy."

They both knew that the approaching Christmas would be Mary's last. When Father O'Brien arrived at her home after Christmas morning Mass, she was awake and waiting for him.

"Merry Christmas, Michael," she said from her bed. "I have a present for you." She held out to him a small, beautifully wrapped gift.

"What's this?" he asked.

"Just a little something I thought you might like. Go ahead, open it."

He untied the ribbon. Carefully, he peeled back the wrapping paper to reveal a small, thin box.

"Go on," Mary urged.

Father O'Brien removed the lid. Inside the box, wrapped in tissue paper, was a shiny silver teaspoon.

It was one of Mary's, although it had been decades since he had last seen any of her silver spoons. Of course, that was entirely his own fault. After their first tea in the mansion, when she had given him a fork on his saucer instead of a teaspoon, he had resolved to have a look at what was in her flatware drawer. Catching him lurking around in the kitchen was all it had taken for her to remove her spoons to some hidden spot in the house. It had been for the best. He doubted if he would have been able to resist them.

"Oh," he breathed, staring at the spoon in the box.

Mary smiled. "Since you have a spoon from nearly everyone else in town, I thought it was time that you had one of mine." She raised a trembling hand, motioning to him.

"Turn it over. There's something on the other side."

An inscription was engraved on the smooth, convex back of the spoon. Father O'Brien had to put on his reading glasses to make out the tiny letters.

"To my dear friend, love, MEHM," he read aloud. His chin quivered. "Oh, Mary, I — I don't know what to say. Well, yes I do. It's just what I always wanted." He was blinking rapidly now, but they both smiled at the truth in his words. "How did you manage this?" he asked.

"Jean helped me," Mary said. "I came up with the idea some weeks ago, and she was kind enough to take a spoon and have it engraved for me." Mary must have noticed the look of panic that appeared on his face, because she added quickly, "Not to worry, though. She doesn't know anything about your . . . collection. In fact, she doesn't even know whom the gift was for."

At once, the tiny spoon became his most prized possession, a symbol of friendship and acceptance. He would keep it in his desk drawer, apart from the others. Mary's spoon was different — a gift untarnished by guilt or greed or sin.

"I have something for Daisy, too . . . a new set of measuring cups. I thought she could use them for her potions," Mary said after a moment.

"She wanted to come see you this evening, so I'll bring her by then," Father O'Brien said, still tracing the delicate edges of his spoon. "I'm sure she'll love them."

When Father O'Brien and Daisy arrived at Mary's on a dark night in early February, he sensed a change in her spirit and the reflection of his own thoughts.

"Hello, my dears." There was physical and emotional pain in her voice. "It's been a year."

"I know," he said. Daisy remained uncharacteristically silent, but went around to the other side of Mary's bed and took her hand.

"I don't have very much longer."

This he also knew, but could not bring himself to acknowledge out loud. Instead, he removed his coat and draped it over the back of his usual seat at her bedside.

"Michael," Mary said before he could sit, "would you give us a minute? There's something I need to tell my Daisy." She smiled at the concerned face of the woman squeezing her hand.

"Of course," he said slowly, backing away from the bed. "I'll wait in the parlor." He glanced with curiosity at Mary before closing the door behind him.

Downstairs, he turned on no lights. A large lamp sat on the end table nearest him, but he felt the darkness of the parlor to be a shield of sorts, a way to diffuse his thoughts into nothingness, to prevent him from staring at his hands clenched in his lap. Certainly Mary was entitled to speak to Daisy alone, but her request to do so was not like her, and it worried him.

After a long while, he heard Mary's bedroom door open. "Father O'Brien?" Daisy called from the top of the stairs. Now he finally switched on the table lamp and stood up.

"Down here, Daisy," he answered. She sniffed and flew down the stairs toward him.

"She wants to see you now. Oh, Father, she told me . . . oh, I never knew, and now I don't know what to do. I love her so much. I don't want her to die, she can't die," Daisy sobbed, clutching him around his waist.

"I know, Daisy, I know," he said, trying to keep control of himself. "So many things happen that we can't help. But we both need to be strong for Mary right now." Gently, he pried Daisy's arms loose and took a step back. "Look, why don't you go to the washroom and dry your eyes while I go up for a few minutes. Yes?"

Daisy sniffed again and nodded. "As soon as I get home, I'm going to try to make a healing potion for her, something stronger than anything I've made so far. Maybe a new, super-strong potion will help."

"That's the spirit, Daisy," Father O'Brien said. "I know Mary would appreciate that, too." He squeezed the little woman's shoulder and started up the stairs.

Mary looked weaker than she had when he had first arrived. She turned toward him as he opened the bedroom door.

"Is Daisy all right?" she asked. "She left pretty quickly. I think she was trying to keep from crying in front of me."

"She's holding up."

"Michael, is everything ready?"

"Almost," he said, sitting down. "Jim Gasaway says most of the paperwork's done, but some can't be finalized until after . . ." He suddenly found himself unable to speak, but Mary nodded.

"I know how I'm going to tell them," she said. He noticed then the sealed envelope and a package wrapped in brown paper resting on her lap. With a shaking hand, she held them out to him. "A letter and gift for the town. I've had the gift for a while, and I wrote the letter today. I think together, they'll explain everything."

"To whom should I give these?" he asked, taking the package and slipping the envelope into the inside pocket of his blazer.

"I want you to read the letter at the town meeting," she said, "and then show them what's inside the package. About a month from now. That should be enough time to finish the arrangements, shouldn't it?"

"A month is plenty," he said. He noticed that Mary's breathing was becoming more labored, as it did when her pain medication was beginning to wear off. "Mary," he said, reaching into his coat pocket, "I brought a refill of your medicine." He placed a full prescription bottle on her nightstand.

"Thank you," she said, closing her eyes. "I'll definitely need it tonight."

Father O'Brien looked at Mary's skin, yellow with returning jaundice, and at the thin outline of her under the bedcovers. *She needs round-the-clock care,* he thought. Her voice had never sounded so weak. "Mary, I think you need to have someone here with you tonight."

"Nonsense," she said. "I'll be just fine. The weekend nurse will be by tomorrow, and I have everything I need right now." Something in the tone of her voice unnerved him, just as her asking to speak to Daisy alone had. A hint of a secret, something that she was keeping from him. Or was it that his own sorrow in seeing her suffer was clouding his perception?

"Just the same, after I take Daisy home, I think I'll come back and stay the night," he said. "You shouldn't be left alone anymore."

"No, Michael, tomorrow is Sunday, and you've got services to prepare. I'll be fine, really. I insist that you go home."

She was adamant. Despite his concern, the last thing he wanted to do was upset her. Perhaps one more night alone wouldn't hurt anything.

"All right," he said finally, "but I don't like the thought of your being here by yourself. Tomorrow, I'm going to make arrangements for a nurse to be here all the time."

A sigh was the only indication that Mary had heard him. After a moment, she turned her head on the pillow. "Michael, could you raise the bed a bit more," she said. "I can hardly see out the window." He pushed a button at the side of her hospital bed, slowly raising it into an upright position. It had started to snow, the kind of large, fluffy flakes that precede a major storm.

"Michael?"

"Yes?"

"There is one last thing I need to tell you,

486

something you don't know, that I intend to reveal to the others in town as well."

She raised her head to look at him. Her expression simultaneously acknowledged his surprise and prevented him from speaking. In a gravelly voice, she half whispered her most private secret, the answer to a question he had asked himself so often.

As she waited for his response, he blinked rapidly. "I wasn't sure, but recently, I've suspected as much," he said finally. "It means so much to me to finally know."

"I wanted to tell you earlier, but I couldn't. Somehow, the time wasn't right. But after the trip into Rutland, everything changed." Mary smiled and leaned back, watching the patches of white fluttering outside her window. "Isn't the snow beautiful?"

"Yes, it is." He was barely able to speak.

"You need to promise me, Michael, that you won't sit here all night. There's no need. Do you promise?"

"Mary, I —"

"Please promise me, Michael."

He put his head in his hands. "I promise. I'll stay only until you fall asleep."

"And you've got the letter and gift?"

"Yes, Mary dear."

With a loud meow, Mary's cat jumped

onto the bed. The Siamese curled up next to her, nudging her hand for attention.

"Hello, Sham-Sham," she said, stroking the cat's head. "When I'm gone, you'll find him a good home, won't you?"

"Of course, Mary, of course." He reached over to her, smoothed a strand of hair away from her face. She smiled with her eyes closed.

"Michael?"

"Yes?"

"Thank you for being my dearest and only friend. Thank you . . . so much." Her voice was soft and a bit slurred. She drifted into sleep before he could reply.

He was so afraid now, afraid that she would be gone by morning, afraid of being without her. He wanted to stay, but he had never broken any promise to her. He couldn't start now, especially if his promise to go home was the last he would ever make to her. He would leave, see that Daisy got home safely, and return to the mansion at first light.

Father O'Brien looked down at Mary as he put on his coat. Sham purred and stared at him with sleepy blue eyes. He said a silent prayer and made the sign of the cross as he stood above them.

"God bless you, Mary dear," he whispered, trying to muster the strength to force himself back downstairs and out into the night.

CHAPTER 21

The town hall was almost full.

Father O'Brien stood in a doorway off the main meeting room. While new additions — a kitchen and a wing for the town offices — had been constructed within the last dozen years or so, the original central meeting room of the town hall building was old, as old as Mill River itself. Inside, the wooden walls stretching up into exposed beams created a wonderful acoustic. The dull floorboards, worn by thousands of footsteps over many decades, creaked as people shuffled in from outside.

The town hall was used for various gatherings throughout the year — the Rotary Club and the Kiwanis held their meetings there. Members of St. John's played bingo in the town hall every Thursday night. Senior citizens came to watch old movies on Saturday afternoons. The old building was the rainy-day site for the town's semiannual yard sale and the regular site for the holiday pitch-in in December and the annual town meeting in March.

The merry throng in the main meeting room greeted each new arrival. Women carried covered dishes to the kitchen at the far side of the building while the men joined clusters of others already talking and laughing. Children darted through the crowd playing tag and hide-and-seek.

Father O'Brien held Mary's small brown package in his hands, and he turned it over and over, slowly, feeling the edge of the taped paper. Watching the townspeople assembling for the meeting, Father O'Brien knew that he should be among them, visiting, making small talk. He was Mill River's only priest, after all. But he was afraid — no, he knew — that if he opened himself up to conversation, he would be peppered with questions about his upcoming announcement. And about Mary.

He would lie low until it was his turn to be heard. It was just as well. His current emotional state would make socializing with all of those people difficult.

For him, this Town Meeting Day was a somber occasion. It was the day he would keep his promise to Mary.

"Well, Father, I dunno how much more

excitement this little town can take." Fitz came up to lean against the doorway beside him. "They're all dying to know about your announcement. I know more than most, and I'm pretty curious myself, if truth be told. And add to that the whole mess with Leroy this past weekend, well." Fitz shook his head. "It's the most that's happened in Mill River in years."

"That's definitely true," Father O'Brien said. "I saw the article in the *Gazette* yesterday."

"Yep. The *Herald* had a story on it, too. And we've got TV stations out of Burlington calling for interviews. We're just now in the beginning stages of the investigation."

"The *Gazette* said that Leroy will be charged with arson and attempted murder."

Fitz nodded. "Yep, and whatever else we can make stick. We're not quite sure yet, but he'll be in the hospital for a while longer, so we've got some time to pull everything together."

"You feel certain he was really the one who started the fire?" Father O'Brien asked.

"Personally, I'm dead sure of it," Fitz said. "And I think we've got all the evidence we'll need to prove it. The whole back of the bakery was covered in fresh graffiti, and the fire department says the cause of the fire was a Molotov cocktail chucked through the back window. We executed a warrant on Leroy's car and found black spray paint, beer bottles, an empty gas container — everything he'd need for homemade bottle-bombs. From the way he was sprawled outside the building, we think one of those bottles exploded on him. Blew off part of his hand and burned his face pretty bad. But here's the kicker — somebody made a bogus burglary call just before the fire. The boys and I rushed out to Doc Richardson's and scared the poor man half to death before we realized what was going on. I called dispatch as soon as I could after the fire and had them trace the 9-1-1 call. Turns out it came from Leroy's cell phone, and he was right downtown here when he made it."

"Oh, dear," Father O'Brien said.

"It's pretty damning, if you'll pardon the expression," Fitz said. "He tried to hide his number with one of those fancy extra services the cell phone companies offer, but those features don't work with the 9-1-1 system. It was stupid of him not to know that."

"Why would he have wanted to burn the bakery in the first place?"

"We've had some ideas about motive," Fitz said. "I thought at first that he wanted to get back at me for putting him on desk duty. Hell, he should've been grateful I didn't fire him after he wrecked the Jeep. But yesterday, we searched his house, too, and you'll never guess what we found."

Father O'Brien raised his eyebrows and shrugged.

"A whole stack of magazines, the kind with pictures of naked women, but all of them had Claudia Simon's face glued in over the faces of the women."

"Claudia Simon? The teacher?"

"Yep. He had a bunch of photos of her, some of 'em with the faces cut out. He must've been watching her for a long time. We think he might've been in her house at some point, too. When we looked through his clothing at the hospital, we found a pair of women's underwear in his coat pocket, probably Claudia's. Kyle said Leroy came on to her real strong a couple weeks ago, but she rejected him. As best we can tell, Leroy heard about her starting to date Kyle and snapped."

"So he was trying to get rid of Kyle?"

"Maybe, and Claudia, too. She was at Kyle's place above the bakery the night of the fire."

"Oh, dear," Father O'Brien said again.

"It's just plain nuts," Fitz agreed. "By the

way, none of what I just told you has been made public yet, so keep it to yourself, would you?"

"Yes, of course," Father O'Brien said.

For several minutes, he stood with Fitz, watching the crowd in the main meeting room. Daisy was among those moving about. He noticed that she carried a small notebook as she made her way from person to person.

"I guess Daisy's taking orders for her St. Patrick's Day potion," Fitz said.

"I was just thinking the same thing," Father O'Brien said. "But look, it's different this year. People aren't trying to avoid her."

Fitz watched Daisy for another moment. "I'll be darned. I guess more than a few folks read the *Gazette* article and realized she might be more credible than they thought."

Daisy, along with Fitz and a few firefighters, had been quoted in the article in the *Gazette.* She had described her chance encounter with Leroy in the woods and her call to the Mill River police. Curious to hear from her just what she had seen, the people in the meeting room greeted her warmly and invited her into their conversations.

"I thought it was an animal," she said to a

group of people nearest the doorway, "but it was a man dressed in black."

"You think Leroy had anything to do with Daisy's trailer burning last November?" Father O'Brien asked.

"Seems probable," Fitz replied. "He was wearing a ski mask the night of the fire, and she actually saw him messing around behind the bakery. She called Ron to report it before we all had to leave for the burglary prank. Leroy might've had it in for Daisy, too, because last October she filed a complaint with me about him. Said he'd threatened to kick her dog after it took a leak on the wheel of his car. Apparently, she was the only witness. I didn't know whether what she claimed was true, but I made Leroy apologize to her anyway. The whole thing sort of blew over, but her trailer burned down less than a month later. Suspicious, huh?"

"She was adamant about having seen a man running away from the fire that night," Father O'Brien said.

"I know," Fitz said. "A man dressed in black. And when she called the station early Saturday morning, she told Ron the guy she saw behind the bakery was the same one that had run from her trailer the night it burned. I don't know if we'll be able to prove anything, but we'll be asking Leroy about Daisy's fire once he's well enough to be interrogated. But anyhow, the similarities are proof enough for me and, from the looks of it, some of the others in town." Fitz squinted down at his watch. "It's just about time, so I'm going to say hello to a few more folks and then call the meeting to order. Why don't you sit with Ruth and me at the supper afterward?"

"Sure thing," Father O'Brien said. Fitz grinned and headed toward a podium at the front of the meeting room. As the elected moderator, it was his responsibility to chair the meeting.

Alone again, Father O'Brien looked over the crowd. Kyle Hansen was there, sitting with his daughter on one side and Claudia Simon on the other. Rowen was such a doll, chattering away to Kyle and Claudia as they looked down at her with bemusement. Father O'Brien was grateful that the little girl still had her father, especially knowing what Fitz had revealed to him.

"So, Miss Simon," Rowen said, looking across her father's lap at Claudia, "are you going to marry my dad?"

Father O'Brien had to stifle a laugh as he watched Claudia's face puckering and reddening.

"Rowen, honey, you're not supposed to ask questions like that," Kyle said to his daughter, smiling. "It's embarrassing."

Claudia was smiling, too, although she looked more flustered than anything else.

"Sorry," Rowen said, more to Kyle than Claudia. "But Dad?"

"Yeah?"

Rowen dropped her voice almost to a whisper, as if sharing a special father-daughter secret. "I like Miss Simon a lot. And if you get married, she could be my new mom, and I wouldn't have to call her 'Miss Simon' anymore."

"Is that so?"

"Uh-huh."

"Well," Kyle said, with mock seriousness, "I'll definitely take that into consideration. You know, Miss Simon and I haven't known each other too long, so I suppose we'll just have to wait and see what happens. But, I'll tell you something."

"What?"

"I like her a lot, too."

"Could everyone take their seats?" Fitz called from the podium. There was no microphone, and he spoke loudly.

Father O'Brien slipped out of the doorway. He passed the crowded front row of chairs, stopping briefly to greet a middle-aged man in a gray suit. As he expected, the last row of chairs was still almost empty, and he lowered himself into a seat. The din of conversation dropped off as others sat down. Fitz took up a gavel at the podium and rapped three times.

"The meeting will come to order," Fitz said. "I'd like to welcome everyone to the annual Mill River Town Meeting. Our agenda is much the same as in past years. We'll elect town officers for the year, then debate and vote on the town and school budgets. Oh, and I believe Father O'Brien has an announcement he'd like to make. My Ruthie and some of our other fine ladies are working to set up our potluck supper, which we'll have after the meeting."

At Fitz's mention of his announcement, many people turned in their seats to look back at him. Father O'Brien only smiled.

"Our first order of business is the election of the town clerk," Fitz said, but Father O'Brien was already tuning out the police chief's voice. He was thinking about the envelope in his breast pocket and the brown package in his lap. He pressed a hand against his pocket to make sure that the envelope was there. He felt it and his reading glasses, too, and was reassured.

The meeting passed in a blur. From time

to time, Father O'Brien heard Fitz's voice booming, "Is there any further discussion?" or sometimes, "Forward your ballots." There was heated debate over whether there was enough money in the school budget to hire an additional teacher's aide and purchase new books for the library. In the end, the library lost.

About an hour and a half into the meeting, Ruth Fitzgerald and several other women began setting warmed covered dishes on a long table on one side of the meeting room. There were hams and fried chicken, homemade stews and baked beans and potato salad. The long table could accommodate only a fraction of the numerous side dishes and casseroles, and the many desserts would have to wait in the kitchen until later.

From his seat at the rear of the meeting room, Father O'Brien could see the heads turning toward the long table. Even the adults were starting to fidget and whisper. He was wondering whether Ruth had brought any tart cherry pie for the potluck supper when he heard Fitz ask, "Is there any further business before we hear from Father O'Brien?"

The room grew very still as the curious faces turned back toward him again.

Fitz waited a few moments. Hearing no requests, he stepped out from behind the podium. "It's all yours, Father," he said, and sat down in a chair off to the side.

Father O'Brien rose and walked to the front of the meeting room. At the podium, he felt the expectant attention of hundreds of people. He straightened his shoulders and looked out at the many familiar faces. He had been alone in front of a crowd so many times during his life, but this was different. The enormous sense of responsibility and loyalty he felt threatened to crush him into the old wooden floor.

He placed the brown package on the podium in front of him before taking his reading glasses and the envelope out of his pocket. With trembling hands, he unfolded his glasses.

It was time.

"About a month ago," he began, "Mill River lost one of its longtime residents. Mary McAllister lived in the white marble house on the hill — all of us have seen it a thousand times. But not more than one or two of you ever saw Mary. That was the way she wanted it, but not for reasons you might imagine.

"I knew Mary well. I was introduced to her and her husband's family shortly after I was assigned to St. John's. That was more than seventy years ago. Mary's wedding was one of the first I ever officiated. Not even a year after that wedding, she'd lost her father and her husband. Her husband was abusive, and he disfigured her before he himself was killed in a car accident.

"You may be wondering why Mary was so reclusive. You see, Mary suffered from social anxiety disorder. She was terribly nervous around other people, and it only became worse as she got older. Physically, she went to pieces around strangers. When I first met her, doctors didn't know how to help someone with her condition. It wasn't even recognized as an illness. Back then, people with Mary's condition were usually put into mental hospitals and rarely got out."

Father O'Brien paused. The people facing him were listening attentively.

"But Mary was lucky. Her husband's grandfather, Conor McAllister, was a kind and decent man. He loved Mary as a granddaughter. He felt responsible for what his grandson had done to her, and he made sure that no one sent her away to a mental hospital. Conor gave her enough money to secure her financially for the rest of her life. He also asked me to look after Mary once he was gone. He was old, he said, and worried that once he died, Mary would have no one.

"I was hesitant to make that promise. I was a young man then, barely a priest, trying to tend to my first congregation, and here I was being asked to look after someone for the unforeseeable future. I knew there was no guarantee — in fact, it was unlikely — that I would be in Mill River all of my life, or Mary's. But I also knew Mary had no one but Conor, and Conor's request was impossible to ignore. I became a priest in part to help people. And so, I promised to do what I could, for as long as I could.

"Over time, Mary came to trust me and we became friends. In fact, she was like a sister to me. After Conor died, I was the only person she would see. Our friendship endured for the rest of her life, until she lost her battle with pancreatic cancer last month.

"You might ask how a person could live in almost total isolation for that long. I asked myself that question often and I have yet to come up with an answer. I asked her often over the years whether she was lonely. She always replied in the negative, and I believe she was telling me the truth, at least in the beginning. After what had happened to her, she needed to feel safe, and she felt completely secure up in her quiet house. Early on, she found plenty to keep herself busy. But as the years passed, she wanted more and more to overcome her anxiety. When she finally worked up the courage to venture out, the experience hurt her terribly. So, she resigned herself to spending the rest of her life in the security of her home. She loved her horses and her Siamese cat, and she struck up an unexpected friendship late in her life." He smiled at Daisy, who was sitting rapt with attention, and she grinned back at him. "She especially loved to read. She learned so much from her books. I think she had one of the sharpest minds I've ever known, even though she never finished high school.

"But the reason I asked to speak to you today is because there are a few things that Mary, and I, thought you should know."

At once, the slight fidgeting that had begun to ripple through the crowd in the meeting room ceased.

"Mary McAllister knew all of you. She used to watch out her windows to see what was going on in town. She read the *Gazette* and listened to the radio. She watched the local news on television. But most of what she knew about you she learned from me."

A murmur of concern rose up from the

townspeople. He could sense what must be going through their minds.

"You needn't worry," Father O'Brien said. "I assure you that I told Mary nothing in violation of any of my vows or duties as a priest. I only provided her information much as one friend or neighbor might do for another."

Father O'Brien scanned the faces watching him. He smiled and looked into the eyes of Ruth Fitzgerald as she stood by the long table. "Mary knew you, Mrs. Fitzgerald. You did her shopping for years without ever having met her, and you saw her only once, but she knew you. She knew when you and Fitz had your twin girls. She saw their picture in the *Gazette* and said they were two of the sweetest babies she had ever seen. After you opened the bakery, she grudgingly admitted that your tart cherry pie was better than hers."

The meeting room tittered, and he shifted his gaze to Kyle Hansen. "Mary knew you, Officer Hansen. She knew that you left a hard-earned position in Boston to make sure that your daughter could grow up in a safe place with the one parent she had left. Mary thought that that kind of love was wonderful, and so often lacking today." Kyle smiled and looked down at Rowen seated beside him.

Claudia Simon sat on the other side of Kyle. Her eyes grew wide as he addressed her next. "Mary knew you, Miss Simon, even though you had lived in Mill River for only a short time. She knew you were an elementary school teacher and a good one at that. She often said to me that without teachers like you, she never would have learned to read. Her limited world would have been infinitely smaller without her books."

Jeanie Wykowski was sitting between her two sons; her husband was on duty at the police station. "Mary knew you, Mrs. Wykowski. Even though you took care of her only at the end of her life, she knew you much longer. She worried about Jimmy when he was hospitalized with pneumonia a few years back, and about Johnny when he got hit with a bat during his first Little League game. She knew how hard you and Ron work to take care of your kids and each other." Jeanie put her arms around her boys and looked as if she would cry.

Father O'Brien looked again at Daisy. "Miss Delaine, you are one of the few who actually got to know Mary. She was a fan of your potions from the beginning. She always made sure I bought them for her." Daisy's face lit up like the bright circle of her flashlight on the snow. "Mary always felt that you and she had something in common, too. She told me once that you were both a little eccentric, and misunderstood by most. Late in her life, when she finally met you in person, she was touched by the kindness that you showed her." Daisy nodded and wiped at her eyes.

"I could stand here and say similar things about each one of you. Through her knowledge of you, Mary felt as if she was a part of Mill River. She appreciated that so much. Even though her condition prevented her from personally interacting with you, knowing about you gave her a sense of belonging, of community. And for all those years, she tried her best to give back to the community the only way she could, in a way that I'll explain shortly. But when Mary learned that she was dying, she decided she hadn't done nearly enough." He blinked rapidly as he pondered what else he should say. Finally, he made a decision and continued.

"This," he said, holding up the envelope, "is a letter from Mary. She wrote it on the day she died. It explains, in her own words, a decision that she made. She also gave me this small package to give to all of you.

These things are the reason I'm up here right now. I promised her that I would read her letter and present this package to you on Town Meeting Day. I suppose I'll start with the letter."

He put on his reading glasses and ripped open the envelope. His breath caught as he unfolded the fine linen stationery. The lines of tentative handwriting on the page were far fewer than he expected. Nevertheless, he said a quick prayer for strength and began to read.

To the dear people of Mill River,
I first intended to write a letter that would explain everything. But then, I decided that there was a better way to go about it, a way that might finally permit you to see me and know me better, much as I have seen and known you for all of these years. I'll ask Father O'Brien to open the small brown package now. Once you see what is inside, all will become clear.

Sincerely,
Mary Elizabeth Hayes McAllister

With his brow furrowed, Father O'Brien looked up from the letter. The people staring back at him appeared to be confused as well. "I'll just open it, then," he said, briefly holding up the package. It took only a moment to tear away the brown paper.

The small package was a DVD.

For a moment, Father O'Brien stared down at it, knowing what must be on the disc and yet not believing Mary could have done it and kept such a secret from him. How had she done it? Mail-ordered a camcorder and discs and recorded herself, perhaps. *That would have been the only way,* he thought, before he suddenly remembered that everyone was watching him expectantly. "It's a DVD recording," he said, raising it again for all to see. He turned to Fitz. "I don't suppose we have some way to watch this, do we?"

"Well, sure," Fitz said. "There's the TV and DVD player for the Saturday movies. It's over there in the supply closet. Hold on a minute." Fitz scrambled up out of his chair and headed for the doorway where Father O'Brien had waited before the start of the meeting. Several hundred pairs of eyes watched Fitz sort through the numerous keys on his key chain until he found the one that unlocked the supply closet. It wasn't more than a few minutes before he had opened the closet and wheeled a tall media cart holding a television and a DVD player to the front of the meeting room. He plugged in the equipment and turned to Father O'Brien.

"I'm not so good with technology," Father O'Brien said, handing the DVD to Fitz. "Would you mind?"

Father O'Brien stepped back and watched as Fitz slid the disc into the player and turned up the volume on the television.

There were a few moments of static, and then Mary's face appeared on the television screen.

The people sitting before him uttered a collective gasp.

Mary was wearing her eye patch. Her face was thin, but not as thin as it had been upon her death, Father O'Brien noticed. She looked alert and a little nervous, and he guessed that the recording had been made months ago, while she still had the ability to move about the mansion.

Mary stared into the camera for a few moments and began to speak.

"My name is Mary McAllister. I am making this recording for the people of Mill River, where I have lived all my life.

"Mine has been a solitary life. Father O'Brien has undoubtedly told you by now about the anxiety I have suffered. It started as a girl, after one of my high school teachers forced himself on me. That terrible experience was the root of an anxiety that became worse and worse. For years, I tried to work up the courage to become part of the community. But even now, the very thought of meeting a new person causes me such anguish that I can barely keep from locking myself away in a room. It is even difficult for me to sit here, knowing that so many people will see this recording. I know that I cannot stop the anxiety. I have merely learned to live with it, to take comfort in my solitude, as best I can.

"Still, like any human being, I have also wished that I might belong, that I might have friends and acquaintances, people to care about and who might care for me. Through the windows of my home, the *Gazette,* and Father O'Brien, you, the people of Mill River, provided me with that sense of belonging."

Mary's voice trembled as a tear slipped from the corner of her eye. She swallowed hard and continued.

"For so many years, I have cared about you. Seeing the town, reading and hearing about you and your families and your lives, always gave me such comfort. It was one-sided, yes, but it sustained me from the time I was widowed, until now, as I sit before you an old woman. I tried to reciprocate this comfort by providing for you in your times of need. I always had so much more than I needed, but I know now that what I provided wasn't nearly enough.

"You see, not long ago, I left Mill River for the first time since I was little more than a teenager. I learned on that day that I was dying. Coming home, seeing my house high up on the hill apart from the town, I realized how much of an outsider I have been. I've not done enough to allow you to get to know me. Yet, without your presence in my life, I would have died long ago.

"It would be impossible to repay you for the happiness you have unknowingly given me. I was so delighted, reading how each of the Fitzgerald twins had been voted homecoming queen — one for football and one for basketball. It was a wonderful thing to hear how Mr. and Mrs. Nesmeyer celebrated their sixtieth wedding anniversary. Those and hundreds or even thousands of other happenings through the years brought such light into my small world.

"I asked myself how I might try to express my gratitude in the time I had left. As much as I long to meet all of you in person, I know that doing so would be impossible for me. I doubt that I could face any of you, and I know that by Town Meeting Day, my time in this world will have passed.

"But I can give to you everything else I have, and this I shall do.

"I know that you are honest, hardworking people. You give of yourselves even if what you have to give is little. Several among you have gone out of your way to show me undeserved kindness. I would be honored to contribute to your well-being and your happiness. You have unknowingly helped me for so long. I hope that you remember me as a friend and neighbor who will always be grateful to you."

Mary paused, taking a deep breath before continuing.

"There is something else I want everyone to know. On the day I learned I was dying, the same day I realized how distant I must be to all of you, I learned something else that brought me great happiness. As I record this message, I have yet to tell anyone. But you need to know. Everyone needs to know.

"I was never able to return to school after the incident with my teacher. I was devastated, yes, but, as I soon discovered, I was also pregnant.

"When I was seventeen years old, I gave birth to a baby daughter. I loved her from the moment I laid eyes on her. I memorized every detail of her cherubic face, down to the shape of the birthmark that extended up onto her cheek. But I was still a child myself, and there was no way I could have provided her with the life she deserved. I gave my daughter up for adoption.

"On the day I was diagnosed with cancer, I met Daisy Delaine for the first time, and I recognized her face and her birthmark. I knew my daughter had come back to me.

"Some might see it as a cruel twist of fate that I found Daisy in the waning days of my life, but I see it as a blessing. I was given time to get to know her, to learn about her life, her upbringing, her dreams. And by now, she knows me as well, and knows who I am. She knows that I have wondered about her — and loved her — all of my life.

"Like me, Daisy has lived in your midst for years but is still isolated. To you, Daisy is a familiar face but an unfamiliar person. I understand that it is human nature to avoid people who are a little different from us. But it isn't easy for any person to exist on the perimeter of relationships, to be tolerated but not welcomed. Know that my daughter is a gentle, beautiful soul. She reaches out to you, our neighbors in Mill River, as best she can. I ask you to open your hearts and return the friendship she so freely offers, to consider her part of your families as I consider you part of mine. After all, one cannot love, or be loved by, too many people.

"I'd like to close this message by speaking directly to my Daisy and to Father O'Brien. First, to Daisy, my beautiful daughter . . . I'm so grateful for having found you. Your kindness and concern for others have made you a truly magical person. Such immense love I have carried for you all of my life, Daisy. I hope only that you will feel that love in your heart for the rest of yours.

"And to my dear Michael . . . to this day, I wonder how I could have been so deserving of the gift of your selfless friendship. In so many ways, you are grace personified. You made and kept the promise of a lifetime for me. You have been my confidant and companion . . . my brother and best friend. You truly gave me the world . . . *my* world, my neighbors, and my hometown. I could never repay such a gift. I can give you only my love, and my hope that it will remain with you after I'm gone."

Mary sniffed once as another tear slid down her cheek. She leaned forward, presumably to stop the recorder, and the television screen filled with static. Fitz slowly reached over and turned off the TV.

His face wet with tears, Father O'Brien looked away from the television screen. The floorboards creaked as he shifted position behind the podium. In the silence of the meeting room, the sound could have been the earth cracking. Many of the women dabbed at their eyes with tissues as they looked at Daisy Delaine, and him, and each other. Most of the men kept their faces turned downward. Father O'Brien took a deep breath. He wasn't finished just yet.

"My dear Miss Delaine," he said, "I think I speak for us all when I say that your mother was an extraordinary woman." A collective murmur of assent rose up from the crowd. He himself was still shocked that Mary had confirmed in the recording what she had whispered to him — that Daisy was hers. The little woman only nodded and smiled, too overwhelmed to speak.

"Jim, why don't you stand up," Father O'Brien said to the man in the gray suit whom he had greeted before the start of the meeting. The man stood and turned to face the seated townspeople. "I'd like to introduce Jim Gasaway. Jim's an attorney from Rutland, and a good friend. He, and his father before him, have handled Mary's affairs since her husband died." Jim raised a hand, smiled at the crowd, and sat down again.

"For the last year, since Mary learned that she was terminally ill, Jim and I have been making arrangements to dispose of her possessions. She insisted on absolute secrecy, and she was adamant that everything she owned be given to Mill River. To you. She wanted to make sure that she helped wherever there was a need.

"It might surprise you to know that Mary has helped all of us for a very long time. Even if you didn't live in Mill River at the time, most of you have heard the famous story of Christmas 1973, when everyone got a new color television. That was all Mary's idea." His voice cracked and he blinked again. "She wanted everyone to be able to see *Charlie Brown.*"

Many in the crowd began to whisper, but he ignored the noise and continued. "Then there was Edna Wilson's medical bill being paid for and the Sears tire truck rolling down Main Street. And all of the little things that happen around here — the birthday cards for kids, new baby gifts, everything. It was Mary's doing all of those years."

The whispering became an excited hum. "I'm sure many of you remember the fire in town this past November — the one that burned Miss Delaine's home. You probably noticed that Daisy had a brand-new mobile home a few days after that fire. What you don't know is that Mary provided that new home for Miss Delaine."

The meeting room was awash in excited chatter, and Father O'Brien waited a moment until the conversation ebbed. "You'll remember that earlier this month, our police department was the recipient of a brand-new Jeep Cherokee to replace a vehicle totaled in an accident. Mary's estate provided that new Jeep."

Father O'Brien looked down at Fitz sitting to his side. The police chief was grinning, but still shaking his head in disbelief.

"There's much more," Father O'Brien said, hushing the meeting room again. "The old Hayes farm, a few miles out on the southern end of town, was owned by Mary's father. That property has been deeded to the town for use as a park and recreation area. As soon as spring arrives, we'll be sprucing it up a bit. It'll have areas for camping and picnicking. We've ordered some playground equipment, too.

"I think Jim will tell you we've been pretty busy over the last year." Father O'Brien smiled at the letter as another tear worked its way down his face. "Other than a few individual gifts, which will be handled privately, most of Mary's considerable estate has been organized into trust funds to benefit the town. There will be an annual allowance for the schools, enough to buy new textbooks for every enrolled student. The school and town libraries will receive an annual sum for the purchase of new titles. In addition, Mary's personal collection of books, numbering over four thousand, will be donated to the town.

"There's another trust fund for emergency health care. Mary knew that not all of you have health insurance, and that sometimes even the best insurance doesn't cover all medical expenses. Each year, a certain amount from the emergency health fund will be divided among people in Mill River who need a little extra help covering their medical expenses."

Father O'Brien glanced to his right, toward the window on the front side of the town hall building. The streetlight outside highlighted a fine stream of snowflakes.

"Mary loved the snow," he said. "I think we all have to love it, to make it through winters up here, don't you?"

Everyone smiled.

"But Mary wanted all of you to be warm

in the wintertime. She knew that paying the steep heating and electric bills during our winters is a struggle for many. Another fund has been set up to provide assistance with those bills to folks who need it. It'll supplement the programs already run by the state. Thanks to Mary, no one in Mill River will ever be cold again.

"A certain amount has been provided to help the town with necessary expenses. Like maintaining our new town park or purchasing a new police Jeep, for instance. You never know when something will break down — or be smashed into a utility pole." Fitz snorted beside him, and several people in the crowd laughed in response. "We also hope to start a mortgage assistance program to help people in Mill River with down payments on houses, but Jim is still ironing out the kinks with that one. I expect that in the next few months, each of your families will receive a mailing describing everything that is being made available to you from Mary's estate. Jim's law office has graciously offered to answer any questions you may have once all of the programs are in place."

Father O'Brien looked down at his watch. He had been standing at the podium for twenty minutes, but it had seemed like hours. A great sense of joy seized him. He had done it, he had kept his promise, and everything was wonderful. He felt waves of disbelief and delight emanating from the townspeople in front of him. Many still had expressions of amazement on their faces.

Mary would have been delighted to see them. He closed his eyes and felt quite certain that, from somewhere, she could.

"Excuse me, Father O'Brien?"

He opened his eyes, scanning the crowd to find the thin voice that had called out to him. Two small, elderly women stood slowly, arm in arm, and looked around at the townspeople. They were dressed differently but had identical faces and hairstyles.

"Yes?" Father O'Brien said. The women looked strangely familiar, but he couldn't place them. The one who had first spoken continued.

"We were just wondering . . . well, everything that Mary has done for Mill River is absolutely delightful, and it's wonderful how she was able to get to know her daughter, Miss Delaine, but we want to know if she left anything behind for the rest of her family."

Father O'Brien stared, confused as to who these women were and why they would be here now, asking such a question.

"Well, she really has no other family. Her

husband's family didn't have much to do with her after her husband's grandfather passed."

"Your first statement is not exactly true, Father," the other woman said. "We are her family. Mary McAllister was our sister-in-law."

He knew them then. The old women were Sara and Emma, Patrick McAllister's younger twin sisters.

"I recognize you," he said, but one of the twins interrupted him.

"You all must understand; we never wanted to avoid Mary. We felt sorry for her, all alone in that house after our brother died. But our mother insisted that no one on our side have any contact with her. We had no choice."

The other sister nodded in agreement. "Our parents threatened to disinherit us if we so much as mentioned her name."

"But we heard about Mary's death, and the announcement to be made at the meeting tonight. And we thought that maybe she would have left something for her family. After all, it was our grandfather who took care of her in the first place."

Father O'Brien was incredulous. He could not fathom the audacity of these women, coming out of nowhere after seventy years to demand part of her estate. He seethed with a suppressed rage he had never before experienced, a rage that had grown from seeing Mary abandoned by the McAllister family. From watching her suffer, day after day, year after year. From doing everything he could to ensure that tonight, this one night, her final wish would become a beautiful reality.

The sisters took no notice of his agitated state, however, and continued to speak in turn.

"You might be wondering why we would come here, being from a wealthy family."

"Or, at least, a family that was wealthy. The marbleworks didn't do very well after Father took over. He never was good with money, and he ran the company into the ground. That, and with so much competition from abroad, well, he had to declare bankruptcy, you see."

"We're not wealthy anymore. In fact, we're no different from anyone else here tonight. Just two ordinary, middle-class ladies."

"We were only hoping that Mary remembered us in her will. It would sure make things a little easier for us."

Father O'Brien felt the townspeople watching him, waiting for him to respond. He was fighting to keep a handle on his emotions, to remain calm, but his temper had risen with such ferocity that he knew he would not be able to control it this time.

"Make it easier for you?" Even he was surprised at the tone of his voice, a cold hiss devoid of compassion. "How dare you come here tonight, asking for anything from Mary, asking for something to make your lives more pleasant, when you did nothing for her when she needed her family the most?"

Father O'Brien took a step forward, out from behind the podium. "You, and everyone else in your family, save Conor McAllister, shut her out. You two chose the promise of future wealth over the well-being of your own sister-in-law. And after the money was gone, after your parents had passed on, did you ever once contact her? No, you didn't. I know because for all those years, *I* was the one who made sure that she survived. *I* gave her a new family, all of these fine people you see around you." Father O'Brien gestured toward the townspeople and felt fresh tears warm his face. After a moment, he lowered his voice and continued. "And tonight, Mary took care of her family, as she'd done for years. But you are not her family. You have no place here."

The people before him were silent, wide-eyed. He had never spoken with such anger before them, but he saw the wry smiles of support for him flash across their faces.

The McAllister twins scowled. "We'll see about that," one of them snapped while the other crossed her arms and glared back at him. "Wills can always be challenged, you know. And what with all of Mary's mental problems? Who knows whether it will hold up in court."

"I do," Jim Gasaway said, standing again. He nodded to Father O'Brien and continued. "Mary didn't know whether any long-absent family members would come crawling out of the woodwork once she passed, but she insisted on leaving five thousand dollars to each surviving member of Patrick's family. No, it's not much, not by today's standards and the total value of her estate, but it's better than nothing. You can contact my office this week, same as everyone else, if you want to put in a claim for the money." Jim Gasaway shook his head. "Even after what you people did to her, she still couldn't bear to shut you out completely. Shocked the hell out of me, frankly. But she wasn't about to be taken advantage of by any of you, either. So Mary's will explicitly states that any member of the McAllister family that brings any sort of legal challenge against her estate will forfeit his or her inheritance. Trust me, I've been doing wills for thirty years, and we made damn sure that hers is airtight. So you can try to challenge it if you want, but you'll lose. Simple as that."

As the McAllister twins stood in silence, Fitz lumbered up from his chair and cleared his throat. "Well, we've got a delicious supper getting cold, and I think you ladies had best be going. I assume you're parked outside?" The police chief ushered Sara and Emma out the door of the town hall and closed it behind them.

When Father O'Brien had composed himself, he looked again at the crowd. The people were still quiet and waiting. He felt that he had said everything he needed to say, except for one thing.

"The last thing I should tell you," he said, "is something that Mary said to me many times, something that we've all seen here again tonight. And that is that in our world, even small gestures of kindness are remembered. I ask you to honor Mary's memory by continuing to be kind to each other, even if you're not sure that someone deserves your kindness. Mary knew that kindness is what brings all of us together as friends and neighbors and family."

CHAPTER 22

On the morning after the town meeting, Mill River looked as it always had. The colors of the sunrise had just given way to a cloudy sky when Father O'Brien appeared in the doorway of the parish house. He looked down Main Street at the quiet, snow-covered buildings and smiled. The excitement that had gripped the town the previous evening had faded away, but he expected it to reappear as word of Mary's generosity spread to residents who had not attended the town meeting.

It had been a wonderful, beautiful evening.

Today would be wonderful, too.

Father O'Brien stooped to lift a small cardboard box and carried it through the snow to his old pickup. The large shipping box containing his spoons was already on the floor on the passenger's side. He placed the small cardboard box on the seat above it. Soon, he would part with both of them.

It took only a few minutes to drive down to the bakery. Ruth and Fitz were expecting him. He had asked to see them both before work on its reconstruction had begun for the day.

"Morning, Father," Ruth said as she held open the front door. Instead of a flour-covered apron, she wore a heavy coat and gloves, and he could see her breath freeze as she spoke. The blackened inside smelled strongly of smoke. "Sorry, there's no heat since they shut off the power. Fitz is upstairs with some of the construction guys, but he'll be down in a minute. Can I get you a hot cup of coffee?"

"How have you got hot coffee with no electricity?"

Ruth laughed. "I've got plenty. I brought a few thermoses over from my sister's. We're staying with her until the repairs are done."

"Ah. In that case, coffee would be wonderful." Ruth nodded and went behind the counter for a mug. Save for a few folding chairs and old card table near the door, the bakery was completely empty. Even the insulation in the walls was gone. He sat down on one of the folding chairs and noticed several men wearing hard hats and carpenter's belts clustered near the back wall . . . or rather, what used to be the back wall. It was now mostly a gaping hole interspersed with temporary support beams and sealed with clear plastic sheeting.

Ruth brought three mugs of coffee as she and Fitz joined him a few minutes later.

"Hard to believe they didn't condemn this place, seeing as how you're missing a wall," he told them.

"We thought the same thing," Fitz said, "but the inspector took a look and said we could stabilize the building and replace the burned-out parts. There'll be more inspections and permits along the way, since it's a public building, but that's fine with us."

"Cheaper than knocking it down and starting over," Ruth added.

"And faster, too. We should be back in the apartment in a few months if the crew keeps to schedule. We'll have to replace the furniture in here, and our clothes and furnishings upstairs that were ruined by the smoke. But Ruthie here's been wanting to update our stuff for a while, so I guess we've got a good excuse now."

"It looks like you'll be all right, then," Father O'Brien said. "What about Kyle Hansen and his daughter? Have they got a place to stay?"

"Yep. Ron Wykowski's got a spare room, so they're all set," Fitz said.

"Rowen even knows their sons from school, so Jean tells me they've been having a great time playing together."

"This whole thing goes back to what you said last night, Father. You know, people pitching in to help each other. That meeting was something else, I tell you," Fitz said. "I don't know how you managed to keep it all a secret for so long."

"I couldn't sleep a wink," Ruth said. "I just kept thinking about it. The whole night, it kept swimming around in my head, like something out of a movie. Something you never expect to happen in the real world."

Father O'Brien smiled at the couple. They were about to be surprised again.

"You're right," he told them. "But it was actually all Mary's idea, even keeping the whole thing a secret. I just helped her make all the arrangements. That's actually the reason I asked to see you both this morning. You'll remember at the meeting that I said a few bequests from Mary's estate would be handled privately?" Ruth and Fitz nodded. "Well, once you opened the bakery, I took some of your pie up to her every week.

"She wanted to know all about you, of course, especially after you started doing her shopping, Ruth. I told her what I knew about you and your family, that your dream was to open a bed-and-breakfast when Fitz retires. She thought it was a good idea, since we're so close to Killington and the other ski resorts. The thing is, buying a house big enough to do that isn't cheap, even if you've saved for years. What I'm trying to tell you two is that Mary wanted you to have her home, for your bed-and-breakfast, if you want it." He sat back in his chair, enjoying the openmouthed, wide-eyed expressions on the Fitzgeralds' faces.

"Us?" Fitz asked. "She wanted *us* to have it?" Father O'Brien nodded and chuckled.

"But we never really met her," Ruth said. "I almost did that day when she tried to come here, but for all those years, I never so much as set a foot in her house. How could she mean for us to have it? I'd guess that she'd want Daisy — her daughter — to have the house. Are you sure there isn't some mistake?"

"Oh, there's no mistake," Father O'Brien said. "I can count on one hand the number of people in Mill River who've seen inside her home. So that has nothing to do with it. Daisy already has a new home and is happy where she is. She'll be well taken care of, don't worry, and she really couldn't manage such a big place. And another thing —

Mary's home was never meant to be used by only one person. As beautiful as it is, she kept most of the rooms shut. It'd be well suited for a bed-and-breakfast. Plenty of space, a gorgeous view. The furnishings would come with it, of course, and even the rooms she lived in have been well kept. You saw some of them, Fitz, the morning she died."

Fitz nodded and looked at his wife. "You wouldn't believe the stuff in there, Ruthie. All antiques, fancy rugs, and pictures. And I didn't really get a great look at everything because the drapes were pulled shut."

"I'm sure it's as stunning inside as it is outside," Ruth said.

"Let me tell you something else," Father O'Brien continued. "That big house was built by Mary's husband's grandfather as a wedding gift. I knew him well enough to understand how much he loved his grandson and Mary. He arranged the purchase of the property and the construction himself, and poured his heart into it. And yet, that house has never reflected all the love and happiness that went into its building. But just imagine, if you two were to open it up, make it feel warm and inviting, it would be extraordinary. It would finally be the home it was meant to be. And I think that's what

Mary wanted."

Ruth and Fitz looked at each other, each apparently waiting to hear what the other was thinking. Fitz spoke first.

"I don't think we know quite what to say, Father. This is sort of a humbling experience . . . it's not every day you get a mansion handed to you."

Ruth nodded. "It's completely overwhelming. But we'd be honored to have Mary's home," she said, her voice a little unsteady. "And I think we could bring out the beauty in it, and the love, as you say. Just imagine what it would be like for the people in town to be welcomed to the house they've wondered about all these years."

"You sure could work miracles with that house, Ruthie," Fitz said, "but we're so short-staffed at the station. As much as I'd like to, I can't retire just yet, not until we hire an officer to take Leroy's place, and another one to replace me. And then there's this place to take care of."

"There's no hurry. We could work on getting the house ready a little at a time. I'll bet it needs a good cleaning and sprucing up, and we'll probably have to get permits and such so it's all right with public building requirements. Once the bakery is back to normal, we could get someone to help with it, and I could focus on the bed-and-breakfast." Ruth's eyes grew bright, and she laid her hand on Fitz's arm. "I'll bet we could have it ready by the time you retire."

"Hmmph." Fitz looked at his wife, then at Father O'Brien, and slapped the table. "Let's do it, then. This is the opportunity of a lifetime."

Father O'Brien took a business card from his coat pocket and pushed it across the table. "This is Jim Gasaway's card. The address of his office in Rutland is on it. He's got all the papers ready to transfer the property, so you'll just need to call and make an appointment to go sign them. You won't have to worry about any legal expenses for the transfer, either. They're all taken care of."

Father O'Brien stayed a few more minutes to finish his coffee. Ruth and Fitz sat with him, holding hands in the chilly, burned-out bakery and grinning like two teenagers on a first date. In a way, they would be starting anew. When he finally went outside to his pickup truck, he smiled and waved to the Fitzgeralds. He had left two happy people even happier, and, with great effort, he had left his teaspoon on the old card table next to his empty coffee mug.

Father O'Brien continued through town

534

and turned onto the highway leading to Rutland. His destination was the county hospital. He would go there and offer his assistance to Leroy Underwood. He didn't look forward to seeing Leroy — it still made him angry to remember how, as a teenager, Leroy had mistreated Mary — but he considered it his duty to visit the troubled young man. Perhaps he could be of help.

He drove past the outpatient clinic, wrestling the memory of Mary's ordeal there out of his mind. After parking by the visitors' entrance, he went inside to the information desk. Leroy, he learned, had been transferred out of the intensive care unit two days ago and was now in a private room under police supervision. An officer from the Rutland County Police Department came down to escort him to Room 422. Once there, he thanked the officer, knocked softly on the door, and went inside.

Leroy was awake. He turned his head toward the door and glanced up at Father O'Brien with a look of surprise and disgust.

"Well, if it ain't Father O'Brien, come to tell ol' Leroy what a bad boy he's been."

"Good morning, Leroy," Father O'Brien said. "I called last night to see if it would be all right to visit you, and they said it'd be fine." He took a step inside the room. It was strange seeing Leroy in a hospital gown instead of a uniform. Part of his face and the end of his right arm were covered by thick white bandages. "As for why I'm here, well, I don't intend to scold you. I only wanted to see how you were doing."

Leroy sneered. "Yeah, I'll bet. As soon as I woke up, they let the cops in here to question me. Like I'd tell 'em anything. Then they sent in some head doctor, tryin' to shrink me or something. I didn't need that, and I sure don't need no priest, either."

"No one sent me here, Leroy," Father O'Brien said, sitting down in a chair near the bed. "I came here today because I always visit members of my congregation who are in the hospital."

"I ain't been to church in years."

"I know that, but you did attend when you were a little boy. You and your sister used to come, remember? You always sat in the front pew, or as close to the front as you could get."

Leroy grunted and turned his face away.

"Has your sister been by to see you?" Father O'Brien asked.

"Yeah," Leroy said slowly. "Yesterday. But I felt worse after she left."

"Why's that?"

" 'Cause once she found out I wasn't

gonna die, she bitched at me for . . . for what happened. Said she wasn't surprised, that I'd been a screw-up all my life, and she expected me to end up like this." Leroy turned his face away again.

Father O'Brien watched him a moment, remembering the little boy with a dirty face and patched-up clothing who used to attend Sunday Mass. Leroy's childhood had been less than ideal, he knew.

"Well, Leroy," Father O'Brien said, "under all that anger, your sister loves you, I'm sure. As for what happened to you, I wasn't at the bakery last Friday evening. I don't know exactly your involvement in the situation. But I do know that no one is perfect, and the most important thing now is that you're alive. It seems to me that you've been given a second chance to turn your life around."

"They're gonna try me for arson and attempted murder, Father. The arraignment's the day after tomorrow. All I wanted to do was impress Claudia, see. Rescue her. I didn't mean for nobody to get hurt, or anything bad to happen, but I'll probably end up in prison. I won't have any real life after that. My sister was right, that's probably the best place for me."

"She was speaking in anger, Leroy. You

must remember that."

"But, Father," Leroy said through clenched teeth, "she was right. I am a screwup. You don't understand, Father. All my life, all I ever wanted was to be like everybody else. With a real family and friends and all. Instead, I ain't never had nothin'. I tried real hard, Father, but what are you supposed to do when the people you work with hate you? When you send a pretty woman two-dozen roses and she blows you off like dirt? I had to make her understand how I feel about her. I saw her with Kyle, and I couldn't take it no more. I love her. And now look at me. By the time they let me outta jail, I'll be an old, scar-faced, one-handed freak." An angry tear squeezed out of the corner of Leroy's eye, and he brushed it away with his left hand.

"Leroy, your recovery will be difficult. You have a lot of healing to do, but listen to me. There are things you can do to make it better. Think back to when you were that little boy in the front pew, when you held strong faith in God. Try to remember that faith and find it again. It will help guide you.

"Psalm 34 tells us to 'depart from evil and do good; seek peace, and pursue it.' Ask for forgiveness for whatever you've done, from God, from those you may have hurt, and

538

try to have faith. It is especially important that you have faith in yourself, Leroy. Whatever the unfortunate circumstances of your upbringing and recent decisions, you made it this far. Think of this as a new beginning, a chance to do good things wherever you may end up after you leave here.

"You must take a hard look at yourself, your actions, and how you treat others. Did you ever stop and ask yourself why people react to you the way they do? Regardless of what you think you deserve, no one is entitled to anything, and you are responsible for your own actions. You cannot force someone to like you or love you, but you can make it difficult for others to dislike you by earning their respect and trust. And to do that, you must respect yourself. Acknowledge your strengths and weaknesses and your mistakes. Decide what you can do to better your life and the lives of others. Make peace with yourself, Leroy, and then pursue it with others."

Leroy had looked away again, but the young man's face was slicked with tears. Perhaps he had gotten through to him.

"One other thing," Father O'Brien said, laying a hand on Leroy's left arm. "Know that I'll be here to help you however I can.

Think about what I've said. Even if you don't agree with me, if you'd like some company, someone to talk to, call me. I'd be happy to visit you, here or wherever. I won't judge you, Leroy, because that's not my job, and any confession you make to me is confidential no matter what." Leroy sniffed and nodded. Father O'Brien stood up from the chair. "You are in my prayers," he said to Leroy, and left the hospital room.

As was the case after most hospital visits, Father O'Brien felt emotionally exhausted. He allowed his thoughts to wander as he drove back to Mill River. Once there, his next stop was the Wykowski house. As he approached it, he saw the police department's new Jeep, with Ron behind the wheel, pull into the driveway long enough for Jean to hop out. Smiling, she shut the door and waved as Ron backed up onto the road and continued on toward the police station.

Father O'Brien pulled up in his pickup before Jean went inside. She backtracked down the walk to meet him as he took the small cardboard box from the seat of his truck.

"Hello, Jean," he said. "I wondered if I might talk to you for a few minutes. I apologize for not calling before coming out here, but I didn't catch you after the meeting last night, and I've been running errands all morning." He wondered if it might be a bad time. Jean's face was flushed, and she appeared to be a bit flustered.

Jean smoothed her tousled hair. "Oh, it's fine, Father. I'm just glad I was here when you stopped by. But come inside, it's freezing," she said, turning toward her front door. "I don't have to be at work until ten this morning. Once Kyle left to take the kids over to school, Ron wanted to show me the new Jeep." They entered the house. "His shift's almost over, so he took me for a quick spin before he had to have it back to the station. Could I take your coat?"

"Thank you, no," he replied. "I'll be here only a moment. I've got another errand to run after this one."

She showed him into the living room and snatched up a few of the miniature cars that were strewn on the floor. "I'm sorry it's kind of a mess in here. Rowen and the boys had a Hot Wheels ramp set up in here yesterday. They like to crash the little cars off the coffee table, you know, like it's a cliff." She deposited the cars in a little pile on the sofa and sat down next to him. Her cheeks were even more flushed now.

"Goodness, a few toy cars are nothing to

worry about," he told her. "I can only imagine what some kids must get into."

Jean smiled. "Yes. If they were here, I would've made sure they picked them up. But anyway, what brings you by?" Her gaze shifted to the small cardboard box on the coffee table. Father O'Brien followed her line of sight and patted the box.

"This. You'll remember last night, at the meeting, when I said that a few bequests from Mary's estate would be handled privately?" Jean nodded. "Well, your care helped Mary so much, and she wanted for you to have what's in this box." He pushed it over to her and waited.

Jean reached for the box and then hesitated. "What is it?"

"Look inside. You'll know what it is, I'm sure."

The expression on her face when she looked down into the box was a mixture of recognition, guilt, and disbelief. She lifted Mary's small, dark jewelry box from the cardboard container and set it down. With one finger, she traced a line across the front of it. Father O'Brien sensed her hesitation. Jean took a deep breath and slowly raised the top. Mary's pearls, cameo, and magnificent diamond ring glowed in the red velvet interior. She clasped a hand over her mouth.

"She didn't have much jewelry in that box," Father O'Brien said, "but what she had was beautiful. She thought that it, and her diamond ring, especially, would bring more happiness to you than it did to her."

Jean looked sideways at him now, tears dribbling down her cheeks. "It's not right that I should have this. I don't deserve this."

"Mary thought you did, and that's all that matters now. I've found she had a knack for knowing what should and shouldn't be done, and I trust in her decision completely."

"Still, I wouldn't feel right wearing her jewelry," Jean said. "There was a time not too long ago that I would've been thrilled to have what's in that box. I don't have much jewelry myself." Father O'Brien noticed that, as she spoke, she traced her left index finger over a diamond ring on her right hand. "But things are different now. I have all the jewelry I want and I love everything I have."

"Well, now Mary's jewelry is yours, too, and what you do with it is up to you. You wouldn't have to wear it, or even keep it, if you don't want to. You could sell it and use the money for something your family needs, maybe a college fund for your boys, or you could put it in a safe-deposit box to save as a family heirloom. It's your decision." He slowly got to his feet and buttoned his coat.

"I don't know what to do," Jean said. She closed the jewelry box and stood up beside him.

"Well, I'm sure whatever you decide will be right," Father O'Brien said. "But I'll leave you to think about it."

"All right."

A loud meow came from near the floor. Sham the Siamese had appeared and was weaving around his ankles.

"Hello, old friend," he said, bending down to scratch behind the cat's ears. "I see you're as fat and happy as ever."

"Too many kitty treats," Jean said, smiling through her tears as she held the door for him. "He might have used up one of his lives in the fire. The vet treated him for smoke inhalation but said he'll be just fine." Jean smiled. "Thank you for coming by, Father."

Once he was back in the cab of his pickup, Father O'Brien took a deep breath. All he had to do now was deal with the large box beside him. He started the engine and backed out of the driveway.

He had visualized for weeks this last thing that he was about to do. If Mary could give away everything she owned, he could most certainly part with the objects that caused him so much secret shame. His stomach turned as he drove back into the center of town, past the bakery, heading toward the little brick post office. It would be difficult, yes, but he had no doubt that he would do it. He would do it for Mary.

Daisy Delaine, in her hooded parka, waved to him from the sidewalk as he passed. Her little gray dog strained on a leash out in front of her. Father O'Brien smiled and raised a hand in return. He would have to find her later on to explain that Mary had set up a trust fund to support her for the rest of her life. It still amazed him how people had sought Daisy's company and conversation the night before, how they had looked at her as if she were a different person — and that was before everyone knew that she was Mary's daughter. Perhaps now, after everything that had happened, things would be different for Daisy.

The three parking spaces in front of the post office were vacant when he arrived. He pulled into the space nearest the door and went around to the passenger's side to get the box. He'd had quite a time getting it from the parish house into the truck. The box weighed probably fifty or sixty pounds.

Now he stood with it in his trembling arms, trying to steady himself enough to nudge the door of the pickup closed with an elbow.

Feeling his arms start to give way, he took a step backward. His heel clipped the curb, just enough to throw him off balance. The shipping box dropped to the snow-covered pavement with a loud *clang*. When he had regained his footing, he looked down and gasped.

There were perhaps three-dozen spoons sparkling in the snow.

Father O'Brien stooped down, hoping no one had seen him. The box had landed on its side, but the force of the impact had caused part of the bottom seam to pop open. Despite his careful packing, he hadn't used enough tape to reinforce it.

He gathered up the spoons as quickly as he could and shoved them back into the box. Several others protruded from the seam, and he pushed those back inside as well. His breath rose in rapid, frozen puffs as he worked. By the time he finished, he was gasping for air, and his fingers were numb from touching the cold metal and from the beginnings of hyperventilation. He glanced around. No one had seen the spoons, and now they were once again hidden from view. He needed only to re-tape the bottom of the box.

He reached into the pocket of his jacket and found it empty.

His roll of mailing tape was back on his desk at the parish house.

He could get some tape inside the post office, but did he dare risk lifting the box again, or leaving it unattended, knowing that its precious contents were not sealed inside? He had no choice. His fingers pressed the old tape back over the open seam. He righted the box and hoped that he could get it inside without dropping it again.

With his hands supporting the weak underside seam, Father O'Brien strained to lift the box. He managed two steps and stopped, looking down at the box and feeling that the few feet to the post office door were actually a few miles.

"Here, Father, let me give you a hand with that," a voice said. Having just come out of the post office, Kyle Hansen rushed over and took the box from his arms.

"What timing! Thank you, Kyle," Father O'Brien said. The muscles in his biceps felt tingly and exhausted. "I guess I didn't realize it would be harder to get that box out of the truck than into it. Oh, but be careful, the bottom isn't taped very well."

"No problem," Kyle said. Father O'Brien held open the door of the post office as Kyle carried the box inside. Although Kyle managed the box easily, he looked surprised at how heavy it was. "Whatcha got in here, Father? A bunch of lead weights?"

Father O'Brien felt the shock of adrenaline as his heartbeat quickened. A rush of panic and shame overcame him. "The weight of atonement," he said, glancing up at Kyle and then averting his eyes. Kyle looked puzzled, but to Father O'Brien's great relief, he asked no further questions.

As Kyle hoisted the shipping box up on the front counter, Father O'Brien stood on tiptoe to peer around it. There was no clerk to be seen, but a sign near a small silver bell on the counter read RING FOR SERVICE. Father O'Brien did as it directed.

"I'll be with you in just a minute," a voice called from the back room.

The priest leaned against the counter and turned to Kyle. "So I hear you had a scare the other night . . . with the bakery."

Kyle nodded. "You probably know all about it by now. Leroy's a piece of work, I tell you. He could've hurt so many people . . . Ruth, Claudia, my daughter if she'd been there. I don't know what I would do if . . ." Kyle shook his head. "I'm just thankful everyone's okay. Claudia spent the night in the hospital, but they let her go home the next day." He paused for a moment and ran a hand through his hair. "The more I think about it, the more ticked off I get."

"I would probably feel frustrated, too," Father O'Brien said. "But you're right, we can be thankful that so many people escaped safely. And I guess it'll all be sorted out in court."

"Yeah, or maybe a plea deal. But Fitz is pushing for a trial, so we'll see." Kyle said. "Hey, I wanted to let you know that Mary's cat is doing really well. He made it through the fire, too."

Father O'Brien's face brightened. "I just saw him, as a matter of fact. I had to stop by to see Jean Wykowski and Sham came out to say hello. I think he remembered me."

Kyle relaxed against the counter beside him and grinned. "Yeah, Ron and Jean are putting us up for a little while until we can get a new place. But Sham's been great. Rowen's got him spoiled. He sleeps on her bed every night and follows her around until she gives him attention. He's pretty comfortable around me, too. I guess for not having been out of that big house his whole life, he's adjusted pretty well."

"I'm so glad," Father O'Brien said. "Mary would've been happy to hear it, too."

"I'm sure she would've," Kyle said. "Claudia and I were talking about it last night. What Mary decided to do for all of us is pretty unbelievable. And Daisy turning out to be her daughter, that blows my mind."

"I know," Father O'Brien replied, chuckling.

"Well, look, I was actually on my way to the station — I've got to relieve Wykowski, so I should get going, but if you ever need help lifting any more boxes of lead, or, uh, whatever you've got in there, give me a call. I'd be glad to help you out."

Father O'Brien smiled. "Thanks, Kyle, I'll do that."

The clerk appeared behind the counter as Kyle left. Father O'Brien turned around to face her.

"I'd like to send this bulk rate," he said.

"You mean Standard Post?"

"Yes, if that's the cheapest. It's pretty heavy. And could you put some more tape across the bottom seam?"

With a strong effort, the clerk managed to slide the package across the counter onto the scale. "Fifty-six pounds and twelve ounces," she said. "Is there anything hazardous or perishable in there?" She produced a large roll of tape and used it to reinforce the bottom of the box.

"Oh, no."

"You need any insurance or delivery confirmation on it?"

"Can I just get the delivery confirmation?" He couldn't imagine what price he would put on the box for insurance purposes. The delivery confirmation, though, would be a comforting thing.

"With standard post, you can only get the confirmation if you purchase insurance."

He thought for a moment. "I guess I could insure it for a hundred dollars," he said. For anyone but himself, even that amount would probably seem too high for a box of assorted spoons.

The clerk was punching numbers into her computer. "Okay, then. Your total comes to thirty-seven dollars and twenty-two cents."

Father O'Brien handed her two twenty-dollar bills. He reread the address on the box one last time. The black lettering was neatly printed: "St. Francis House and Soup Kitchen, 39 Boylston St., Boston, MA, 02116." He remembered writing that address on the box, all the while hoping, knowing, that his spoons would be used and appreciated. There were always so many hungry people in big cities like Boston. He touched the box, the mailing tape reinforcing the seams, the corner where he had included his own return address. He blinked several times. He would never see his spoons again.

"Father? Here's your change, Father." The clerk held the bills and coins out to him. "Shouldn't take any longer than five to seven business days to get there, but it'll probably be more like two days since Massachusetts is pretty close to here."

"Thank you," he said. He blinked again and took a step back. The clerk tried to lift the box, then called into the sorting room for someone to help. A burly, bearded man in a postal uniform came puffing around the corner. Father O'Brien watched as the two eased the box down from the counter and into a cart. The man pushed the cart away with him into the back room.

Father O'Brien turned toward the door. "Have a nice day," the clerk called to him, but he barely heard her.

It was over.

The sun broke through the clouds as he left the post office. Outside the brick building, a thin ray of sunlight fixed directly on his balding head, illuminating the few remaining hairs on top that refused to lie flat. He felt the warmth of the ray spreading throughout him. He had done what was right. All his life, he had tried and tried to do what was right. He had kept his word, honored the people he served, revered the God he worshipped. Thanks to Mary, he looked forward to his next visit to the confessional. He had finally overcome his greatest sin.

The sunshine on his head was a sign, he was certain.

He and Daisy still had to plan a memorial service for Mary. It would be a private service, with only himself, Daisy, and maybe a few others attending. So many times over the years, he and Mary had strolled among the maple trees on her property, eating the sweet icicles that formed when maple sap flowed from a broken branch and froze solid. He would select a location on her father's farm to serve as her final resting place. It would be somewhere Mary might have chosen herself — somewhere with sugar maples, where sapsicles would form in the early spring, and with a beautiful view of the place where she had been so happy in her youth.

After that, what would he do with the rest of his life? He had lived through more than nine decades, but how much longer did he have? That would be uncertain until the end, but this much he did know: He would always help people. He would eat tart cherry pie. He would remember Mary, her strength and acceptance and generosity, and keep an eye on her daughter. He would never steal again but would admire spoons from a distance. Most of all, he would continue to do the best he could.

That was all anyone could do.

ACKNOWLEDGMENTS

Many people gave the generous gift of time by reading early drafts of this book and improving it through their critique and encouragement. Thanks to "test-readers" Tim and Beverly Trushel, Tess Alleyne, Susan Dunbar, Michelle Johnson-Weider, Heather Burnham, Diane Nesmeyer, Heather Lowell, Gary Endicott (who also explained the nuances of Molotov cocktails), Matt McGhie, Janell Bentz, Janine Johnson, Anne Williams, Patricia Clements, Barry Gold, and Kristin Banks, my aunt Sheila Wheeler, and my cousins Shannon McCracken and Angela Hawkins. Also, thanks to my friend and "author big sis," Elizabeth Letts, for her advice and insight, and to Cynthia Webb and the rest of the staff at the Paoli Public Library, for their wonderful hometown support.

To those who gave this novel a boost in electronic or social media in one form or another — Jenny Bent, for her tweets, Chris Meeks, for a fabulous blog interview, Greg Doublet, for the initial feature on *Ereader News Today* that introduced this novel to readers in e-book form, Alexandra Alter, for a humbling article in *The Wall Street Journal*, Amy Edelman, for her many mentions on *IndieReader.com,* and Karen Dionne and the rest of the wonderful people of the Backspace writers' community — thank you so much. I greatly appreciate all of you and everything you did to help me.

I would like to thank Robert Pye of the Vermont Marble Museum, for sharing his expertise in the history of the Vermont marble industry, and Jim Simonds and Carol Wagner of the Building and Zoning Department, City of Rutland, Vermont, for information relating to fire damage of public buildings. Thanks also to Chris Kiefer of the Rutland County Sheriff's Office for taking the time to answer my questions about small-town police departments, and to Detective First Class Mark Baxter with the Howard County, Maryland, Police Department for explaining police procedure for responding to burglaries in progress.

I would like to thank my publisher, Libby McGuire, as well as Kim Hovey and Jennifer Hershey, for their support in getting my first novel further out into the world. Many thanks also to my publicist, Lindsey Kennedy, and to Susan Corcoran in the publicity department; to my marketing manager, Maggie Oberrender; to my copy editor, Briony Everroad, and my production editor, Jennifer Rodriguez; to Marietta Anastassatos and Richard Tuschman, the designer and illustrator, respectively, who created the gorgeous cover for this story; and to the rest of the wonderful people at Ballantine whose great care and effort have gone into the publishing and launch of this novel.

To my incredibly gifted editor and kindred spirit, Kara Cesare — I am so thrilled and thankful to have been able to work with you on this first novel. Your sage advice is always spot-on. I couldn't ask for a better partner or in-house champion of my writing, and I greatly appreciate the effort and enthusiasm you put into the publication of this book.

I am continually grateful for the patience, support, advice, encouragement, and expertise of my wonderful literary agent, Laurie Liss. There are few agents who would take a chance on, and invest years of time and effort in, a quiet story by a completely unknown writer. Laurie did just that, and without her extraordinary effort and determination, this book would never have been published.

A special thank-you to the people closest to me — my law school classmates and "brunch buddies" Tammy Baxter and Michele Knorr, and to my longtime friends Ruth Uyesugi, Angie Swedhin, Deidre Woods, Sherri Miller, and Elizabeth San Miguel. I am also grateful for the unwavering support and enthusiasm of my immediate family — my mother, Linda Tomasallo; father and stepmother, Dennis and Susan Tomasallo; sisters Carrie and Molly Tomasallo; and grandmother Helen Richardson.

Finally, a special thank-you to my husband, Tim, for reading new passages even after sleepless nights on call at the hospital, for maintaining and upgrading my computer and other technology necessary for my writing, and for always, always believing in me.

■ ■ ■ ■

The Mill River Recluse

A NOVEL
Darcie Chan

■ ■ ■ ■

A Reader's Guide

A LETTER FROM THE AUTHOR

Dear Reader,

The novel that you are holding in your hands — *The Mill River Recluse* — is my first novel. For most authors, writing a first novel is a learning experience and a labor of love. Trying to get a first novel published is quite another matter. Frustration and disappointment abound. The paths to traditional publication are paved with rejection letters from agents and publishers. Self-publishing these days also presents a host of difficulties. Producing a quality story on one's own is just the first step; an author must then get that story noticed in an ever-expanding ocean of content. *The Mill River Recluse* has taken me down both paths, culminating in an amazing, rollercoaster ride that I never expected to experience.

My central story idea for *The Mill River*

561

Recluse had a real-life origin. The basic concept for the book was inspired by a gentleman named Sol Strauss who lived in Paoli, Indiana, the small town in which I lived during high school and where my mother was born and raised. Mr. Strauss, a Jewish man who fled Nazi Germany, operated a dry goods store in Paoli in the 1940s. Even though Mr. Strauss lived quietly alone above his shop and never seemed to be fully embraced by the town's predominantly Christian population, he considered Paoli to be his adopted community. When he died, the town was shocked to learn that he had bequeathed to it a substantial sum, which was to be used for charitable purposes to benefit the people of Paoli.

The Sol Strauss Supporting Organization Fund is still in operation today. Among other things, it provides clothing and other necessities for needy children and an annual supply of new books for the high school English department. Residents of Paoli may also apply to the fund for assistance in carrying out a project that would benefit the town. The fund is the legacy of Mr. Strauss, who continues to be remembered for his extreme and unexpected generosity.

I remembered what Mr. Strauss had done when I was brainstorming ideas for a first novel. I thought it would be interesting and challenging to build a story around a character who is misunderstood or different in some way, and to show that even someone who is seemingly far removed from his or her community may in fact be more special and integral than anyone could imagine.

I began writing for a few hours after work most evenings, and it took two and a half years to complete a first draft. I polished the manuscript as best I could, and I was ecstatic when Laurie Liss, an agent with Sterling Lord Literistic in New York, agreed to shop it around for me. Despite Laurie's valiant efforts, though, my novel didn't sell. I put the manuscript in a drawer and resolved that someday, I would write a second book and try again. Life went on.

I didn't write much during the next several years. My job grew increasingly demanding, my husband finished his residency and accepted a position necessitating a move to a different state, and we had a baby. (I'm still trying to catch up on sleep missed for all those reasons!)

But, when my son was a toddler, I started reading articles about how e-books had exploded in popularity. Even more interesting was the fact that apparently it had become very easy for an individual writer to self-publish a book in electronic form. I thought of *The Mill River Recluse* languishing in my drawer. I figured I had nothing to lose and released it as an e-book in May 2011.

Soon, I realized that no one would find my novel among all the other e-books out there unless I did some sort of marketing for it. After all, publishing companies invest in marketing and publicity for their books. As an individual with a modest budget, there was no way I could fund a major marketing campaign, but I arranged for a few inexpensive online ads to get my novel on readers' radar screens. I kept the price of my book very low, to encourage people to take a chance on a story by a completely unknown writer. I also set up a website, Twitter account, and Facebook author page. And then, I waited.

Sales started to trickle in. During the first month, I sold around a hundred copies. I was so thrilled! To think, a hundred people had bought my book! My husband, Tim, and I grabbed up our little boy and did a happy dance in the kitchen. "Wow, maybe you'll be able to sell a thousand," I remember him saying. I doubted that, but I thought perhaps a few hundred more sales might be possible.

In late June, a feature of my novel popped up on a large website that recommends e-books to readers. Within two days, another six hundred copies sold! After the feature ended, the pace of sales accelerated. Reviews from readers started coming in — and most of them were the kind of glowing, positive reviews that authors dream of receiving. I was hearing directly from those readers, too.

One gentleman sent me an email to tell me that he loved the book, but that he had had to wait until his wife had left the house to read the last few pages. The reason? He didn't want his wife to see him become "a blubbering mess." Another woman wrote to tell me that she had read my book aloud to her mother in the hospital, and it brought her mother great comfort during her last days of life. Both of those messages, as well as many others I received, left *me* in tears. And the emails and Facebook messages kept coming from readers of all ages throughout the United States and the rest of the world.

By mid-July, I knew something extraordinary was happening. I kept my agent in the loop, of course, but I was shocked when she called me in mid-August and left a cryptic message on my answering machine.

"Darcie, it's Laurie. Check your email."

I scrambled around and got to my computer. She had sent me an advance copy of the latest *New York Times* best-seller list.

The Mill River Recluse appeared on it at #12.

To this day, there are no words that are adequate to describe everything I felt in that moment.

My novel remained on the *New York Times* and *USA Today* bestseller lists for the next several months, and the wonderful notes from readers kept coming. I thought that surely, finally, things had peaked, but I was wrong.

In late November 2011, I was contacted by Alexandra Alter, a book reporter for *The Wall Street Journal.* She wanted to interview me for a feature story about my writing journey up to that point. Alexandra was cheerful and pleasant when she came to my home on the Friday after Thanksgiving. I didn't feel at all nervous or odd about speaking with her until she told me that, during the previous week, she had gone up to Maine to interview Stephen King.

I am still mortified when I envision how far my mouth must have dropped open before I regained control of it.

The Wall Street Journal ran Alexandra's article on December 9, 2011. It appeared on the front page of the Friday magazine, with a full-color photo spread inside and additional teasers on the front page of the whole paper. By late afternoon, the online version of the story had been picked up by *Yahoo! News,* and my photo was among those circulating on the Yahoo! homepage. Pandemonium ensued.

My phone began ringing off the hook. Other writers were calling, wanting advice or simply to get together for coffee. Other reporters were calling, wanting interviews. (I changed my number to an unlisted one immediately!) My website email inbox was accumulating emails faster than I could scroll down the page. My colleagues were incredulous, as most of them had no idea I'd written a novel years before and had recently, casually decided to self-publish it. Several of my clients emailed, sending me links to the article and saying things like, "Oh my God, is this *you*?" Laurie was fielding phone calls from publishing companies and film studios. My family and my closest friends, scattered in a half dozen states across the country, were calling and emailing ecstatic messages of support.

I was a quivering mess. All I could do was sit and hug my son. I knew that things had changed permanently for me at that point.

Within a few weeks, I received an offer from Ballantine Books, a division of Random House, to write two new novels. It was an offer to make my childhood dream a reality. The question was, could I continue to work as an attorney and write books in my spare time? Or, did I have to choose between the two?

I loved my legal career and the many colleagues with whom I'd worked for more than a decade. But I knew that I couldn't live the rest of my life wondering whether I could have had a successful career as a writer, and there was no way I could give writing my best shot if I was constrained by the restrictions that applied to me as an employee of the federal government. It was a difficult decision, but I resigned my attorney position to write full-time in March 2012.

To date, *The Mill River Recluse* has sold more than 700,000 electronic copies and has been or will be published in nine foreign languages, in addition to its publication in English. The story of its self-publication as an e-book was featured in a documentary film called *Out of Print,* which was directed by Vivienne Roumani-Denn and narrated by Meryl Streep. But now, finally, I feel as if the roller coaster has slowed, and my life is returning to normal. A *new* normal.

In the short time that I've been a writer — which is a description of myself that I'm still getting used to — I've learned a few things. First, you should always expect the unexpected. And, there is sometimes more than one path that will enable you to achieve a dream. For me, being able to get my first novel in front of readers changed my career and my life. I will always be grateful for every person who reads *The Mill River Recluse,* especially those first e-book readers who gave it a chance and took the time to review it, mention it to a friend, or send me a note of encouragement. Those readers — *my* readers — made my dream of being an author come true. I only hope that this first novel and my future books return to them — and to you — the same great happiness and enjoyment I have experienced in writing them.

My very best wishes,
Darcie Chan
May 2014

QUESTIONS AND TOPICS
FOR DISCUSSION

1. *The Mill River Recluse* is not written in a single timeline, but instead uses alternating timelines that link near the end. What did you think of this structure? Was it effective in driving the story forward, or was it disorienting? Did you prefer one timeline over the other?

2. Of all the characters in *The Mill River Recluse,* with which one did you most identify, and why? If you could meet one of the characters for coffee, who would it be and why?

3. The opening scene of the book is of Mary McAllister taking her own life to avoid having to suffer further agonizing pain and certain eventual natural death resulting from her metastatic cancer. Do you think Father O'Brien knew Mary planned to take her own life when he left the marble man-

sion that last night? What do you think about Mary's decision to take things into her own hands? Did this scene give you pause?

4. How does Mary McAllister evolve from a shy teenager into a woman held prisoner by social anxiety and agoraphobia? Do you agree with the way in which Father O'Brien tried to help her? Would you have done anything differently had you been in his position?

5. Patrick McAllister is shockingly cruel, particularly toward the most vulnerable people and the animals in his life. Do you think that Patrick became the person he did because of his parents and their relationship with him?

6. Unlike Patrick McAllister, Leroy Underwood had a very underprivileged upbringing. During Leroy's visit with Father O'Brien in the hospital, he sheds tears. Do you think his tears were a sign of remorse? Are he and Patrick McAllister different kinds of "bad people," or do you think their character defects are of a similar nature?

7. Despite his animosity toward Leroy, Father O'Brien visits him in the hospital to

offer him support and comfort. Can you describe a time in your own life when you had to put aside your feelings to do something that you knew was right?

8. Of all the potions Daisy concocts, is there one that you believe you could drink if you had to? How would you react if Daisy showed up at your door peddling her wares?

9. Father O'Brien has been obsessed with spoons his entire life, but the reason for his attraction to those particular objects is never discussed or revealed. Do you have any theories as to why he is so drawn to spoons — so drawn, in fact, that he is willing to break his vows and steal them — as opposed to some other kind of item? Do you believe he has truly kicked his "spoon habit"?

10. Claudia Simon's struggle to eat healthy food is almost sabotaged by a box of Entenmann's powdered sugar doughnuts. Is there a food that you have trouble resisting?

11. Jean Wykowski struggles with middle age and a life that seems to have settled into a predictable routine. Instead of "borrowing" Mary's ring, what advice would you give her to add a little excitement and variety in her life?

12. Near the end of the novel, the people of Mill River learn that they have actually had a kind of relationship with Mary McAllister for years, and that Mary is a very different person than many of them had imagined her to be. Are there other relationships in the novel in which one of the characters learns something new or unexpected about another?

13. Which character do you feel experiences the most personal growth throughout the course of the story, and why?

14. How did you feel upon finishing *The Mill River Recluse*? Did anything about the story or characters linger in your mind or change the way you view certain people or situations?

ABOUT THE AUTHOR

Darcie Chan is the *New York Times* best-selling author of the eBook sensation *The Mill River Recluse* and the novel *The Mill River Redemption.* She has been featured in *The New York Times, USA Today,* and *The Wall Street Journal.* For fourteen years, Chan worked as an attorney drafting environmental and natural resource legislation for the U.S. Senate. She now writes fiction full time and lives north of New York City with her husband and son.

www.darciechan.com

www.facebook.com/pages/Darcie-Chan-Author/193245487387883

www.twitter.com/DarcieChan

The employees of Thorndike Press hope you have enjoyed this Large Print book. All our Thorndike, Wheeler, and Kennebec Large Print titles are designed for easy reading, and all our books are made to last. Other Thorndike Press Large Print books are available at your library, through selected bookstores, or directly from us.

For information about titles, please call:
(800) 223-1244

or visit our Web site at:
http://gale.cengage.com/thorndike

To share your comments, please write:
Publisher
Thorndike Press
10 Water St., Suite 310
Waterville, ME 04901